LAFCADIO HEARN
Short Stories

LAFCADIO HEARN
HEARN
Short Stories

ARCTURUS

ARCTURUS

This edition published in 2018 by Arcturus Publishing Limited
26/27 Bickels Yard, 151–153 Bermondsey Street,
London SE1 3HA

ISBN: 978-1-78888-402-0
AD006606UK

Printed in China

Contents

Introduction

....

Lafcadio Hearn was born in 1850 in Levkás, Greece. His unusual name came from the island of his birth, though he did not spend long there, moving to Ireland when he was only two years old. His parents' marriage was not a happy one, and his mother moved back to Greece in 1857, leaving Lafcadio in the care of his aunt, Sarah Holmes Brenane.

In 1869, Hearn decided to emigrate to the United States. He made his way to Cincinnati, Ohio, and he spent his first years there doing menial jobs to survive. His talent as a writer landed him a position as a journalist with the *Cincinnati Daily Enquirer* in 1872, and he distinguished himself through his sensationalist writing and exceptionally graphic accounts of local murders. In 1874, he married Alethea Foley, an African-American woman, but fell foul of Ohio's anti-miscegenation law and was fired from the *Enquirer*. The relationship with Foley was short lived, and he divorced in 1877.

Cincinnati no longer held the same appeal for Hearn, and so he moved to New Orleans in 1878, where he became fascinated by Creole culture and developed an interest in supernatural phenomena and the blurred boundaries between myth and reality which became enduring features of his life.

It was around this time that Hearn began writing fiction. His first stories were little more than sketches that blurred the boundaries between fact and fiction. Rarely more than a few paragraphs, they were a chance for him to demonstrate his unique gift to evoke an atmosphere that drew on his own experiences, but his stories found appeal in national magazines like *Harper's Weekly*. However, his wanderlust could not be restrained for long, and, in 1887, Hearn left to spend two years in Martinique as a correspondent.

Returning to America, Hearn never felt truly at home and his life remained unsatisfying. He became increasingly disenchanted with Western society. In 1890, he made the most important decision of his life when he accepted a commission to visit Japan as a correspondent. It was a revelatory experience: Lafcadio fully embraced the traditional culture of his new home. He married a Japanese woman, Koizumi Setsu, and became an ardent supporter of traditional Japanese practices. Learning the language and adopting traditional dress, Hearn became more Japanese than the Japanese themselves.

He took it upon himself to preserve the legends and stories of ancient Japan from the onslaught of modernization and economic progress. A fervent admirer of Japanese culture, he aimed to share his fondness with a wider audience and recorded the folklore of the local population in the form of short stories written in English. These were some of his most powerful works, bringing to life the magic and mystery of the east.

This anthology includes stories from his collections *Stray Leaves*, *Creole Sketches*, *Some Chinese Ghosts*, *Japanese Fairy Tales*, *In Ghostly Japan*, *Shadowings*, *Kwaidan: Stories and Studies of Strange Things*, and *The Romance of the Milky Way*. Hearn's writing displays extraordinary breadth, ranging from fairy tales to horror to mythology. Regardless of the subject matter, the authenticity of his work shines through, presenting a window into other worlds.

All in White

"**N**o," he said, "I did not stay long in Havana. I should think it would be a terrible place to live in. Somehow, in spite of all the tropical brightness, the city gave me the idea of a huge sepulchre at times. One feels in those narrow streets as though entombed. Pretty women?—I suppose so, yes; but I saw only one. It was in one of the quaint streets which make you think that the Spaniards learned to build their cities from the Moors—a chasm between lofty buildings, and balconies jutting out above to break the view of the narrow strip of blue sky. Nobody was in the street except myself; and the murmur of the city's life seemed to come from afar, like a ghostly whisper. The silence was so strange that I felt as if walking on the pavement of a church, and disturbing the religious quiet with my footsteps.

I stopped before a great window—no glass, but iron bars only;—and behind the iron bars lay the only beautiful woman I saw in Havana by daylight. She could not have been more than eighteen—a real Spanish beauty—dark, bewitching, an oval face with noble features, and long eyelashes resting on the cheek. She was dead! All in white—like the phantom bride of the German tradition—white robes, white satin shoes, and one white tropical flower in her black hair, shining like a star. I do not know what it was; but its perfume came to me through the window, sweet and strange. The young woman, sleeping there all in white, against the darkness of the silent chamber within, fascinated me. I felt as if it was not right to look at her so long; yet I could not help it. Candles were burning at her head and feet; and in the stillness of the hot air their yellow flames did not even tremble. Suddenly I heard a heavy tramping at the end of the street. A battalion of Spanish soldiers were coming towards me. There was no means of proceeding; and I had no time to retreat. The street was so narrow that I was obliged to put my back to the wall in order to let them pass.

They passed in dead silence—I only heard the tread of the men, mechanically regular and heavily echoing. They were all in white. Every man looked at me as he passed by; and every look was dark, sinister, suspicious. I was anxious to escape those thousands of Spanish eyes; but I could not have done it without turning my face to the wall. I do not think one of them looked at the dead girl at all; but each one looked at me, and forced me to look at him, I dared not smile—not one of the swarthy faces smiled. The situation became really unpleasant. It was like one of those nightmares in which you are obliged to witness an endless procession of phantoms, each one of whom compels you to look at it. If I had even heard a single *carajo Americano*, I should have felt relieved; but all passed me in dead silence. I was transpierced by the black steel of at least two thousand Spanish eyes, and every eye looked at me as if I had been detected in some awful crime. Yet why they did not look at that window instead of looking at me, I cannot tell. After they had passed, I looked an instant at the dead girl again; and it seemed to me that I saw the ghost of a smile—a cynical, mocking smile about her lips. She was well avenged—if her consecrated rest had been disturbed by my heretic eyes. I can still smell the white flower; and I can see even the silk stitches in the white satin shoes—the motion-less yellow tongues of the candles—the thin dead face that seemed to smile, and the thousand sinister faces that smiled not, and dared me to smile."

The Little Red Kitten

The kitten would have looked like a small red lion, but that its ears were positively enormous—making the head like one of those little demons sculptured in mediæval stone-work which have wings instead of ears. It ate beefsteak and cockroaches, caterpillars and fish, chicken and butterflies, mosquito-hawks and roast mutton, hash and tumble-bugs, beetles and pigs' feet, crabs and spiders, moths and poached eggs, oysters and earth-worms, ham and mice, rats and rice pudding—until its belly became a realization of Noah's Ark. On this diet it soon acquired strength to whip all the ancient cats in the neighborhood, and also to take under its protection a pretty little salmon-colored cat of the same sex, which was too weak to defend itself and had been unmercifully mauled every night before the tawny sister enforced reform in the shady yard of the old Creole house. The red kitten was not very big, but was very solid and more agile than a monkey. Its flaming emerald eyes were always watching, and its enormous ears always on the alert; and woe to the cat who dared approach the weak little sister with hostile intentions. The two always slept together—the little speckled one resting its head upon the body of its protector; and the red kitten licked its companion every day like a mother washing her baby. Wherever the red kitten went the speckled kitten followed; they hunted all kinds of creeping things together, and even formed a criminal partnership in kitten stealing. One day they were forcibly separated; the red kitten being locked up in the closet under the stairs to keep it out of mischief during dinner hours, as it had evinced an insolent determination to steal a stuffed crab from the plate of Madame R. Thus temporarily deprived of its guide, philosopher, and friend, the speckled kitten unfortunately wandered under a rocking-chair violently agitated by a heavy gentleman who was reading the "Bee"; and with a sharp little cry of agony it gave up its gentle ghost. Everybody stopped eating; and there was a general outburst of indignation and sorrow. The heavy gentleman got very red in the face, and said he had not intended to do it. *"Tonnerre d'une pipe;—nom d'un petit bonhomme!"*—he might have been a little more careful! …An hour later the red kitten was vainly seeking its speckled companion—all ears and eyes. It uttered strange little cries, and vainly waited for the customary reply. Then it commenced to look everywhere— upstairs, downstairs, on the galleries, in the corners, among the shrubbery, never supposing in its innocent mind that a little speckled body was lying far away upon a heap of garbage and ashes. Then it became very silent; purring when offered food, but eating nothing…. At last a sudden thought seemed to strike it. It had never seen the great world which rumbled beyond the archway of the old courtyard; perhaps its little sister had wandered out there. So it would go and seek her. For the first time it wandered beyond the archway and saw the big world it had never seen before—miles of houses and myriads of people and great cotton-floats thundering by, and great wicked dogs which murder kittens. But the little red one crept along beside the houses in the narrow strip of shadow, sometimes trembling when the big wagons rolled past, and some- times hiding in doorways when it saw a dog, but still bravely seeking the lost sister…. It came to a great wide street—five times wider than the narrow street before the old Creole house; and the sun was so hot, so hot. The little creature was so tired and hungry, too. Perhaps somebody would help it to find the way. But nobody seemed to notice the red kitten, with its funny ears and great bright eyes. It opened its little pink mouth and cried; but nobody stopped. It could not understand that. Whenever it had cried that way at home, somebody had come to pet it. Suddenly a fire-engine came roaring up the street, and a great crowd of people were running after it. Then the kitten got very, very frightened; and tried to run out of the way, but its poor little brain was so confused and there was so much noise and shouting.... Next morning two little bodies lay side by side on the ashes—miles away from the old Creole house. The little tawny kitten had found its speckled sister.

The Night
of All Saints

T he Night of All Saints—a night clear and deep and filled with a glory of white moonlight.

And a low sweet Wind came up from the West, and wandered among the tombs, whispering to the Shadows.

And there were flowers among the tombs.

They looked into the face of the moon, and from them a thousand invisible perfumes arose into the night.

And the Wind blew upon the flowers until their soft eyelids began to close and their perfume grew fainter in the moonlight. And the Wind sought in vain to arouse them from the dreamless sleep into which they were sinking.

For the perfume of a flower is but the presence of its invisible soul; and the flowers drooped in the moonlight, and at the twelfth hour they closed their eyes forever and the incense of their lives passed away from them.

Then the Wind mourned awhile among the old white tombs; and whispered to the cypress trees and to the Shadows, "Were not these offerings?"

And the Shadows and the cypresses bowed weirdly in mysterious reply. But the Wind asked, *To Whom?* And the Shadows kept silence with the cypresses.

Then the Wind entered like a ghost into the crannies of the white sepulchres, and whispered in the darkness, and coming forth shuddered and mourned.

And the Shadows shuddered also; and the cypresses sighed in the night.

"It is a mystery," sobbed the Wind, "and passeth my understanding. Wherefore these offerings to those who dwell in the darkness where even dreams are dead?"

But the trees and the Shadows answered not and the hollow tombs uttered no voice.

Then came a Wind out of the South, murmuring to the orange groves, and lifting the long tresses of the palms with the breath of his wings, and bearing back to the ancient place of tombs the souls of a thousand flowers. And the Wind of the South whispered to the souls of the flowers, "Answer, little spirits, answer my mourning brother."

And the flower-souls answered, making fragrant all the white streets of the white city of the dead:—

"We are the offerings of love bereaved to the All-loving—the sacrifices of the fatherless to the All-father. We know not of the dead—the Infinite secret hath not been revealed to us;—we know only that they sleep under the eye of Him who never sleeps. Thou hast seen the flowers die; but their perfumes live in the wings of the winds and sweeten all God's world. Is it not so with that fragrance of good deeds, which liveth after the deed hath been done—or the memories of dead loves which soften the hearts of the living?"

And the cypresses together with the Shadows bowed answeringly; and the West Wind, ceasing to mourn, spread his gauzy wings in flight toward the rising of the sun.

The moon, sinking, made longer the long shadows; the South Wind caressed the cypresses, and, bearing with him ghosts of the flowers, rose in flight toward the dying fires of the stars.

The Devil's Carbuncle

Ricard Palma, the Lima correspondent of La Raza Latina, *has been collecting some curious South American traditions which date back to the Spanish Conquest. The following legend, entitled "El Carbunclo del Diablo," is one of these:—*

When Juan de la Torre, one of the celebrated *Conqistadores*, discovered and seized an immense treasure in one of the *huacas* near the city of Lima, the Spanish soldiers became seized with a veritable mania for treasure-seeking among the old forts and cemeteries of the Indians. Now there were there *ballesteros* belonging to the company of Captain Diego Gumiel, who had formed a partnership for the purpose of seeking fortunes among the *huacas* of Miraflores, and who had already spent weeks upon weeks in digging for treasure without finding the smallest article of value.

On Good Friday, in the year 1547, without any respect for the sanctity of the day—for to human covetousness nothing is sacred—the three *ballesteros*, after vainly sweating and panting all morning and afternoon, had not found anything except a mummy—not even a trinket or bit of pottery worth three *pesetas*. Thereupon they gave themselves over to the Father of Evil—cursing all the Powers of Heaven, and blaspheming so horribly that the Devil himself was obliged to stop his ears with cotton.

By this time the sun had set; and the adventurers were preparing to return to Lima, cursing the niggardly Indians for the unpardonable stupidity of not having been entombed in state upon beds of solid gold or silver, when one of the Spaniards gave the mummy so ferocious a kick that it rolled a considerable distance. A glimmering jewel dropped from the skeleton, and rolled slowly after the mummy.

"*Canario!*" cried one of the soldiers, "what kind of a taper is that? *Santa Maria!* what a glorious carbuncle!"

And he was about to walk toward the jewel, when the one who had kicked the corpse, and who was a great bully, held him back with the words:—

"Halt, comrade! May I never be sad if that carbuncle does not belong to me; for it was I who found the mummy!

"May the Devil carry thee away! I first saw it shine, and may I die before any other shall possess it!"

"*Cepos quedos!*" thundered the third, unsheathing his sword, and making it whistle round his head. "So I am nobody?"

"*Caracolines!* not even the Devil's wife shall wring it from me," cried the bully, unsheathing his dagger.

And a tremendous fight began among the three comrades.

The following day some *Mitayos* found the dead body of one of the combatants, and the other two riddled with wounds, begging for a confessor. Before they died they related the story of the carbuncle, and told how it illumined the combat with a sinister and lurid light. But the carbuncle was never found after. Tradition ascribes its origin to the Devil; and it is said that each Good Friday night travelers may perceive its baleful rays twinkling from the *huaca* Juliana, rendered famous by this legend.

The Ghostly Kiss

The theatre was full. I cannot remember what they were playing. I did not have time to observe the actors. I only remember how vast the building seemed. Looking back, I saw an ocean of faces stretching away almost beyond the eye's power of definition to the far circles where the seats rose tier above tier in lines of illumination. The ceiling was blue, and in the midst a great mellow lamp hung suspended like a moon, at a height so lofty that I could not see the suspending chain. All the seats were black. I fancied that the theatre was hung with hangings of black velvet, bordered with a silver fringe that glimmered like tears. The audience were all in white.

All in white!—I asked myself whether I was not in some theatre of some tropical city—why all in white? I could not guess. I fancied at moments that I could perceive a moonlit landscape through far distant oriel windows, and the crests of palms casting moving shadows like gigantic spiders. The air was sweet with a strange and a new perfume; it was a drowsy air—a poppied air, in which the waving of innumerable white fans made no rustle, no sound.

There was a strange stillness and a strange silence. All eyes were turned toward the stage, except my own. I gazed in every direction but that of the stage! I cannot imagine why it was that I rarely looked toward the stage. No one noticed me; no one appeared to perceive that I was the only person in all that vast assembly clad in black—a tiny dark speck in a sea of white light.

Gradually the voices of the actors seemed to me to become fainter and fainter—thin sounds like whispers from another world—a world of ghosts!—and the music seemed not music, but only an echo in the mind of the hearer, like a memory of songs heard and forgotten in forgotten years.

There were faces that I thought strangely familiar—faces I fancied I had seen somewhere else in some other time. But none recognized me.

A woman sat before me—a fair woman with hair as brightly golden as the locks of Aphrodite. I asked my heart why it beat so strangely when I turned my eyes upon her. I felt as if it sought to leap from my breast and fling itself all palpitating under her feet. I watched the delicate movements of her neck, where a few loose bright curls were straying, like strands of gold clinging to a column of ivory;—the soft curve of the cheek flushed by a faint ruddiness like the velvet surface of a half-ripe peach;—the grace of the curving lips—lips sweet as those of the Cnidian Venus, which even after two thousand years still seem humid, as with the kisses of the last lover. But the eyes I could not see.

And a strange desire rose within me—an intense wish to kiss those lips. My heart said, Yes;—my reason whispered, No. I thought of the ten thousand thousand eyes that might suddenly be turned upon me. I looked back; and it seemed to me as if the whole theatre had grown vaster! The circles of seats had receded;—the great centre lamp seemed to have mounted higher;—the audience seemed vast as that we dream of in visions of the Last Judgment. And my heart beat so violently that I heard its passionate pulsation, louder than the voices of the actors and I feared lest it should betray me to all the host of white-clad men and women above me. But none seemed to hear or to see me. I trembled as I thought of the consequences of obeying the mad impulse that became every moment more over-powering and uncontrollable.

And my heart answered, "One kiss of those lips were worth the pain of ten thousand deaths."

I do not remember that I arose. I only remember finding myself beside her, close to her, breathing her perfumed breath, and gazing into eyes deep as the amethystine heaven of a tropical night. I pressed my lips passionately to hers;—I felt a thrill of inexpressible delight and triumph;—I felt the warm soft lips curl back to meet mine, and give me back my kiss!

And a great fear suddenly came upon me. And all the multitude of white-clad men and women arose in silence; and ten thousand thousand eyes looked upon me.

I heard a voice, faint, sweet—such a voice as we hear when dead loves visit us in dreams.

"Thou hast kissed me: the compact is sealed forever."

And raising my eyes once more I saw that all the seats were graves and all the white dresses shrouds. Above me a light still shone in the blue roof, but only the light of a white moon in the eternal azure of heaven. White tombs stretched away in weird file to the verge of the horizon;—where it had seemed to me that I beheld a play, I saw only a lofty mausoleum;—and I knew that the perfume of the night was but the breath of flowers dying upon the tombs!

Metempsychosis

"Those theories which you call wild dreams," cried the Doctor, rising to his feet as he spoke, his features glowing with enthusiasm under the moon, "are but the mystic veils with which the eternal Isis veils her awful face. Your deep German philosophy is shallow—your modern pantheism vaguer than smoke—compared with the mighty knowledge of the East. The theories of the greatest modern thinkers were taught in India before the name of Rome was heard in the world; and our scientific researches of to-day simply confirm most ancient Oriental beliefs, which we, in our ignorance, have spoken of as dreams of madmen."

"Yes, but surely, you cannot otherwise characterize the idea of the transmigration of souls?"

"Ah! souls, souls," replied the stranger, drawing at his cigar until it glowed like a carbuncle in the night—"we have nothing to do with souls, but with facts. The metempsychosis is only the philosophic symbol of a vast natural fact, grotesque only to those who understand it not;—just as the most hideous Indian idol, diamond-eyed and skull-chapleted, represents to the Brahmin a hidden truth incomprehensible to the people. Conscious of the eternity of Matter and Force;—knowing that the substance of whirling universes, like clay in the hands of the potter, has been and is being and will be forever fashioned into myriad shifting forms;—knowing that shapes alone are evanescent, and that each atom of our living bodies has been from the beginning and will always be, even after the mountains have melted like wax in the heat of a world's dissolution—it is impossible to regard the theory of transmigration as a mere fantasy. Each particle of our flesh has lived before our birth through millions of transmigrations more wonderful than any poet has dared to dream of; and the life-force that throbs in the heart of each one of us has throbbed for all time in the eternal metempsychosis of the universe. Each atom of our blood has doubtless circulated, before our very civilization commenced, through the veins of millions of living creatures—soaring, crawling, or dwelling in the depths of the sea; and each molecule that floats in a sunbeam has, perhaps, vibrated to the thrill of human passion. The soil under my foot has lived and loved; and Nature, refashioning the paste in her awful laboratory into new forms of being, shall make this clay to live and hope and suffer again. Dare I even whisper to you of the past transformations of the substance of the rosiest lips you have kissed, or the brightest eyes which have mirrored your look? We have lived innumerable lives in the past; we have lived in the flowers, in the birds, in the emerald abysses of the ocean;—we have slept in the silence of solid rocks, and moved in the swells of the thunder-chanting sea;—we have been women as well as men;—we have changed our sex a thousand times like the angels of the Talmud; and we shall continue the everlasting transmigration long after the present universe has passed away and the fires of the stars have burned themselves out. Can one know these things and laugh at the theories of the East?"

"But the theory of Cycles—"

"It is not less of a solemn truth. Knowing that Force and Matter are eternal, we know also that the kaleidoscope of changing shapesmust whirl forever. But as the colored particles within a kaleidoscope are limited, only a certain number of combinations may be produced. Are not the elements of eternal matter limited?

If so, their combinations must also be; and as the everlasting force must forever continue to create forms, it can only repeat its work. Then, we must believe that all which has already happened must have happened before throughout all time, and will happen again at vast intervals through all eternity. It is not the first time we have sat together on the night of September 6;—we have done so in other Septembers, yet the same; and in other New Orleanses, the same yet not the same. We must have done it centrillions of times before, and will do it centrillions of times again through the æons of the future. I shall be again as I am, yet different; I shall smoke the same cigar, yet a different one. The same chair with the same scratches on its polished back will be there for you to sit in; and we shall hold the same conversation. The same good-natured lady will bring us a bottle of wine of the same quality; and the same persons will be reunited in this quaint Creole house. Trees like these will fling their shadows on the pavement; and above us shall we again behold as now the golden swarm of worlds sparkling in the abysses of the infinite night. There will be new stars and a new universe, yet we shall know it only as we know it at this moment that centrillions of years ago we must have suffered and hoped and loved as we do in these weary years. Good-bye, friends!"

He flung the stump of his cigar among the vines, where it expired in a shower of rosy sparks; and his footsteps died away forever. NAY, not forever; for though we should see him no more in this life, shall we not see him again throughout the Cycles and the Æons? YEA, alas, forever; for even though we should see him again throughout the Cycles and the Æons, will it not be so that he always departeth under the same circumstances and at the same moment, *in sæcula sæculorum?*

The Undying One

I have lived for three thousand years; I am weary of men and of the world: this earth has become too small for such as I; this sky seems a gray vault of lead about to sink down and crush me.

There is not a silver hair in my head; the dust of thirty centuries has not dimmed my eyes. Yet I am weary of the earth.

I speak a thousand tongues; and the faces of the continents are familiar to me as the characters of a book; the heavens have unrolled themselves before mine eyes as a scroll; and the entrails of the earth have no secrets for me.

I have sought knowledge in the deepest deeps of ocean gulfs;—in the waste places where sands shift their yellow waves, with a dry and bony sound;—in the corruption of charnel houses and the hidden horrors of the catacombs;—amid the virgin snows of Dwalagiri;—in the awful labyrinths of forests untrodden by man;—in the wombs of dead volcanoes;—in lands where the surface of lake or stream is studded with the backs of hippopotami or enameled with the mail of crocodiles;—at the extremities of the world where spectral glaciers float over inky seas;—in those strange parts where no life is, where the mountains are rent asunder by throes of primeval earthquake, and where the eyes behold only a world of parched and jagged ruin, like the Moon—of dried-up seas and river channels worn out by torrents that ceased to roll long ere the birth of man.

All the knowledge of all the centuries, all the craft and skill and cunning of man in all things—are mine, and yet more!

For Life and Death have whispered me their most ancient secrets; and all that men have vainly sought to learn has for me no mystery. Have I not tasted all the pleasures of this petty world—pleasures that would have consumed to ashes a frame less mighty than my own?

I have built temples with the Egyptians, the princes of India, and the Cæsars;—I have aided conquerors to vanquish a world;—I have reveled through nights of orgiastic fury with rulers of Thebes and Babylon;—I have been drunk with wine and blood!

The kingdoms of the earth and all their riches and glory have been mine.

With that lever which Archimedes desired I have uplifted empires and overthrown dynasties. Nay! like a god, I have held the world in the hollow of my hand.

All that the beauty of youth and the love of woman can give to make joyful the hearts of men, have I possessed;—no Assyrian king, no Solomon, no ruler of Samarcand, no Caliph of Bagdad, no Rajah of the most eastern East, has ever loved as I; and in my myriad loves I have beheld the realization of all that human thought had conceived or human heart desired or human hand crystallized into that marble of Pentelicus called imperishable—yet less enduring than these iron limbs of mine.

And ruddy I remain like that rosy granite of Egypt on which kings carved their dreams of eternity.

But I am weary of this world!

I have attained all that I sought; I have desired nothing that I have not obtained—save that I now vainly desire and yet shall never obtain.

There is no comrade for me in all this earth; no mind that can comprehend me; no heart that can love me for what I am.

Should I utter what I know, no living creature could understand;

should I write my knowledge no human brain could grasp my thought. Wearing the shape of a man, capable of doing all that man can do—yet more perfectly than man can ever do—I must live as these my frail companions, and descend to the level of their feeble minds, and imitate their puny works, though owning the wisdom of a god! How mad were those Greek dreamers who sang of gods descending to the level of humanity that they might love a woman!

In other centuries I feared to beget a son—a son to whom I might have bequeathed my own immortal youth;—jealous that I was of sharing my secret with any terrestrial creature! Now the time has past. No son of mine born in this age, of this degenerate race, could ever become a worthy companion for me. Oceans would change their beds, and new continents arise from the emerald gulfs, and new races appear upon the earth ere he could comprehend the least of my thoughts!

The future holds no pleasure in reserve for me:—I have foreseen the phases of a myriad million years. All that has been will be again:—all that will be has been before. I am solitary as one in a desert; for men have become as puppets in my eyes, and the voice of living woman hath no sweetness for my ears.

Only to the voices of the winds and of the sea do I hearken;—yet do even these weary me, for they murmured me the same music and chanted me the same hymns, among aged woods or ancient rocks, three thousand years ago!

To-night I shall have seen the moon wax and wane thirty-six thousand nine hundred times! And my eyes are weary of gazing upon its white face.

Ah! I might be willing to live on through endless years, could I but transport myself to other glittering worlds, illuminated by double suns and encircled by galaxies of huge moons!—other worlds in which I might find knowledge equal to my own, and minds worthy of my companionship—and—perhaps—women that I might love—not hollow Emptinesses, not El-women like the spectres of Scandinavian fable, and like the frail mothers of this puny terrestrial race, but creatures of immortal beauty worthy to create immortal children!

Alas!—there is a power mightier than my will, deeper than my knowledge—a Force "deaf as fire, blind as the night," which binds me forever to this world of men.

Must I remain like Prometheus chained to his rock in never-ceasing pain, with vitals eternally gnawed by the sharp beak of the vulture of Despair, or dissolve this glorious body of mine forever?

I might live till the sun grows dim and cold; yet am I too weary to live longer.

I shall die utterly—even as the beast dieth, even as the poorest being dieth that bears the shape of man; and leave no written thought behind that human thought can ever grasp. I shall pass away as a flying smoke, as a shadow, as a bubble in the crest of a wave in mid-ocean, as the flame of a taper blown out; and none shall ever know that which I was. This heart that has beaten unceasingly for three thousand years; these feet that have trod the soil of all parts of the earth; these hands that have moulded the destinies of nations; this brain that contains a thousandfold more wisdom than all the children of the earth ever knew, shall soon cease to be. And yet to shatter and destroy the wondrous mechanism of this brain—a brain worthy of the gods men dream of—a temple in which all the archives of terrestrial knowledge are stored!

The moon is up! O death-white dead world!—couldst thou too feel, how gladly wouldst thou cease thy corpselike circlings in the Night of Immensity and follow me to that darker immensity where even dreams are dead!

The Vision of the Dead Creole

he waters of the Gulf were tepid in the warmth of the tropical night. A huge moon looked down upon me as I swam toward the palm-fringed beach; and looking back I saw the rigging of the vessel sharply cut against its bright face. There was no sound! The sea-ripples kissed the brown sands silently, as if afraid; faint breezes laden with odors of saffron and cinnamon and drowsy flowers came over the water;—the stars seemed vaster than in other nights;—the fires of the Southern Cross burned steadily without one diamond-twinkle;—I paused a moment in terror;—for it seemed I could hear the night breathe—in long, weird sighs. The fancy passed as quickly as it came. The ship's bells struck the first hour of the morning. I stood again on the shore where I had played as a child, and saw through the palms the pale houses of the quaint city beyond, whence I had fled with blood upon my hands twenty-seven long years before.

Was it a witch-night, that the city slumbered so deep a sleep and the *sereno* slept at his post as I passed? I know not, but it was well for him that he slept! I passed noiselessly as the Shadow of Death through the ancient gates, and through the shadows flung down by the projecting balconies, and along the side of the plaza unilluminated by the gaze of the tropical moon, and where the towers of the cathedral made goblin shapes of darkness on the pavement; and along narrow ways where the star-sprinkled blue of heaven above seemed but a ribbon of azure, jagged and gashed along its edges by sharp projections of balconies; and beyond again into the white moonshine, where orange trees filled the warm air with a perfume as that of a nuptial chamber; and beyond, yet farther, where ancient cypresses with roots and branches gnarled and twisted as by the tortures of a thousand years of agony, bowed weirdly over the Place of Tombs.

Gigantic spiders spun their webs under the moon between the walls of the tombs;—vipers glided over my feet;—the vampire hovered above under the stars; and fireflies like corpse-lights circled about the resting-places of the dead. Great vines embraced the marbles green with fungus-growths; the ivy buried its lizard feet in the stones;—*lianas* had woven a veil, thick as that of Isis, across the epitaphs carven above the graves. But I found HER tomb! I would have reached it, as I had sworn, even in the teeth of Death and Hell!

I tore asunder the venomous plants which clung to the marble like reptiles;—but the blood poured from my hands upon her name;—and I could not find one unreddened spot to kiss. And I heard the blood from my fingers dripping with a thick, dead sound, as of molten lead, upon the leaves of the uptorn plants at my feet.

And the dead years rose from their graves of mist and stood around me! I saw the moss-green terrace where I received her first kiss that filled my veins with madness;—the marble urns with their carved bas-reliefs of naked dancing boys;—the dead fountain choked with water-lilies;—the monstrous flowers that opened their hearts to the moon. And SHE!—the sinuous outlines of that body of Corinthian bronze unconcealed by the feathery lightness of the white robe she wore;—the Creole eyes;—the pouting and passionate mouth;—and that cruel, sphinx-smile, that smile of Egypt, eternally pitiless, eternally mystical—the smile she wore when I flung myself like a worm before her to kiss her feet, and vainly shrieked to her to trample upon me, to spit upon me! And after my fierce moment of vengeance, the smile of Egypt still remained upon her dark face, as though moulded in everlasting bronze.

There was no rustle among the *lianas*, no stir among the dead leaves; yet SHE stood again before me! My heart seemed to cease its beatings;—a chill as of those nights in which I had sailed Antarctic seas passed over me! Robed in white as in the buried years, with lights like fireflies in her hair, and the same dark, elfish smile!

And suddenly the chill passed away with a fierce cataclysm of the blood, as though each of its cells were heated by volcanic fire;—for the strange words of the Hebrew canticle came to me like a far echo—

LOVE IS STRONG AS DEATH!

I burst the fetters with which horror had chained my voice;—I spake to her; I wept—I wept tears of blood!

And the old voice came to me, argentine and low and mockingly sweet as the voices of birds that call to each other through the fervid West Indian night—

"I knew thou wouldst come back to me—howsoever long thou mightst wander under other skies and over other seas.

"Didst thou dream that I was dead? Nay, I die not so quickly! I have lived through all these years. I shall live on; and thou must return hither again to visit me like a thief in the night.

"Knowest thou how I have lived? I have lived in the bitter tears thou hast wept through all these long years;—the agony of the remorse that seized thee in silent nights and lonesome wastes;—in the breath of thy youth and life exhaled in passionate agony when no human eyes beheld thee;—in the images that haunt thy dreams and make it a horror for thee to find thyself alone! Yet wouldst thou kiss me –"

I looked upon her again in the white light;—I saw the same weirdly beautiful face, the same smile of the sphinx;—I saw the vacant tomb yawning to its entrails;—I saw its shadow—my shadow—lying sharply upon the graves;—and I saw that the tall white figure before me *cast no shadow before the moon!*

And suddenly under the stars, sonorous and vibrant as far cathedral bells, the voices of the awakening watchmen chanted—*Ave Maria Purísima!—las tres de la mañana, y tiempo sereno!*

The Name on the Stone

"**A**s surely as the wild bird seeks the summer, you will come back," she whispered. "Is there a drop of blood in your veins that does not grow ruddier and warmer at the thought of me? Does not your heart beat quicker at this moment because I am here? It belongs to me;—it obeys me in spite of your feeble will;—it will remain my slave when you are gone. You have bewitched yourself at my lips; I hold you as a bird is held by an invisible thread; and my thread, invisible and intangible, is stronger than your will. Fly: but you can no longer fly beyond the circle in which my wish confines you. Go: but I shall come to you in dreams of the night; and you will be awakened by the beating of your own heart to find yourself alone with darkness and memory. Sleep in whose arms you will, I shall come like a ghost between you; kiss a thousand lips, but it will be I that shall receive them. Though you circle the earth in your wanderings, you will never be able to leave my memory behind you; and your pulse will quicken at recollections of me whether you find yourself under Indian suns or Northern lights. You lie when you say you do not love me!—your heart would fling itself under my feet could it escape from its living prison! You will come back."

And having vainly sought rest through many vainly spent years, I returned to her. It was a night of wild winds and fleeting shadows and strange clouds that fled like phantoms before the storm and across the face of the moon. "You are a cursed witch," I shrieked, "but I have come back!"

And she, placing a finger—white as the waxen tapers that are burned at the feet of the dead—upon my lips, only smiled and whispered, "Come with me."

And I followed her.

The thunder muttered in the east; the horizon pulsated with lightnings; the night-birds screamed as we reached the iron gates of the burial-ground, which swung open with a groan at her touch.

Noiselessly she passed through the ranges of the graves; and I saw the mounds flame when her feet touched them—flame with a cold white dead flame like the fire of the glow-worm.

Was it an illusion of broken moonlight and flying clouds, or did the dead rise and follow us like a bridal train?

And was it only the vibration of the thunder, or did the earth quake when I stood upon *that* grave?

"Look not behind you even for an instant," she muttered, "or you are lost."

But there came to me a strange desire to read the name graven upon the moss-darkened stone; and even as it came the storm unveiled the face of the moon.

And the dark shadow at my side whispered, "Read it not!"

And the moon veiled herself again. "I cannot go! I cannot go!" I whispered passionately, "until I have read the name upon this stone."

Then a flash of lightning in the east revealed to me the name; and an agony of memory came upon me; and I shrieked it to the flying clouds and the wan lights of heaven!

Again the earth quaked under my feet; and a white Shape rose from the bosom of the grave like an exhalation and stood before me: I felt the caress of lips shadowy as those of the fair phantom women who haunt the dreams of youth; and the echo of a dead voice, faint as the whisper of a summer wind, murmured:—"Love, love is stronger than Death!—I come back from the eternal night to save thee!"

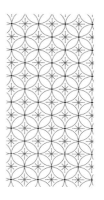

Aphrodite and the King's Prisoner

Columns of Corinthian marble stretching away in mighty perspective and rearing their acanthus capitals a hundred feet above the polished marble from which they rose;— antique mosaics from the years of Hadrian;—Pompeiian frescoes limning all the sacrifices made to Aphrodite;—naked bronzes uplifting marvelous candelabra;—fantastically beautiful oddities in terra cotta;—miracles of art in Pentelic marble;—tripods supporting vessels of burning spices which filled the palace with perfumes as intoxicating as the Song of Solomon;—and in the midst of all a range of melodious fountains amid whose waters white nymphs showed their smooth thighs of stone and curved their marble figures into all the postures that harmonize with beauty. Vast gardens of myrtle and groves of laurel, mystic and shadowy as those of Daphne, surrounded the palace with a world of deep green, broken only at intervals by the whiteness of Parian dryads;—flowers formed a living carpet upon the breadth of the terraces, and a river washed the eastern walls and marble stairways of the edifice. It was a world of wonders and of marvels, of riches and rarities, though created by the vengeance of a king. There was but one human life amid all that enchantment of Greek marble, of petrified loveliness and beauty made motionless in bronze. No servants were ever seen;—no voice was ever heard;—there was no exit from that strange paradise. It was said that the king's prisoner was served by invisible hands;—

that tables covered with luxurious viands rose up through the marble pavements at regular hours;—and the fumes of the richest wines of the Levant, sweetened with honey, perfumed the chamber chosen for his repasts. All that art could inspire, all that gold might obtain, all that the wealth of a world could create were for him—save only the sound of a human voice and the sight of a human face. To madden in the presence of unattainable loveliness, to consume his heart in wild longings to realize the ravishing myth of Pygmalion, to die of a dream of beauty—such was the sentence of the king!

Lovelier than all other lovelinesses created in stone or gem or eternal bronze by the hands of men whose lives were burnt out in longings for a living idol worthy of their dreams of perfect beauty—a figure of Aphrodite displayed the infinite harmony of her naked loveliness upon a pedestal of black marble, so broad and so highly polished that it reflected the divine poem of her body like a mirror of ebony—the Foam-born rising from the silent deeps of a black Ægean. The delicate mellowness of the antique marble admirably mocked the tint of human flesh;—a tropical glow, a golden warmth seemed to fill the motionless miracle—this dream of love frozen into marble by a genius greater than Praxiteles; no modem restorer had given to the attitude of this bright divinity the Christian anachronism of shame. With arms extended as if to welcome a lover, all the exquisite curves of her bosom faced the eyes of the beholder; and with one foot slightly advanced she seemed in the act of stepping forward to bestow a kiss. And a brazen tablet let into the black marble of the pedestal bore, in five learned tongues, the strange inscription:—

"Created by the hand of one maddened by love, I madden all who gaze upon me. Mortal, condemned to live in solitude with me, prepare thyself to die of love at my feet. The old gods, worshiped by youth and beauty, are dead; and no immortal power can place a living heart in this stony bosom or lend to these matchless limbs the warm flexibility and rosiness of life."

Around the chamber of the statue ran a marble wainscoting chiseled with Bacchanal bas-reliefs—a revel of rude dryads and fauns linking themselves in amorous interlacings;—upon an altar of porphyry flickered the low flame of the holy fire fed with leaves of the myrtle sacred to love;—doves for the sacrifice were cooing and wooing in the marble court without;—a sound of crystal water came from a fountain near the threshold, where beautiful feminine monsters, whose lithe flanks blended into serpent coils, upheld in their arms of bronze the fantastic cup from which the living waters leapt; a balmy, sensuous air, bearing on its wings the ghosts of perfumes known to the voluptuaries of Corinth, filled the softly lighted sanctuary;—and on either side of the threshold stood two statues, respectively in white and black marble—Love, the blond brother of Death; Death, the dark brother of Love, with torch forever extinguished.

And the King knew that the Prisoner kept alive the sacred fire, and poured out the blood of the doves at the feet of the goddess, who smiled with the eternal smile of immortal youth and changeless loveliness and the consciousness of the mighty witchery of her enchanting body. For secret watchers came to the palace and said:—

"When he first beheld the awful holiness of her beauty, he fell prostrate as one bereft of life, and long so remained."

And the King musingly made answer:—

"Aphrodite is no longer to be appeased with the blood of doves, but only with the blood of men—men of mighty hearts and volcanic passion. He is youthful and strong and an artist!—and he must soon die. Let the weapons of death be mercifully placed at the feet of Aphrodite, that her victim may be able to offer himself up in sacrifice."

* * *

Now the secret messengers were eunuchs. And they came again to the palace, and whispered in the ears of the silver-bearded King:—

"He has again poured out the blood of the doves, and he sings the sacred Hymn of Homer, and kisses her marble body until his lips bleed;—and the goddess still smiles the smile of perfect loveliness that is pitiless."

And the King answered:—

"It is even as I desire."

A second time the messengers came to the palace, and whispered in the ears of the iron-eyed King:—

"He bathes her feet with his tears: his heart is tortured as though crushed by fingers of marble; he no longer eats or slumbers, neither drinks he the waters of the Fountain of Bronze;—and the goddess still smiles the mocking smile of eternal and perfect loveliness that is without pity and without mercy." And the King answered:—

"It is even as I had wished."

So one morning, in the first rosy flush of sunrise, they found the Prisoner dead, his arms madly flung about the limbs of the goddess in a last embrace, and his cheek resting upon her marble foot. All the blood of his heart, gushing from a wound in his breast, had been poured out upon the pedestal of black marble; and it trickled down over the brazen tablet inscribed with five ancient tongues, and over the mosaic pavement, and over the marble threshold past the statue of Love who is the brother of Death, and the statue of Death who is the brother of Love, until it mingled with the waters of the Fountain of Bronze from which the sacrificial doves did drink.

And around the bodies of the serpent-women the waters blushed rosily; and above the dead, the goddess still smiled the sweet and mocking smile of eternal and perfect loveliness that hath no pity.

"Thrice seven days he has lived at her feet," muttered the King;

"yet even I, hoary with years, dare not trust myself to look upon her for an hour!" And a phantom of remorse, like a shadow from Erebus, passed across his face of granite. "Let her be broken in pieces," he said, "even as a vessel of glass is broken."

But the King's servants, beholding the white witchery of her rhythmic limbs, fell upon their faces; and there was no man found to raise his hand against the Medusa of beauty whose loveliness withered men's hearts as leaves are crisped by fire. And Aphrodite smiled down upon them with the smile of everlasting youth and immortal beauty and eternal mockery of human passion.

The Fountain of Gold

This is the tale told in the last hours of a summer night to the old Spanish priest in the Hôtel Dieu, by an aged wanderer from the Spanish Americas; and I write it almost as I heard it from the priest's lips.

"I could not sleep. The strange odors of the flowers; the sense of romantic excitement which fills a vivid imagination in a new land; the sight of a new heaven illuminated by unfamiliar constellations, and a new world which seemed to me a very garden of Eden—perhaps all of these added to beget the spirit of unrest which consumed me as with a fever. I rose and went out under the stairs. I heard the heavy breathing of the soldiers, whose steel corselets glimmered in the ghostly light;—the occasional snorting of the horses;—the regular tread of the sentries guarding the sleep of their comrades. An inexplicable longing came upon me to wander alone into the deep forest beyond, such a longing as in summer days in Seville had seized me when I heard the bearded soldiers tell of the enchantment of the New World. I did not dream of danger; for in those days I feared neither God nor devil, and the Commander held me the most desperate of that desperate band of men. I strode out beyond the lines;—the grizzled sentry growled out a rough protest as I received his greeting in sullen silence;—I cursed him and passed on.

* * *

47

"The deep sapphire of that marvelous Southern night paled to pale amethyst; then the horizon brightened into yellow behind the crests of the palm trees; and at last the diamond-fires of the Southern Cross faded out. Far behind me I heard the Spanish bugles, ringing their call through the odorous air of that tropical morning, quaveringly sweet in the distance, faint as music from another world. Yet I did not dream of retracing my steps. As in a dream I wandered on under the same strange impulse, and the bugle-call again rang out, but fainter than before. I do not know if it was the strange perfume of the strange flowers, or the odors of the spice-bearing trees, or the caressing warmth of the tropical air, or witchcraft; but a new sense of feeling came to me. I would have given worlds to have been able to weep: I felt the old fierceness die out of my heart;—wild doves flew down from the trees and perched upon my shoulders, and I laughed to find myself caressing them—I whose hands were red with blood, and whose heart was black with crime.

"And the day broadened and brightened into a paradise of emerald and gold; birds no larger than bees, but painted with strange metallic fires of color, hummed about me;—parrots chattered in the trees;—apes swung themselves with fantastic agility from branch to branch;—a million million blossoms of inexpressible beauty opened their silky hearts to the sun;—and the drowsy perfume of the dreamy woods became more intoxicating. It seemed to me a land of witchcraft, such as the Moors told us of in Spain, when they spoke of countries lying near the rising of the sun. And it came to pass that I found myself dreaming of the Fountain of Gold which Ponce de Leon sought.

"Then it seemed to me that the trees became loftier. The palms looked older than the deluge, and their cacique-plumes seemed to touch the azure of heaven. And suddenly I found myself within a great clear space, ringed in by the primeval trees so lofty that all within their circle was bathed in verdant shadow. The ground was carpeted with moss and odorous herbs and flowers, so thickly growing that the foot made no sound upon their elastic leaves and petals; and from the circle of the trees on every side the land sloped down to a vast basin filled with sparkling water, and there was a lofty jet in the midst of the basin, such as I had seen in the Moorish courts of Granada. The water was deep and clear as the eyes of a woman in her first hours of love;—I saw gold-sprinkled sands far below, and rainbow lights where the rain of the fountain made ripples. It seemed strange to me that the jet leaped from nothing formed by the hand of man; it was as though a mighty underflow forced it upward in a gush above the bright level of the basin. I unbuckled my armor and doffed my clothing, and plunged into the fountain with delight. It was far deeper than I expected; the crystalline purity of the water had deceived me—I could not even dive to the bottom. I swam over to the fountain jet and found to my astonishment that while the waters of the basin were cool as the flow of a mountain spring, the leaping column of living crystal in its centre was warm as blood!

"I felt an inexpressible exhilaration from my strange bath; I gamboled in the water like a boy; I even cried aloud to the woods and the birds; and the parrots shouted back my cries from the heights of the palms. And, leaving the fountain, I felt no fatigue or hunger; but when I lay down a deep and leaden sleep came upon me—such a sleep as a child sleeps in the arms of its mother.

"When I awoke a woman was bending over me. She was wholly unclad, and with her perfect beauty, and the tropical tint of her skin, she looked like a statue of amber. Her flowing black hair was interwoven with white flowers; her eyes were very large, and dark and deep, and fringed with silky lashes. She wore no ornaments of gold, like the Indian girls I had seen—only the white flowers in her hair. I looked at her wonderingly as upon an angel; and with her tall and slender grace she seemed to me, indeed, of another world. For the first time in all that dark life of mine, I felt fear in the presence of a woman; but a fear not unmixed with pleasure. I spoke to her in Spanish; but she only opened her dark eyes more widely, and smiled. I made signs; she brought me fruits and clear water in a gourd; and as she bent over me again, I kissed her.

"Why should I tell of our love, Padre?—let me only say that those were the happiest years of my life. Earth and heaven seemed to have embraced in that strange land; it was Eden; it was paradise; never-wearying love, eternal youth! No other mortal ever knew such happiness as I;—yet none ever suffered so agonizing a loss. We lived upon fruits and the water of the Fountain;—our bed was the moss and the flowers; the doves were our playmates;—the stars our lamps. Never storm or cloud;—never rain or heat;—only the tepid summer drowsy with sweet odors, the songs of birds and murmuring water; the waving palms, the jewel-breasted minstrels of the woods who chanted to us through the night. And we never left the little valley. My armor and my good rapier rusted away; my garments were soon worn out; but there we needed no raiment, it was all warmth and light and repose. 'We shall never grow old here,' she whispered. But when I asked her if that was, indeed, the Fountain of Youth, she only smiled and placed her finger upon her lips. Neither could I ever learn her name. I could not acquire her tongue; yet she had learned mine with marvelous quickness. We never had a quarrel;—I could never find heart to even frown upon her. She was all gentleness, playfulness, loveliness—but what do you care, Padre, to hear all these things?

* * *

"Did I say our happiness was perfect? No: there was one strange cause of anxiety which regularly troubled me. Each night, while lying in her arms, I heard the Spanish bugle-call—far and faint and ghostly as a voice from the dead. It seemed like a melancholy voice calling to me. And whenever the sound floated to us, I felt that she trembled, and wound her arms faster about me, and she would weep until I kissed away her tears. And through all those years I heard the bugle-call. Did I say years?—nay, *centuries!*—for in that land one never grows old; I heard it through centuries after all my companions were dead."

(The priest crossed himself under the lamplight, and murmured a prayer. "Continue, *hijo mio*," he said at last; "tell me all.")

"It was anger, Padre; I wished to see for myself where the sounds came from that tortured my life. And I know not why she slept so deeply that night. As I bent over to kiss her, she moaned in her dreams, and I saw a crystal tear glimmer on the dark fringe of her eyes—and then that cursed bugle-call—"

The old man's voice failed a moment. He gave a feeble cough, spat blood, and went on:—

"I have little time to tell you more, Padre. I never could find my way back again to the valley. I lost her forever. When I wandered out among men, they spoke another language that I could not speak; and the world was changed. When I met Spaniards at last, they spoke a tongue unlike what I heard in my youth. I did not dare to tell my story. They would have confined me with madmen. I speak the Spanish of other centuries; and the men of my own nation mock my quaint ways. Had I lived much in this new world of yours, I should have been regarded as mad, for my thoughts and ways are not of to-day; but I have spent my life among the swamps of the tropics, with the python and the cayman, in the heart of untrodden forests and by the shores of rivers that have no names, and the ruins of dead Indian cities—until my strength died and my hair became white in looking for her."

"My son," cried the old priest, "banish these evil thoughts. I have heard your story; and any, save a priest, would believe you mad. I believe all you have told me;—the legends of the Church contain much that is equally strange. You have been a great sinner in your youth; and God has punished you by making your sins the very instrument of your punishment. Yet has He not preserved you through the centuries that you might repent? Banish all thoughts of the demon who still tempts you in the shape of a woman; repent and commend your soul to God, that I may absolve you."

"Repent!" said the dying man, fixing upon the priest's face his great black eyes, which flamed up again as with the fierce fires of his youth; "repent, father? I cannot repent! I love her!—I love her! And if there be a life beyond death, I shall love her through all time and eternity:—more than my own soul I love her!—more than my hope of heaven!—more than my fear of death and hell!"

The priest fell on his knees, and, covering his face, prayed fervently. When he lifted his eyes again, the soul had passed away unabsolved; but there was such a smile upon the dead face that the priest wondered, and, forgetting the *Miserere* upon his lips, involuntarily muttered: "He hath found Her at last." And the east brightened; and touched by the magic of the rising sun, the mists above his rising formed themselves into a Fountain of Gold.

At the Cemetery

"**C**ome with me," he said, "that you may see the contrast between poverty and riches, between the great and the humble, even among the ranks of the dead;—for verily it hath been said that there are sermons in stones."

And I passed with him through the Egyptian gates, and beyond the pylons into the Alley of Cypresses; and he showed me the dwelling-place of the rich in the City of Eternal Sleep—the ponderous tombs of carven marble, the white angels that mourned in stone, the pale symbols of the urns, and the names inscribed upon tablets of granite in letters of gold. But I said to him: "These things interest me not;—these tombs are but traditions of the wealth once owned by men who dwell now where riches avail nothing and all rest together in the dust."

Then my friend laughed softly to himself, and taking my hand led me to a shadowy place where the trees bent under their drooping burdens of gray moss, and made waving silhouettes against the catacombed walls which girdle the cemetery. There the dead were numbered and piled away thickly upon the marble shelves, like those documents which none may destroy but which few care to read—the Archives of our Necropolis. And he pointed to a marble tablet closing the aperture of one of the little compartments in the lowest range of the catacombs, almost level with the grass at our feet.

There was no inscription, no name, no wreath, no vase. But some hand had fashioned a tiny flower-bed in front of the tablet—a little garden about twelve inches in width and depth—and had hemmed it about with a border of pink-tinted seashells, and had covered the black mould over with white sand, through which the green leaves and buds of the baby plants sprouted up.

"Nothing but love could have created that," said my companion, as a shadow of tenderness passed over his face;—"and that sand has been brought here from a long distance, and from the shores of the sea."

Then I looked and remembered wastes that I had seen, where sand-waves shifted with a dry and rustling sound, where no life was and no leaf grew, where all was death and barrenness. And here were flowers blooming in the midst of sand!—the desert blossoming!—love living in the midst of death! And I saw the print of a hand, a child's hand—the tiny fingers that had made this poor little garden and smoothed the sand over the roots of the flowers.

"There is no name upon the tomb," said the voice of the friend who stood beside me; "yet why should there be?"

Why, indeed? I answered. Why should the world know the sweet secret of that child's love? Why should unsympathetic eyes read the legend of that grief? Is it not enough that those who loved the dead man know his place of rest, and come hither to whisper to him in his dreamless sleep?

I said *he;* for somehow or other the sight of that little garden created a strange fancy in my mind, a fancy concerning the dead. The shells and the sand were not the same as those usually used in the cemeteries. They had been brought from a great distance—from the moaning shores of the Mexican Gulf.

So that visions of a phantom sea arose before me; and mystic ships rocking in their agony upon shadowy waves;—and dreams of wild coasts where the weed-grown skeletons of wrecks lie buried in the ribbed sand.

And I thought—Perhaps this was a sailor and perhaps the loving ones who come at intervals to visit his place of rest waited and watched and wept for a ship that never came back.

But when the sea gave up its dead, they bore him to his native city, and laid him in this humble grave, and brought hither the sand that the waves had kissed, and the pink-eared shells within whose secret spirals the moan of ocean lingers forever.

And from time to time his child comes to plant a frail blossom, and smooth the sand with her tiny fingers, talking softly the while,— perhaps only to herself—perhaps to that dead father who comes to her in dreams.

Aïda

To Thebes, the giant city of a hundred gates, the city walled up to heaven, come the tidings of war from the south. Dark Ethiopia has risen against Egypt, the power "shadowing with wings" has invaded the kingdom of the Pharaohs, to rescue from captivity the beautiful Aïda, daughter of Amonasro, monarch of Ethiopia. Aïda is the slave of the enchanting Amneris, daughter of Pharaoh. Radames, chief among the great captains of Egypt, is beloved by Amneris; but he has looked upon the beauty of the slave-maiden, and told her in secret the story of his love.

And Radames, wandering through the vastness of Pharaoh's palace, dreams of Aïda, and longs for power. Visions of grandeur tower before him like the colossi of Osiris in the temple courts; hopes and fears agitate his soul, as varying winds from desert or sea bend the crests of the *dhoums* to the four points of heaven. In fancy he finds himself seated at the king's right hand, clad with the robes of honor, and wearing the ring of might;—second only to the most powerful of the Pharaohs. He lifts Aïda to share his greatness; he binds her brows with gold, and restores her to the land of her people. And even as he dreams, Ramphis, the deep-voiced priest, draws nigh, bearing the tidings of war and of battle-thunder rolling up from the land "shadowing with wings," which is beyond the river of Ethiopia. The priest has consulted with the Veiled Goddess—Isis, whose awful face no man may see and live. And the

Veiled One has chosen the great captain who shall lead the hosts of Egypt. "O happy man!—would that it were I!" cries Radames. But the priest utters not the name, and passes down the avenue of mighty pillars, and out into the day beyond.

Amneris, the daughter of Pharaoh, speaks words of love to Radames. His lips answer, but his heart is cold. And the subtle mind of the Egyptian maiden divines the fatal secret. Shall she hate her slave?

The priests summon the people of Egypt together; the will of the goddess is made manifest by the lips of Pharaoh himself. Radames shall lead the hosts of Egypt against the dark armies of Ethiopia. A roar of acclamation goes up to heaven. Aïda fears and weeps; it is against her beloved father, Amonasro, that her lover must lead the armies of the Nile. Radames is summoned to the mysterious halls of the Temple of Phthah:—through infinitely extending rows of columns illumined by holy flames he is led to the inner sanctuary itself. The linen-mantled priest performs the measure of their ancient and symbolic dance; the warriors clad in consecrated armor; about his loins is girt a sacred sword; and the vast temple re-echoes through all its deeps of dimness the harmonies of the awful hymn to the Eternal Spirit of Fire.

The ceremony is consummated.

The monarch proclaims tremendous war. Thebes opens her hundred mouths of brass and vomits forth her nations of armies. The land shakes to the earthquake of the chariot-roll;—numberless as ears of corn are the spear-blades of bronze;—the jaws of Egypt have opened to devour her enemies!

Aïda has confessed her love in agony; Amneris has falsely told her that her lover has fallen in battle. And the daughter of Pharaoh is strong and jealous.

* * *

As the white moon moves around the earth, as the stars circle in Egypt's rainless heaven, so circle the dancing-girls in voluptuous joy before the king—gauze-robed or clad only with jeweled girdles;—their limbs, supple as the serpents charmed by the serpent charmer, curve to the music of harpers harping upon fantastic harps. The earth quakes again; there is a sound in the distance as when a mighty tide approaches the land—a sound as of the thunder-chanting sea. The hosts of Egypt return. The chariots roar through the hundred gates of Thebes. Innumerable armies defile before the granite terraces of the Palace. Radames comes in the glory of his victory. Pharaoh descends from his throne to embrace him. "Ask what thou wilt, O Radames, even though it be the half of my kingdom!"

And Radames asks for the life of his captives. Amonasro is among them; and Aïda, beholding him, fears with an exceeding great fear. Yet none but she knows Amonasro; for he wears the garb of a soldier—none but she, and Radames. The priests cry for blood. But the king must keep his vow. The prisoners are set free. And Radames must wed the tall and comely Amneris, Pharaoh's only daughter.

It is night over Egypt. To Ramphis, the deep-voiced priest, tall Amneris must go. It is the eve of her nuptials. She must pray to the Veiled One, the mystic mother of love, to bless her happy union. Within the temple burn the holy lights; incense smoulders in the tripods of brass; solemn hymns resound through the vast-pillared sanctuary. Without, under the stars, Aïda glides like a shadow to meet her lover.

It is not her lover who comes. It is her father! "Aïda," mutters the deep but tender voice of Amonasro, "thou hast the daughter of Pharaoh in thy power! Radames loves thee! Wilt thou see again the blessed land of thy birth?—wilt thou inhale the balm of our forests?—wilt thou gaze upon our valleys and behold our temples of gold, and pray to the gods of thy fathers? Then it will only be needful for thee to learn what path the Egyptians will follow! Our people have risen in arms again! Radames loves thee!—he will tell thee all! What! dost thou hesitate? Refuse!—and they who died to free thee from captivity shall arise from the black gulf to curse thee! Refuse!—and the shade of thy mother will return from the tomb to curse thee! Refuse!—and I, thy father, shall disown thee and invoke upon thy head my everlasting curse!"

Radames comes! Amonasro, hiding in the shadow of the palms, hears all. Radames betrays his country to Aïda. "Save thyself!—fly with me!" she whispers to her lover. "Leave thy gods; we shall worship together in the temples of my country. The desert shall be our nuptial couch!—the silent stars the witness of our love. Let my black hair cover thee as a tent;—my eyes sustain thee;—my kisses console thee." And as she twines about him and he inhales the perfume of her lips and feels the beating of her heart, Radames forgets country and honor and faith and fame; and the fatal word is spoken. *Napata!*—Amonasro, from the shadows of the palm trees, shouts the word in triumph! There is a clash of brazen blades; Radames is seized by priests and soldiers: Amonasro and his daughter fly under cover of the night.

Vainly tall Amneris intercedes with the deep-voiced priest. Ramphis has spoken the word: "He shall die!" Vainly do the priests call upon Radames to defend himself against their terrible accusations. His lips are silent. He must die the death of traitors. They sentence him to living burial under the foundations of the temple, under the feet of the granite gods.

Under the feet of the deities they have made the tomb of Radames—a chasm wrought in a mountain of hewn granite. Above it the weird-faced gods with beards of basalt have sat for a thousand years. Their eyes of stone have beheld the courses of the stars change in heaven; generations have worshiped at their feet of granite. Rivers have changed their courses; dynasties have passed away since first they took their seats upon their thrones of mountain rock, and placed their giant hands upon their knees. Changeless as the granite hill from whose womb they were delivered by hieratic art, they watch over the face of Egypt, far-gazing through the pillars of the temple into the palm-shadowed valley beyond. Their will is inexorable as the hard rock of which their forms are wrought; their faces have neither pity nor mercy, because they are the faces of gods!

The priests close up the tomb; they chant their holy and awful hymn. Radames finds his Aïda beside him. She had concealed herself in the darkness that she might die in his arms.

The footsteps of the priests, the sacred hymn, die away. Alone in the darkness above, at the feet of the silent gods, there is a sound as of a woman's weeping. It is Amneris, the daughter of the king. Below in everlasting gloom the lovers are united at once in love and death. And Osiris, forever impassible, gazes into the infinite night with tearless eyes of stone.

A Creole Mystery

They came together from Havana, mistress and servant. The mistress had a strange and serpentine sort of beauty;—the litheness of a snake in every movement;—the fascination of an ophidian;—and great eyes that flamed like black opals. One felt on meeting her that the embraces of lianas and of ivy were less potent to fetter than hers—and to fetter forever. Her voice was remarkably sweet, but had strangely deep tones in it;—and her laugh caused a feeling of unpleasant surprise. It was a mocking, weird, deep laugh, uttered without any change of features; there was no smile, no movement of the facial muscles; the lips simply opened and the laugh came pealing from her white throat, while the eyes, large, brilliant, and sinister with mockery, fixed themselves with motionless lids upon the face of the person present. But she seldom laughed.

None knew who she was. She was a mystery to the French people of the quarter. Her rooms were luxuriously furnished and hung in blue satin. At long intervals strangers called upon her—men of olivaceous complexion and hair tropically black with dead-blue lights in it. They spoke only in Spanish; and their interviews lasted far into the night. Sometimes they seemed to be gay. Gossipy people said they heard the popping of champagne corks; and a perfume of Havana tobacco floated out of the windows and hung about the shrubbery that enshrouded the veranda. Sometimes, however, there were sinister sounds as of men's voices raised in anger, and at intervals the deep laugh of the mysterious woman, long and loud and clear, and vibrant with mockery.

The servant was a mulattress, tall and solidly constructed as a caryatid of bronze. She was not less of a mystery than her mistress. She spoke French and Spanish with equal facility, but these only on rare occasions. Generally no mute in the seraglio of a Sultan could be more silent or more impassible. She never smiled. She never gossiped. She never seemed to hear or to see; yet she saw and heard all. Only a strange face could attract her attention—for a brief moment, during which she gazed upon it with an indescribable look that seemed potent enough to burn what it touched. It was a look that made its living object feel that his face was photographed in her brain and would be equally vivid there fifty years after. The foreigners who came were received by her in silence and without scrutiny. Their faces were doubtless familiar. None of them ever spoke to her. She seemed to be more than a Doppelgänger, and to appear in five or six different rooms at the same time. Nothing could transpire unperceived by her; though she seemed never to look at anything. Her feet were never heard. She moved like a phantom through the house, opening and closing doors noiselessly as a ghost. She always suddenly appeared when least expected. When looked for, she was never to be found. Her mistress never called her. When needed, she appeared to rise suddenly from the floor, like those Genii of Arabian fables summoned by a voiceless wish. She never played with the children; and these hushed their voices when she glided by them in silence. With a subtle intelligence seemingly peculiar to her, she answered questions before they were fully asked. She never seemed to sleep. Persons who visited the house were as certain to meet her at the entrance three hours before sunrise as at any other hours. She appeared to be surprised at nothing, and to anticipate everything. She was even a greater mystery, if possible, than her mistress.

At last the swarthy foreigners called more frequently and the interviews grew stormier. It was said that sometimes the conversations were held in Catalan; and that when Catalan was spoken there were angrier words and wickeder laughing. And one night the interviews were so terrible that all the old-fashioned French folks in the quarter put their heads out of the windows to listen. There were sounds as of broken glass and passionate blows given to the mahogany table. And the strange laughter suddenly ceased.

Next morning the postman calling to deliver a registered letter found the rooms empty. The spectral servant was gone. The sinister mistress was gone. The furniture was all there; and the only records of the night's mystery were two broken glasses and stains of wine on the rich carpet. The bed had been undisturbed. The clock still ticked on its marble pedestal. The wind moved the blue silk hangings. A drowsy perfume of woman lingered in the rooms like incense. The wardrobes retained their wealth of silks and laces. The piano remained open. A little Angora cat was playing with a spool of silk under the table. A broken fan lay on the luxuriously padded rocking-chair; and a bouquet of camellias lay dying upon the mantelpiece.

The letter was never delivered. The rooms remained as they were, until mould and dust came to destroy the richness of their upholstery. The strangers never came back, nor did any ever hear what became of them. The mystery remains unexplained. The letter remains in the dead-letter office. But I would like to open it and find out what is in it;—wouldn't you?

El Vómito

The mother was a small and almost grotesque personage, with a somewhat mediæval face, oaken colored and long and full of Gothic angularity; only her eyes were young, full of vivacity and keen comprehension. The daughter was tall and slight and dark; a skin with the tint of Mexican gold; hair dead black and heavy with snaky ripples in it that made one think of Medusa; eyes large and of almost sinister brilliancy, heavily shadowed and steady as a falcon's; she had that lengthened grace of dancing figures on Greek vases, but on her face reigned the motionless beauty of bronze—never a smile or frown. The mother, a professed sorceress, who told the fortunes of veiled women by the light of a lamp burning before a skull, did not seem to me half so weird a creature as the daughter. The girl always made me think of Southey's witch, kept young by enchantment to charm Thalaba.

The house was a mysterious ruin: walls green with morbid vegetation of some fungous kind; humid rooms with rotting furniture of a luxurious and antiquated pattern; shrieking stairways; yielding and groaning floors; corridors forever dripping with a cold sweat; bats under the roof and rats under the floor; snails moving up and down by night in wakes of phosphorescent slime; broken shutters, shattered glass, lockless doors, mysterious icy draughts, and elfish noises. Outside there was a kind of savage garden—torchon trees, vines bearing spotted and suspicious flowers, Spanish bayonets growing in broken urns, agaves, palmettoes, something that looked like green elephant's ears, a monstrous and ill-smelling species of lily with a phallic pistil, and many vegetable eccentricities I have never seen before. In a little stable-yard at the farther end were dyspeptic chickens, nostalgic ducks, and a most ancient and rheumatic horse, whose feet were always in water, and who made nightmare moanings through all the hours of darkness. There were also dogs that never barked and spectral cats that never had a kittenhood. Still the very ghastliness of the place had its fantastic charm for me. I remained; the drowsy Southern spring came to vitalize vines and lend a Japanese monstrosity to the tropical jungle under my balconied window. Unfamiliar and extraordinary odors floated up from the spotted flowers; and the snails crawled upstairs less frequently than before. Then a fierce and fevered summer!

It was late in the night when I was summoned to the Cuban's bedside:—a night of such stifling and motionless heat as precedes a Gulf storm: the moon, magnified by the vapors, wore a spectral nimbus; the horizon pulsed with feverish lightnings. Its white flicker made shadowy the lamp-flame in the sick-room at intervals. I bade them close the windows. "*El Vómito?*"—already delirious; strange ravings; the fine dark face phantom-shadowed by death; singular and unfamiliar symptoms of pulsation and temperature; extraordinary mental disturbance. Could this be *Vómito?* There was an odd odor in the room—ghostly, faint, but sufficiently perceptible to affect the memory:—I suddenly remembered the balcony overhanging the African wildness of the garden, the strange vines that clung with webbed feet to the ruined wall, and the peculiar, heavy, sickly, somnolent smell of the spotted blossoms!—And as I leaned over the patient, I became aware of another perfume in the room, a perfume that impregnated the pillow—the odor of a woman's hair, the incense of a woman's youth mingling with the phantoms of the flowers, as ambrosia with venom, life with death, a breath from paradise with an exhalation from hell. From the bloodless lips of the sufferer, as from the mouth of one oppressed by some hideous dream, escaped the name of the witch's daughter. And suddenly the house shuddered through all its framework, as if under the weight of invisible blows:—a mighty shaking of walls and windows—the storm knocking at the door.

I found myself alone with her; the moans of the dying could not be shut out; and the storm knocked louder and more loudly, demanding entrance. *"It is not the fever,"* I said. "I have lived in lands of tropical fever; your lips are even now humid with his kisses, and you have condemned him. My knowledge avails nothing against this infernal craft; but I know also that you must know the antidote which will baffle death;—this man shall not die!—I do not fear you!—I will denounce you!—He shall not die!"

For the first time I beheld her smile—the smile of secret strength that scorns opposition. Gleaming through the diaphanous whiteness of her loose robe, the lamplight wrought in silhouette the serpentine grace of her body like the figure of an Egyptian dancer in a mist of veils, and her splendid hair coiled about her like the viperine locks of a gorgon.

"La voluntad de mi madre!" she answered calmly. "You are too late! You shall not denounce us! Even could you do so, you could prove nothing. Your science, as you have said, is worth nothing here. Do you pity the fly that nourishes the spider? You shall do nothing so foolish, señor doctor, but you will certify that the stranger has died of the *vómito*. You do not know anything; you shall not know anything. You will be recompensed. We are rich."—Without, the knocking increased, as if the thunder sought to enter: I, within,

looked upon her face, and the face was passionless and motionless as the face of a woman of bronze.

She had not spoken, but I felt her serpent litheness wound about me, her heart beating against my breast, her arms tightening about my neck, the perfume of her hair and of her youth and of her breath intoxicating me as an exhalation of enchantment. I could not speak; I could not resist; spellbound by a mingling of fascination and pleasure, witchcraft and passion, weakness and fear—and the storm awfully knocked without, as if summoning the stranger; and his moaning ceased.

Whence she came, the mother, I know not. She seemed to have risen from beneath:—

"The doctor is conscientious!—he cares for his patient well. The stranger will need his excellent attention no more. The conscientious doctor has accepted his recompense; he will certify what we desire—will he not, *hija mia?*"

And the girl mocked me with her eyes, and laughed fiercely.

A Kiss Fantastical

Curves of cheek and throat, and shadow of loose hair—the dark flash of dark eyes under the silk of black lashes—a passing vision light as a dream of summer—the sweet temptations of seventeen years' grace—womanhood at its springtime, when the bud is bursting through the blossom—the patter of feet that hardly touch ground in their elastic movement,—the light loose dress, moulding its softness upon the limbs beneath it, betraying much, suggesting the rest;—an apparition seen only for a moment passing through the subdued light of a vineshaded window, briefly as an object illuminated by lightning—yet such a moment may well be recorded by the guardian angels of men's lives.

"Croyez-vous ça?" suddenly demands a metallically sonorous voice at the other side of the table.

"Pardon!—qu'est-ce que c'est?" asks the stranger, in the tone of one suddenly awakened, internally annoyed at being disturbed, yet anxious to appear deeply interested. They had been talking of Japan—and the traveler, suddenly regaining the clue of the conversation, spoke of a bath-house at Yokohama, and of strange things he had seen there, until the memory of the recent vision mingled fantastically with recollections of the Japanese bathing-house, and he sank into another reverie, leaving the untasted cup of black coffee before him to mingle its dying aroma with the odor of the cigarettes.

* * *

For there are living apparitions that affect men more deeply than fancied visits from the world of ghosts;—numbing respiration momentarily, making the blood to gather about the heart like a great weight, hushing the voice to a murmur, creating an indescribable oppression in the throat—until nature seeks relief in a strong sigh that fills the lungs with air again and cools for a brief moment the sudden fever of the veins. The vision may endure but an instant— seen under a gleam of sunshine, or through the antiquated gateway one passes from time to time on his way to the serious part of the city; yet that instant is enough to change the currents of the blood, and slacken the reins of the will, and make us deaf and blind and dumb for a time to the world of SOLID FACT. The whole being is momentarily absorbed, enslaved by a vague and voiceless desire to touch her, to kiss her, to bite her.

The lemon-gold blaze in the west faded out; the blue became purple; and in the purple the mighty arch of stars burst into illumination, with its myriad blossoms of fire white as a woman's milk. A Spanish officer improved a momentary lull in the conversation by touching a guitar, and all eyes turned toward the musician, who suddenly wrung from his instrument the nervous, passionate, semi-barbaric melody of a Spanish dance. For a moment he played to an absolutely motionless audience; the very waving of the fans ceased, the listeners held their breath. Then two figures glided through the vine-framed doorway, and took their seats. One was the Vision of a few hours before—a type of semi-tropical grace, with the bloom of Southern youth upon her dark skin. The other immediately impressed the stranger as the ugliest little Mexican woman he had ever seen in the course of a long and experienced life.

She was grotesque as a Chinese image of Buddha, no taller than a child of ten, but very broadly built. Her skin had the ochre tint of new copper; her forehead was large and disagreeably high; her nose flat; her cheek-bones very broad and prominent; her eyes small, deeply set, and gray as pearls; her mouth alone small, passionate, and pouting, with rather thick lips, relieved the coarseness of her face. Although so compactly built, she had no aspect of plumpness or fleshiness:—she had the physical air of one of those little Mexican fillies which are all nerve and sinew. Both women were in white; and the dress of the little Mexican was short enough to expose a very pretty foot and well-turned ankle.

Another beautiful woman would scarcely have diverted the stranger's attention from the belle of the party that night; but that Mexican was so infernally ugly, and so devilishly comical, that he could not remove his eyes from her grotesque little face. He could not help remarking that her smile was pleasing if not pretty, and her teeth white as porcelain; that there was a strong, good-natured originality about her face, and that her uncouthness was only apparent, as she was the most accomplished dancer in the room. Even the belle's movements seemed heavy compared with hers; she appeared to dance as lightly as the hummingbird moves from blossom to blossom. By and by he found to his astonishment that this strange creature could fascinate without beauty and grace, and play coquette without art; also that her voice had pretty bird tones in it; likewise that the Spanish captain was very much interested in her, and determined to monopolize her as much as possible for the rest of the evening. And the stranger felt oddly annoyed thereat; and sought to console himself by the reflection that she was the most fantastically ugly little creature he had seen in his whole life. But for some mysterious reason consolation refused to come. "Well, I am going back to Honduras to-morrow," he thought—"and there thoughts of women will give me very little concern."

"I protest against this kissing," cried the roguish host in a loud voice, evidently referring to something that had just taken place in the embrasure of the farther window. "*On fait venir l'eau dans la bouche!* Monopoly is strictly prohibited. Our rights and feelings must be taken into just consideration." Frenzied applause followed. What difference did it make?—they were the world's Bohemians— here to-day, there to-morrow!—before another moonrise they would be scattered west and south;—the ladies ought to kiss them all for good luck.

So the kiss of farewell was given under the great gate, overhung by vine-tendrils drooping like a woman's hair love-loosened.

The beauty's lips shrank from the pressure of the stranger's;— it was a fruitless phantom sort of kiss. "*Y yo, señor,*" cried the little Mexican, standing on tiptoe as she threw her arms about his neck. Everybody laughed except the recipient of the embrace. He had received an electric shock of passion which left him voiceless and speechless, and it seemed to him that his heart had ceased to beat.

Those carmine-edged lips seemed to have a special life of their own as of the gymnotus—as if crimsoned by something more lava-warm than young veins: they pressed upon his mouth with the motion of something that at once bites and sucks blood irresistibly but softly, like the great bats which absorb the life of sleepers in tropical forests;—there was something moist and cool and supple indescribable in their clinging touch, as of beautiful snaky things which, however firmly clasped, slip through the hand with boneless strength;—they could not themselves be kissed because they mesmerized and mastered the mouth presented to them;—their touch for the instant paralyzed the blood, but only to fill its motionless currents with unquenchable fires as strange as of a tropical volcano, so that the heart strove to rise from its bed to meet them, and all the life of the man seemed to have risen to his throat only to strangle there in its effort at self-release. A feeble description, indeed; but how can such a kiss be described?

Six months later the stranger came back from Honduras, and deposited some small but heavy bags in the care of his old host. Then he called the old man aside, and talked long and earnestly and passionately, like one who makes a confession.

The landlord burst into a good-natured laugh, *"Ah la drôle!—la vilaine petite drôle!* So she made you crazy also. *Mon cher,* you are not the only one, *pardieu!* But the idea of returning here on account of one kiss, and then to be too late, after all! She is gone, my friend, gone. God knows where. Such women are birds of passage. You might seek the whole world and never find her; again, you might meet her when least expected. But you are too late. She married the *guitarrista."*

The Gipsy's Story

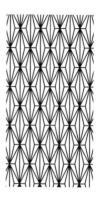

The summer's day had been buried in Charlemagne splendors of purple and gold; the Spanish sable of the night glittered with its jewel-belt of stars. The young moon had not yet lifted the silver horns of her Moslem standard in the far east. We were sailing over lukewarm waves, rising and falling softly as the breast of a sleeper; winds from the south bore to us a drowsy perfume of lemon-blossoms; and the yellow lights among the citron trees seemed, as we rocked upon the long swell, like the stars of Joseph's dream doing obeisance. Far beyond them a giant pharos glared at us with its single Cyclopean eye of bloodshot fire, dyeing the face of the pilot crimson as a pomegranate. At intervals the sea amorously lipped the smooth flanks of the vessel with a sharp sound; and ghostly fires played about our prow. Seated upon a coil of rope a *guitarrista* sang, improvising as he sang, one of those sweetly monotonous ballads which the Andalusian gypsies term *soleariyas*. Even now the rich tones of that solitary voice vibrate in our memory, almost as on that perfumed sea, under the light of summer stars:—

> *Sera,*
> *Para mi er mayo delirio*
> *Berte y no poerte habla.*

Gacho,
Gacho que no hab ya motas
Es un barco sin timon.

Por ti,
Las horitas e la noche
Me las paso sin dormi.

Sereno,
No de oste la boz tan arta
Que quieo dormi y no pueo.

Marina,
Con que te lavas la cara
Que la tienes tan dibina?

Why he told me his story I know not: I know only that our hearts understood each other.

"Of my mother," he said, "I knew little when a child; I only remember her in memories vague as dreams, and perhaps in dreams also. For there are years of our childhood so mingled with dreams that we cannot discern through memory the shadow from the substance. But in those times I was forever haunted by a voice that spoke a tongue only familiar to me in after years, and by a face I do not ever remember to have kissed.

"A clear, dark face, strong and delicate, with sharp crescent brows and singularly large eyes, liquidly black, bending over me in my sleep—the face of a tall woman. There was something savage even in the tenderness of the great luminous eyes—such a look as the hunter finds in the eyes of fierce birds when he climbs to their nests above the clouds; and this dark dream-face filled me with strange love and fear. The hair, flowing back from her temples in long ripples of jet, was confined by a broad silver comb curved and gleaming like a new moon.

"And at last when these dreams came upon me, and the half-fierce, loving eyes looked upon me in the night, I would awake and go out under the stars and sob.

"A vast unrest possessed me; a new heat throbbed in my veins, and I heard forever flute-tones of a strange voice, speaking in an unknown tongue;—but far, far off, like the sounds of words broken and borne away in fragments by some wandering wind.

"Ocean breezes sang in my ears the song of waves—of waves chanting the deep hymn that no musician can learn—the mystic hymn whereof no human ear may ever discern the words—the magical hymn that is older than the world, and weirder than the moon.

"The winds of the woods bore me odors of tears of spicy gums and the sounds of bird-voices sweeter than the plaint of running water, and whispers of shaking shadows, and the refrain of that mighty harp-song which the pines sing, and the vaporous souls of flowers, and the mysteries of succubus-vines that strangle the oaks with love.

"Winds also, piercing and cold as Northern eyes, came to me from the abysses of the rocks, and from peaks whose ermine of snow has never since the being of the world felt the pressure of a bird's foot; and they sang Runic chants of mountain freedom, where the lightnings cross their flickerings. And with these winds came also shadows of birds, far circling above me, with eyes fierce and beautiful as the eyes of my dream.

"So that a great envy came upon me of the winds and waves and birds that circle forever with the eternal circling of the world. Nightly the large eyes, half fierce, half tender, glimmered through my sleep:—phantom winds called to me, and shadowy seas chanted through their foam-flecked lips runes weird as the Runes of Odin.

"And I hated cities with the hatred of the camel—the camel that sobs and moans on beholding afar, on the yellow rim of the desert, the corpse-white finger of a minaret pointing to the dome of Mahomet's heaven.

"Also I hated the rumble of traffic and the roar of the race for gold; the shadows of palaces on burning streets; the sound of toiling feet; the black breath of towered chimneys; and the vast machines, forever laboring with sinews of brass, and panting with heart of steam and steel.

"Only loved I the eyes of night and the women eyes that haunted me—the silence of rolling plains, the whispers of untrodden woods, the shadows of flying birds and fleeting clouds, the heaving emerald of waves, the silver lamentation of brooks, the thunder roll of that mighty hymn of hexameters which the ocean must eternally sing to the stars.

"Once, and once only, did I speak to my father of the dark and beautiful dream that floated to me on the misty waves of sleep. Once, and once only; for I beheld his face grow whiter than the face of Death.

"Encompassed about by wealth and pleasure, I still felt like a bird in a cage of gold. Books I loved only because they taught me mysteries of sky and sea—the alchemy of suns, the magic of seasons, the marvels of lands to which we long forever to sail, yet may never see. But I loved wild rides by night, and long wrestling with waves silver-kissed by the moon, and the musky breath of woods, where wild doves wandered from shadow to shadow, cooing love. And the strange beauty of the falcon face, that haunted me forever, chilled my heart to the sun-haired maidens who sought our home, fair like tall idols of ivory and gold.

"Often, in the first pinkness of dawn, I rose from a restless sleep to look upon a mirror; thirsting to find in my own eyes some dark kindred with the eyes of my dreams; and often I felt in my veins the blood of a strange race, not my father's.

"I saw birds flying to the perfumed South; I watched the sea gulls seeking warmer coasts; I cursed the hawks for their freedom—I cursed the riches that were the price of my bondage to civilization, the pleasures that were the guerdon of my isolation among a people not my own.

—"'O that I were a cloud,' I cried, 'to drift forever with the hollow wind!—O that I were a wave to pass from ocean to ocean, and chant my freedom in foam upon the rocks of a thousand coasts!—O that I might live even as the eagle, who may look into the face of the everlasting sun!'

"So the summer of my life came upon me, with a madness of longing for freedom—a freedom as of winds and waves and birds— and a vague love for that unknown people whose wild blood made fever in my veins—until one starless night I fled my home forever.

"I slumbered in the woods at last; the birds were singing in the emerald shadows above when I awoke. A tall girl, lithe as a palm, swarthy as Egypt, was gazing upon me. My heart almost ceased to beat. I beheld in the wild beauty of her dark face as it were the shadow of the face that had haunted me; and in the midnight of her eyes the eyes of my dream. Circles of thin gold were in her ears;— her brown arms and feet were bare. She smiled not; but, keeping her great wild eyes fixed upon mine, addressed me in a strange tongue. Strange as India—yet not all strange to me; for at the sound of its savage syllables dusky chambers of memory long unvisited reopened their doors and revealed forgotten things. The tongue was the tongue spoken to me in dreams through all those restless years. And she, perceiving that I understood, although I spoke not, pointed to far tents beyond the trees, and ascending spirals of lazy smoke.

"'Whithersoever we go, thou shalt also go,' she murmured. 'Thou art of our people; the blood that flows in thy veins is also mine. We have long waited and watched for thee, summer by summer, in those months when the great longing comes upon us all. For thy mother was of my people; and thou who hast sucked her breasts mayst not live with the pale children of another race. The heaven is our tent; the birds guide our footsteps south and north; the stars lead us to the east and west. My people have sought word of thee even while wandering in lands of sunrise. Our blood is stronger than wine; our kindred dearer than gold. Thou wilt leave riches, pleasures, honors, and the life of cities for thy heart's sake; and I will be thy sister.'

"And I, having kissed her, followed her to the tents of her people—my people—the world wanderers of the most ancient East."

The One Pill-Box

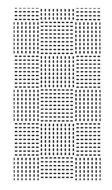

Like Nebuchadnezzar's furnace, the sun seemed to blaze with sevenfold heat; the sky glowed like steel in the process of blistering; a haze yellow as the radiance above a crucible gilded the streets; the great plants swooned in the garden—fainting flowers laid their heads on the dry clay; the winds were dead; the Yellow Plague filled the city with invisible exhalations of death. A silence as of cemeteries weighed down upon the place; commerce slept a wasting slumber; the iron muscles and brazen bones of wealth machinery relaxed, and lungs of steel ceased their panting; the ships had spread their white wings and flown; the wharves were desolate; the cotton-presses ceased their mighty mastication, and no longer uttered their titanic sighs.

The English mill-master had remained at his post, with the obstinate courage of his race, until stricken down. There was a sound in his ears as of rushing waters; darkness before his eyes: the whispering of the nurses, the orders of the physicians, the tinkling of glasses and spoons, the bubbling of medicine poured out, the sound of doors softly opened and closed, and of visits made on tiptoe, he no longer heard or remembered. The last object his eyes had rested upon was a tiny white-and-red pill-box, lying on the little table beside the bed.

The past came to him in shadowy pictures between dark intervals of half-conscious suffering—of such violent pain in thighs and loins as he remembered to have felt long years before after some frightful fall from a broken scaffolding. The sound in his ears of rushing water gradually sharpened into a keener sound—like the hum of machinery, like the purring of revolving saws, gnawing their meal of odorous wood with invisibly rapid teeth. Odors of cypress and pine, walnut and oak, seemed to float to his nostrils—with sounds of planing and beveling, hammering and polishing, subdued laughter of workmen, loud orders, hurrying feet, and above all the sharp, trilling purr of the hungry saws, and the shaking rumble of the hundred-handed engines.

He was again in the little office, fresh with odors of resinous woods—seated at the tall desk whose thin legs trembled with the palpitation of the engine's heart. It seemed to him there was a vast press of work to be done—enormous efforts to be made—intricate contracts to be unknotted—huge estimates to be made out—agonizing errors to be remedied—frightful miscalculations to be corrected—a world of anxious faces impatiently watching him. Figures and diagrams swam before his eyes—plans of facades—mathematical calculations for stairways—difficult angles of roofs—puzzling arrangements of corridors. The drawings seemed to vary their shape with fantastic spitefulness; squares lengthened into parallelograms and distorted themselves into rhomboids—circles mockingly formed themselves into ciphers—triangles became superimposed, like the necromantic six-pointed star. Then numerals mingled with the draw-ings—columns of magical figures which could never be added up, because they seemed to lengthen themselves at will with serpent elasticity—a mad procession of confused notes in addition and subtraction, in division and multiplication, danced before him. And the world of anxious faces watched yet more impatiently.

* * *

All was dark again; the merciless pain in loins and thighs had returned with sharp consciousness of the fever, and the insufferable heat and skull-splitting headache—heavy blankets and miserable helplessness—and the recollection of the very, very small pill-box on the table. Then it seemed to him there were other pill-boxes— three! nine! twenty-seven! eighty-one! one hundred and sixty-two! one hundred and sixty-two very small pill-boxes.

He seemed to be wandering in a cemetery, under blazing sunlight and in a blinding glare of whitewashed tombs, whose skeletons of brick were left bare in leprous patches by the falling away of the plastering. And, wandering, he came to a deep wall, catacombed from base to summit with the resting-places of ten thousand dead; and there was one empty place—one black void—inscribed with a name strangely like his own. And a great weariness and faintness came upon him; and the pains, returning, carried back his thoughts to the warmth and dimness of the sick-room.

It seemed to him that this could not be death—he was too weary even to die! But they would put him into the hollow void in the wall!—they might: he would not resist, he felt no fear. He could rest there very well even for a hundred years. He had a gimlet somewhere!—they would let him take it with him;—he could bore a tiny little hole in the wall so that a thread of sunlight would creep into his resting-place every day, and he could hear the voices of the world about him. Yet perhaps he should never be able to leave that dark damp place again!—It was very possible; seeing that he was so tired. And there was so much to be arranged first: there were estimates and plans and contracts; and nobody else could make them out; and everything would be left in such confusion! And perhaps he might not even be able to think in a little while; all the knowledge he had stored up would be lost; nobody could think much or say much after having been buried. And he thought again of the pill-boxes—one hundred and sixty-two very small pill-boxes. No; there were exactly three hundred and sixty-six! Perhaps that was because it was leap year.

Everything must be arranged at once!—at once! The pill-boxes would do; he could breathe his thoughts into them and close them tightly—recollections of estimates, corrections of plans, directions to the stair-builders, understanding with contractors, orders to the lumber dealers, instructions to Texan and Mississippi agents, answers to anxious architects, messages to the senior partner, explanations to the firm of X and W. Then it seemed to him that each little box received its deposit of memories, and became light as flame, buoyant as a bubble;—rising in the air to float halfway between floor and ceiling. A great anxiety suddenly came upon him;—the windows were all open, and the opening of the door might cause a current. All these little thoughts would float away!—yet he could not rise to lock the door! The boxes were all there, floating above him light as motes in a sunbeam:—there were so many now that he could not count them! If the nurse would only stay away! …Then all became dark again—a darkness as of solid ebony, heavy, crushing, black, blank, universal….

All lost! Brutally the door opened and closed again with a cruel clap of thunder…. Yellow lightnings played circling before his eyes…. The pill-boxes were gone! But was not that the face of the doctor, anxious and kindly? The burning day was dead; the sick man turned his eyes to the open windows, and beheld the fathomless purple of the night, and the milky blossoms of the stars. And he strove to speak, but could not! The light of a shaded lamp falling upon the table illuminated a tiny object, blood-scarlet by day, carmine under the saffron artificial light. *There was only one pill-box.*

The Book of Thoth

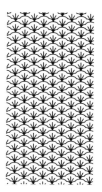

An Egyptian tale of weirdness, as told in a demotic papyrus found in the necropolis of Deir-el-Medineh among the ruins of hundred-gated Thebes.... Written in the thirty-fifth year of the reign of some forgotten Ptolomæus, and in the month of Tybi completed by a scribe famous among magicians.... Dedicated, doubtless, to Thoth, Lord of all Scribes, Grand Master of all Sorcerers; whose grace had been reverently invoked upon whomsoever might speak well concerning the same papyrus....

Thoth, the divine, lord of scribes, most excellent of workers, prince of wizards, once, it is said, wrote with his own hand a book surpassing all other books, and containing two magical formulas only. Whosoever could recite the first of these formulas would become forthwith second only to the gods—for by its simple utterance the mountains and the valleys, the ocean and the clouds, the heights of heaven and the deeps of hell, would be made subject unto his will; while the birds of air, the reptiles of darkness, and the fishes of the waters, would be thereby compelled to appear, and to make manifest the thoughts secreted within their hearts. But whosoever could recite the second formula might never know death—for even though buried within the entrails of the earth, he would still behold heaven through the darkness and hear the voices of earth athwart the silence; even in the necropolis he would still see the rising and setting of the sun, and the Cycle of the Gods, and the waxing and waning of the moon, and the eternal lights of the firmament.

And the god Thoth deposited his book within a casket of gold, and the casket of gold within a casket of silver, and the casket of silver within a casket of ivory and ebony, and the casket of ivory and ebony within a casket of palm-wood, and the casket of palm-wood within a casket of bronze, and the casket of bronze within a casket of iron. And he buried the same in the bed of the great river of Egypt where it flows through the Nome of Coptos; and immortal river monsters coiled about the casket to guard it from all magicians.

Now, of all magicians, Noferkephtah, the son of King Minibphtah (to whom be life, health, and strength forevermore!), first by cunning discovered the place where the wondrous book was hidden, and found courage to possess himself thereof. For after he had well paid the wisest of the ancient priests to direct his way, Noferkephtah obtained from his father Pharaoh a royal cangia, well supplied and stoutly manned, wherein he journeyed to Coptos in search of the hidden treasure. Coming to Coptos after many days, he created him a magical boat and a magical crew by reciting mystic words; and he and the shadowy crew with him toiled to find the casket; and by the building of dams they were enabled to find it. Then Noferkephtah prevailed also against the immortal serpent by dint of sorcery; and he obtained the book, and read the mystic formulas, and made himself second only to the gods.

But the divinities, being wroth with him, caused his sister and wife Ahouri to fall into the Nile, and his son also. Noferkephtah indeed compelled the river to restore them; but although the power of the book maintained their life after a strange fashion, they lived not as before, so that he had to bury them in the necropolis at

Coptos. Seeing these things and fearing to return to the king alone, he tied the book above his heart, and also allowed himself to drown. The power of the book, indeed, maintained his life after a strange fashion; but he lived not as before, so that they took him back to Thebes as one who had passed over to Amenthi, and there laid him with his fathers, and the book also.

Yet, by the power of the book, he lived within the darkness of the tomb, and beheld the sun rising, and the Cycle of the Gods, and the phases of the moon, and the stars of the night. By the power of the book, also, he summoned to him the shadow of his sister Ahouri, buried at Coptos—whom he had made his wife according to the custom of the Egyptians; and there was light within their dwelling-place. Thus Noferkephtah knew ghostly happiness in the company of the Ka, or shadow, of his wife Ahouri, and the Ka of his son Mikhonsou.

Now, four generations had passed since the time of King Minibphtah; and the Pharaoh of Egypt was Ousirmari. Ousirmari had two sons who were learned among the Egyptians—Satni was the name of the elder; Anhathorerôou that of the younger. There was not in all Egypt so wise a scribe as Satni. He knew how to read the sacred writings, and the inscriptions upon the amulets, and the sentences within the tombs, and the words graven upon the stelæ, and the books of that sacerdotal library called the "Double House of Life." Also he knew the composition of all formulas of sorcery and of all sentences which spirits obey, so that there was no enchanter like him in all Egypt. And Satni heard of Noferkephtah and the book of Thoth from a certain aged priest, and resolved that he would obtain it. But the aged priest warned him, saying, "Beware thou dost not wrest the book from Noferkephtah, else thou wilt be enchanted by him, and compelled to bear it back to him within the tomb, and do great penance."

Nevertheless Satni sought and obtained permission of the king to descend into the necropolis of Thebes, and to take away, if he might, the book from thence. So he went thither with his brother.

Three days and three nights the brothers sought for the tomb of Noferkephtah in the immeasurable city of the dead; and after they had threaded many miles of black corridors, and descended into many hundred burial pits, and were weary with the deciphering of innumerable inscriptions by quivering light of lamps, they found his resting-place at last. Now, when they entered the tomb their eyes were dazzled; for Noferkephtah was lying there with his wife Ahouri beside him; and the book of Thoth, placed between them, shed such a light around, that it seemed like the brightness of the sun. And when Satni entered, the Shadow of Ahouri rose against the light; and she asked him, "Who art thou?"

Then Satni answered: "I am Satni, son of King Ousirmari; and I come for the book of Thoth which is between thee and Noferkephtah; and if thou wilt not give it me, I shall wrest it away by force."

But the Shadow of the woman replied to him: "Nay, be not unreasoning in thy words! Do not ask for this book. For we, in obtaining it, were deprived of the pleasure of living upon earth for the term naturally allotted us; neither is this enchanted life within the tomb like unto the life of Egypt. Nowise can the book serve thee; therefore listen rather to the recital of all those sorrows which befell us by reason of this book...."

But after hearing the story of Ahouri, the heart of Satni remained as bronze; and he only repeated: "If thou wilt not give me the book which is between thee and Noferkephtah, I shall wrest it away by force."

Then Noferkephtah rose up within the tomb, and laughed, saying: "O Satni, if thou art indeed a true scribe, win this book from me by thy skill! If thou art not afraid, play against me a game for the possession of this book—a game of *fifty-two!*" Now there was a chess-board within the tomb.

Then Satni played a game of chess with Noferkephtah, while the Kas, the Shadows, the Doubles of Ahouri, and the large-eyed boy looked on. But the eyes with which they gazed upon him, and the eyes of Noferkephtah also, strangely disturbed him, so that Satni's brain whirled, and the web of his thought became entangled, and he lost! Noferkephtah laughed, and uttered a magical word, and placed the chess-board upon Satni's head; and Satni sank to his knees into the floor of the tomb.

Again they played, and the result was the same. Then Noferkephtah uttered another magical word, and again placed the chess-board upon Satni's head; and Satni sank to his hips into the floor of the tomb.

Once more they played, and the result was the same. Then Noferkephtah uttered a third magical word, and laid the chess-board on Satni's head, and Satni sank up to his ears into the floor of the tomb!

Then Satni shrieked to his brother to bring him certain talismans quickly; and the brother fetched the talismans, and placed them upon Satni's head, and by magical amulets saved him from the power of Noferkephtah. But having done this, Anhathorerôou fell dead within the tomb.

And Satni put forth his hand and took the book from Noferkephtah, and went out of the tomb into the corridors; while the book lighted the way for him, so that a great brightness traveled before him, and deep blackness went after him. Into the darkness Ahouri followed him, lamenting, and crying out: "Woe! Woe upon us! The light that gave life is taken from us; the hideous Nothingness will come upon us! Now, indeed, will annihilation enter into the tomb!" But Noferkephtah called Ahouri to him, and bade her cease to weep, saying to her: "Grieve not after the book; for I shall make him bring it back to me, with a fork and stick in his hand and a lighted brazier upon his head."

But when the king Ousirmari heard of all that had taken place, he became very much alarmed for his son, and said to him: "Behold! Thy folly has already caused the death of thy brother Anhathorerôou; take heed, therefore, lest it bring about thine own destruction likewise. Noferkephtah dead is even a mightier magician than thou. Take back the book forthwith, lest he destroy thee."

And Satni replied: "Lo! Never have I owned a sensual wish, nor done evil to *living* creature; how, then, can the dead prevail against me? It is only the foolish scribe—the scribe who hath not learned the mastery of passions—that may be overcome by enchantment."

And he kept the book.

Now it came to pass that a few days after, while Satni stood upon the parvise of the temple of Pthah, he beheld a woman so beautiful that from the moment his eyes fell upon her he ceased to act like one living, and all the world grew like a dream about him. And while the young woman was praying in the temple, Satni heard that her name was Thoutboui, daughter of a prophet. Whereupon he sent a messenger to her, saying: "Thus declares my master: I, the Prince Satni, son of King Ousirmari, do so love thee that I feel as one about to die.... If thou wilt love me as I desire, thou shalt have kingliest gifts; otherwise, know that I have the power to bury thee alive among the dead, so that none may ever see thee again."

And Thoutboui on hearing these words appeared not at all astonished, nor angered, nor terrified; but her great black eyes laughed, and she answered, saying: "Tell thy master, Prince Satni, son of King Ousirmari, to visit me within my house at Bubastes, whither I am even now going,"... Thereupon she went away with her retinue of maidens.

So Satni hastened forthwith to Bubastes by the river, and to the house of Thoutboui, the prophet's daughter. In all the place there was no house like unto her house; it was lofty and long, and surrounded by a garden all encircled with a white wall. And Satni followed Thoutboui's serving-maid into the house, and by a coiling stairway to an upper chamber wherein were broad beds of ebony and ivory, and rich furniture curiously carved, and tripods with burning perfumes, and tables of cedar with cups of gold. And the walls were coated with lapis-lazuli inlaid with emerald, making a strange and pleasant light.... Thoutboui appeared upon the threshold, robed in textures of white, transparent as the dresses of those dancing women limned upon the walls of the Pharaohs' palace; and as she stood against the light, Satni, beholding the litheness of her limbs, the flexibility of her body, felt his heart cease to beat within him, so that he could not speak. But she served him with wine, and took from his hands the gifts which he had brought—and she suffered him to kiss her.

Then said Thoutboui: "Not lightly is my love to be bought with gifts. Yet will I test thee, since thou dost so desire. If thou wilt be loved by me, therefore, make over to me by deed all thou hast—thy gold and thy silver, thy lands and houses, thy goods and all that belongs to thee. So that the house wherein I dwell may become thy house!"

And Satni, looking into the long black jewels of her eyes, forgot the worth of all that he possessed; and a scribe was summoned, and the scribe drew up the deed giving to Thoutboui all the goods of Satni.

Then said Thoutboui: "Still will I test thee, since thou dost so desire. If thou wilt have my love, make over to me thy children, also, as my slaves, lest they should seek dispute with my children concerning that which was thine. So that the house in which I dwell may become thy house!"

And Satni, gazing upon the witchery of her bosom, curved like ivory carving, rounded like the eggs of the ostrich, forgot his loving children; and the deed was written…. Even at that moment a messenger came, saying: "O Satni, thy children are below, and await thee." And he said: "Bid them ascend hither."

Then said Thoutboui: "Still will I test thee, since thou dost so desire. If thou wilt have my love, let thy children be put to death, lest at some future time they seek to claim that which thou hast given. So that the house in which I dwell may be thy house!"

And Satni, enchanted with the enchantment of her pliant stature, of her palmy grace, of her ivorine beauty, forgot even his fatherhood, and answered: "Be it so; were I ruler of heaven, even heaven would I give thee for a kiss."

Then Thoutboui had the children of Satni slain before his eyes; yet he sought not to save them! She bade her servant cast their bodies from the windows to the cats and to the dogs below; yet Satni lifted not his hand to prevent it! And while he drank wine with Thoutboui, he could hear the growling of the animals that were eating the flesh of his children. But he only moaned to her: "Give me thy love! I am as one in hell for thy sake!" And she arose, and, entering another chamber, turned and held out her wonderful arms to him, and drew him to her with the sorcery of her unutterable eyes….

But as Satni sought to clasp her and to kiss her, lo! Her ruddy mouth opened and extended and broadened and deepened—yawning wider, darker, quickly, vastly—a blackness as of necropoles, a vastness as of Amenthi! And Satni beheld only a gulf before him, deepening and shadowing like night; and from out the gulf a burst of tempest roared up, and bore him with it, and whirled him abroad as a leaf. And his senses left him….

… When he came again to himself, he was lying naked at the entrance of the subterranean sepulchres; and a great horror and despair came upon him, so that he purposed ending his life. But the servants of the king found him, and bore him safely to his father. And Ousirmari heard the ghostly tale.

Then said Ousirmari: "O Satni, Noferkephtah dead is a mightier magician than even thou living. Know, my son, first of all that thy children are alive and well in my own care; know, also, that the woman by whose beauty thou wert bewitched, and for whom thou hast in thought committed all heinous crimes, was a phantom wrought by Noferkephtah's magic. Thus, by exciting thee to passion, did he bring thy magical power to nought. And now, my dear son, haste with the book to Noferkephtah, lest thou perish utterly, with all thy kindred."

So Satni took the book of Thoth, and, carrying a fork and stick in his hands and a lighted brazier upon his head, carried it to the Theban necropolis and into the tomb of Noferkephtah. And Ahouri clapped her hands, and smiled to see the light again return. And Noferkephtah laughed, saying: "Did I not tell thee beforehand?" "Aye!" said Ahouri, "thou wert enchanted, O Satni!" But Satni, prostrating himself before Noferkephtah, asked how he might make atonement.

"O Satni," answered Noferkephtah, "my wife and my son are indeed buried at Coptos; these whom thou seest here are their Doubles only—their Shadows, their Kas—maintained with me by enchantment. Seek out their resting-place at Coptos, therefore, and bury their bodies with me, that we may all be thus reunited, and that thou mayst do penance.".…

So Satni went to Coptos, and there found an ancient priest, who told him the place of Ahouri's sepulture, saying: "The father of the father of my father told it to my father's father, who told it to my father.".… Then Satni found the bodies, and restored to Noferkephtah his wife and his son; and thus did penance. After which the tomb of Noferkephtah was sealed up forever by Pharaoh's order; and no man knoweth more the place of Noferkephtah's sepulture.

The Fountain Maiden

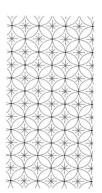

A legend of that pacific land where garments are worn by none save the dead; where the beauty of youth is as the beauty of statues of amber; where through eternal summer even the mountains refuse to don a girdle of cloud....

> "MIGHTY OMATAIANUKU!
> Dark Avaava the Tall!
> Tall Outuutu!
> Shadow the way for us!
> Tower as the cocoa-palms before us!
> Bend ye as dreams above the slumberers!
> Make deeper the sleep of the sleepers!

"Sleep, ye crickets of the threshold! Sleep, ye never reposing ants! Sleep, ye shining beetles of the night!

"Winds, cease ye from whispering! Restless grass, pause in thy rustling! Leaves of the palms, be still! Reeds of the water-ways, sway not! Blue river, cease thy lipping of the banks!

"Slumber, ye beams of the house, ye posts, great and small, ye rafters and ridge-poles, thatchings of grass, woven work of reeds, windows bamboo-latticed, doors that squeak like ghosts, low-glimmering fires of sandal-wood—slumber ye all!

O Omataianuku!
Tall Outuutu!
Dark Avaava!
Make shadowy the way for us!
Tower as the cocoa-palms before us!
Bend ye as dreams above the slumberers!
Make deeper the sleep of the sleepers—
Deeper the sleep of the winds—
Deeper the sleep of the waters—
Dimmer the dimness of night!
Veil ye the moon with your breathings!
Make fainter the fires of the stars!
In the name of the weird ones:
Omataianuku!
Outuuturoraa!
Ovaavaroroa!
Sleep!
Sleep!"

So, with the rising of each new moon, was heard the magical song of the thieves—the first night, low as the humming of the wind among the cocoa-palms; louder and louder each succeeding night, and clearer and sweeter, until the great white face of the full moon flooded the woods with light, and made silver pools about the columns of the palms. For the magic of the full moon was mightier than the witchcraft of the song; and the people of Rarotonga slept not. But of other nights the invisible thieves did carry away many coconuts and taros, and plantains and bananas, despite the snares set for them by the people of Rarotonga. And it was observed with terror that coconuts were removed from the crests of trees so lofty that no human hand might have reached them.

* * *

But the chief Aki, being one night by the fountain Vaipiki, which gushes out from the place of waters that flow below the world, beheld rising up from the water, just as the thin moon looked into it, a youth and a girl whiter than the moon herself, naked as fishes, beautiful as dreams. And they began to sing a song, at whose sound Aki, hidden among the pandanus leaves, stopped his ears—the wizard-song, *E tira Omataianuku, E tira Outuuturoroa!* And the winds were stilled, and the waves sank to sleep, and the palm-leaves ceased to nod, and the song of the crickets was hushed.

Then Aki, devising to capture them, set a great fish-net deep within the fountain, and waited for their return. The vast silence of the night deepened; the smoke of the mountain of fire, blood-tinted from below, hung motionless in the sky, like a giant's plume of feathers. At last the winds of the sea began their ghost whisperings among the palm-groves; a cricket chirped, and a million insect-chants responded; the new moon plunged one of her pale horns into the ocean; the east whitened and changed hue like the belly of a shark. The spell was broken, the day was dawning.

And Aki beheld the White Ones returning, bearing with them fruits and nuts and fragrant herbs. Rising suddenly from his hiding-place among the leaves, he rushed upon them; and they leaped into the fountain, like fishes, leaving their fruits scattered upon the brink. But, lo! They were caught in the net!

Then Aki strove to pull the net on shore; and, being a strong man, he easily moved it. But, in turning, the male leaped through the opening of the net, and flashed like a salmon through the deeps down to the unknown abyss of waters below, so that Aki caught the girl only. Vainly she struggled in the net; and her moon-white body took opalescent gleams, like the body of a beautiful fish in the hands of the captor. Vainly she wept and pleaded; and Aki blocked up the bottom of the fountain with huge blocks of coral, lest, slipping away from him, she might disappear again. But, looking upon the strangeness of her beauty, he kissed her and comforted her; and she ceased at last to weep. Her eyes were large and dark, like a tropical heaven flashed with stars.

So it came to pass that Aki loved her; more than his own life he loved her. And the people wondered at her beauty; for light came from her as she moved, and when she swam in the river her passage was like the path of the moon on waters—a quivering column of brightness. Only, it was noticed that this luminous beauty waxed and waned contrariwise to the waxing and waning of the moon: her whiteness was whitest at the time of the new moon; it almost ceased to glow when the face of the moon was full. And whensoever the new moon rose, she wept silently, so that Aki could not comfort her, even after having taught her the words of love in the tongue of his own people—the tongue, many-voweled, that wooes the listener like the mockery of a night-bird's song.

Thus many years passed away, and Aki became old; but she seemed ever the same, for the strange race to which she belonged never grow old. Then it was noticed that her eyes became deeper and sweeter—weirdly sweet; and Aki knew that he would become a father in his age. Yet she wept and pleaded with him, saying:

"Lo! I am not of thy race, and at last I must leave thee. If thou lovest me, sever this white body of mine, and save our child; for if it suckle me, I must dwell ten years longer in this world to which I do not belong. Thou canst not hurt me thus; for though I seem to die, yet my body will live on—thou mayst not wound me more than water is wounded by axe or spear! For I am of the water and the light, of moonshine and of wind! And I may not suckle thy child."…

But Aki, fearing that he might lose both her and the child,

pleaded with her successfully. And the child was beautiful as a white star, and she nursed it for ten happy years.

But, the ten years having passed, she kissed Aki, and said to him, "Alas! I must now leave thee, lest I die utterly; take thou away, therefore, the coral rocks from the fountain." And kissing him once more, she vowed to come back again, so that he complied at last with her request. She would have had him go with her; but he could not, being only mortal man. Then she passed away in the fountain deeps, like a gleam of light.

The child grew up very tall and beautiful, but not like his mother—white only like strangers from beyond the sea. In his eyes there was, nevertheless, a strange light, brightest at the time of the new moon, waning with its waxing.... One night there came a great storm: the cocoa-palms bent like reeds, and a strange voice came with the wind, crying, calling! At dawn the white youth was gone, nor did human eyes ever behold him again.

But Aki lived beyond a hundred years, waiting for the return by the Vaipiki fountain, until his hair was whiter than the summer clouds. At last the people carried him away, and laid him in his house on a bed of pandanus leaves; and all the women watched over him, lest he should die.

... It was the night of a new month, and the rising of the new moon. Suddenly a low sweet voice was heard, singing the old song that some remembered after the passing of half a hundred years. Sweeter and sweeter it grew; higher rose the moon! The crickets ceased to sing; the cocoa-palms refused obeisance to the wind. And a heaviness fell upon the watchers, who, with open eyes, could move no limb, utter no voice. Then all were aware of a White Woman, whiter than moonlight, lithe-fashioned as a lake-fish, gliding between the ranks of the watchers; and, taking Aki's gray head upon her bright breast, she sang to him, and kissed him, and stroked his aged face....

The sun arose; the watchers awakened. They bent over Aki, and it seemed that Aki slept lightly. But when they called him, he answered not; when they touched him, he stirred not. He slept forever!...

The Bird Wife

There the Moon becometh old and again young many times, as one that dieth often and is reanimated as often by enchantment; while the Sun moveth in a circle of pallid mists, and setteth not. But when he setteth at last, it is still light; for the dead make red fires in the sky above the icebergs until after many, many dim months he riseth again.

All things there are white, save the black sea and the wan fogs; and yet it is hard to discover where the water ends and the land begins, for that part of the world the gods forgot to finish. The ice-peaks grow and diminish, and shift their range northward and southward, and change their aspects grotesquely. There are Faces in the ice that lengthen and broaden; and Forms as of vanished creatures. When it is full moon the innumerable multitude of dogs, that live upon dead fish, howl all together at the roaring sea; and the great bears hearing huddle themselves together on the highest heights of the glaciers, and thence hurl down sharp white crags upon the dogs. Above all, rising into the Red Lights, there is a mountain which has been a fountain of living fire ever since the being of the world; and all the surface of the land about is heaped with monstrous bones. But this is summer in that place; in winter there is no sound but the groaning of the ice, the shrieking of the winds, the gnashing of the teeth of the floes.

Now there are men in those parts, whose houses are huts of snow, lighted by lamps fed with the oil of sea-creatures; and the wild dogs obey them. But they live in fear of the Havstramb, that monster which has the form of an armless man and the green color of ancient ice; they fear the Margige, shaped like a woman, which cries under the ice on which their huts repose; and the goblin Bear whose fangs are icicles; and the Kajarissat, which are the spirits of the icebergs, drawing the kayaks under the black water; and the ghostly ivory-hunter who drives his vapory and voiceless team over ice thinner than the scales of fish; and the white Spectre that lies in wait for those who lose their way by night, having power to destroy all whom he can excite to laughter by weird devices; and the white-eyed deer which must not be pursued. There also is the home of the warlocks, the wizards, the Iliseetsut—creators of the Tupilek.

Now the Tupilek is of all awful things the most awful, of all unutterable things the most unutterable.

For that land is full of bones—the bones of sea monsters and of earth monsters, the skulls and ribs of creatures that perished in eons ere man was born; and there are mountains, there are islands, of these bones. Sometimes great merchants from far southern countries send thither ivory-hunters with sledges and innumerable dogs to risk their lives for those white teeth, those terrific tusks, which protrude from the ice and from the sand, that is not deep enough to cover them. And the Iliseetsut seek out the hugest of these bones, and wrap them in a great whale skin, together with the hearts and the brains of many sea creatures and earth animals; and they utter strange words over them. Then the vast mass quivers and groans and shapes itself into a form more hideous, more enormous, than any form created by the gods; it moves upon many feet; it sees with many eyes; it devours with innumerable teeth; it obeys the will of its creator; it is a Tupilek!

* * *

And all things change form in that place—even as the ice shifts its shapes fantastically, as the boundaries of the sand eternally vary, as bone becomes earth and earth seems to become bone. So animals also take human likeness, birds assume human bodies; for there is sorcery in all things there. Thus it came to pass, one day, that a certain ivory-hunter beheld a flock of sea-birds change themselves into women; and creeping cautiously over the white snow—himself being clad in white skins—he came suddenly upon them, and caught hold of the nearest one with a strong hand, while the rest, turning again to birds, flew southward with long weird screams.

Slender was the girl, like a young moon, and as white; and her eyes black and soft, like those of the wild gulls. So the hunter—finding that she struggled not, but only wept—felt pity for her, and, taking her into his warm hut of snow, clothed her in soft skins and fed her with the heart of a great fish. Then, his pity turning to love, she became his wife.

Two years they lived thus together, and he fed her with both fish and flesh, being skillful in the use of the net and the bow; but always while absent he blocked up the door of the hut, lest she might change into a bird again, and so take wing. After she had borne him two children, nevertheless, his fear passed from him, like the memory of a dream; and she followed him to the chase, managing the bow with wonderful skill. But she prevailed upon him that he should not smite the wild gulls.

So they lived and so loved until the children became strong and swift.

Then it came to pass one day, while they were hunting all together, that many birds had been killed; and she called to the children, "Little ones, bring me quickly some feathers!" And they came to her with their hands full; and she laid the feathers upon their arms and upon her own shoulders, and shrieked to them, "Fly! Ye are of the race of birds, ye are the Wind's children!"

Forthwith their garments fell from them; and, being changed into wild gulls, mother and children rose in the bright icy air, circling and circling, higher and higher, against the sky. Thrice above the weeping father they turned in spiral flight, thrice screamed above the peaks of glimmering ice, and, sweeping suddenly toward the far south, whirred away forever.

The Soul of the Great Bell

She hath spoken, and her words still resound in his ears.

HAO-KHIEOU-TCHOUAN: c. ix

The water-clock marks the hour in the *Ta-chung sz'*—in the Tower of the Great Bell: now the mallet is lifted to smite the lips of the metal monster—the vast lips inscribed with Buddhist texts from the sacred *Fa-hwa-King*, from the chapters of the holy *Ling-yen-King*! Hear the great bell responding!—how mighty her voice, though tongueless!—KO-NGAI! All the little dragons on the high-tilted eaves of the green roofs shiver to the tips of their gilded tails under that deep wave of sound; all the porcelain gargoyles tremble on their carven perches; all the hundred little bells of the pagodas quiver with desire to speak. KO-NGAI!—all the green-and-gold tiles of the temple are vibrating; the wooden goldfish above them are writhing against the sky; the uplifted finger of Fo shakes high over the heads of the worshippers through the blue fog of incense! KO-NGAI!—What a thunder tone was that! All the lacquered goblins on the palace cornices wriggle their fire-colored tongues! And after each huge shock, how wondrous the multiple echo and the great golden moan and, at last, the sudden sibilant sobbing in the ears when the immense tone faints away in broken whispers of silver—as though a woman should whisper, "*Hiai!*" Even so the

great bell hath sounded every day for well-nigh five hundred years—
Ko-Ngai: first with stupendous clang, then with immeasurable moan
of gold, then with silver murmuring of *"Hiai!"* And there is not a
child in all the many-colored ways of the old Chinese city who
does not know the story of the great bell—who cannot tell you why
the great bell says *Ko-Ngai* and *Hiai!*

Now, this is the story of the great bell in the Ta-chung sz', as the
same is related in the *Pe-Hiao-Tou-Choue*, written by the learned
Yu-Pao-Tchen, of the City of Kwang-tchau-fu.

Nearly five hundred years ago the Celestially August, the Son
of Heaven, Yong-Lo, of the "Illustrious," or Ming, dynasty,
commanded the worthy official Kouan-Yu that he should have a
bell made of such size that the sound thereof might be heard for
one hundred *li*. And he further ordained that the voice of the bell
should be strengthened with brass, and deepened with gold, and
sweetened with silver; and that the face and the great lips of it
should be graven with blessed sayings from the sacred books, and
that it should be suspended in the centre of the imperial capital, to
sound through all the many-colored ways of the City of Pe-king.

Therefore the worthy mandarin Kouan-Yu assembled the master-
moulders and the renowned bellsmiths of the empire, and all men
of great repute and cunning in foundry work; and they measured
the materials for the alloy, and treated them skilfully, and prepared
the moulds, the fires, the instruments, and the monstrous melting-pot
for fusing the metal. And they labored exceedingly, like giants—
neglecting only rest and sleep and the comforts of life; toiling both
night and day in obedience to Kouan-Yu, and striving in all things
to do the behest of the Son of Heaven.

But when the metal had been cast, and the earthen mould separated from the glowing casting, it was discovered that, despite their
great labor and ceaseless care, the result was void of worth; for the

metals had rebelled one against the other—the gold had scorned alliance with the brass, the silver would not mingle with the molten iron. Therefore the moulds had to be once more prepared, and the fires rekindled, and the metal remelted, and all the work tediously and toilsomely repeated. The Son of Heaven heard, and was angry, but spake nothing.

A second time the bell was cast, and the result was even worse. Still the metals obstinately refused to blend one with the other; and there was no uniformity in the bell, and the sides of it were cracked and fissured, and the lips of it were slagged and split asunder; so that all the labor had to be repeated even a third time, to the great dismay of Kouan-Yu. And when the Son of Heaven heard these things, he was angrier than before; and sent his messenger to Kouan-Yu with a letter, written upon lemon-colored silk, and sealed with the seal of the Dragon, containing these words:—

"From the Mighty Yong-Lo, the Sublime Tait-Sung, the Celestial and August—whose reign is called 'Ming,'—to Kouan-Yu the Fuh-yin: Twice thou hast betrayed the trust we have deigned graciously to place in thee; if thou fail a third time in fulfilling our command, thy head shall be severed from thy neck. Tremble, and obey!"

Now, Kouan-Yu had a daughter of dazzling loveliness, whose name—Ko-Ngai—was ever in the mouths of poets, and whose heart was even more beautiful than her face. Ko-Ngai loved her father with such love that she had refused a hundred worthy suitors rather than make his home desolate by her absence; and when she had seen the awful yellow missive, sealed with the Dragon-Seal, she fainted away with fear for her father's sake. And when her senses and her strength returned to her, she could not rest or sleep for thinking of her parent's danger, until she had secretly sold some of her jewels, and with the money so obtained had hastened to an astrologer, and paid him a great price to advise her by what means her father might be saved from the peril impending over him. So the astrologer made observations of the heavens, and marked the aspect of the Silver Stream (which we call the Milky Way), and examined the signs of the Zodiac—the *Hwang-tao*, or Yellow Road—and consulted the table of the Five *Hin*, or Principles of the Universe, and the mystical books of the alchemists. And after a long silence, he made answer to her, saying: "Gold and brass will never meet in wedlock, silver and iron never will embrace, until the flesh of a maiden be melted in the crucible; until the blood of a virgin be mixed with the metals in their fusion." So Ko-Ngai returned home sorrowful at heart; but she kept secret all that she had heard, and told no one what she had done.

At last came the awful day when the third and last effort to cast the great bell was to be made; and Ko-Ngai, together with her waiting-woman, accompanied her father to the foundry, and they took their places upon a platform overlooking the toiling of the moulders and the lava of liquefied metal. All the workmen wrought their tasks in silence; there was no sound heard but the muttering of the fires. And the muttering deepened into a roar like the roar of typhoons approaching, and the blood-red lake of metal slowly brightened like the vermilion of a sunrise, and the vermilion was transmuted into a radiant glow of gold, and the gold whitened blindingly, like the silver face of a full moon. Then the workers ceased to feed the raving flame, and all fixed their eyes upon the eyes of Kouan-Yu; and Kouan-Yu prepared to give the signal to cast.

But ere ever he lifted his finger, a cry caused him to turn his head; and all heard the voice of Ko-Ngai sounding sharply sweet as a bird's song above the great thunder of the fires—"*For thy sake, O my Father!*" And even as she cried, she leaped into the white flood of metal; and the lava of the furnace roared to receive her, and spattered monstrous flakes of flame to the roof, and burst over the verge of the earthen crater, and cast up a whirling fountain of many-colored fires, and subsided quakingly, with lightnings and with thunders and with mutterings.

Then the father of Ko-Ngai, wild with his grief, would have leaped in after her, but that strong men held him back and kept firm grasp upon him until he had fainted away and they could bear him like one dead to his home. And the serving-woman of Ko-Ngai, dizzy and speechless for pain, stood before the furnace, still holding in her hands a shoe, a tiny, dainty shoe, with embroidery of pearls and flowers—the shoe of her beautiful mistress that was. For she had sought to grasp Ko-Ngai by the foot as she leaped, but had only been able to clutch the shoe, and the pretty shoe came off in her hand; and she continued to stare at it like one gone mad.

But in spite of all these things, the command of the Celestial and August had to be obeyed, and the work of the moulders to be finished, hopeless as the result might be. Yet the glow of the metal seemed purer and whiter than before; and there was no sign of the beautiful body that had been entombed therein. So the ponderous casting was made; and lo! when the metal had become cool, it was found that the bell was beautiful to look upon, and perfect in form, and wonderful in color above all other bells. Nor was there any trace found of the body of Ko-Ngai; for it had been totally absorbed by the precious alloy, and blended with the well-blended brass and gold, with the intermingling of the silver and the iron. And when they sounded the bell, its tones were found to be deeper and mellower and mightier than the tones of any other bell—reaching even beyond the distance of one hundred *li*, like a pealing of summer thunder; and yet also like some vast voice uttering a name, a woman's name—the name of Ko-Ngai!

And still, between each mighty stroke there is a long low moaning heard; and ever the moaning ends with a sound of sobbing and of complaining, as though a weeping woman should murmur, "*Hiai!*" And still, when the people hear that great golden moan they keep silence; but when the sharp, sweet shuddering comes in the air, and the sobbing of "*Hiai!*" then, indeed, all the Chinese mothers in all the many-colored ways of Pe-king whisper to their little ones: "*Listen! that is Ko-Ngai crying for her shoe! That is Ko-Ngai calling for her shoe!*"

The Story of Ming-Y

THE ANCIENT WORDS OF KOUEI—MASTER OF MUSICIANS
IN THE COURTS OF THE EMPEROR YAO:—

When ye make to resound the stone melodious, the Ming-Khieou—When ye touch the lyre that is called Kin, or the guitar that is called Ssé—Accompanying their sound with song—Then do the grandfather and the father return; Then do the ghosts of the ancestors come to hear.

Sang the Poet Tching-Kou: "Surely the Peach-Flowers blossom over the tomb of Sië-Thao."

D o you ask me who she was—the beautiful Sië-Thao? For a thousand years and more the trees have been whispering above her bed of stone. And the syllables of her name come to the listener with the lisping of the leaves; with the quivering of many-fingered boughs; with the fluttering of lights and shadows; with the breath, sweet as a woman's presence, of numberless savage flowers—*Sië-Thao*. But, saving the whispering of her name, what the trees say cannot be understood; and they alone remember the years of Sië-Thao. Something about her you might, nevertheless, learn from any of those *Kiang-kou-jin*—those famous Chinese story-tellers, who nightly narrate to listening crowds, in consideration of a few *tsien*, the legends of the past. Something concerning her you may also find in the book entitled "Kin-Kou-Ki-Koan," which signifies in our tongue: "The Marvellous Happenings of Ancient and of Recent Times." And perhaps of all things therein written, the most marvellous is this memory of Sië-Thao:—

Five hundred years ago, in the reign of the Emperor Houng-Wou, whose dynasty was *Ming*, there lived in the City of Genii, the city of Kwang-tchau-fu, a man celebrated for his learning and for his piety, named Tien-Pelou. This Tien-Pelou had one son, a beautiful boy, who for scholarship and for bodily grace and for polite accomplishments had no superior among the youths of his age. And his name was Ming-Y.

Now when the lad was in his eighteenth summer, it came to pass that Pelou, his father, was appointed Inspector of Public Instruction at the city of Tching-tou; and Ming-Y accompanied his parents thither. Near the city of Tching-tou lived a rich man of rank, a high commissioner of the government, whose name was Tchang, and who wanted to find a worthy teacher for his children. On hearing of the arrival of the new Inspector of Public Instruction, the noble Tchang visited him to obtain advice in this matter; and happening to meet and converse with Pelou's accomplished son, immediately engaged Ming-Y as a private tutor for his family.

Now as the house of this Lord Tchang was situated several miles from town, it was deemed best that Ming-Y should abide in the house of his employer. Accordingly the youth made ready all things necessary for his new sojourn; and his parents, bidding him farewell, counseled him wisely, and cited to him the words of Lao-tseu and of the ancient sages:

"By a beautiful face the world is filled with love; but Heaven may never be deceived thereby. Shouldst thou behold a woman coming from the East, look thou to the West; shouldst thou perceive a maiden approaching from the West, turn thine eyes to the East."

If Ming-Y did not heed this counsel in after days, it was only because of his youth and the thoughtlessness of a naturally joyous heart.

And he departed to abide in the house of Lord Tchang, while the autumn passed, and the winter also.

When the time of the second moon of spring was drawing near, and that happy day which the Chinese call *Hoa-tchao*, or, "The Birthday of a Hundred Flowers," a longing came upon Ming-Y to see his parents; and he opened his heart to the good Tchang, who not only gave him the permission he desired, but also pressed into his hand a silver gift of two ounces, thinking that the lad might wish to bring some little memento to his father and mother. For it is the Chinese custom, on the feast of Hoa-tchao, to make presents to friends and relations.

That day all the air was drowsy with blossom perfume, and vibrant with the droning of bees. It seemed to Ming-Y that the path he followed had not been trodden by any other for many long years; the grass was tall upon it; vast trees on either side interlocked their mighty and moss-grown arms above him, beshadowing the way; but the leafy obscurities quivered with bird-song, and the deep vistas of the wood were glorified by vapors of gold, and odorous with flower-breathings as a temple with incense. The dreamy joy of the day entered into the heart of Ming-Y; and he sat him down among the young blossoms, under the branches swaying against the violet sky, to drink in the perfume and the light, and to enjoy the great sweet silence. Even while thus reposing, a sound caused him to turn his eyes toward a shady place where wild peach-trees were in bloom; and he beheld a young woman, beautiful as the pinkening blossoms themselves, trying to hide among them. Though he looked for a moment only, Ming-Y could not avoid discerning the loveliness of her face, the golden purity of her complexion, and the brightness of her long eyes, that sparkled under a pair of brows as daintily curved as the wings of the silkworm butterfly outspread. Ming-Y at once turned his gaze away, and, rising quickly, proceeded on his journey. But so much embarrassed did he feel at the idea of those charming eyes peeping at him through the leaves, that he suffered the money he had been carrying in his sleeve to fall, without being aware of it. A few moments later he heard the patter of light feet running behind him, and a woman's voice calling him by name. Turning his face in great surprise, he saw a comely servant-maid, who said to him, "Sir, my mistress bade me pick up and return you this silver which you dropped upon the road." Ming-Y thanked the girl gracefully, and requested her to convey his compliments to her mistress. Then he proceeded on his way through the perfumed silence, athwart the shadows that dreamed along the forgotten path, dreaming himself also, and feeling his heart beating with strange quickness at the thought of the beautiful being that he had seen.

It was just such another day when Ming-Y, returning by the same path, paused once more at the spot where the gracious figure had momentarily appeared before him. But this time he was surprised to perceive, through a long vista of immense trees, a dwelling that had previously escaped his notice—a country residence, not large, yet elegant to an unusual degree. The bright blue tiles of its curved and serrated double roof, rising above the foliage, seemed to blend their color with the luminous azure of the day; the green-and-gold designs of its carven porticos were exquisite artistic mockeries of leaves and flowers bathed in sunshine. And at the summit of terrace-steps before it, guarded by great porcelain tortoises, Ming-Y saw standing the mistress of the mansion—the idol of his passionate fancy—accompanied by the same waiting-maid who had borne to her his message of gratitude. While Ming-Y looked, he perceived that their eyes were upon him; they smiled and conversed together as if speaking about him; and, shy though he was, the youth found courage to salute the fair one from a distance. To his astonishment, the young servant beckoned him to approach; and opening a rustic gate half veiled by trailing plants bearing crimson flowers, Ming-Y advanced along the verdant alley leading to the terrace, with mingled feelings of surprise and timid joy. As he drew near, the beautiful lady withdrew from sight; but the maid waited at the broad steps to receive him, and said as he ascended:

"Sir, my mistress understands you wish to thank her for the trifling service she recently bade me do you, and requests that you will enter the house, as she knows you already by repute, and desires to have the pleasure of bidding you good-day."

Ming-Y entered bashfully, his feet making no sound upon a matting elastically soft as forest moss, and found himself in a reception-chamber vast, cool, and fragrant with scent of blossoms freshly gathered. A delicious quiet pervaded the mansion; shadows of flying birds passed over the bands of light that fell through the half-blinds of bamboo; great butterflies, with pinions of fiery color, found their way in, to hover a moment about the painted vases, and pass out again into the mysterious woods. And noiselessly as they, the young mistress of the mansion entered by another door, and kindly greeted the boy, who lifted his hands to his breast and bowed low in salutation. She was taller than he had deemed her, and supplely-slender as a beauteous lily; her black hair was interwoven with the creamy blossoms of the *chu-sha-kih*; her robes of pale silk took shifting tints when she moved, as vapors change hue with the changing of the light.

"If I be not mistaken," she said, when both had seated themselves after having exchanged the customary formalities of politeness, "my honored visitor is none other than Tien-chou, surnamed Ming-Y, educator of the children of my respected relative, the High Commissioner Tchang. As the family of Lord Tchang is my family also, I cannot but consider the teacher of his children as one of my own kin."

"Lady," replied Ming-Y, not a little astonished, "may I dare to inquire the name of your honored family, and to ask the relation which you hold to my noble patron?"

"The name of my poor family," responded the comely lady, "is *Ping*—an ancient family of the city of Tching-tou. I am the daughter of a certain Sië of Moun-hao; Sië is my name, likewise; and I was married to a young man of the Ping family, whose name was Khang. By this marriage I became related to your excellent patron; but my husband died soon after our wedding, and I have chosen this solitary place to reside in during the period of my widowhood."

There was a drowsy music in her voice, as of the melody of brooks, the murmurings of spring; and such a strange grace in the manner of her speech as Ming-Y had never heard before. Yet, on learning that she was a widow, the youth would not have presumed to remain long in her presence without a formal invitation; and after having sipped the cup of rich tea presented to him, he arose to depart. Sië would not suffer him to go so quickly.

"Nay, friend," she said; "stay yet a little while in my house, I pray you; for, should your honored patron ever learn that you had been here, and that I had not treated you as a respected guest, and regaled you even as I would him, I know that he would be greatly angered. Remain at least to supper."

So Ming-Y remained, rejoicing secretly in his heart, for Sië seemed to him the fairest and sweetest being he had ever known, and he felt that he loved her even more than his father and his mother. And while they talked the long shadows of the evening slowly blended into one violet darkness; the great citron-light of the sunset faded out; and those starry beings that are called the Three Councillors, who preside over life and death and the destinies of men, opened their cold bright eyes in the northern sky. Within the mansion of Sië the painted lanterns were lighted; the table was laid for the evening repast; and Ming-Y took his place at it, feeling little inclination to eat, and thinking only of the charming face before him. Observing that he scarcely tasted the dainties laid upon his plate, Sië pressed her young guest to partake of wine; and they drank several cups together. It was a purple wine, so cool that the cup into which it was poured became covered with vapory dew; yet it seemed to warm the veins with strange fire. To Ming-Y, as he drank, all things became more luminous as by enchantment; the walls of the chamber appeared to recede, and the roof to heighten; the lamps glowed like stars in their chains, and the voice of Sië floated to the boy's ears like some far melody heard through the spaces of a drowsy night. His heart swelled; his tongue loosened; and words flitted from his lips that he had fancied he could never dare to utter. Yet Sië sought not to restrain him; her lips gave no smile; but her long bright eyes seemed to laugh with pleasure at his words of praise, and to return his gaze of passionate admiration with affectionate interest.

"I have heard," she said, "of your rare talent, and of your many elegant accomplishments. I know how to sing a little, although I cannot claim to possess any musical learning; and now that I have the honor of finding myself in the society of a musical professor, I will venture to lay modesty aside, and beg you to sing a few songs with me. I should deem it no small gratification if you would condescend to examine my musical compositions."

"The honor and the gratification, dear lady," replied Ming-Y, "will be mine; and I feel helpless to express the gratitude which the offer of so rare a favor deserves."

The serving-maid, obedient to the summons of a little silver gong, brought in the music and retired. Ming-Y took the manuscripts, and began to examine them with eager delight. The paper upon which they were written had a pale yellow tint, and was light as a fabric of gossamer; but the characters were antiquely beautiful, as though they had been traced by the brush of Heï-song Ché-Tchoo himself—that divine Genius of Ink, who is no bigger than a fly; and the signatures attached to the compositions were the signatures of Youen-tchin, Kao-pien, and Thou-mou—mighty poets and musicians of the dynasty of Thang! Ming-Y could not repress a scream of delight at the sight of treasures so inestimable and so unique; scarcely could he summon resolution enough to permit them to leave his hands even for a moment. "O Lady!" he cried, "these are veritably priceless things, surpassing in worth the treasures of all kings. This indeed is the handwriting of those great masters who sang five hundred years before our birth. How marvellously it has been preserved! Is not this the wondrous ink of which it was written: *Po-nien-jou-chi, i-tien-jou-ki*—'After centuries I remain firm as stone, and the letters that I make like lacquer'? And how divine the charm of this composition!—the song of Kao-pien, prince of poets, and Governor of Sze-tchouen five hundred years ago!"

"Kao-pien! darling Kao-pien!" murmured Sië, with a singular light in her eyes. "Kao-pien is also my favorite. Dear Ming-Y, let us chant his verses together, to the melody of old—the music of those grand years when men were nobler and wiser than to-day."

And their voices rose through the perfumed night like the voices of the wonder-birds—of the Fung-hoang—blending together in liquid sweetness. Yet a moment, and Ming-Y, overcome by the witchery of his companion's voice, could only listen in speechless ecstasy, while the lights of the chamber swam dim before his sight, and tears of pleasure trickled down his cheeks.

So the ninth hour passed; and they continued to converse, and to drink the cool purple wine, and to sing the songs of the years of Thang, until far into the night. More than once Ming-Y thought of departing; but each time Sië would begin, in that silver-sweet voice of hers, so wondrous a story of the great poets of the past, and of the women whom they loved, that he became as one entranced; or she would sing for him a song so strange that all his senses seemed to die except that of hearing. And at last, as she paused to pledge him in a cup of wine, Ming-Y could not restrain himself from putting his arm about her round neck and drawing her dainty head closer to him, and kissing the lips that were so much ruddier and sweeter than the wine. Then their lips separated no more;—the night grew old, and they knew it not.

The birds awakened, the flowers opened their eyes to the rising sun, and Ming-Y found himself at last compelled to bid his lovely enchantress farewell. Sië, accompanying him to the terrace, kissed him fondly and said, "Dear boy, come hither as often as you are able—as often as your heart whispers you to come. I know that you are not of those without faith and truth, who betray secrets; yet, being so young, you might also be sometimes thoughtless; and I pray you never to forget that only the stars have been the witnesses of our love. Speak of it to no living person, dearest; and take with you this little souvenir of our happy night."

And she presented him with an exquisite and curious little thing—a paper-weight in likeness of a couchant lion, wrought from a jade-stone yellow as that created by a rainbow in honor of Kong-fu-tze. Tenderly the boy kissed the gift and the beautiful hand that gave it. "May the Spirits punish me," he vowed, "if ever I knowingly give you cause to reproach me, sweetheart!" And they separated with mutual vows.

That morning, on returning to the house of Lord Tchang, Ming-Y told the first falsehood which had ever passed his lips. He averred that his mother had requested him thenceforward to pass his nights at home, now that the weather had become so pleasant; for, though the way was somewhat long, he was strong and active, and needed both air and healthy exercise. Tchang believed all Ming-Y said, and offered no objection. Accordingly the lad found himself enabled to pass all his evenings at the house of the beautiful Sië. Each night they devoted to the same pleasures which had made their first acquaintance so charming: they sang and conversed by turns; they played at chess—the learned game invented by Wu-Wang, which is an imitation of war; they composed pieces of eighty rhymes upon the flowers, the trees, the clouds, the streams, the birds, the bees. But in all accomplishments Sië far excelled her young sweetheart. Whenever they played at chess, it was always Ming-Y's general, Ming-Y's *tsiang*, who was surrounded and vanquished; when they composed verses, Sië's poems were ever superior to his in harmony of word-coloring, in elegance of form, in classic loftiness of thought. And the themes they selected were always the most difficult—those of the poets of the Thang dynasty; the songs they sang were also the songs of five hundred years before—the songs of Youen-tchin, of Thou-mou, of Kao-pien above all, high poet and ruler of the province of Sze-tchouen.

So the summer waxed and waned upon their love, and the luminous autumn came, with its vapors of phantom gold, its shadows of magical purple.

Then it unexpectedly happened that the father of Ming-Y, meeting his son's employer at Tching-tou, was asked by him: "Why must your boy continue to travel every evening to the city, now that the winter is approaching? The way is long, and when he returns in the morning he looks fordone with weariness. Why not permit him to slumber in my house during the season of snow?" And the father of Ming-Y, greatly astonished, responded: "Sir, my son has not visited the city, nor has he been to our house all this summer. I fear that he must have acquired wicked habits, and that he passes his nights in evil company—perhaps in gaming, or in drinking with the women of the flower-boats." But the High Commissioner returned: "Nay! that is not to be thought of. I have never found any evil in the boy, and there are no taverns nor flower-boats nor any places of dissipation in our neighborhood. No doubt Ming-Y has found some amiable youth of his own age with whom to spend his evenings, and only told me an untruth for fear that I would not otherwise permit him to leave my residence. I beg that you will say nothing to him until I shall have sought to discover this mystery; and this very evening I shall send my servant to follow after him, and to watch whither he goes."

Pelou readily assented to this proposal, and promising to visit Tchang the following morning, returned to his home. In the evening, when Ming-Y left the house of Tchang, a servant followed him unobserved at a distance. But on reaching the most obscure portion of the road, the boy disappeared from sight as suddenly as though the earth had swallowed him. After having long sought after him in vain, the domestic returned in great bewilderment to the house, and related what had taken place. Tchang immediately sent a messenger to Pelou.

In the meantime Ming-Y, entering the chamber of his beloved, was surprised and deeply pained to find her in tears. "Sweetheart," she sobbed, wreathing her arms around his neck, "we are about to be separated forever, because of reasons which I cannot tell you. From the very first I knew this must come to pass; and nevertheless it seemed to me for the moment so cruelly sudden a loss, so unexpected a misfortune, that I could not prevent myself from weeping! After this night we shall never see each other again, beloved, and I know that you will not be able to forget me while you live; but I know also that you will become a great scholar, and that honors and riches will be showered upon you, and that some beautiful and loving woman will console you for my loss. And now let us speak no more of grief; but let us pass this last evening joyously, so that your recollection of me may not be a painful one, and that you may remember my laughter rather than my tears."

She brushed the bright drops away, and brought wine and music and the melodious *kin* of seven silken strings, and would not suffer Ming-Y to speak for one moment of the coming separation. And she sang him an ancient song about the calmness of summer lakes reflecting the blue of heaven only, and the calmness of the heart also, before the clouds of care and of grief and of weariness darken its little world. Soon they forgot their sorrow in the joy of song and wine; and those last hours seemed to Ming-Y more celestial than even the hours of their first bliss.

But when the yellow beauty of morning came their sadness returned, and they wept. Once more Sië accompanied her lover to the terrace-steps; and as she kissed him farewell, she pressed into his hand a parting gift—a little brush-case of agate, wonderfully chiseled, and worthy the table of a great poet. And they separated forever, shedding many tears.

Still Ming-Y could not believe it was an eternal parting. "No!" he thought, "I shall visit her tomorrow; for I cannot now live without her, and I feel assured that she cannot refuse to receive me." Such were the thoughts that filled his mind as he reached the house of Tchang, to find his father and his patron standing on the porch awaiting him. Ere he could speak a word, Pelou demanded: "Son, in what place have you been passing your nights?"

Seeing that his falsehood had been discovered, Ming-Y dared not make any reply, and remained abashed and silent, with bowed head, in the presence of his father. Then Pelou, striking the boy violently with his staff, commanded him to divulge the secret; and at last, partly through fear of his parent, and partly through fear of the law which ordains that *"the son refusing to obey his father shall be punished with one hundred blows of the bamboo,"* Ming-Y faltered out the history of his love.

Tchang changed color at the boy's tale. "Child," exclaimed the

High Commissioner, "I have no relative of the name of Ping; I have never heard of the woman you describe; I have never heard even of the house which you speak of. But I know also that you cannot dare to lie to Pelou, your honored father; there is some strange delusion in all this affair."

Then Ming-Y produced the gifts that Sië had given him—the lion of yellow jade, the brush-case of carven agate, also some original compositions made by the beautiful lady herself. The astonishment of Tchang was now shared by Pelou. Both observed that the brush-case of agate and the lion of jade bore the appearance of objects that had lain buried in the earth for centuries, and were of a workmanship beyond the power of living man to imitate; while the compositions proved to be veritable master-pieces of poetry, written in the style of the poets of the dynasty of Thang.

"Friend Pelou," cried the High Commissioner, "let us immediately accompany the boy to the place where he obtained these miraculous things, and apply the testimony of our senses to this mystery. The boy is no doubt telling the truth; yet his story passes my understanding." And all three proceeded toward the place of the habitation of Sië.

But when they had arrived at the shadiest part of the road, where the perfumes were most sweet and the mosses were greenest, and the fruits of the wild peach flushed most pinkly, Ming-Y, gazing through the groves, uttered a cry of dismay. Where the azure-tiled roof had risen against the sky, there was now only the blue emptiness of air; where the green-and-gold facade had been, there was visible only the flickering of leaves under the aureate autumn light; and where the broad terrace had extended, could be discerned only a ruin—a tomb so ancient, so deeply gnawed by moss, that the name graven upon it was no longer decipherable. The home of Sië had disappeared!

All suddenly the High Commissioner smote his forehead with his hand, and turning to Pelou, recited the well-known verse of the ancient poet Tching-Kou:—

"Surely the peach-flowers blossom over the tomb of sië-thao."

"Friend Pelou," continued Tchang, "the beauty who bewitched your son was no other than she whose tomb stands there in ruin before us! Did she not say she was wedded to Ping-Khang? There is no family of that name, but Ping-Khang is indeed the name of a broad alley in the city near. There was a dark riddle in all that she said. She called herself Sië of Moun-Hiao: there is no person of that name; there is no street of that name; but the Chinese characters *Moun* and *hiao*, placed together, form the character 'Kiao.' Listen! The alley Ping-Khang, situated in the street Kiao, was the place where dwelt the great courtesans of the dynasty of Thang! Did she not sing the songs of Kao-pien? And upon the brush-case and the paper-weight she gave your son, are there not characters which read, '*Pure object of art belonging to Kao, of the city of Pho-hai*'? That city no longer exists; but the memory of Kao-pien remains, for he was governor of the province of Sze-tchouen, and a mighty poet. And when he dwelt in the land of Chou, was not his favorite the beautiful wanton Sië—Sië-Thao, unmatched for grace among all the women of her day? It was he who made her a gift of those manuscripts of song; it was he who gave her those objects of rare art. Sië-Thao died not as other women die. Her limbs may have crumbled to dust; yet something of her still lives in this deep wood—her Shadow still haunts this shadowy place."

Tchang ceased to speak. A vague fear fell upon the three. The thin mists of the morning made dim the distances of green, and deepened the ghostly beauty of the woods. A faint breeze passed by, leaving a trail of blossom-scent—a last odor of dying flowers—thin as that which clings to the silk of a forgotten robe; and, as it passed, the trees seemed to whisper across the silence, "*Sië-Thao.*"

Fearing greatly for his son, Pelou sent the lad away at once to the city of Kwang-tchau-fu. And there, in after years, Ming-Y obtained high dignities and honors by reason of his talents and his learning; and he married the daughter of an illustrious house, by whom he became the father of sons and daughters famous for their virtues and their accomplishments. Never could he forget Sië-Thao; and yet it is said that he never spoke of her—not even when his children begged him to tell them the story of two beautiful objects that always lay upon his writing-table: a lion of yellow jade, and a brush-case of carven agate.

The Legend of Tchi-Niu

A SOUND OF GONGS, A SOUND OF SONG—THE SONG OF
THE BUILDERS BUILDING THE DWELLINGS OF THE DEAD:—

Khiû tchî yîng-yîng.
Toû tchî hoûng-hoûng.
Tchŏ tchî tông-tông.
Siŏ liú pîng-pîng.

Jn the quaint commentary accompanying the text of that holy book of Lao-tseu called *Kan-ing-p'ien* may be found a little story so old that the name of the one who first told it has been forgotten for a thousand years, yet so beautiful that it lives still in the memory of four hundred millions of people, like a prayer that, once learned, is forever remembered. The Chinese writer makes no mention of any city nor of any province, although even in the relation of the most ancient traditions such an omission is rare; we are only told that the name of the hero of the legend was Tong-yong, and that he lived in the years of the great dynasty of Han, some twenty centuries ago.

Tong-Yong's mother had died while he was yet an infant; and when he became a youth of nineteen years his father also passed away, leaving him utterly alone in the world, and without resources of any sort; for, being a very poor man, Tong's father had put himself to great straits to educate the lad, and had not been able to lay by even one copper coin of his earnings. And Tong lamented greatly to find himself so destitute that he could not honor the memory of that good father by having the customary rites of burial performed, and a carven tomb erected upon a propitious site. The poor only are friends of the poor; and among all those whom Tong knew; there was no one able to assist him in defraying the expenses of the funeral. In one way only could the youth obtain money—by selling himself as a slave to some rich cultivator; and this he at last decided to do. In vain his friends did their utmost to dissuade him; and to no purpose did they attempt to delay the accomplishment of his sacrifice by beguiling promises of future aid. Tong only replied that he would sell his freedom a hundred times, if it were possible, rather than suffer his father's memory to remain unhonored even for a brief season. And furthermore, confiding in his youth and strength, he determined to put a high price upon his servitude—a price which would enable him to build a handsome tomb, but which it would be well-nigh impossible for him ever to repay.

Accordingly he repaired to the broad public place where slaves and debtors were exposed for sale, and seated himself upon a bench of stone, having affixed to his shoulders a placard inscribed with the terms of his servitude and the list of his qualifications as a laborer. Many who read the characters upon the placard smiled disdainfully at the price asked, and passed on without a word; others lingered only to question him out of simple curiosity; some commended him with hollow praise; some openly mocked his unselfishness, and laughed at his childish piety. Thus many hours wearily passed, and Tong had almost despaired of finding a master, when there rode up a high official of the province—a grave and handsome man, lord of a thousand slaves, and owner of vast estates. Reining in his Tartar horse, the official halted to read the placard and to consider the value of the slave. He did not smile, or advise, or ask any questions; but having observed the price asked, and the fine strong limbs of the youth, purchased him without further ado, merely ordering his attendant to pay the sum and to see that the necessary papers were made out.

Thus Tong found himself enabled to fulfil the wish of his heart, and to have a monument built which, although of small size, was destined to delight the eyes of all who beheld it, being designed by cunning artists and executed by skilful sculptors. And while it was yet designed only, the pious rites were performed, the silver coin was placed in the mouth of the dead, the white lanterns were hung at the door, the holy prayers were recited, and paper shapes of all things the departed might need in the land of the Genii were consumed in consecrated fire. And after the geomancers and the necromancers had chosen a burial-spot which no unlucky star could shine upon, a place of rest which no demon or dragon might ever disturb, the beautiful *chih* was built. Then was the phantom money strewn along the way; the funeral procession departed from the dwelling of the dead, and with prayers and lamentation the mortal remains of Tong's good father were borne to the tomb.

Then Tong entered as a slave into the service of his purchaser, who allotted him a little hut to dwell in; and thither Tong carried with him those wooden tablets, bearing the ancestral names, before which filial piety must daily burn the incense of prayer, and perform the tender duties of family worship.

Thrice had spring perfumed the breast of the land with flowers, and thrice had been celebrated that festival of the dead which is called *Siu-fan-ti*, and thrice had Tong swept and garnished his father's tomb and presented his fivefold offering of fruits and meats. The period of mourning had passed, yet he had not ceased to mourn for his parent.

The years revolved with their moons, bringing him no hour of joy, no day of happy rest; yet he never lamented his servitude, or failed to perform the rites of ancestral worship—until at last the fever of the rice-fields laid strong hold upon him, and he could not arise from his couch; and his fellow-laborers thought him destined to die. There was no one to wait upon him, no one to care for his needs, inasmuch as slaves and servants were wholly busied with the duties of the household or the labor of the fields—all departing to toil at sunrise and returning weary only after the sundown.

Now, while the sick youth slumbered the fitful slumber of exhaustion one sultry noon, he dreamed that a strange and beautiful woman stood by him, and bent above him and touched his forehead with the long, fine fingers of her shapely hand. And at her cool touch a weird sweet shock passed through him, and all his veins tingled as if thrilled by new life. Opening his eyes in wonder, he saw verily bending over him the charming being of whom he had dreamed, and he knew that her lithe hand really caressed his throbbing forehead. But the flame of the fever was gone, a delicious coolness now penetrated every fibre of his body, and the thrill of which he had dreamed still tingled in his blood like a great joy. Even at the same moment the eyes of the gentle visitor met his own, and he saw they were singularly beautiful, and shone like splendid black jewels under brows curved like the wings of the swallow. Yet their calm gaze seemed to pass through him as light through crystal; and a vague awe came upon him, so that the question which had risen to his lips found no utterance. Then she, still caressing him, smiled and said: "I have come to restore thy strength and to be thy wife. Arise and worship with me."

Her clear voice had tones melodious as a bird's song; but in her gaze there was an imperious power which Tong felt he dare not resist. Rising from his couch, he was astounded to find his strength wholly restored; but the cool, slender hand which held his own led him away so swiftly that he had little time for amazement. He would have given years of existence for courage to speak of his misery, to declare his utter inability to maintain a wife; but something irresistible in the long dark eyes of his companion forbade him to speak; and as though his inmost thought had been discerned by that wondrous gaze, she said to him, in the same clear voice, "*I will provide.*" Then shame made him blush at the thought of his wretched aspect and tattered apparel; but he observed that she also was poorly attired, like a woman of the people—wearing no ornament of any sort, nor even shoes upon her feet. And before he had yet spoken to her, they came before the ancestral tablets; and there she knelt with him and prayed, and pledged him in a cup of wine—brought he knew not from whence—and together they worshiped Heaven and Earth. Thus she became his wife.

A mysterious marriage it seemed, for neither on that day nor at any future time could Tong venture to ask his wife the name of her family, or of the place whence she came, and he could not answer any of the curious questions which his fellow-laborers put to him concerning her; and she, moreover, never uttered a word about herself, except to say that her name was Tchi. But although Tong had such awe of her that while her eyes were upon him he was as one having no will of his own, he loved her unspeakably; and the thought of his serfdom ceased to weigh upon him from the hour of his marriage. As through magic the little dwelling had become transformed: its misery was masked with charming paper devices— with dainty decorations created out of nothing by that pretty jugglery of which woman only knows the secret.

Each morning at dawn the young husband found a well-prepared and ample repast awaiting him, and each evening also upon his return; but the wife all day sat at her loom, weaving silk after a fashion unlike anything which had ever been seen before in that province. For as she wove, the silk flowed from the loom like a slow current of glossy gold, bearing upon its undulations strange forms of violet and crimson and jewel-green: shapes of ghostly horsemen riding upon horses, and of phantom chariots dragon-drawn, and of standards of trailing cloud. In every dragon's beard glimmered the mystic pearl; in every rider's helmet sparkled the gem of rank. And each day Tchi would weave a great piece of such figured silk; and the fame of her weaving spread abroad. From far and near people thronged to see the marvelous work; and the silk-merchants of great cities heard of it, and they sent messengers to Tchi, asking her that she should weave for them and teach them her secret. Then she wove for them, as they desired, in return for the silver cubes which they brought her; but when they prayed her to teach them, she laughed and said, "Assuredly I could never teach you, for no one among you has fingers like mine." And indeed no man could discern her fingers when she wove, any more than he might behold the wings of a bee vibrating in swift flight.

The seasons passed, and Tong never knew want, so well did his beautiful wife fulfil her promise—"*I will provide*"; and the cubes of bright silver brought by the silk-merchants were piled up higher and higher in the great carven chest which Tchi had bought for the storage of the household goods.

One morning, at last, when Tong, having finished his repast, was about to depart to the fields, Tchi unexpectedly bade him remain; and opening the great chest, she took out of it and gave him a document written in the official characters called *li-shu*. And Tong, looking at it, cried out and leaped in his joy, for it was the certificate of his manumission. Tchi had secretly purchased her husband's freedom with the price of her wondrous silks!

"Thou shalt labor no more for any master," she said, "but for thine own sake only. And I have also bought this dwelling, with all which is therein, and the tea-fields to the south, and the mulberry groves hard by—all of which are thine."

Then Tong, beside himself for gratefulness, would have prostrated himself in worship before her, but that she would not suffer it.

Thus he was made free; and prosperity came to him with his freedom; and whatsoever he gave to the sacred earth was returned to him centupled; and his servants loved him and blessed the beautiful Tchi, so silent and yet so kindly to all about her. But the silk-loom soon remained untouched, for Tchi gave birth to a son—a boy so beautiful that Tong wept with delight when he looked upon him. And thereafter the wife devoted herself wholly to the care of the child.

Now it soon became manifest that the boy was not less wonderful than his wonderful mother. In the third month of his age he could speak; in the seventh month he could repeat by heart the proverbs of the sages, and recite the holy prayers; before the eleventh month he could use the writing-brush with skill, and copy in shapely characters the precepts of Lao-tseu. And the priests of the temples came to behold him and to converse with him, and they marveled at the charm of the child and the wisdom of what he said; and they blessed Tong, saying: "Surely this son of thine is a gift from the Master of Heaven, a sign that the immortals love thee. May thine eyes behold a hundred happy summers!"

It was in the Period of the Eleventh Moon: the flowers had passed away, the perfume of the summer had flown, the winds were growing chill, and in Tong's home the evening fires were lighted. Long the husband and wife sat in the mellow glow—he speaking much of his hopes and joys, and of his son that was to be so grand a man, and of many paternal projects; while she, speaking little, listened to his words, and often turned her wonderful eyes upon him with an answering smile. Never had she seemed so beautiful before; and Tong, watching her face, marked not how the night waned, nor how the fire sank low, nor how the wind sang in the leafless trees without.

All suddenly Tchi arose without speaking, and took his hand in hers and led him, gently as on that strange wedding-morning, to the cradle where their boy slumbered, faintly smiling in his dreams. And in that moment there came upon Tong the same strange fear that he knew when Tchi's eyes had first met his own—the vague fear that love and trust had calmed, but never wholly cast out, like unto the fear of the gods. And all unknowingly, like one yielding to the pressure of mighty invisible hands, he bowed himself low before her, kneeling as to a divinity. Now, when he lifted his eyes again to her face, he closed them forthwith in awe; for she towered before him taller than any mortal woman, and there was a glow about her as of sunbeams, and the light of her limbs shone through her garments. But her sweet voice came to him with all the tenderness of other hours, saying: *"Lo! my beloved, the moment has come in which I must forsake thee; for I was never of mortal born, and the Invisible may incarnate themselves for a time only. Yet I leave with thee the pledge of our love—this fair son, who shall ever be to thee as faithful and as fond as thou thyself hast been. Know, my beloved, that I was sent to thee even by the Master of Heaven, in reward of thy filial piety, and that I must now return to the glory of His house: I AM THE GODDESS TCHI-NIU."*

Even as she ceased to speak, the great glow faded; and Tong, re-opening his eyes, knew that she had passed away forever—mysteriously as pass the winds of heaven, irrevocably as the light of a flame blown out. Yet all the doors were barred, all the windows unopened. Still the child slept, smiling in his sleep. Outside, the darkness was breaking; the sky was brightening swiftly; the night was past. With splendid majesty the East threw open high gates of gold for the coming of the sun; and, illuminated by the glory of his coming, the vapors of morning wrought themselves into marvelous shapes of shifting color—into forms weirdly beautiful as the silken dreams woven in the loom of Tchi-Niu.

The Return of Yen-Tchin-King

Before me ran, as a herald runneth, the Leader of the Moon;
And the Spirit of the Wind followed after me—quickening his flight.

LI-SAO

In the thirty-eighth chapter of the holy book, *Kan-ing-p'ien*, wherein the Recompense of Immortality is considered, may be found the legend of Yen-Tchin-King. A thousand years have passed since the passing of the good Tchin-King; for it was in the period of the greatness of Thang that he lived and died.

Now, in those days when Yen-Tchin-King was Supreme Judge of one of the Six August Tribunals, one Li-hi-lié, a soldier mighty for evil, lifted the black banner of revolt, and drew after him, as a tide of destruction, the millions of the northern provinces. And learning of these things, and knowing also that Hi-lié was the most ferocious of men, who respected nothing on earth save fearlessness, the Son of Heaven commanded Tchin-King that he should visit Hi-lié and strive to recall the rebel to duty, and read unto the people who followed after him in revolt the Emperor's letter of reproof and warning. For Tchin-King was famed throughout the provinces for his wisdom, his rectitude, and his fearlessness; and the Son of

Heaven believed that if Hi-lié would listen to the words of any living man steadfast in loyalty and virtue, he would listen to the words of Tchin-King. So Tchin-King arrayed himself in his robes of office, and set his house in order; and, having embraced his wife and his children, mounted his horse and rode away alone to the roaring camp of the rebels, bearing the Emperor's letter in his bosom. "I shall return; fear not!" were his last words to the gray servant who watched him from the terrace as he rode.

And Tchin-King at last descended from his horse, and entered into the rebel camp, and, passing through that huge gathering of war, stood in the presence of Hi-lié. High sat the rebel among his chiefs, encircled by the wave-lightning of swords and the thunders of ten thousand gongs: above him undulated the silken folds of the Black Dragon, while a vast fire rose bickering before him. Also Tchin-King saw that the tongues of that fire were licking human bones, and that skulls of men lay blackening among the ashes. Yet he was not afraid to look upon the fire, nor into the eyes of Hi-lié; but drawing from his bosom the roll of perfumed yellow silk upon which the words of the Emperor were written, and kissing it, he made ready to read, while the multitude became silent. Then, in a strong, clear voice he began:—

"The words of the Celestial and August, the Son of Heaven, the Divine Ko-Tsu-Tchin-Yao-ti, unto the rebel Li-Hi-lié and those that follow him."

And a roar went up like the roar of the sea—a roar of rage, and the hideous battle-moan, like the moan of a forest in storm—*"Hoo! hoo-oo-oo-oo!"*—and the sword-lightnings brake loose, and the thunder of the gongs moved the ground beneath the messenger's feet. But Hi-lié waved his gilded wand, and again there was silence. "Nay!" spake the rebel chief; "let the dog bark!" So Tchin-King spake on:—

"*Knowest thou not, O most rash and foolish of men, that thou leadest the people only into the mouth of the Dragon of Destruction? Knowest thou not, also, that the people of my kingdom are the first-born of the Master of Heaven? So it hath been written that he who doth needlessly subject the people to wounds and death shall not be suffered by Heaven to live! Thou who wouldst subvert those laws founded by the wise—those laws in obedience to which may happiness and prosperity alone be found—thou art committing the greatest of all crimes—the crime that is never forgiven!*

"*O my people, think not that I your Emperor, I your Father, seek your destruction. I desire only your happiness, your prosperity, your greatness; let not your folly provoke the severity of your Celestial Parent. Follow not after madness and blind rage; hearken rather to the wise words of my messenger.*"

"*Hoo! hoo-oo-oo-oo-oo!*" roared the people, gathering fury. "*Hoo! hoo-oo-oo-oo!*"—till the mountains rolled back the cry like the rolling of a typhoon; and once more the pealing of the gongs paralyzed voice and hearing. Then Tchin-King, looking at Hi-lié, saw that he laughed, and that the words of the letter would not again be listened to. Therefore he read on to the end without looking about him, resolved to perform his mission in so far as lay in his power. And having read all, he would have given the letter to Hi-lié; but Hi-lié would not extend his hand to take it. Therefore Tchin-King replaced it in his bosom, and folding his arms, looked Hi-lié calmly in the face, and waited. Again Hi-lié waved his gilded wand; and the roaring ceased, and the booming of the gongs, until nothing save the fluttering of the Dragon-banner could be heard. Then spake Hi-lié, with an evil smile—

"Tchin-King, O son of a dog! if thou dost not now take the oath of fealty, and bow thyself before me, and salute me with the salutation of Emperors—even with the *luh-kao*, the triple prostration—into that fire thou shalt be thrown."

But Tchin-King, turning his back upon the usurper, bowed himself a moment in worship to Heaven and Earth; and then rising suddenly, ere any man could lay hand upon him, he leaped into the towering flame, and stood there, with folded arms, like a God.

Then Hi-lié leaped to his feet in amazement, and shouted to his men; and they snatched Tchin-King from the fire, and wrung the flames from his robes with their naked hands, and extolled him, and praised him to his face. And even Hi-lié himself descended from his seat, and spoke fair words to him, saying: "O Tchin-King, I see thou art indeed a brave man and true, and worthy of all honor; be seated among us, I pray thee, and partake of whatever it is in our power to bestow!"

But Tchin-King, looking upon him unswervingly, replied in a voice clear as the voice of a great bell—

"Never, O Hi-lié, shall I accept aught from thy hand, save death, so long as thou shalt continue in the path of wrath and folly. And never shall it be said that Tchin-King sat him down among rebels and traitors, among murderers and robbers."

Then Hi-lié in sudden fury, smote him with his sword; and Tchin-King fell to the earth and died, striving even in his death to bow his head toward the South—toward the place of the Emperor's palace—toward the presence of his beloved Master.

Even at the same hour the Son of Heaven, alone in the inner chamber of his palace, became aware of a Shape prostrate before his feet; and when he spake, the Shape arose and stood before him, and he saw that it was Tchin-King. And the Emperor would have questioned him; yet ere he could question, the familiar voice spake, saying:

"Son of Heaven, the mission confided to me I have performed; and thy command hath been accomplished to the extent of thy humble servant's feeble power. But even now must I depart, that I may enter the service of another Master."

And looking, the Emperor perceived that the Golden Tigers upon the wall were visible through the form of Tchin-King; and a strange coldness, like a winter wind, passed through the chamber; and the figure faded out. Then the Emperor knew that the Master of whom his faithful servant had spoken was none other than the Master of Heaven.

Also at the same hour the gray servant of Tchin-King's house beheld him passing through the apartments, smiling as he was wont to smile when he saw that all things were as he desired. "Is it well with thee, my lord?" questioned the aged man. And a voice answered him: "It is well"; but the presence of Tchin-King had passed away before the answer came.

So the armies of the Son of Heaven strove with the rebels. But the land was soaked with blood and blackened with fire; and the corpses of whole populations were carried by the rivers to feed the fishes of the sea; and still the war prevailed through many a long red year. Then came to aid the Son of Heaven the hordes that dwell in the desolations of the West and North—horsemen born, a nation of wild archers, each mighty to bend a two-hundred-pound bow until the ears should meet. And as a whirlwind they came against rebellion, raining raven-feathered arrows in a storm of death; and they prevailed against Hi-lié and his people. Then those that survived destruction and defeat submitted, and promised allegiance; and once more was the law of righteousness restored. But Tchin-King had been dead for many summers.

And the Son of Heaven sent word to his victorious generals that they should bring back with them the bones of his faithful servant, to be laid with honor in a mausoleum erected by imperial decree. So the generals of the Celestial and August sought after the nameless grave and found it, and had the earth taken up, and made ready to remove the coffin.

But the coffin crumbled into dust before their eyes; for the worms had gnawed it, and the hungry earth had devoured its substance, leaving only a phantom shell that vanished at touch of the light. And lo! as it vanished, all beheld lying there the perfect form and features of the good Tchin-King. Corruption had not touched him, nor had the worms disturbed his rest, nor had the bloom of life departed from his face. And he seemed to dream only—comely to see as upon the morning of his bridal, and smiling as the holy images smile, with eyelids closed, in the twilight of the great pagodas.

Then spoke a priest, standing by the grave: "O my children, this is indeed a Sign from the Master of Heaven; in such wise do the Powers Celestial preserve them that are chosen to be numbered with the Immortals. Death may not prevail over them, neither may corruption come nigh them. Verily the blessed Tchin-King hath taken his place among the divinities of Heaven!"

Then they bore Tchin-King back to his native place, and laid him with highest honors in the mausoleum which the Emperor had commanded; and there he sleeps, incorruptible forever, arrayed in his robes of state. Upon his tomb are sculptured the emblems of his greatness and his wisdom and his virtue, and the signs of his office, and the Four Precious Things: and the monsters which are holy symbols mount giant guard in stone about it; and the weird Dogs of Fo keep watch before it, as before the temples of the gods.

The Tradition of the Tea-Plant

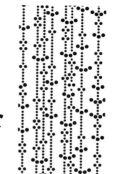

SANG A CHINESE HEART FOURTEEN HUNDRED YEARS
AGO:—

There is Somebody of whom I am thinking.
Far away there is Somebody of whom I am thinking.
A hundred leagues of mountains lie between us:—
Yet the same Moon shines upon us, and the passing
Wind breathes upon us both.

"Good is the continence of the eye;
Good is the continence of the ear;
Good is the continence of the nostrils;
Good is the continence of the tongue;
Good is the continence of the body;
Good is the continence of speech;
Good is all...."

Again the Vulture of Temptation soared to the highest heaven of his contemplation, bringing his soul down, down, reeling and fluttering, back to the World of Illusion. Again the memory made dizzy his thought, like the perfume of some venomous flower. Yet he had seen the bayadere for an instant only, when passing through Kasí upon his way to China—to the vast empire of souls that thirsted after the refreshment of Buddha's law, as sun-parched fields thirst for the life-giving rain. When she called him, and dropped her little gift into his mendicant's bowl, he had indeed lifted his fan before his face, yet not quickly enough; and the penalty of that fault had followed him a thousand leagues— pursued after him even into the strange land to which he had come to hear the words of the Universal Teacher. Accursed beauty! surely framed by the Tempter of tempters, by Mara himself, for the perdition of the just! Wisely had Bhagavat warned his disciples: "O ye Çramanas, women are not to be looked upon! And if ye chance to meet women, ye must not suffer your eyes to dwell upon them; but, maintaining holy reserve, speak not to them at all. Then fail not to whisper unto your own hearts, 'Lo, we are Çramanas, whose duty it is to remain uncontaminated by the corruptions of this world, even as the Lotos, which suffereth no vileness to cling unto its leaves, though it blossom amid the refuse of the wayside ditch.'" Then also came to his memory, but with a new and terrible meaning, the words of the Twentieth-and-Third of the Admonitions:—

"Of all attachments unto objects of desire, the strongest indeed is the attachment to form. Happily, this passion is unique; for were there any other like unto it, then to enter the Perfect Way were impossible."

How, indeed, thus haunted by the illusion of form, was he to fulfil the vow that he had made to pass a night and a day in perfect and unbroken meditation? Already the night was beginning! Assuredly, for sickness of the soul, for fever of the spirit, there was no physic save prayer. The sunset was swiftly fading out. He strove to pray:—

"O the Jewel in the Lotos!

"Even as the tortoise withdraweth its extremities into its shell, let me, O Blessed One, withdraw my senses wholly into meditation!

"O the Jewel in the Lotos!

"For even as rain penetrateth the broken roof of a dwelling long uninhabited, so may passion enter the soul uninhabited by meditation.

"*O the Jewel in the Lotos!*

"Even as still water that hath deposited all its slime, so let my soul, O Tathgāta, be made pure! Give me strong power to rise above the world, O Master, even as the wild bird rises from its marsh to follow the pathway of the Sun!

"*O the Jewel in the Lotos!*

"By day shineth the sun, by night shineth the moon; shineth also the warrior in harness of war; shineth likewise in meditations the Çramana. But the Buddha at all times, by night or by day, shineth ever the same, illuminating the world.

"*O the Jewel in the Lotos!*

"Let me cease, O thou Perfectly Awakened, to remain as an Ape in the World-forest, forever ascending and descending in search of the fruits of folly. Swift as the twining of serpents, vast as the growth of lianas in a forest, are the all-encircling growths of the Plant of Desire.

"*O the Jewel in the Lotos!*"

Vain his prayer, alas! vain also his invocation! The mystic meaning of the holy text—the sense of the Lotos, the sense of the Jewel—had evaporated from the words, and their monotonous utterance now served only to lend more dangerous definition to the memory that tempted and tortured him. *O the jewel in her ear!* What lotos-bud more dainty than the folded flower of flesh, with its dripping of diamond-fire! Again he saw it, and the curve of the cheek beyond, luscious to look upon as beautiful brown fruit. How true the Two Hundred and Eighty-Fourth verse of the Admonitions!—"So long as a man shall not have torn from his heart even the smallest rootlet of that liana of desire which draweth his thought toward women, even so long shall his soul remain fettered." And there came to his mind also the Three Hundred and Forty-Fifth verse of the same blessed book, regarding fetters:

"In bonds of rope, wise teachers have said, there is no strength; nor in fetters of wood, nor yet in fetters of iron. Much stronger than any of these is the fetter of *concern for the jeweled earrings of women*."

"Omniscient Gotama!" he cried—"all-seeing Tathgāta! How multiform the Consolation of Thy Word! how marvelous Thy understanding of the human heart! Was this also one of Thy temptations?—one of the myriad illusions marshaled before Thee by Mara in that night when the earth rocked as a chariot, and the sacred trembling passed from sun to sun, from system to system, from universe to universe, from eternity to eternity?"

O the jewel in her ear! The vision would not go! Nay, each time it hovered before his thought it seemed to take a warmer life, a fonder look, a fairer form; to develop with his weakness; to gain force from his enervation. He saw the eyes, large, limpid, soft, and black as a deer's; the pearls in the dark hair, and the pearls in the pink mouth; the lips curling to a kiss, a flower-kiss; and a fragrance seemed to float to his senses, sweet, strange, soporific—a perfume of youth, an odor of woman. Rising to his feet, with strong resolve he pronounced again the sacred invocation; and he recited the holy words of the *Chapter of Impermanency*:

"Gazing upon the heavens and upon the earth ye must say, *These are not permanent*. Gazing upon the mountains and the rivers, ye must say, *These are not permanent*. Gazing upon the forms and upon the faces of exterior beings, and beholding their growth and their development, ye must say, *These are not permanent*."

And nevertheless! how sweet illusion! The illusion of the great sun; the illusion of the shadow-casting hills; the illusion of waters, formless and multiform; the illusion of—Nay, nay I what impious fancy! Accursed girl! yet, yet! why should he curse her? Had she ever done aught to merit the malediction of an ascetic? Never, never! Only her form, the memory of her, the beautiful phantom of her, the accursed phantom of her! What was she? An illusion creating illusions, a mockery, a dream, a shadow, a vanity, a vexation of spirit! The fault, the sin, was in himself, in his rebellious thought, in his untamed memory. Though mobile as water, intangible as vapor, Thought, nevertheless, may be tamed by the Will, may be harnessed to the chariot of Wisdom—must be!—that happiness be found. And he recited the blessed verses of the "Book of the Way of the Law":—

"All forms are only temporary." When this great truth is fully comprehended by any one, then is he delivered from all pain. This is the Way of Purification.

"All forms are subject unto pain." When this great truth is fully comprehended by any one, then is he delivered from all pain. This is the Way of Purification.

"All forms are without substantial reality." When this great truth is fully comprehended by any one, then is he delivered from all pain. This is the way of ...

Her form, too, unsubstantial, unreal, an illusion only, though comeliest of illusions? She had given him alms! Was the merit of the giver illusive also—illusive like the grace of the supple fingers that gave? Assuredly there were mysteries in the Abhidharma impenetrable, incomprehensible!... It was a golden coin, stamped with the symbol of an elephant—not more of an illusion, indeed, than the gifts of Kings to the Buddha! Gold upon her bosom also, less fine than the gold of her skin. Naked between the silken sash and the narrow breast-corslet, her young waist curved glossy and pliant as a bow. Richer the silver in her voice than in the hollow *pagals* that made a moonlight about her ankles! But her smile!—the little teeth like flower-stamens in the perfumed blossom of her mouth!

O weakness! O shame! How had the strong Charioteer of Resolve thus lost his control over the wild team of fancy! Was this languor of the Will a signal of coming peril, the peril of slumber? So strangely vivid those fancies were, so brightly definite, as about to take visible form, to move with factitious life, to play some unholy drama upon the stage of dreams! "O Thou Fully Awakened!" he cried aloud, "help now thy humble disciple to obtain the blessed wakefulness of perfect contemplation! let him find force to fulfil his vow! suffer not Mara to prevail against him!" And he recited the eternal verses of the Chapter of Wakefulness:—

"*Completely and eternally awake are the disciples of Gotama!* Unceasingly, by day and night, their thoughts are fixed upon the Law.

"*Completely and eternally awake are the disciples of Gotama!* Unceasingly, by day and night, their thoughts are fixed upon the Community.

"*Completely and eternally awake are the disciples of Gotama!* Unceasingly, by day and night, their thoughts are fixed upon the Body.

"*Completely and eternally awake are the disciples of Gotama!* Unceasingly, by day and night, their minds know the sweetness of perfect peace.

"*Completely and eternally awake are the disciples of Gotama!* Unceasingly, by day and night, their minds enjoy the deep peace of meditation."

There came a murmur to his ears; a murmuring of many voices, smothering the utterances of his own, like a tumult of waters. The stars went out before his sight; the heavens darkened their infinities: all things became viewless, became blackness; and the great murmur deepened, like the murmur of a rising tide; and the earth seemed to sink from beneath him. His feet no longer touched the ground; a sense of supernatural buoyancy pervaded every fibre of his body: he felt himself floating in obscurity; then sinking softly, slowly, like a feather dropped from the pinnacle of a temple. Was this death? Nay, for all suddenly, as transported by the Sixth Supernatural Power, he stood again in light—a perfumed, sleepy light, vapory, beautiful—that bathed the marvelous streets of some Indian city. Now the nature of the murmur became manifest to him; for he moved with a mighty throng, a people of pilgrims, a nation of worshippers. But these were not of his faith; they bore upon their foreheads the smeared symbols of obscene gods! Still, he could not escape from their midst; the mile-broad human torrent bore him irresistibly with it, as a leaf is swept by the waters of the Ganges. Rajahs were there with their trains, and princes riding upon elephants, and Brahmins robed in their vestments, and swarms of voluptuous dancing-girls, moving to chant of *kabit* and *damāri*. But whither, whither? Out of the city into the sun they passed, between avenues of banyan, down colonnades of palm. But whither, whither?

Blue-distant, a mountain of carven stone appeared before them—the Temple, lifting to heaven its wilderness of chiseled pinnacles, flinging to the sky the golden spray of its decoration. Higher it grew with approach, the blue tones changed to gray, the outlines sharpened in the light. Then each detail became visible: the elephants of the pedestals standing upon tortoises of rock; the great grim faces of the capitals; the serpents and monsters writhing among the friezes; the many-headed gods of basalt in their galleries of fretted niches, tier above tier; the pictured foulnesses, the painted lusts, the divinities of abomination. And, yawning in the sloping precipice of sculpture, beneath a frenzied swarming of gods and Gopia—a beetling pyramid of limbs and bodies interlocked—the Gate, cavernous and shadowy as the mouth of Siva, devoured the living multitude.

The eddy of the throng whirled him with it to the vastness of the interior. None seemed to note his yellow robe, none even to observe his presence. Giant aisles intercrossed their heights above him; myriads of mighty pillars, fantastically carven, filed away to invisibility behind the yellow illumination of torch-fires. Strange images, weirdly sensuous, loomed up through haze of incense. Colossal figures, that at a distance assumed the form of elephants or garuda-birds, changed aspect when approached, and revealed as the secret of their design an interplaiting of the bodies of women; while one divinity rode all the monstrous allegories—one divinity or demon, eternally the same in the repetition of the sculptor, universally visible as though self-multiplied. The huge pillars themselves were symbols, figures, carnalities; the orgiastic spirit of that worship lived and writhed in the contorted bronze of the lamps, the twisted gold of the cups, the chiseled marble of the tanks....

How far had he proceeded? He knew not; the journey among those countless columns, past those armies of petrified gods, down lanes of flickering lights, seemed longer than the voyage of a caravan, longer than his pilgrimage to China! But suddenly, inexplicably, there came a silence as of cemeteries; the living ocean seemed to have ebbed away from about him, to have been engulfed within abysses of subterranean architecture! He found himself alone in some strange crypt before a basin, shell-shaped and shallow, bearing in its centre a rounded column of less than human height, whose smooth and spherical summit was wreathed with flowers. Lamps similarly formed, and fed with oil of palm, hung above it. There was no other graven image, no visible divinity. Flowers of countless varieties lay heaped upon the pavement; they covered its surface like a carpet, thick, soft; they exhaled their ghosts beneath his feet. The perfume seemed to penetrate his brain—a perfume sensuous, intoxicating, unholy; an unconquerable languor mastered his will, and he sank to rest upon the floral offerings.

The sound of a tread, light as a whisper, approached through the heavy stillness, with a drowsy tinkling of *pagals*, a tintinnabulation of anklets. All suddenly he felt glide about his neck the tepid smoothness of a woman's arm. *She, she!* his Illusion, his Temptation;

but how transformed, transfigured!—preternatural in her loveliness, incomprehensible in her charm! Delicate as a jasmine-petal the cheek that touched his own; deep as night, sweet as summer, the eyes that watched him. *"Heart's-thief,"* her flower-lips whispered— *"heart's-thief, how have I sought for thee! How have I found thee! Sweets I bring thee, my beloved; lips and bosom; fruit and blossom. Hast thirst? Drink from the well of mine eyes! Wouldst sacrifice? I am thine altar! Wouldst pray? I am thy God!"*

Their lips touched; her kiss seemed to change the cells of his blood to flame. For a moment Illusion triumphed; Mara prevailed!... With a shock of resolve the dreamer awoke in the night—under the stars of the Chinese sky.

Only a mockery of sleep! But the vow had been violated, the sacred purpose unfulfilled! Humiliated, penitent, but resolved, the ascetic drew from his girdle a keen knife, and with unfaltering hands severed his eyelids from his eyes, and flung them from him. "O Thou Perfectly Awakened!" he prayed, "thy disciple hath not been overcome save through the feebleness of the body; and his vow hath been renewed. Here shall he linger, without food or drink, until the moment of its fulfilment." And having assumed the hieratic posture—seated himself with his lower limbs folded beneath him, and the palms of his hands upward, the right upon the left, the left resting upon the sole of his upturned foot—he resumed his meditation.

Dawn blushed; day brightened. The sun shortened all the shadows of the land, and lengthened them again, and sank at last upon his funeral pyre of crimson-burning cloud. Night came and glittered and passed. But Mara had tempted in vain. This time the vow had been fulfilled, the holy purpose accomplished.

And again the sun arose to fill the World with laughter of light; flowers opened their hearts to him; birds sang their morning hymn of fire worship; the deep forest trembled with delight; and far upon the plain, the eaves of many-storied temples and the peaked caps of the city-towers caught aureate glory. Strong in the holiness of his accomplished vow, the Indian pilgrim arose in the morning glow. He started for amazement as he lifted his hands to his eyes. What! was everything a dream? Impossible! Yet now his eyes felt no pain; neither were they lidless; not even so much as one of their lashes was lacking. What marvel had been wrought? In vain he looked for the severed lids that he had flung upon the ground; they had mysteriously vanished. But lo! there where he had cast them two wondrous shrubs were growing, with dainty leaflets eyelid-shaped, and snowy buds just opening to the East.

Then, by virtue of the supernatural power acquired in that mighty meditation, it was given the holy missionary to know the secret of that newly created plant—the subtle virtue of its leaves. And he named it, in the language of the nation to whom he brought the Lotos of the Good Law, "*TE*"; and he spake to it, saying:—

"Blessed be thou, sweet plant, beneficent, life-giving, formed by the spirit of virtuous resolve! Lo! the fame of thee shall yet spread unto the ends of the earth; and the perfume of thy life be borne unto the uttermost parts by all the winds of heaven! Verily, for all time to come men who drink of thy sap shall find such refreshment that weariness may not overcome them nor languor seize upon them;—neither shall they know the confusion of drowsiness, nor any desire for slumber in the hour of duty or of prayer. Blessed be thou!"

And still, as a mist of incense, as a smoke of universal sacrifice, perpetually ascends to heaven from all the lands of earth the pleasant vapor of TE, created for the refreshment of mankind by the power of a holy vow, the virtue of a pious atonement.

The Tale of the Porcelain-God

It is written in the FONG-HO-CHIN-TCH'OUEN, *that whenever the artist Thsang-Kong was in doubt, he would look into the fire of the great oven in which his vases were baking, and question the Guardian-Spirit dwelling in the flame. And the Spirit of the Oven-fires so aided him with his counsels, that the porcelains made by Thsang-Kong were indeed finer and lovelier to look upon than all other porcelains. And they were baked in the years of Khang-hí—sacredly called Jin Houang-tí.*

Who first of men discovered the secret of the *Kao-ling*, of the *Pe-tun-tse*—the bones and the flesh, the skeleton and the skin, of the beauteous Vase? Who first discovered the virtue of the curd-white clay? Who first prepared the ice-pure bricks of *tun*: the gathered-hoariness of mountains that have died for age; blanched dust of the rocky bones and the stony flesh of sun-seeking Giants that have ceased to be? Unto whom was it first given to discover the divine art of porcelain?

Unto Pu, once a man, now a god, before whose snowy statues bow the myriad populations enrolled in the guilds of the potteries. But the place of his birth we know not; perhaps the tradition of it may have been effaced from remembrance by that awful war which in our own day consumed the lives of twenty millions of the Black-haired Race, and obliterated from the face of the world even the wonderful City of Porcelain itself—the City of King-te-chin, that of old shone like a jewel of fire in the blue mountain-girdle of Feou-liang.

Before his time indeed the Spirit of the Furnace had being; had issued from the Infinite Vitality; had become manifest as an emanation of the Supreme Tao. For Hoang-ti, nearly five thousand years ago, taught men to make good vessels of baked clay; and in his time all potters had learned to know the God of Oven-fires, and turned their wheels to the murmuring of prayer. But Hoang-ti had been gathered unto his fathers for thrice ten hundred years before that man was born destined by the Master of Heaven to become the Porcelain-God.

And his divine ghost, ever hovering above the smoking and the toiling of the potteries, still gives power to the thought of the shaper, grace to the genius of the designer, luminosity to the touch of the enamelist. For by his heaven-taught wisdom was the art of porcelain created; by his inspiration were accomplished all the miracles of Thao-yu, maker of the *Kia-yu-ki*, and all the marvels made by those who followed after him;—

All the azure porcelains called *You-kouo-thien-tsing*; brilliant as a mirror, thin as paper of rice, sonorous as the melodious stone *Khing*, and colored, in obedience to the mandate of the Emperor Chi-tsong, "blue as the sky is after rain, when viewed through the rifts of the clouds." These were, indeed, the first of all porcelains, likewise called *Tchai-yao*, which no man, howsoever wicked, could find courage to break, for they charmed the eye like jewels of price;—

And the *Jou-yao*, second in rank among all porcelains, sometimes mocking the aspect and the sonority of bronze, sometimes blue as summer waters, and deluding the sight with mucid appearance of thickly floating spawn of fish;—

And the *Kouan-yao*, which are the Porcelains of Magistrates, and third in rank of merit among all wondrous porcelains, colored with colors of the morning—skyey blueness, with the rose of a great dawn blushing and bursting through it, and long-limbed marsh-birds flying against the glow;

Also the *Ko-yao*—fourth in rank among perfect porcelains—of fair, faint, changing colors, like the body of a living fish, or made in the likeness of opal substance, milk mixed with fire; the work of Sing-I, elder of the immortal brothers Tchang;

Also the *Ting-yao*—fifth in rank among all perfect porcelains—white as the mourning garments of a spouse bereaved, and beautiful with a trickling as of tears—the porcelains sung of by the poet Son-tong-po;

Also the porcelains called *Pi-se-yao*, whose colors are called "hidden," being alternately invisible and visible, like the tints of ice beneath the sun—the porcelains celebrated by the far-famed singer Sin-in;

Also the wondrous *Chu-yao*—the pallid porcelains that utter a mournful cry when smitten—the porcelains chanted of by the mighty chanter, Thou-chao-ling;

Also the porcelains called *Thsin-yao*, white or blue, surface-wrinkled as the face of water by the fluttering of many fins.... And ye can see the fish!

Also the vases called *Tsi-hong-khi*, red as sunset after a rain; and the *T'o-t'ai-khi*, fragile as the wings of the silkworm-moth, lighter than the shell of an egg;

Also the *Kia-tsing*—fair cups pearl-white when empty, yet, by some incomprehensible witchcraft of construction, seeming to swarm with purple fish the moment they are filled with water;

Also the porcelains called *Yao-pien*, whose tints are transmuted by the alchemy of fire; for they enter blood-crimson into the heat, and change there to lizard-green, and at last come forth azure as the cheek of the sky;

Also the *Ki-tcheou-yao*, which are all violet as a summer's night; and the *Hing-yao* that sparkle with the sparklings of mingled silver and snow;

Also the *Sieouen-yao*—some ruddy as iron in the furnace, some diaphanous and ruby-red, some granulated and yellow as the rind of an orange, some softly flushed as the skin of a peach;

Also the *Tsoui-khi-yao*, crackled and green as ancient ice is; and the *Tchou-fou-yao*, which are the Porcelains of Emperors, with dragons wriggling and snarling in gold; and those *yao* that are pink-ribbed and have their angles serrated as the claws of crabs are;

Also the *Ou-ni-yao*, black as the pupil of the eye, and as lustrous; and the *Hou-tien-yao*, darkly yellow as the faces of men of India; and the *Ou-kong-yao*, whose color is the dead-gold of autumn-leaves;

Also the *Long-kang-yao*, green as the seedling of a pea, but bearing also paintings of sun-silvered cloud, and of the Dragons of Heaven;

Also the *Tching-hoa-yao*—pictured with the amber bloom of grapes and the verdure of vine-leaves and the blossoming of poppies, or decorated in relief with figures of fighting crickets;

Also the *Khang-hi-nien-ts'ang-yao*, celestial azure sown with star-dust of gold; and the *Khien-long-nien-thang-yao*, splendid in sable and silver as a fervid night that is flashed with lightnings.

Not indeed the *Long-Ouang-yao*—painted with the lascivious *Pi-hi*, with the obscene *Nan-niu-ssé-sie*, with the shameful *Tchun-hoa*, or "Pictures of Spring"; abominations created by command of the wicked Emperor Moutsong, though the Spirit of the Furnace hid his face and fled away;

But all other vases of startling form and substance, magically articulated, and ornamented with figures in relief, in cameo, in transparency—the vases with orifices belled like the cups of flowers, or cleft like the bills of birds, or fanged like the jaws of serpents, or pink-lipped as the mouth of a girl; the vases flesh-colored and purple-veined and dimpled, with ears and with earrings; the vases in likeness of mushrooms, of lotos-flowers, of lizards, of horse-footed dragons woman-faced; the vases strangely translucid, that simulate the white glimmering of grains of prepared rice, that counterfeit the vapory lace-work of frost, that imitate the efflorescences of coral;—

Also the statues in porcelain of divinities: the Genius of the Hearth; the Long-pinn who are the Twelve Deities of Ink; the blessed Lao-tseu, born with silver hair; Kong-fu-tse, grasping the scroll of written wisdom; Kouan-in, sweetest Goddess of Mercy, standing snowy-footed upon the heart of her golden lily; Chi-nong, the god who taught men how to cook; Fo, with long eyes closed in meditation, and lips smiling the mysterious smile of Supreme Beatitude; Cheou-lao, god of Longevity, bestriding his aërial steed, the white-winged stork; Pou-t'ai, Lord of Contentment and of Wealth, obese and dreamy; and that fairest Goddess of Talent, from whose beneficent hands eternally streams the iridescent rain of pearls.

And though many a secret of that matchless art that Pu bequeathed unto men may indeed have been forgotten and lost forever, the story of the Porcelain-God is remembered; and I doubt not that any of the aged *Jeou-yen-liao-kong*, any one of the old blind men of the great potteries, who sit all day grinding colors in the sun, could tell you Pu was once a humble Chinese workman, who grew to be a great artist by dint of tireless study and patience and by the inspiration of Heaven. So famed he became that some deemed him an alchemist, who possessed the secret called *White-and-Yellow*, by which stones might be turned into gold; and others thought him a magician, having the ghastly power of murdering men with horror of nightmare, by hiding charmed effigies of them under the tiles of their own roofs; and others, again, averred that he was an astrologer who had discovered the mystery of those Five

Hing which influence all things—those Powers that move even in the currents of the star-drift, in the milky *Tien-ho*, or River of the Sky. Thus, at least, the ignorant spoke of him; but even those who stood about the Son of Heaven, those whose hearts had been strengthened by the acquisition of wisdom, wildly praised the marvels of his handicraft, and asked each other if there might be any imaginable form of beauty which Pu could not evoke from that beauteous substance so docile to the touch of his cunning hand.

And one day it came to pass that Pu sent a priceless gift to the Celestial and August: a vase imitating the substance of ore-rock, all aflame with pyritic scintillation—a shape of glittering splendor with chameleons sprawling over it; chameleons of porcelain that shifted color as often as the beholder changed his position. And the Emperor, wondering exceedingly at the splendor of the work, questioned the princes and the mandarins concerning him that made it. And the princes and the mandarins answered that he was a workman named Pu, and that he was without equal among potters, knowing secrets that seemed to have been inspired either by gods or by demons. Whereupon the Son of Heaven sent his officers to Pu with a noble gift, and summoned him unto his presence.

So the humble artisan entered before the Emperor, and having performed the supreme prostration—thrice kneeling, and thrice nine times touching the ground with his forehead—awaited the command of the August.

And the Emperor spake to him, saying: "Son, thy gracious gift hath found high favor in our sight; and for the charm of that offering we have bestowed upon thee a reward of five thousand silver *liang*. But thrice that sum shall be awarded thee so soon as thou shalt have fulfilled our behest. Hearken, therefore, O matchless artificer! it is now our will that thou make for us a vase having the tint and the aspect of living flesh, but—mark well our desire!—*of flesh made to creep by the utterance of such words as poets utter—flesh moved by an Idea, flesh horripilated by a Thought!* Obey, and answer not! We have spoken."

Now Pu was the most cunning of all the *P'ei-se-kong*—the men who marry colors together; of all the *Hoa-yang-kong*, who draw the shapes of vase-decoration; of all the *Hoei-sse-kong*, who paint in enamel; of all the *T'ien-thsai-kong*, who brighten color; of all the *Chao-lou-kong*, who watch the furnace-fires and the porcelain-ovens. But he went away sorrowing from the Palace of the Son of Heaven, notwithstanding the gift of five thousand silver *liang* which had been given to him. For he thought to himself: "Surely the mystery of the comeliness of flesh, and the mystery of that by which it is moved, are the secrets of the Supreme Tao. How shall man lend the aspect of sentient life to dead clay? Who save the Infinite can give soul?"

Now Pu had discovered those witchcrafts of color, those surprises of grace, that make the art of the ceramist. He had found the secret of the *feng-hong*, the wizard flush of the Rose; of the *hoa-hong*, the delicious incarnadine; of the mountain-green called *chan-lou*; of the pale soft yellow termed *hiao-hoang-yeou*; and of the *hoang-kin*, which is the blazing beauty of gold. He had found those eel-tints, those serpent-greens, those pansy-violets, those furnace-crimsons, those carminates and lilacs, subtle as spirit-flame, which our enamelists of the Occident long sought without success to reproduce. But he trembled at the task assigned him, as he returned to the toil of his studio, saying: "How shall any miserable man render in clay the quivering of flesh to an Idea—the inexplicable horripilation of a Thought? Shall a man venture to mock the magic of that Eternal Moulder by whose infinite power a million suns are shapen more readily than one small jar might be rounded upon my wheel?"

Yet the command of the Celestial and August might never be

disobeyed; and the patient workman strove with all his power to fulfil the Son of Heaven's desire. But vainly for days, for weeks, for months, for season after season, did he strive; vainly also he prayed unto the gods to aid him; vainly he besought the Spirit of the Furnace, crying: "O thou Spirit of Fire, hear me, heed me, help me! how shall I—a miserable man, unable to breathe into clay a living soul—how shall I render in this inanimate substance the aspect of flesh made to creep by the utterance of a Word, sentient to the horripilation of a Thought?"

For the Spirit of the Furnace made strange answer to him with whispering of fire: "*Vast thy faith, weird thy prayer! Has Thought feet, that man may perceive the trace of its passing? Canst thou measure me the blast of the Wind?*"

Nevertheless, with purpose unmoved, nine-and-forty times did Pu seek to fulfil the Emperor's command; nine-and-forty times he strove to obey the behest of the Son of Heaven. Vainly, alas! did he consume his substance; vainly did he expend his strength; vainly did he exhaust his knowledge: success smiled not upon him; and Evil visited his home, and Poverty sat in his dwelling, and Misery shivered at his hearth.

Sometimes, when the hour of trial came, it was found that the colors had become strangely transmuted in the firing, or had faded into ashen pallor, or had darkened into the fuliginous hue of forest-mould. And Pu, beholding these misfortunes, made wail to the Spirit of the Furnace, praying: "O thou Spirit of Fire, how shall I render the likeness of lustrous flesh, the warm glow of living color, unless thou aid me?"

And the Spirit of the Furnace mysteriously answered him with murmuring of fire: "*Canst thou learn the art of that Infinite Enameler who hath made beautiful the Arch of Heaven—whose brush is Light; whose paints are the Colors of the Evening?*"

Sometimes, again, even when the tints had not changed, after the pricked and labored surface had seemed about to quicken in the heat, to assume the vibratility of living skin—even at the last hour all the labor of the workers proved to have been wasted; for the fickle substance rebelled against their efforts, producing only crinklings grotesque as those upon the rind of a withered fruit, or granulations like those upon the skin of a dead bird from which the feathers have been rudely plucked. And Pu wept, and cried out unto the Spirit of the Furnace: "O thou Spirit of Flame, how shall I be able to imitate the thrill of flesh touched by a Thought, unless thou wilt vouchsafe to lend me thine aid?"

And the Spirit of the Furnace mysteriously answered him with muttering of fire: *"Canst thou give ghost unto a stone? Canst thou thrill with a Thought the entrails of the granite hills?"*

Sometimes it was found that all the work indeed had not failed; for the color seemed good, and all faultless the matter of the vase appeared to be, having neither crack nor wrinkling nor crinkling; but the pliant softness of warm skin did not meet the eye; the flesh-tinted surface offered only the harsh aspect and hard glimmer of metal. All their exquisite toil to mock the pulpiness of sentient substance had left no trace; had been brought to nought by the breath of the furnace. And Pu, in his despair, shrieked to the Spirit of the Furnace: "O thou merciless divinity! O thou most pitiless god!—thou whom I have worshiped with ten thousand sacrifices!—for what fault hast thou abandoned me? for what error hast thou forsaken me? How may I, most wretched of men! ever render the aspect of flesh made to creep with the utterance of a Word, sentient to the titillation of a Thought, if thou wilt not aid me?"

And the Spirit of the Furnace made answer unto him with roaring of fire: *"Canst thou divide a Soul? Nay!... Thy life for the life of thy work!—thy soul for the soul of thy Vase!"*

And hearing these words Pu arose with a terrible resolve swelling at his heart, and made ready for the last and fiftieth time to fashion his work for the oven.

One hundred times did he sift the clay and the quartz, the *kao-ling* and the *tun*; one hundred times did he purify them in clearest water; one hundred times with tireless hands did he knead the creamy paste, mingling it at last with colors known only to himself. Then was the vase shapen and reshapen, and touched and retouched by the hands of Pu, until its blandness seemed to live, until it appeared to quiver and to palpitate, as with vitality from within, as with the quiver of rounded muscle undulating beneath the integument. For the hues of life were upon it and infiltrated throughout its innermost substance, imitating the carnation of blood-bright tissue, and the reticulated purple of the veins; and over all was laid the envelope of sun-colored *Pe-kia-ho*, the lucid and glossy enamel, half diaphanous, even like the substance that it counterfeited—the polished skin of a woman. Never since the making of the world had any work comparable to this been wrought by the skill of man.

Then Pu bade those who aided him that they should feed the furnace well with wood of *tcha*; but he told his resolve unto none. Yet after the oven began to glow, and he saw the work of his hands blossoming and blushing in the heat, he bowed himself before the Spirit of Flame, and murmured: "O thou Spirit and Master of Fire, I know the truth of thy words! I know that a Soul may never be divided! Therefore my life for the life of my work!—my soul for the soul of my Vase!"

And for nine days and for eight nights the furnaces were fed unceasingly with wood of *tcha*; for nine days and for eight nights men watched the wondrous vase crystallizing into being, rose-lighted by the breath of the flame. Now upon the coming of the ninth night, Pu bade all his weary comrades retire to, rest, for that the work was well-nigh done, and the success assured. "If you find me not here at sunrise," he said, "fear not to take forth the vase; for I know that the task will have been accomplished according to the command of the August." So they departed.

But in that same ninth night Pu entered the flame, and yielded up his ghost in the embrace of the Spirit of the Furnace, giving his life for the life of his work—his soul for the soul of his Vase.

And when the workmen came upon the tenth morning to take forth the porcelain marvel, even the bones of Pu had ceased to be; but lo! the Vase lived as they looked upon it: seeming to be flesh moved by the utterance of a Word, creeping to the titillation of a Thought. And whenever tapped by the finger it uttered a voice and a name—the voice of its maker, the name of its creator: PU.

And the son of Heaven, hearing of these things, and viewing the miracle of the vase, said unto those about him: "Verily, the Impossible hath been wrought by the strength of faith, by the force of obedience! Yet never was it our desire that so cruel a sacrifice should have been; we sought only to know whether the skill of the matchless artificer came from the Divinities or from the Demons— from heaven or from hell. Now, indeed, we discern that Pu hath taken his place among the gods." And the Emperor mourned exceedingly for his faithful servant. But he ordained that godlike honors should be paid unto the spirit of the marvelous artist, and that his memory should be revered forevermore, and that fair statues of him should be set up in all the cities of the Celestial Empire, and above all the toiling of the potteries, that the multitude of workers might unceasingly call upon his name and invoke his benediction upon their labors.

The Goblin-Spider

• •

In very ancient books it is said that there used to be many goblin-spiders in Japan.

Some folks declare there are still some goblin-spiders. During the daytime they look just like common spiders; but very late at night, when everybody is asleep, and there is no sound, they become very, very big, and do awful things. Goblin-spiders are supposed also to have the magical power of taking human shape— so as to deceive people. And there is a famous Japanese story about such a spider.

There was once, in some lonely part of the country, a haunted temple. No one could live in the building because of the goblins that had taken possession of it. Many brave samurai went to that place at various times for the purpose of killing the goblins. But they were never heard of again after they had entered the temple.

At last one who was famous for his courage and his prudence, went to the temple to watch during the night. And he said to those who accompanied him there:—"If in the morning I am still alive, I shall drum upon the drum of the temple." Then he was left alone, to watch by the light of a lamp.

As the night advanced he crouched down under the altar, which supported a dusty image of Buddha. He saw nothing strange and heard no sound till after midnight. Then there came a goblin, having but half a body and one eye, and said: *"Hitokusai!"* ["There is the smell of a man!"] But the samurai did not move. The goblin went away.

Then there came a priest and played upon a *samisen* so wonderfully that the samurai felt sure it was not the playing of a man. So he leaped up with his sword drawn. The priest, seeing him, burst out laughing, and said:—"So you thought I was a goblin? Oh no! I am only the priest of this temple; but I have to play to keep off the goblins. Does not this *samisen* sound well? Please play a little."

And he offered the instrument to the samurai who grasped it very cautiously with his left hand. But instantly the *samisen* changed into a monstrous spider web, and the priest into a goblin and the warrior found himself caught fast in the web by the left hand. He struggled bravely, and struck at the spider with his sword, and wounded it; but he soon became entangled still more in the net, and could not move.

However, the wounded spider crawled away—and the sun rose. In a little while the people came and found the samurai in the horrible web, and freed him. They saw tracks of blood upon the floor, and followed the tracks out of the temple to a hole in the deserted garden. Out of the hole issued a frightful sound of groaning. They found the wounded goblin in the hole, and killed it.

Fragment

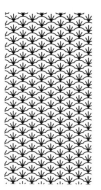

And it was at the hour of sunset that they came to the foot of the mountain. There was in that place no sign of life—neither token of water, nor trace of plant, nor shadow of flying bird—nothing but desolation rising to desolation. And the summit was lost in heaven.

Then the Bodhisattva said to his young companion:—"What you have asked to see will be shown to you. But the place of the Vision is far; and the way is rude. Follow after me, and do not fear: strength will be given you."

Twilight gloomed about them as they climbed. There was no beaten path, nor any mark of former human visitation; and the way was over an endless heaping of tumbled fragments that rolled or turned beneath the foot. Sometimes a mass dislodged would clatter down with hollow echoings;—sometimes the substance trodden would burst like an empty shell…. Stars pointed and thrilled; and the darkness deepened.

"Do not fear, my son," said the Bodhisattva, guiding: "danger there is none, though the way be grim."

Under the stars they climbed—fast, fast—mounting by help of power superhuman. High zones of mist they passed; and they saw below them, ever widening as they climbed, a soundless flood of cloud, like the tide of a milky sea.

Hour after hour they climbed;—and forms invisible yielded to their tread with dull soft crashings;—and faint cold fires lighted and died at every breaking.

And once the pilgrim-youth laid hand on a something smooth that was not stone—and lifted it—and dimly saw the cheekless gibe of death.

"Linger not thus, my son!" urged the voice of the teacher;—"the summit that we must gain is very far away!"

On through the dark they climbed—and felt continually beneath them the soft strange breakings—and saw the icy fires worm and die—till the rim of the night turned grey, and the stars began to fail, and the east began to bloom.

Yet still they climbed—fast, fast—mounting by help of power superhuman. About them now was frigidness of death—and silence tremendous.... A gold flame kindled in the east.

Then first to the pilgrim's gaze the steeps revealed their nakedness;—and a trembling seized him—and a ghastly fear. For there was not any ground—neither beneath him nor about him nor above him—but a heaping only, monstrous and measureless, of skulls and fragments of skulls and dust of bone—with a shimmer of shed teeth strown through the drift of it, like the shimmer of scrags of shell in the wrack of a tide.

"Do not fear, my son!" cried the voice of the Bodhisattva;—"only the strong of heart can win to the place of the Vision!"

Behind them the world had vanished. Nothing remained but the clouds beneath, and the sky above, and the heaping of skulls between—up-slanting out of sight.

Then the sun climbed with the climbers; and there was no warmth in the light of him, but coldness sharp as a sword. And the horror of stupendous height, and the nightmare of stupendous depth, and the terror of silence, ever grew and grew, and weighed upon the pilgrim, and held his feet—so that suddenly all power departed from him, and he moaned like a sleeper in dreams.

....

"Hasten, hasten, my son!" cried the Bodhisattva: "the day is brief, and the summit is very far away."

But the pilgrim shrieked—"I fear! I fear unspeakably!—and the power has departed from me!"

"The power will return, my son," made answer the Bodhisattva.... "Look now below you and above you and about you, and tell me what you see."

"I cannot," cried the pilgrim, trembling and clinging; "I dare not look beneath! Before me and about me there is nothing but skulls of men."

"And yet, my son," said the Bodhisattva, laughing softly—"and yet you do not know of what this mountain is made."

The other, shuddering, repeated:—"I fear!—unutterably I fear!... there is nothing but skulls of men!"

"A mountain of skulls it is," responded the Bodhisattva. "But know, my son, that all of them ARE YOUR OWN! Each has at some time been the nest of your dreams and delusions and desires. Not even one of them is the skull of any other being. All—all without exception—have been yours, in the billions of your former lives."

A Passional Karma

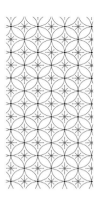

O ne of the never-failing attractions of the Tōkyō stage is the performance, by the famous Kikugorō and his company, of the *Botan-Dōrō*, or "Peony-Lantern." This weird play, of which the scenes are laid in the middle of the last century, is the dramatization of a romance by the novelist Encho, written in colloquial Japanese, and purely Japanese in local color, though inspired by a Chinese tale. I went to see the play; and Kikugorō made me familiar with a new variety of the pleasure of fear. "Why not give English readers the ghostly part of the story?"— asked a friend who guides me betimes through the mazes of Eastern philosophy. "It would serve to explain some popular ideas of the supernatural which Western people know very little about. And I could help you with the translation."

I gladly accepted the suggestion; and we composed the following summary of the more extraordinary portion of Encho's romance. Here and there we found it necessary to condense the original narrative; and we tried to keep close to the text only in the conversational passages—some of which happen to possess a particular quality of psychological interest.

—This is the story of the Ghosts in the Romance of the Peony-Lantern:—

I

There once lived in the district of Ushigomé, in Yedo, a *hatamoto*[1] called Iijima Heizayémon, whose only daughter, Tsuyu, was beautiful as her name, which signifies "Morning Dew." Iijima took a second wife when his daughter was about sixteen; and, finding that O-Tsuyu could not be happy with her mother-in-law, he had a pretty villa built for the girl at Yanagijima, as a separate residence, and gave her an excellent maidservant, called O-Yoné, to wait upon her.

O-Tsuyu lived happily enough in her new home until one day when the family physician, Yamamoto Shijō, paid her a visit in company with a young samurai named Hagiwara Shinzaburō, who resided in the Nedzu quarter. Shinzaburō was an unusually handsome lad, and very gentle; and the two young people fell in love with each other at sight. Even before the brief visit was over, they contrived—unheard by the old doctor—to pledge themselves to each other for life. And, at parting, O-Tsuyu whispered to the youth—"*Remember! If you do not come to see me again, I shall certainly die!*"

Shinzaburō never forgot those words; and he was only too eager to see more of O-Tsuyu. But etiquette forbade him to make the visit alone: he was obliged to wait for some other chance to accompany the doctor, who had promised to take him to the villa a second time. Unfortunately the old man did not keep this promise. He had perceived the sudden affection of O-Tsuyu; and he feared that her father would hold him responsible for any serious results. Iijima Heizayémon had a reputation for cutting off heads. And the more Shijō thought about the possible consequences of his

---

1   The *hatamoto* were samurai forming the special military force of the Shogun. The name literally signifies "Banner-Supporters." These were the highest class of samurai—not only as the immediate vassals of the Shogun, but as a military aristocracy.

introduction of Shinzaburō at the Iijima villa, the more he became afraid. Therefore he purposely abstained from calling upon his young friend.

Months passed; and O-Tsuyu, little imagining the true cause of Shinzaburō's neglect, believed that her love had been scorned. Then she pined away, and died. Soon afterwards, the faithful servant O-Yoné also died, through grief at the loss of her mistress; and the two were buried side by side in the cemetery of Shin-Banzui-In—a temple which still stands in the neighborhood of Dango-Zaka, where the famous chrysanthemum-shows are yearly held.

II

Shinzaburō knew nothing of what had happened; but his disappointment and his anxiety had resulted in a prolonged illness. He was slowly recovering, but still very weak, when he unexpectedly received another visit from Yamamoto Shijō. The old man made a number of plausible excuses for his apparent neglect. Shinzaburō said to him:—"I have been sick ever since the beginning of spring;— even now I cannot eat anything…. Was it not rather unkind of you never to call? I thought that we were to make another visit together to the house of the Lady Iijima; and I wanted to take to her some little present as a return for our kind reception. Of course I could not go by myself."

Shijō gravely responded—"I am very sorry to tell you that the young lady is dead!"

"Dead!" repeated Shinzaburō, turning white—"did you say that she is dead?"

The doctor remained silent for a moment, as if collecting himself: then he resumed, in the quick light tone of a man resolved not to take trouble seriously:—

"My great mistake was in having introduced you to her; for it seems that she fell in love with you at once. I am afraid that you must have said something to encourage this affection—when you were in that little room together. At all events, I saw how she felt towards you; and then I became uneasy—fearing that her father might come to hear of the matter, and lay the whole blame upon me. So—to be quite frank with you—I decided that it would be better not to call upon you; and I purposely stayed away for a long time. But, only a few days ago, happening to visit Iijima's house, I heard, to my great surprise, that his daughter had died, and that her servant O-Yoné had also died. Then, remembering all that had taken place, I knew that the young lady must have died of love for you…. [Laughing] Ah, you are really a sinful fellow! Yes, you are! [Laughing] Isn't it a sin to have been born so handsome that the girls die for love of you? [Seriously] Well, we must leave the dead to the dead. It is no use to talk further about the matter;—all that you now can do for her is to repeat the Nembutsu[2].… Good-bye."

And the old man retired hastily—anxious to avoid further converse about the painful event for which he felt himself to have been unwittingly responsible.

III

Shinzaburō long remained stupefied with grief by the news of O-Tsuyu's death. But as soon as he found himself again able to think clearly, he inscribed the dead girl's name upon a mortuary tablet, and placed the tablet in the Buddhist shrine of his house, and set offerings before it, and recited prayers. Every day thereafter

---

2   The invocation *Namu Amida Butsu!* ("Hail to the Buddha Amitabha!"), repeated, as a prayer, for the sake of the dead.

he presented offerings, and repeated the Nembutsu; and the memory of O-Tsuyu was never absent from his thought.

Nothing occurred to change the monotony of his solitude before the time of the Bon—the great Festival of the Dead—which begins upon the thirteenth day of the seventh month. Then he decorated his house, and prepared everything for the festival;—hanging out the lanterns that guide the returning spirits, and setting the food of ghosts on the *shōryōdana*, or Shelf of Souls. And on the first evening of the Bon, after sun-down, he kindled a small lamp before the tablet of O-Tsuyu, and lighted the lanterns.

The night was clear, with a great moon—and windless, and very warm. Shinzaburō sought the coolness of his veranda. Clad only in a light summer-robe, he sat there thinking, dreaming, sorrowing;— sometimes fanning himself; sometimes making a little smoke to drive the mosquitoes away. Everything was quiet. It was a lonesome neighborhood, and there were few passers-by. He could hear only the soft rushing of a neighboring stream, and the shrilling of night-insects.

But all at once this stillness was broken by a sound of women's *geta*[3] approaching—*kara-kon, kara-kon*;—and the sound drew nearer and nearer, quickly, till it reached the live-hedge surrounding the garden. Then Shinzaburō, feeling curious, stood on tiptoe, so as to look over the hedge; and he saw two women passing. One, who was carrying a beautiful lantern decorated with peony-flowers,[4] appeared to be a servant;—the other was a slender girl of about

---

3   *Komageta* in the original. The *geta* is a wooden sandal, or clog, of which there are many varieties—some decidedly elegant. The *komageta*, or "pony-geta" is so-called because of the sonorous hoof-like echo which it makes on hard ground.

4   The sort of lantern here referred to is no longer made. It was totally unlike the modern domestic band-lantern, painted with the owner's crest; but it was not altogether unlike some forms of lanterns still manufactured for the Festival of the Dead, and called *Bon-dōrō*. The flowers ornamenting it were not painted: they were artificial flowers of crepe-silk, and were attached to the top of the lantern.

seventeen, wearing a long-sleeved robe embroidered with designs of autumn-blossoms. Almost at the same instant both women turned their faces toward Shinzaburō;—and to his utter astonishment, he recognized O-Tsuyu and her servant O-Yoné.

They stopped immediately; and the girl cried out—"Oh, how strange!... Hagiwara Sama!"

Shinzaburō simultaneously called to the maid:—"O-Yoné! Ah, you are O-Yoné!—I remember you very well."

"Hagiwara Sama!" exclaimed O-Yoné in a tone of supreme amazement. "Never could I have believed it possible!... Sir, we were told that you had died."

"How extraordinary!" cried Shinzaburō. "Why, I was told that both of you were dead!"

"Ah, what a hateful story!" returned O-Yoné. "Why repeat such unlucky words?... Who told you?"

"Please to come in," said Shinzaburō;—"here we can talk better. The garden-gate is open."

So they entered, and exchanged greeting; and when Shinzaburō had made them comfortable, he said:—

"I trust that you will pardon my discourtesy in not having called upon you for so long a time. But Shijō, the doctor, about a month ago, told me that you had both died."

"So it was he who told you?" exclaimed O-Yoné. "It was very wicked of him to say such a thing. Well, it was also Shijō who told us that you were dead. I think that he wanted to deceive you—which was not a difficult thing to do, because you are so confiding and trustful. Possibly my mistress betrayed her liking for you in some words which found their way to her father's ears; and, in that case, O-Kuni—the new wife—might have planned to make the doctor tell you that we were dead, so as to bring about a separation. Anyhow, when my mistress heard that you had died, she wanted to cut off her hair immediately, and to become a nun.

But I was able to prevent her from cutting off her hair; and I persuaded her at last to become a nun only in her heart. Afterwards her father wished her to marry a certain young man; and she refused. Then there was a great deal of trouble—chiefly caused by O-Kuni;—and we went away from the villa, and found a very small house in Yanaka-no-Sasaki. There we are now just barely able to live, by doing a little private work.... My mistress has been constantly repeating the Nembutsu for your sake. To-day, being the first day of the Bon, we went to visit the temples; and we were on our way home—thus late—when this strange meeting happened."

"Oh, how extraordinary!" cried Shinzaburō. "Can it be true?—or is it only a dream? Here I, too, have been constantly reciting the Nembutsu before a tablet with her name upon it! Look!" And he showed them O-Tsuyu's tablet in its place upon the Shelf of Souls.

"We are more than grateful for your kind remembrance," returned O-Yoné, smiling.... "Now as for my mistress,"—she continued, turning towards O-Tsuyu, who had all the while remained demure and silent, half-hiding her face with her sleeve—"as for my mistress, she actually says that she would not mind being disowned by her father for the time of seven existences,[5] or even being killed by him, for your sake! Come! will you not allow her to stay here to-night?"

Shinzaburō turned pale for joy. He answered in a voice trembling with emotion:—"Please remain; but do not speak loud—because there

---

5 "For the time of seven existences,"—that is to say, for the time of seven successive lives. In Japanese drama and romance it is not uncommon to represent a father as disowning his child "for the time of seven lives." Such a disowning is called *shichi-shō madé no mandō,* a disinheritance for seven lives—signifying that in six future lives after the present the erring son or daughter will continue to feel the parental displeasure.

is a troublesome fellow living close by—a *ninsomi*[6] called Hakuōdō Yusai, who tells people's fortunes by looking at their faces. He is inclined to be curious; and it is better that he should not know."

The two women remained that night in the house of the young samurai, and returned to their own home a little before daybreak. And after that night they came every night for seven nights—whether the weather were foul or fair—always at the same hour. And Shinzaburō became more and more attached to the girl; and the twain were fettered, each to each, by that bond of illusion which is stronger than bands of iron.

IV

Now there was a man called Tomozō, who lived in a small cottage adjoining Shinzaburō's residence, Tomozō and his wife O-Miné were both employed by Shinzaburō as servants. Both seemed to be devoted to their young master; and by his help they were able to live in comparative comfort.

One night, at a very late hour, Tomozō heard the voice of a woman in his master's apartment; and this made him uneasy. He feared that Shinzaburo, being very gentle and affectionate, might be made the dupe of some cunning wanton—in which event the domestics would be the first to suffer. He therefore resolved to watch; and on the following night he stole on tiptoe to Shinzaburō's dwelling, and looked through a chink in one of the sliding shutters. By the glow of a night-lantern within the sleeping-room, he was able to perceive that his master and a strange woman were talking together under the mosquito-net. At first he could not see the woman

---

6   The profession is not yet extinct. The *ninsomi* uses a kind of magnifying glass (or magnifying-mirror sometimes) called *tengankyō* or *ninsomégané*.

distinctly. Her back was turned to him;—he only observed that she was very slim, and that she appeared to be very young—judging from the fashion of her dress and hair.[7] Putting his ear to the chink, he could hear the conversation plainly. The woman said:—

"And if I should be disowned by my father, would you then let me come and live with you?"

Shinzaburō answered:—

"Most assuredly I would—nay, I should be glad of the chance. But there is no reason to fear that you will ever be disowned by your father; for you are his only daughter, and he loves you very much. What I do fear is that some day we shall be cruelly separated."

She responded softly:—

"Never, never could I even think of accepting any other man for my husband. Even if our secret were to become known, and my father were to kill me for what I have done, still—after death itself—I could never cease to think of you. And I am now quite sure that you yourself would not be able to live very long without me."… Then clinging closely to him, with her lips at his neck, she caressed him; and he returned her caresses.

Tomozō wondered as he listened—because the language of the woman was not the language of a common woman, but the language of a lady of rank.[8] Then he determined at all hazards to get one glimpse of her face; and he crept round the house, backwards and forwards, peering through every crack and chink. And at last he was able to see;—but therewith an icy trembling seized him; and the hair of his head stood up.

For the face was the face of a woman long dead—and the fingers

---

7   The color and form of the dress, and the style of wearing the hair, are by Japanese custom regulated according to the age of the woman.

8   The forms of speech used by the samurai, and other superior classes, differed considerably from those of the popular idiom; but these differences could not be effectively rendered into English.

caressing were fingers of naked bone—and of the body below the waist there was not anything: it melted off into thinnest trailing shadow. Where the eyes of the lover deluded saw youth and grace and beauty, there appeared to the eyes of the watcher horror only, and the emptiness of death. Simultaneously another woman's figure, and a weirder, rose up from within the chamber, and swiftly made toward the watcher, as if discerning his presence. Then, in uttermost terror, he fled to the dwelling of Hakuōdō Yusai, and, knocking frantically at the doors, succeeded in arousing him.

V

Hakuōdō Yusai, the *ninsomi*, was a very old man; but in his time he had traveled much, and he had heard and seen so many things that he could not be easily surprised. Yet the story of the terrified Tomozō both alarmed and amazed him. He had read in ancient Chinese books of love between the living and the dead; but he had never believed it possible. Now, however, he felt convinced that the statement of Tomozō was not a falsehood, and that something very strange was really going on in the house of Hagiwara. Should the truth prove to be what Tomozō imagined, then the young samurai was a doomed man.

"If the woman be a ghost,"—said Yusai to the frightened servant, "—if the woman be a ghost, your master must die very soon—unless something extraordinary can be done to save him. And if the woman be a ghost, the signs of death will appear upon his face. For the spirit of the living is *yōki*, and pure;—the spirit of the dead is *inki*, and unclean: the one is Positive, the other Negative. He whose bride is a ghost cannot live. Even though in his blood there existed the force of a life of one hundred years, that force must quickly perish.... Still, I shall do all that I can to save Hagiwara Sama. And in the meantime,

Tomozō, say nothing to any other person—not even to your wife—about this matter. At sunrise I shall call upon your master."

VI

When questioned next morning by Yusai, Shinzaburō at first attempted to deny that any women had been visiting the house; but finding this artless policy of no avail, and perceiving that the old man's purpose was altogether unselfish, he was finally persuaded to acknowledge what had really occurred, and to give his reasons for wishing to keep the matter a secret. As for the lady Iijima, he intended, he said, to make her his wife as soon as possible.

"Oh, madness!" cried Yusai—losing all patience in the intensity of his alarm. "Know, sir, that the people who have been coming here, night after night, are dead! Some frightful delusion is upon you!... Why, the simple fact that you long supposed O-Tsuyu to be dead, and repeated the Nembutsu for her, and made offerings before her tablet, is itself the proof!... The lips of the dead have touched you!—the hands of the dead have caressed you!... Even at this moment I see in your face the signs of death—and you will not believe!... Listen to me now, sir—I beg of you—if you wish to save yourself: otherwise you have less than twenty days to live. They told you—those people—that they were residing in the district of Shitaya, in Yanaka-no-Sasaki. Did you ever visit them at that place? No!—of course you did not! Then go to-day—as soon as you can—to Yanaka-no-Sasaki, and try to find their home!..."

And having uttered this counsel with the most vehement earnestness, Hakuōdō Yusai abruptly took his departure.

Shinzaburō, startled though not convinced, resolved after a moment's reflection to follow the advice of the *ninsomi*, and to go to Shitaya. It was yet early in the morning when he reached the quarter of Yanaka-no-Sasaki, and began his search for the dwelling of O-Tsuyu. He went through every street and side-street, read all the names inscribed at the various entrances, and made inquiries whenever an opportunity presented itself. But he could not find anything resembling the little house mentioned by O-Yone; and none of the people whom he questioned knew of any house in the quarter inhabited by two single women. Feeling at last certain that further research would be useless, he turned homeward by the shortest way, which happened to lead through the grounds of the temple Shin-Banzui-In.

Suddenly his attention was attracted by two new tombs, placed side by side, at the rear of the temple. One was a common tomb, such as might have been erected for a person of humble rank: the other was a large and handsome monument; and hanging before it was a beautiful peony-lantern, which had probably been left there at the time of the Festival of the Dead. Shinzaburō remembered that the peony-lantern carried by O-Yoné was exactly similar; and the coincidence impressed him as strange. He looked again at the tombs; but the tombs explained nothing. Neither bore any personal name—only the Buddhist *kaimyō*, or posthumous appellation. Then he determined to seek information at the temple. An acolyte stated, in reply to his questions, that the large tomb had been recently erected for the daughter of Iijima Heizayémon, the *hatamoto* of Ushigomé; and that the small tomb next to it was that of her servant O-Yoné, who had died of grief soon after the young lady's funeral.

Immediately to Shinzaburō's memory there recurred, with another and sinister meaning, the words of O-Yoné:—"We went away, and found a very small house in Yanaka-no-Sasaki. There we are now just barely able to live—by doing a little private work...." Here was indeed the very small house—and in Yanaka-no-Sasaki. But the little private work...?

Terror-stricken, the samurai hastened with all speed to the house of Yusai, and begged for his counsel and assistance. But Yusai declared himself unable to be of any aid in such a case. All that he could do was to send Shinzaburō to the high-priest Ryōseki, of Shin-Banzui-In, with a letter praying for immediate religious help.

VII

The high-priest Ryōseki was a learned and a holy man. By spiritual vision he was able to know the secret of any sorrow, and the nature of the karma that had caused it. He heard unmoved the story of Shinzaburō, and said to him:—

"A very great danger now threatens you, because of an error committed in one of your former states of existence. The karma that binds you to the dead is very strong; but if I tried to explain its character, you would not be able to understand. I shall therefore tell you only this—that the dead person has no desire to injure you out of hate, feels no enmity towards you: she is influenced, on the contrary, by the most passionate affection for you. Probably the girl has been in love with you from a time long preceding your present life—from a time of not less than three or four past existences; and it would seem that, although necessarily changing her form and condition at each succeeding birth, she has not been able to cease from following after you. Therefore it will not be an easy thing to escape from her influence.... But now I am going to lend you this powerful *mamoni*.[9] It is a pure gold image of that Buddha called

---

9　The Japanese word *mamori* has significations at least as numerous as those attaching to our own term "amulet." It would be impossible, in a mere footnote, even to suggest the variety of Japanese religious objects to which the name is given. In this instance, the *mamori* is a very small image, probably enclosed in a miniature shrine of lacquer-work or metal, over which a silk cover is drawn. Such little images were often worn by samurai on the person. I was recently shown a miniature figure of Kwannon, in an iron case, which had been carried by an officer through the Satsuma war. He observed, with good reason, that it had probably saved his life; for it had stopped a bullet of which the dent was plainly visible.

the Sea-Sounding Tathāgata—Kai-On-Nyōrai—because his preaching of the Law sounds through the world like the sound of the sea. And this little image is especially a *shiryō-yoké*,[10]—which protects the living from the dead. This you must wear, in its covering, next to your body—under the girdle.... Besides, I shall presently perform in the temple, a *Segaki*-service[11] for the repose of the troubled spirit.... And here is a holy sutra, called *Ubō-Darani-Kyō*, or "Treasure-Raining Sutra":[12] you must be careful to recite it every night in your house—without fail.... Furthermore I shall give you this package of *o-fuda*;[13]—you must paste one of them over every opening of your house—no matter how small. If you do this, the power of the holy texts will prevent the dead from entering. But— whatever may happen—do not fail to recite the sutra."

Shinzaburō humbly thanked the high-priest; and then, taking with him the image, the sutra, and the bundle of sacred texts, he made all haste to reach his home before the hour of sunset.

---

10 From *shiryō*, a ghost, and *yokeru*, to exclude. The Japanese have two kinds of ghosts proper in their folklore: the spirits of the dead, *shiryō*; and the spirits of the living, *ikiryō*. A house or a person may be haunted by an *ikiryō* as well as by a *shiryō*.

11 A special service—accompanying offerings of food, etc., to those dead having no living relatives or friends to care for them—is thus termed. In this case, however, the service would be of a particular and exceptional kind.

12 The name would be more correctly written *Ubō-Darani-Kyō*. It is the Japanese pronunciation of the title of a very short sutra translated out of Sanscrit into Chinese by the Indian priest Amoghavajra, probably during the eighth century. The Chinese text contains transliterations of some mysterious Sanscrit words—apparently talismanic words—like those to be seen in Kern's translation of the Saddharma-Pundarika, ch. xxvi.

13 *O-fuda* is the general name given to religious texts used as charms or talismans. They are sometimes stamped or burned upon wood, but more commonly written or printed upon narrow strips of paper. *O-fuda* are pasted above house-entrances, on the walls of rooms, upon tablets placed in household shrines, etc. Some kinds are worn about the person;—others are made into pellets, and swallowed as spiritual medicine. The text of the larger *o-fuda* is often accompanied by curious pictures or symbolic illustrations.

VIII

With Yusai's advice and help, Shinzaburō was able before dark to fix the holy texts over all the apertures of his dwelling. Then the *ninsomi* returned to his own house—leaving the youth alone. Night came, warm and clear. Shinzaburō made fast the doors, bound the precious amulet about his waist, entered his mosquito-net, and by the glow of a night-lantern began to recite the *Ubō-Darani-Kyō*. For a long time he chanted the words, comprehending little of their meaning;—then he tried to obtain some rest. But his mind was still too much disturbed by the strange events of the day. Midnight passed; and no sleep came to him. At last he heard the boom of the great temple-bell of Dentsu-In announcing the eighth hour.[14]

It ceased; and Shinzaburō suddenly heard the sound of *geta* approaching from the old direction—but this time more slowly: *karan-koron, karan-koron*! At once a cold sweat broke over his forehead. Opening the sutra hastily, with trembling hand, he began again to recite it aloud. The steps came nearer and nearer—reached the live hedge—stopped! Then, strange to say, Shinzaburō felt unable to remain under his mosquito-net: something stronger even than his fear impelled him to look; and, instead of continuing to recite the *Ubō-Darani-Kyō*, he foolishly approached the shutters, and through a chink peered out into the night. Before the house he saw O-Tsuyu standing, and O-Yoné with the peony-lantern; and both of them were gazing at the Buddhist texts pasted above the entrance. Never before—not even in what time

---

14 According to the old Japanese way of counting time, this *yatsudoki* or eighth hour was the same as our two o'clock in the morning. Each Japanese hour was equal to two European hours, so that there were only six hours instead of our twelve; and these six hours were counted backwards in the order—9, 8, 7, 6, 5, 4. Thus the ninth hour corresponded to our midday, or midnight; half-past nine to our one o'clock; eight to our two o'clock. Two o'clock in the morning, also called "the Hour of the Ox," was the Japanese hour of ghosts and goblins.

she lived—had O-Tsuyu appeared so beautiful; and Shinzaburō felt his heart drawn towards her with a power almost resistless. But the terror of death and the terror of the unknown restrained; and there went on within him such a struggle between his love and his fear that he became as one suffering in the body the pains of the Shō-netsu hell.[15]

Presently he heard the voice of the maid-servant, saying:—

"My dear mistress, there is no way to enter. The heart of Hagiwara Sama must have changed. For the promise that he made last night has been broken; and the doors have been made fast to keep us out.... We cannot go in to-night.... It will be wiser for you to make up your mind not to think any more about him, because his feeling towards you has certainly changed. It is evident that he does not want to see you. So it will be better not to give yourself any more trouble for the sake of a man whose heart is so unkind."

But the girl answered, weeping:—

"Oh, to think that this could happen after the pledges which we made to each other!... Often I was told that the heart of a man changes as quickly as the sky of autumn;—yet surely the heart of Hagiwara Sama cannot be so cruel that he should really intend to exclude me in this way!... Dear Yoné, please find some means of taking me to him.... Unless you do, I will never, never go home again."

Thus she continued to plead, veiling her face with her long sleeves—and very beautiful she looked, and very touching; but the fear of death was strong upon her lover.

O-Yoné at last made answer—"My dear young lady, why will you trouble your mind about a man who seems to be so cruel?... Well, let us see if there be no way to enter at the back of the house: come with me!"

---

15   *En-netsu* or *Shō-netsu* (Sanscrit "Tapana") is the sixth of the Eight Hot Hells of Japanese Buddhism. One day of life in this hell is equal in duration to thousands (some say millions) of human years.

And taking O-Tsuyu by the hand, she led her away toward the rear of the dwelling; and there the two disappeared as suddenly as the light disappears when the flame of a lamp is blown out.

IX

Night after night the shadows came at the Hour of the Ox; and nightly Shinzaburō heard the weeping of O-Tsuyu. Yet he believed himself saved—little imagining that his doom had already been decided by the character of his dependents.

Tomozō had promised Yusai never to speak to any other person—not even to O-Miné—of the strange events that were taking place. But Tomozō was not long suffered by the haunters to rest in peace. Night after night O-Yoné entered into his dwelling, and roused him from his sleep, and asked him to remove the *o-fuda* placed over one very small window at the back of his master's house. And Tomozō, out of fear, as often promised her to take away the *o-fuda* before the next sundown; but never by day could he make up his mind to remove it—believing that evil was intended to Shinzaburo. At last, in a night of storm, O-Yoné startled him from slumber with a cry of reproach, and stooped above his pillow, and said to him: "Have a care how you trifle with us! If, by to-morrow night, you do not take away that text, you shall learn how I can hate!" And she made her face so frightful as she spoke that Tomozō nearly died of terror.

O-Miné, the wife of Tomozō, had never till then known of these visits: even to her husband they had seemed like bad dreams. But on this particular night it chanced that, waking suddenly, she heard the voice of a woman talking to Tomozō. Almost in the same moment the talking ceased; and when O-Miné looked about her, she saw, by the light of the night-lamp, only her husband—shuddering and white with fear. The stranger was gone; the doors were fast: it seemed impossible that anybody could have entered. Nevertheless the jealousy of the wife had been aroused; and she began to chide and to question Tomozō in such a manner that he thought himself obliged to betray the secret, and to explain the terrible dilemma in which he had been placed.

Then the passion of O-Miné yielded to wonder and alarm; but she was a subtle woman, and she devised immediately a plan to save her husband by the sacrifice of her master. And she gave Tomozō a cunning counsel—telling him to make conditions with the dead.

They came again on the following night at the Hour of the Ox; and O-Miné hid herself on hearing the sound of their coming— *karan-koron, karan-koron!* But Tomozo went out to meet them in the dark, and even found courage to say to them what his wife had told him to say:—

"It is true that I deserve your blame;—but I had no wish to cause you anger. The reason that the *o-fuda* has not been taken away is that my wife and I are able to live only by the help of Hagiwara Sama, and that we cannot expose him to any danger without bringing misfortune upon ourselves. But if we could obtain the sum of a hundred *ryō* in gold, we should be able to please you, because we should then need no help from anybody. Therefore if you will give us a hundred *ryō*, I can take the *o-fuda* away without being afraid of losing our only means of support."

When he had uttered these words, O-Yoné and O-Tsuyu looked at each other in silence for a moment. Then O-Yoné said:—

"Mistress, I told you that it was not right to trouble this man,—as we have no just cause of ill will against him. But it is certainly useless to fret yourself about Hagiwara Sama, because his heart has changed towards you. Now once again, my dear young lady, let me beg you not to think any more about him!"

But O-Tsuyu, weeping, made answer:—

"Dear Yoné, whatever may happen, I cannot possibly keep myself from thinking about him! You know that you can get a hundred *ryō* to have the *o-fuda* taken off…. Only once more, I pray, dear Yoné!—only once more bring me face to face with Hagiwara Sama,—I beseech you!" And hiding her face with her sleeve, she thus continued to plead.

"Oh! why will you ask me to do these things?" responded O-Yoné. "You know very well that I have no money. But since you will persist in this whim of yours, in spite of all that I can say, I suppose that I must try to find the money somehow, and to bring it here to-morrow night…." Then, turning to the faithless Tomozō, she said:—"Tomozō, I must tell you that Hagiwara Sama now wears upon his body a *mamori* called by the name of *Kai-On-Nyōrai*, and that so long as he wears it we cannot approach him. So you will have to get that *mamori* away from him, by some means or other, as well as to remove the *o-fuda*."

Tomozō feebly made answer:—

"That also I can do, if you will promise to bring me the hundred *ryō*."

"Well, mistress," said O-Yoné, "you will wait—will you not—until to-morrow night?"

"Oh, dear Yoné!" sobbed the other—"have we to go back to-night again without seeing Hagiwara Sama? Ah! it is cruel!"

And the shadow of the mistress, weeping, was led away by the shadow of the maid.

X

Another day went, and another night came, and the dead came with it. But this time no lamentation was heard without the house of Hagiwara; for the faithless servant found his reward at the Hour of the Ox, and removed the *o-fuda*. Moreover he had been able, while his master was at the bath, to steal from its case the golden *mamori*, and to substitute for it an image of copper; and he had buried the *Kai-On-Nyōrai* in a desolate field. So the visitants found nothing to oppose their entering. Veiling their faces with their sleeves they rose and passed, like a streaming of vapor, into the little window from over which the holy text had been torn away. But what happened thereafter within the house Tomozō never knew.

The sun was high before he ventured again to approach his master's dwelling, and to knock upon the sliding-doors. For the first time in years he obtained no response; and the silence made him afraid. Repeatedly he called, and received no answer. Then, aided by O-Miné, he succeeded in effecting an entrance and making his way alone to the sleeping-room, where he called again in vain. He rolled back the rumbling shutters to admit the light; but still within the house there was no stir. At last he dared to lift a corner of the mosquito-net. But no sooner had he looked beneath than he fled from the house, with a cry of horror.

Shinzaburō was dead—hideously dead;—and his face was the face of a man who had died in the uttermost agony of fear;—and lying beside him in the bed were the bones of a woman! And the bones of the arms, and the bones of the hands, clung fast about his neck.

XI

Hakuōdō Yusai, the fortune-teller, went to view the corpse at the prayer of the faithless Tomozō. The old man was terrified and astonished at the spectacle, but looked about him with a keen eye. He soon perceived that the *o-fuda* had been taken from the little window at the back of the house; and on searching the body of Shinzaburō, he discovered that the golden *mamori* had been taken from its wrapping, and a copper image of Fudō put in place of it. He suspected Tomozō of the theft; but the whole occurrence was so very extraordinary that he thought it prudent to consult with the priest Ryōseki before taking further action. Therefore, after having made a careful examination of the premises, he betook himself to the temple Shin-Banzui-In, as quickly as his aged limbs could bear him.

Ryōseki, without waiting to hear the purpose of the old man's visit, at once invited him into a private apartment.

"You know that you are always welcome here," said Ryōseki. "Please seat yourself at ease…. Well, I am sorry to tell you that Hagiwara Sama is dead."

Yusai wonderingly exclaimed:—"Yes, he is dead;—but how did you learn of it?"

The priest responded:—

"Hagiwara Sama was suffering from the results of an evil karma; and his attendant was a bad man. What happened to Hagiwara Sama was unavoidable;—his destiny had been determined from a time long before his last birth. It will be better for you not to let your mind be troubled by this event."

Yusai said:—

"I have heard that a priest of pure life may gain power to see into the future for a hundred years; but truly this is the first time in my existence that I have had proof of such power…. Still, there is another matter about which I am very anxious…."

"You mean," interrupted Ryōseki, "the stealing of the holy *mamori*, the *Kai-On-Nyōrai*. But you must not give yourself any concern about that. The image has been buried in a field; and it will be found there and returned to me during the eighth month of the coming year. So please do not be anxious about it."

More and more amazed, the old *ninsomi* ventured to observe:—

"I have studied the *In-Yō*,[16] and the science of divination; and I make my living by telling people's fortunes;—but I cannot possibly understand how you know these things."

Ryōseki answered gravely:—

"Never mind how I happen to know them.... I now want to speak to you about Hagiwara's funeral. The House of Hagiwara has its own family-cemetery, of course; but to bury him there would not be proper. He must be buried beside O-Tsuyu, the Lady Iijima; for his karma-relation to her was a very deep one. And it is but right that you should erect a tomb for him at your own cost, because you have been indebted to him for many favors."

Thus it came to pass that Shinzaburō was buried beside O-Tsuyu, in the cemetery of Shin-Banzui-In, in Yanaka-no-Sasaki.

– Here ends the story of the Ghosts in the Romance of the Peony-Lantern.—

My friend asked me whether the story had interested me; and I answered by telling him that I wanted to go to the cemetery of Shin-Banzui-In—so as to realize more definitely the local color of the author's studies.

"I shall go with you at once," he said. "But what did you think of the personages?"

"To Western thinking," I made answer, "Shinzaburō is a despicable creature. I have been mentally comparing him with the true lovers of our old ballad-literature. They were only too glad to follow a dead sweetheart into the grave; and nevertheless, being Christians, they believed that they had only one human life to enjoy in this world. But Shinzaburō was a Buddhist—with a million lives behind

---

16 The Male and Female principles of the universe, the Active and Passive forces of Nature. Yusai refers here to the old Chinese nature-philosophy—better known to Western readers by the name FENG-SHUI.

him and a million lives before him; and he was too selfish to give up even one miserable existence for the sake of the girl that came back to him from the dead. Then he was even more cowardly than selfish. Although a samurai by birth and training, he had to beg a priest to save him from ghosts. In every way he proved himself contemptible; and O-Tsuyu did quite right in choking him to death."

"From the Japanese point of view, likewise," my friend responded, "Shinzaburō is rather contemptible. But the use of this weak character helped the author to develop incidents that could not otherwise, perhaps, have been so effectively managed. To my thinking, the only attractive character in the story is that of O-Yoné: type of the old-time loyal and loving servant—intelligent, shrewd, full of resource—faithful not only unto death, but beyond death.... Well, let us go to Shin-Banzui-In."

We found the temple uninteresting, and the cemetery an abomination of desolation. Spaces once occupied by graves had been turned into potato-patches. Between were tombs leaning at all angles out of the perpendicular, tablets made illegible by scurf, empty pedestals, shattered water-tanks, and statues of Buddhas without heads or hands. Recent rains had soaked the black soil—leaving here and there small pools of slime about which swarms of tiny frogs were hopping. Everything—excepting the potato-patches—seemed to have been neglected for years. In a shed just within the gate, we observed a woman cooking; and my companion presumed to ask her if she knew anything about the tombs described in the Romance of the Peony-Lantern.

"Ah! the tombs of O-Tsuyu and O-Yoné?" she responded, smiling;—" you will find them near the end of the first row at the back of the temple—next to the statue of Jizō."

Surprises of this kind I had met with elsewhere in Japan.

We picked our way between the rain-pools and between the green ridges of young potatoes—whose roots were doubtless feeding on the substance of many another O-Tsuyu and O-Yoné;—and we reached at last two lichen-eaten tombs of which the inscriptions seemed almost obliterated. Beside the larger tomb was a statue of Jizō, with a broken nose.

"The characters are not easy to make out," said my friend—"but wait!".... He drew from his sleeve a sheet of soft white paper, laid it over the inscription, and began to rub the paper with a lump of clay. As he did so, the characters appeared in white on the blackened surface.

"'*Eleventh day, third month—Rat, Elder Brother, Fire—Sixth year of Horeki* [A. D. 1756].'... This would seem to be the grave of some innkeeper of Nedzu, named Kichibei. Let us see what is on the other monument."

With a fresh sheet of paper he presently brought out the text of a kaimyō, and read—

"'*En-myō-In, Hō-yō-I-tei-ken-shi, Hō-ni*':—'*Nun-of-the-Law, Illustrious, Pure-of-heart-and-will, Famed-in-the-Law—inhabiting the Mansion-of-the-Preaching-of-Wonder.*'.... The grave of some Buddhist nun."

"What utter humbug!" I exclaimed. "That woman was only making fun of us."

"Now," my friend protested, "you are unjust to the woman! You came here because you wanted a sensation; and she tried her very best to please you. You did not suppose that ghost-story was true, did you?"

Jngwa-Banashi[17]

The daimyo's wife was dying, and knew that she was dying. She had not been able to leave her bed since the early autumn of the tenth Bunsei. It was now the fourth month of the twelfth Bunsei,—the year 1829 by Western counting; and the cherry-trees were blossoming. She thought of the cherry-trees in her garden, and of the gladness of spring. She thought of her children. She thought of her husband's various concubines—especially the Lady Yukiko, nineteen years old.

"My dear wife," said the daimyo, "you have suffered very much for three long years. We have done all that we could to get you well—watching beside you night and day, praying for you, and often fasting for your sake, But in spite of our loving care, and in spite of the skill of our best physicians, it would now seem that the end of your life is not far off. Probably we shall sorrow more than you will sorrow because of your having to leave what the Buddha so truly termed 'this burning-house of the world.' I shall order to be performed—no matter what the cost—every religious rite that

---

17 Lit., "a tale of *ingwa*." *Ingwa* is a Japanese Buddhist term for evil karma, or the evil consequence of faults committed in a former state of existence. Perhaps the curious title of the narrative is best explained by the Buddhist teaching that the dead have power to injure the living only in consequence of evil actions committed by their victims in some former life. Both title and narrative may be found in the collection of weird stories entitled *Hyaku-Monogatari*.

can serve you in regard to your next rebirth; and all of us will pray without ceasing for you, that you may not have to wander in the Black Space, but nay quickly enter Paradise, and attain to Buddhahood."

He spoke with the utmost tenderness, pressing her the while. Then, with eyelids closed, she answered him in a voice thin as the voice of in insect:—

"I am grateful—most grateful—for your kind words…. Yes, it is true, as you say, that I have been sick for three long years, and that I have been treated with all possible care and affection…. Why, indeed, should I turn away from the one true Path at the very moment of my death?… Perhaps to think of worldly matters at such a time is not right;—but I have one last request to make—only one…. Call here to me the Lady Yukiko;—you know that I love her like a sister. I want to speak to her about the affairs of this household."

Yukiko came at the summons of the lord, and, in obedience to a sign from him, knelt down beside the couch. The daimyo's wife opened her eyes, and looked at Yukiko, and spoke:—"Ah, here is Yukiko!… I am so pleased to see you, Yukiko!… Come a little closer—so that you can hear me well: I am not able to speak loud…. Yukiko, I am going to die. I hope that you will be faithful in all things to our dear lord;—for I want you to take my place when I am gone…. I hope that you will always be loved by him—yes, even a hundred times more than I have been—and that you will very soon be promoted to a higher rank, and become his honored wife…. And I beg of you always to cherish our dear lord: never allow another woman to rob you of his affection…. This is what I wanted to say to you, dear Yukiko…. Have you been able to understand?"

"Oh, my dear Lady," protested Yukiko, "do not, I entreat you, say such strange things to me! You well know that I am of poor and mean condition:—how could I ever dare to aspire to become the wife of our lord!"

"Nay, nay!" returned the wife, huskily—"this is not a time for words of ceremony: let us speak only the truth to each other. After my death, you will certainly be promoted to a higher place; and I now assure you again that I wish you to become the wife of our lord—yes, I wish this, Yukiko, even more than I wish to become a Buddha!... Ah, I had almost forgotten!—I want you to do something for me, Yukiko. You know that in the garden there is a *yaë-zakura*,[18] which was brought here, the year before last, from Mount Yoshino in Yamato. I have been told that it is now in full bloom;—and I wanted so much to see it in flower! In a little while I shall be dead;—I must see that tree before I die. Now I wish you to carry me into the garden—at once, Yukiko—so that I can see it.... Yes, upon your back, Yukiko;—take me upon your back...."

While thus asking, her voice had gradually become clear and strong—as if the intensity of the wish had given her new force: then she suddenly burst into tears. Yukiko knelt motionless, not knowing what to do; but the lord nodded assent.

"It is her last wish in this world," he said. "She always loved cherry-flowers; and I know that she wanted very much to see that Yamato-tree in blossom. Come, my dear Yukiko, let her have her will."

As a nurse turns her back to a child, that the child may cling to it, Yukiko offered her shoulders to the wife, and said:—

"Lady, I am ready: please tell me how I best can help you."

"Why, this way!"—responded the dying woman, lifting herself with an almost superhuman effort by clinging to Yukiko's shoulders. But as she stood erect, she quickly slipped her thin hands down over the shoulders, under the robe, and clutched the breasts of the girl, and burst into a wicked laugh.

---

18 *Yaë-zakura, yaë-no-sakura*, a variety of Japanese cherry-tree that bears double-blossoms.

"I have my wish!" she cried—"I have my wish for the cherry-bloom,[19]—but not the cherry-bloom of the garden!... I could not die before I got my wish. Now I have it!—oh, what a delight!"

And with these words she fell forward upon the crouching girl, and died.

The attendants at once attempted to lift the body from Yukiko's shoulders, and to lay it upon the bed. But—strange to say!—this seemingly easy thing could not be done. The cold hands had attached themselves in some unaccountable way to the breasts of the girl—appeared to have grown into the quick flesh. Yukiko became senseless with fear and pain.

Physicians were called. They could not understand what had taken place. By no ordinary methods could the hands of the dead woman be unfastened from the body of her victim;—they so clung that any effort to remove them brought blood. This was not because the fingers held: it was because the flesh of the palms had united itself in some inexplicable manner to the flesh of the breasts!

At that time the most skilful physician in Yedo was a foreigner,—a Dutch surgeon. It was decided to summon him. After a careful examination he said that he could not understand the case, and that for the immediate relief of Yukiko there was nothing to be done except to cut the hands from the corpse. He declared that it would be dangerous to attempt to detach them from the breasts. His advice was accepted; and the hands were amputated at the wrists. But they remained clinging to the breasts; and there they soon darkened and dried up—like the hands of a person long dead.

Yet this was only the beginning of the horror.

Withered and bloodless though they seemed, those hands were

---

19   In Japanese poetry and proverbial phraseology, the physical beauty of a woman is compared to the cherry-flower; while feminine moral beauty is compared to the plum-flower.

not dead. At intervals they would stir—stealthily, like great grey spiders. And nightly thereafter—beginning always at the Hour of the Ox,[20]—they would clutch and compress and torture. Only at the Hour of the Tiger the pain would cease.

Yukiko cut off her hair, and became a mendicant-nun—taking the religious name of Dassetsu. She had an *ibai* (mortuary tablet) made, bearing the *kaimyō* of her dead mistress—"Myō-Kō-In-Den Chizan-Ryō-Fu Daishi";—and this she carried about with her in all her wanderings; and every day before it she humbly besought the dead for pardon, and performed a Buddhist service in order that the jealous spirit might find rest. But the evil karma that had rendered such an affliction possible could not soon be exhausted. Every night at the Hour of the Ox, the hands never failed to torture her, during more than seventeen years—according to the testimony of those persons to whom she last told her story, when she stopped for one evening at the house of Noguchi Dengozayémon, in the village of Tanaka in the district of Kawachi in the province of Shimotsuké. This was in the third year of Kōkwa (1846). Thereafter nothing more was ever heard of her.

---

20 In ancient Japanese time, the Hour of the Ox was the special hour of ghosts. It began at 2 A.M., and lasted until 4 A.M.—for the old Japanese hour was double the length of the modern hour. The Hour of the Tiger began at 4 A.M.

The Reconciliation

here was a young Samurai of Kyōto who had been reduced to poverty by the ruin of his lord, and found himself obliged to leave his home, and to take service with the Governor of a distant province. Before quitting the capital, this Samurai divorced his wife—a good and beautiful woman—under the belief that he could better obtain promotion by another alliance. He then married the daughter of a family of some distinction, and took her with him to the district whither he had been called.

But it was in the time of the thoughtlessness of youth, and the sharp experience of want, that the Samurai could not understand the worth of the affection so lightly cast away. His second marriage did not prove a happy one; the character of his new wife was hard and selfish; and he soon found every cause to think with regret of Kyōto days. Then he discovered that he still loved his first wife— loved her more than he could ever love the second; and he began to feel how unjust and how thankless he had been. Gradually his repentance deepened into a remorse that left him no peace of mind. Memories of the woman he had wronged—her gentle speech, her smiles, her dainty, pretty ways, her faultless patience—continually haunted him. Sometimes in dreams he saw her at her loom, weaving as when she toiled night and day to help him during the years of their distress: more often he saw her kneeling alone in the desolate little room where he had left her, veiling her tears with her poor worn sleeve. Even in the hours of official duty, his thoughts would wander back to her: then he would ask himself how she was living, what she was doing. Something in his heart assured him that she could not accept another husband, and that she never would refuse to pardon him. And he secretly resolved to seek her out as soon as he could return to Kyōto—then to beg her forgiveness, to take her back, to do everything that a man could do to make atonement. But the years went by.

At last the Governor's official term expired, and the Samurai was free. "Now I will go back to my dear one," he vowed to himself. "Ah, what a cruelty—what a folly to have divorced her!" He sent his second wife to her own people (she had given him no children); and hurrying to Kyōto, he went at once to seek his former companion—not allowing himself even the time to change his travelling-garb.

When he reached the street where she used to live, it was late in the night—the night of the tenth day of the ninth month;—and the city was silent as a cemetery. But a bright moon made everything visible; and he found the house without difficulty. It had a deserted look: tall weeds were growing on the roof. He knocked at the sliding-doors, and no one answered. Then, finding that the doors had not been fastened from within, he pushed them open, and entered. The front room was matless and empty: a chilly wind was blowing through crevices in the planking; and the moon shone through a ragged break in the wall of the alcove. Other rooms presented a like forlorn condition. The house, to all seeming, was unoccupied. Nevertheless, the Samurai determined to visit one other apartment at the further end of the dwelling—a very small room that had been his wife's favorite resting-place. Approaching the sliding-screen that closed it, he was startled to perceive a glow within. He pushed the screen aside, and uttered a cry of joy; for he saw her there—sewing by the light of a paper-lamp. Her eyes at the same instant met his own; and with a happy smile she greeted him—asking only:—"When did you come back to Kyōto? How did you find your way here to me, through all those black rooms?" The years had not changed her. Still she seemed as fair and young as in his fondest memory of her;—but sweeter than any memory there came to him the music of her voice, with its trembling of pleased wonder.

Then joyfully he took his place beside her, and told her all:— how deeply he repented his selfishness—how wretched he had been without her—how constantly he had regretted her—how long he had hoped and planned to make amends;—caressing her the while, and asking her forgiveness over and over again. She answered him, with loving gentleness, according to his heart's desire—entreating him to cease all self-reproach. It was wrong, she said, that he should have allowed himself to suffer on her account: she had always felt that she was not worthy to be his wife. She knew that he had separated from her, notwithstanding, only because of poverty; and while he lived with her, he had always been kind; and she had never ceased to pray for his happiness. But even if there had been a reason for speaking of amends, this honorable visit would be ample amends;—what greater happiness than thus to see him again, though it were only for a moment? "Only for a moment!" he answered, with a glad laugh—"say, rather, for the time of seven existences! My loved one, unless you forbid, I am coming back to live with you always—always—always! Nothing shall ever separate us again. Now I have means and friends: we need not fear poverty. To-morrow my goods will be brought here; and my servants will come to wait upon you; and we shall make this house beautiful.... To-night," he added, apologetically, "I came thus late—without even changing my dress—only because of the longing I had to see you, and to tell you this." She seemed greatly pleased by these words; and in her turn she told him about all that had happened in Kyōto since the time of his departure—excepting her own sorrows, of which she sweetly refused to speak. They chatted far into the night: then she conducted him to a warmer room, facing south—a room that had been their bridal chamber in former time. "Have you no one in the house to help you?" he asked, as she began to prepare the couch for him. "No," she answered, laughing cheerfully: "I could not afford a servant;—so I have been living all alone." "You will have plenty of servants to-morrow," he said—"good servants—and everything else that you need." They lay down to rest—not to sleep: they had too much to tell each other;—and they talked of the past and the present and the future, until the dawn was gray. Then, involuntarily, the Samurai closed his eyes, and slept.

When he awoke, the daylight was streaming through the chinks of the sliding-shutters; and he found himself, to his utter amazement, lying upon the naked boards of a mouldering floor.... Had he only dreamed a dream? No: she was there;—she slept.... He bent above her—and looked—and shrieked;—for the sleeper had no face!... Before him, wrapped in its grave-sheet only, lay the corpse of a woman—a corpse so wasted that little remained save the bones, and the long black tangled hair.

Slowly—as he stood shuddering and sickening in the sun—the icy horror yielded to a despair so intolerable, a pain so atrocious, that he clutched at the mocking shadow of a doubt. Feigning ignorance of the neighborhood, he ventured to ask his way to the house in which his wife had lived.

"There is no one in that house," said the person questioned. "It used to belong to the wife of a Samurai who left the city several years ago. He divorced her in order to marry another woman before he went away; and she fretted a great deal, and so became sick. She had no relatives in Kyōto, and nobody to care for her; and she died in the autumn of the same year—on the tenth day of the ninth month...."

A Legend of Fugen-Bosatsu

There was once a very pious and learned priest, called Shōku Shōnin, who lived in the province of Harima. For many years he meditated daily upon the chapter of Fugen-Bosatsu [the Bodhisattva Samantabhadra] in the Sûtra of the Lotos of the Good Law; and he used to pray, every morning and evening, that he might at some time be permitted to behold Fugen-Bosatsu as a living presence, and in the form described in the holy text.[21]

One evening, while he was reciting the Sûtra, drowsiness overcame him; and he fell asleep leaning upon his *kyōsoku*.[22] Then he dreamed; and in his dream a voice told him that, in order to see Fugen-Bosatsu, he must go to the house of a certain courtesan,

---

21 The priest's desire was probably inspired by the promises recorded in the chapter entitled "The Encouragement of Samantabhadra" (see Kern's translation of the Saddharma Pundarîka in the *Sacred Books of the East*—pp 433-4):—"Then the Bodhisattva Mahâsattva Samantabhadra said to the Lord: ... 'When a preacher who applies himself to this Dharmaparyâya shall take a walk, then, O Lord, will I mount a white elephant with six tusks, and betake myself to the place where that preacher is walking, in order to protect this Dharmaparyâya. And when that preacher, applying himself to this Dharmaparyâya, forgets, be it but a single word or syllable, then will I mount the white elephant with six tusks, and show my face to that preacher, and repeat this entire Dharmaparyâya."—But these promises refer to "the end of time."

22 The *kyōsoku* is a kind of padded arm-rest, or arm-stool, upon which the priest leans one arm while reading. The use of such an arm-rest is not confined, however, to the Buddhist clergy.

known as the "Yujō-no-Chōja,"[23] who lived in the town of Kanzaki. Immediately upon awakening he resolved to go to Kanzaki;—and, making all possible haste, he reached the town by the evening of the next day.

When he entered the house of the *yujō*, he found many persons already there assembled—mostly young men of the capital, who had been attracted to Kanzaki by the fame of the woman's beauty. They were feasting and drinking; and the *yujō* was playing a small hand-drum (*tsuzumi*), which she used very skilfully, and singing a song. The song which she sang was an old Japanese song about a famous shrine in the town of Murozumi; and the words were these:—

Within the sacred water-tank[24] of Murozumi in Suwō,
Even though no wind be blowing,
The surface of the water is always rippling.

The sweetness of the voice filled everybody with surprise and delight. As the priest, who had taken a place apart, listened and wondered, the girl suddenly fixed her eyes upon him; and in the same instant he saw her form change into the form of Fugen-Bosatsu, emitting from her brow a beam of light that seemed to pierce beyond the limits of the universe, and riding a snow-white elephant with six tusks. And still she sang—but the song also was now transformed; and the words came thus to the ears of the priest:—

---

23 A *yujō*, in old days, was a singing-girl as well as a courtesan. The term "Yujō-no-Chōja," in this case, would mean simply "the first (or best) of *yujō*."

24 *Mitarai. Mitarai* (or *mitarashi*) is the name especially given to the water-tanks, or water-fonts—of stone or bronze—placed before Shintō shrines in order that the worshipper may purify his lips and hands before making prayer. Buddhist tanks are not so named.

On the Vast Sea of Cessation,
Though the Winds of the Six Desires
and of the Five Corruptions never blow,
Yet the surface of that deep is always covered
With the billowings of Attainment to the Reality-in-Itself.

Dazzled by the divine ray, the priest closed his eyes: but through their lids he still distinctly saw the vision. When he opened them again, it was gone: he saw only the girl with her hand-drum, and heard only the song about the water of Murozumi. But he found that as often as he shut his eyes he could see Fugen-Bosatsu on the six-tusked elephant, and could hear the mystic Song of the Sea of Cessation. The other persons present saw only the *yujō*: they had not beheld the manifestation.

Then the singer suddenly disappeared from the banquet-room— none could say when or how. From that moment the revelry ceased; and gloom took the place of joy. After having waited and sought for the girl to no purpose, the company dispersed in great sorrow. Last of all, the priest departed, bewildered by the emotions of the evening. But scarcely had he passed beyond the gate, when the *yujō* appeared before him, and said:—"Friend, do not speak yet to any one of what you have seen this night." And with these words she vanished away—leaving the air filled with a delicious fragrance.

The monk by whom the foregoing legend was recorded, comments upon it thus:—The condition of a *yujō* is low and miserable, since she is condemned to serve the lusts of men. Who therefore could imagine that such a woman might be the *nirmanakaya*, or incarnation, of a Bodhisattva. But we must remember that the Buddhas and the Bodhisattvas may appear in this world in countless different forms; choosing, for the purpose of their divine compassion, even the most humble or contemptible shapes when such shapes can serve them to lead men into the true path, and to save them from the perils of illusion.

The Screen-Maiden

Says the old Japanese author, Hakubai-En Rosui:—[25]
"In Chinese and in Japanese books there are related many stories—both of ancient and of modern times—about pictures that were so beautiful as to exercise a magical influence upon the beholder. And concerning such beautiful pictures—whether pictures of flowers or of birds or of people, painted by famous artists—it is further told that the shapes of the creatures or the persons, therein depicted, would separate themselves from the paper or the silk upon which they had been painted, and would perform various acts;—so that they became, by their own will, really alive. We shall not now repeat any of the stories of this class which have been known to everybody from ancient times. But even in modern times the fame of the pictures painted by Hishigawa Kichibei—'Hishigawa's Portraits'—has become widespread in the land."

He then proceeds to relate the following story about one of the so-called portraits:—

---

25 He died in the eighteenth year of Kyōhō (1733). The painter to whom he refers—better known to collectors as Hishigawa Kichibei Moronobu—flourished during the latter part of the seventeenth century. Beginning his career as a dyer's apprentice, he won his reputation as an artist about 1680, when he may be said to have founded the *Ukiyo-yé* school of illustration. Hishigawa was especially a delineator of what are called *fūryū*, ("elegant manners")—the aspects of life among the upper classes of society.

There was a young scholar of Kyōto whose name was Tokkei. He used to live in the street called Muromachi. One evening, while on his way home after a visit, his attention was attracted by an old single-leaf screen (*tsuitaté*), exposed for sale before the shop of a dealer in second-hand goods. It was only a paper-covered screen; but there was painted upon it the full-length figure of a girl which caught the young man's fancy. The price asked was very small: Tokkei bought the screen, and took it home with him.

When he looked again at the screen, in the solitude of his own room, the picture seemed to him much more beautiful than before. Apparently it was a real likeness—the portrait of a girl fifteen or sixteen years old; and every little detail in the painting of the hair, eyes, eyelashes, mouth, had been executed with a delicacy and a truth beyond praise. The *manajiri*[26] seemed "like a lotos-blossom courting favor"; the lips were "like the smile of a red flower"; the whole young face was inexpressibly sweet. If the real girl so portrayed had been equally lovely, no man could have looked upon her without losing his heart. And Tokkei believed that she must have been thus lovely;—for the figure seemed alive—ready to reply to anybody who might speak to it.

Gradually, as he continued to gaze at the picture, he felt himself bewitched by the charm of it. "Can there really have been in this world," he murmured to himself, "so delicious a creature? How gladly would I give my life—nay, a thousand years of life!—to hold her in my arms even for a moment!" (The Japanese author says "for a few seconds.") In short, he became enamored of the picture—so much enamored of it as to feel that he never could love any woman except the person whom it represented. Yet that person,

---

26 Also written *méjiri*—the exterior canthus of the eye. The Japanese (like the old Greek and the old Arabian poets) have many curious dainty words and similes to express particular beauties of the hair, eyes, eyelids, lips, fingers, etc.

if still alive, could no longer resemble the painting: perhaps she had been buried long before he was born!

Day by day, nevertheless, this hopeless passion grew upon him. He could not eat; he could not sleep: neither could he occupy his mind with those studies which had formerly delighted him. He would sit for hours before the picture, talking to it—neglecting or forgetting everything else. And at last he fell sick—so sick that he believed himself going to die.

Now among the friends of Tokkei there was one venerable scholar who knew many strange things about old pictures and about young hearts. This aged scholar, hearing of Tokkei's illness, came to visit him, and saw the screen, and understood what had happened. Then Tokkei, being questioned, confessed everything to his friend, and declared:—"If I cannot find such a woman, I shall die."

The old man said:—

"That picture was painted by Hishigawa Kichibei—painted from life. The person whom it represented is not now in the world. But it is said that Hishigawa Kichibei painted her mind as well as her form, and that her spirit lives in the picture. So I think that you can win her."

Tokkei half rose from his bed, and stared eagerly at the speaker.

"You must give her a name," the old man continued;—"and you must sit before her picture every day, and keep your thoughts constantly fixed upon her, and call her gently by the name which you have given her, *until she answers you....*"

"Answers me!" exclaimed the lover, in breathless amazement.

"Oh, yes," the adviser responded, "she will certainly answer you. But you must be ready, when she answers you, to present her with what I am going to tell you...."

"I will give her my life!" cried Tokkei.

"No," said the old man;—"you will present her with a cup of

wine that has been bought at one hundred different wine-shops. Then she will come out of the screen to accept the wine. After that, probably she herself will tell you what to do."

With these words the old man went away. His advice aroused Tokkei from despair. At once he seated himself before the picture, and called it by the name of a girl—(what name the Japanese narrator has forgotten to tell us)—over and over again, very tenderly. That day it made no answer, nor the next day, nor the next. But Tokkei did not lose faith or patience; and after many days it suddenly one evening answered to its name—

"*Hai!*" (Yes.)

Then quickly, quickly, some of the wine from a hundred different wine-shops was poured out, and reverentially presented in a little cup. And the girl stepped from the screen, and walked upon the matting of the room, and knelt to take the cup from Tokkei's hand—asking, with a delicious smile:—

"How could you love me so much?"

Says the Japanese narrator: "She was much more beautiful than the picture—beautiful to the tips of her finger-nails—beautiful also in heart and temper—lovelier than anybody else in the world." What answer Tokkei made to her question is not recorded: it will have to be imagined.

"But will you not soon get tired of me?" she asked.

"Never while I live!" he protested.

"And after—?" she persisted;—for the Japanese bride is not satisfied with love for one life-time only.

"Let us pledge ourselves to each other," he entreated, "for the time of seven existences."

"If you are ever unkind to me," she said, "I will go back to the screen."

* * *

They pledged each other. I suppose that Tokkei was a good boy—for his bride never returned to the screen. The space that she had occupied upon it remained a blank.

Exclaims the Japanese author—
"How very seldom do such things happen in this world!"

The Corpse-Rider

The body was cold as ice; the heart had long ceased to beat: yet there were no other signs of death. Nobody even spoke of burying the woman. She had died of grief and anger at having been divorced. It would have been useless to bury her—because the last undying wish of a dying person for vengeance can burst asunder any tomb and rift the heaviest graveyard stone. People who lived near the house in which she was lying fled from their homes. They knew that she was only *waiting for the return of the man who had divorced her.*

At the time of her death he was on a journey. When he came back and was told what had happened, terror seized him. "If I can find no help before dark," he thought to himself, "she will tear me to pieces." It was yet only the Hour of the Dragon;[27] but he knew that he had no time to lose.

He went at once to an *inyōshi*[28] and begged for succor. The *inyōshi* knew the story of the dead woman; and he had seen the body. He said to the supplicant:—"A very great danger threatens you. I will try to save you. But you must promise to do whatever

---

27 *Tatsu no Koku*, or the Hour of the Dragon, by old Japanese time, began at about eight o'clock in the morning.

28 *Inyōshi*, a professor or master of the science of *in-yō*—the old Chinese nature-philosophy, based upon the theory of a male and a female principle pervading the universe.

I shall tell you to do. There is only one way by which you can be saved. It is a fearful way. But unless you find the courage to attempt it, she will tear you limb from limb. If you can be brave, come to me again in the evening before sunset." The man shuddered; but he promised to do whatever should be required of him.

At sunset the *inyōshi* went with him to the house where the body was lying. The *inyōshi* pushed open the sliding-doors, and told his client to enter. It was rapidly growing dark. "I dare not!" gasped the man, quaking from head to foot;—"I dare not even look at her!" "You will have to do much more than look at her," declared the *inyōshi*;—"and you promised to obey. Go in!" He forced the trembler into the house and led him to the side of the corpse.

The dead woman was lying on her face. "Now you must get astride upon her," said the *inyōshi*, "and sit firmly on her back, as if you were riding a horse.... Come!—you must do it!" The man shivered so that the *inyōshi* had to support him—shivered horribly; but he obeyed. "Now take her hair in your hands," commanded the *inyōshi*—"half in the right hand, half in the left.... So!... You must grip it like a bridle. Twist your hands in it—both hands—tightly. That is the way!... Listen to me! You must stay like that till morning. You will have reason to be afraid in the night—plenty of reason. But whatever may happen, never let go of her hair. If you let go— even for one second—she will tear you into gobbets!"

The *inyōshi* then whispered some mysterious words into the ear of the body, and said to its rider:—"Now, for my own sake, I must leave you alone with her.... Remain as you are!... Above all things, remember that you must not let go of her hair." And he went away—closing the doors behind him.

* * *

Hour after hour the man sat upon the corpse in black fear;—and the hush of the night deepened and deepened about him till he screamed to break it. Instantly the body sprang beneath him, as to cast him off; and the dead woman cried out loudly, "Oh, how heavy it is! Yet I shall bring that fellow here now!"

Then tall she rose, and leaped to the doors, and flung them open, and rushed into the night—always bearing the weight of the man. But he, shutting his eyes, kept his hands twisted in her long hair—tightly, tightly—though fearing with such a fear that he could not even moan. How far she went, he never knew. He saw nothing: he heard only the sound of her naked feet in the dark— *picha-picha, picha-picha*—and the hiss of her breathing as she ran.

At last she turned, and ran back into the house, and lay down upon the floor exactly as at first. Under the man she panted and moaned till the cocks began to crow. Thereafter she lay still.

But the man, with chattering teeth, sat upon her until the *inyōshi* came at sunrise. "So you did not let go of her hair!"—observed the *inyōshi*, greatly pleased. "That is well... Now you can stand up." He whispered again into the ear of the corpse, and then said to the man:—"You must have passed a fearful night; but nothing else could have saved you. Hereafter you may feel secure from her vengeance."

The conclusion of this story I do not think to be morally satisfying. It is not recorded that the corpse-rider became insane, or that his hair turned white: we are told only that "he worshiped the *inyōshi* with tears of gratitude." A note appended to the recital is equally disappointing. "It is reported," the Japanese author says, "that a grandchild of the man [*who rode the corpse*] still survives, and that a grandson of the *inyōshi* is at this very time living in a village called Otokunoi-mura [*probably pronounced Otonoi-mura*]."

This village-name does not appear in any Japanese directory of to-day. But the names of many towns and villages have been changed since the foregoing story was written.

The Sympathy of Benten

Jn Kyōto there is a famous temple called Amadera. Sadazumi Shinnō, the fifth son of the Emperor Seiwa, passed the greater part of his life there as a priest; and the graves of many celebrated persons are to be seen in the temple-grounds.

But the present edifice is not the ancient Amadera. The original temple, after the lapse of ten centuries, fell into such decay that it had to be entirely rebuilt in the fourteenth year of Genroku (AD1701).

A great festival was held to celebrate the rebuilding of the Amadera; and among the thousands of persons who attended that festival there was a young scholar and poet named Hanagaki Baishū. He wandered about the newly-laid-out grounds and gardens, delighted by all that he saw, until he reached the place of a spring at which he had often drunk in former times. He was then surprised to find that the soil about the spring had been dug away, so as to form a square pond, and that at one corner of this pond there had been set up a wooden tablet bearing the words *Tanjō-Sui* ("Birth-Water").[29] He also saw that a small, but very handsome temple of the Goddess Benten had been erected beside

---

29   The word *tanjō* (birth) should here be understood in its mystical Buddhist meaning of new life or rebirth, rather than in the Western signification of birth.

the pond. While he was looking at this new temple, a sudden gust of wind blew to his feet a *tanzaku*,[30] on which the following poem had been written:—

Shirushi aréto
Iwai zo somuru
Tama hōki,
Toruté bakari no
Chigiri narétomo.

This poem—a poem on first love (*hatsu koi*), composed by the famous Shunrei Kyō—was not unfamiliar to him; but it had been written upon the *tanzaku* by a female hand, and so exquisitely that he could scarcely believe his eyes. Something in the form of the characters—an indefinite grace—suggested that period of youth between childhood and womanhood; and the pure rich color of the ink seemed to bespeak the purity and goodness of the writer's heart.[31]

Baishū carefully folded up the *tanzaku*, and took it home with him. When he looked at it again the writing appeared to him even more wonderful than at first. His knowledge in calligraphy assured him only that the poem had been written by some girl who was

30 *Tanzaku* is the name given to the long strips or ribbons of paper, usually colored, upon which poems are written perpendicularly. Poems written upon *tanzaku* are suspended to trees in flower, to wind-bells, to any beautiful object in which the poet has found an inspiration.

31 It is difficult for the inexperienced European eye to distinguish in Chinese or Japanese writing those characteristics implied by our term "hand"—in the sense of individual style. But the Japanese scholar never forgets the peculiarities of a hand-writing once seen; and he can even guess at the approximate age of the writer. Chinese and Japanese authors claim that the color (quality) of the ink used tells something of the character of the writer. As every person grounds or prepares his or her own ink, the deeper and clearer black would at least indicate something of personal carefulness and of the sense of beauty.

very young, very intelligent, and probably very gentle-hearted. But this assurance sufficed to shape within his mind the image of a very charming person; and he soon found himself in love with the unknown. Then his first resolve was to seek out the writer of the verses, and, if possible, make her his wife.... Yet how was he to find her? Who was she? Where did she live? Certainly he could hope to find her only through the favor of the Gods.

But presently it occurred to him that the Gods might be very willing to lend their aid. The *tanzaku* had come to him while he was standing in front of the temple of Benten-Sama; and it was to this divinity in particular that lovers were wont to pray for happy union. This reflection impelled him to beseech the Goddess for assistance. He went at once to the temple of Benten-of-the-Birth-Water (*Tanjō-sui-no-Benten*) in the grounds of the Amadera; and there, with all the fervor of his heart, he made his petition:—"O Goddess, pity me!—help me to find where the young person lives who wrote the *tanzaku*!—vouchsafe me but one chance to meet her—even if only for a moment!" And after having made this prayer, he began to perform a seven days' religious service (*nanuka-mairi*)[32] in honor of the Goddess; vowing at the same time to pass the seventh night in ceaseless worship before her shrine.

Now on the seventh night—the night of his vigil—during the hour when the silence is most deep, he heard at the main gateway of the temple-grounds a voice calling for admittance. Another voice from within answered; the gate was opened; and Baishū saw an old man of majestic appearance approaching with slow steps. This venerable person was clad in robes of ceremony; and he wore upon

---

32   There are many kinds of religious exercises called *mairi*. The performer of a *nanuka-mairi* pledges himself to pray at a certain temple every day for seven days in succession.

his snow-white head a black cap (*eboshi*) of the form indicating high rank. Reaching the little temple of Benten, he knelt down in front of it, as if respectfully awaiting some order. Then the outer door of the temple was opened; the hanging curtain of bamboo behind it, concealing the inner sanctuary, was rolled half-way up; and a *chigo*[33] came forward—a beautiful boy, with long hair tied back in the ancient manner. He stood at the threshold, and said to the old man in a clear loud voice:—

"There is a person here who has been praying for a love-union not suitable to his present condition, and otherwise difficult to bring about. But as the young man is worthy of Our pity, you have been called to see whether something can be done for him. If there should prove to be any relation between the parties from the period of a former birth, you will introduce them to each other."

On receiving this command, the old man bowed respectfully to the *chigo*: then, rising, he drew from the pocket of his long left sleeve a crimson cord. One end of this cord he passed round Baishū's body, as if to bind him with it. The other end he put into the flame of one of the temple-lamps; and while the cord was there burning, he waved his hand three times, as if to summon somebody out of the dark.

Immediately, in the direction of the Amadera, a sound of coming steps was heard; and in another moment a girl appeared—a charming girl, fifteen or sixteen years old. She approached gracefully, but very shyly—hiding the lower part of her face with a fan; and she knelt down beside Baishū. The *chigo* then said to Baishū:—

"Recently you have been suffering much heart-pain; and this

---

33 The term *chigo* usually means the page of a noble household, especially an Imperial page. The *chigo* who appears in this story is of course a supernatural being—the court-messenger of the Goddess, and her mouthpiece.

desperate love of yours has even impaired your health. We could not allow you to remain in so unhappy a condition; and We therefore summoned the Old-Man-under-the-Moon[34] to make you acquainted with the writer of that *tanzaku*. She is now beside you."

With these words, the *chigo* retired behind the bamboo curtain. Then the old man went away as he had come; and the young girl followed him. Simultaneously Baishū heard the great bell of the Amadera sounding the hour of dawn. He prostrated himself in thanksgiving before the shrine of Benten-of-the-Birth-Water, and proceeded homeward—feeling as if awakened from some delightful dream—happy at having seen the charming person whom he had so fervently prayed to meet—unhappy also because of the fear that he might never meet her again.

But scarcely had he passed from the gateway into the street, when he saw a young girl walking alone in the same direction that he was going; and, even in the dusk of the dawn, he recognized her at once as the person to whom he had been introduced before the temple of Benten. As he quickened his pace to overtake her, she turned and saluted him with a graceful bow. Then for the first time he ventured to speak to her; and she answered him in a voice of which the sweetness filled his heart with joy. Through the yet silent streets they walked on, chatting happily, till they found themselves before the house where Baishū lived. There he paused—spoke to the girl of his hopes and fears. Smiling, she asked:—"Do you not know that I was sent for to become your wife?" And she entered with him.

Becoming his wife, she delighted him beyond expectation by

---

34 *Gekkawō*. This is a poetical appellation for the God of Marriage, more usually known as *Musubi-no-kami*. Throughout this story there is an interesting mingling of Shintō and Buddhist ideas.

the charm of her mind and heart. Moreover, he found her to be much more accomplished than he had supposed. Besides being able to write so wonderfully, she could paint beautiful pictures; she knew the art of arranging flowers, the art of embroidery, the art of music; she could weave and sew; and she knew everything in regard to the management of a house.

It was in the early autumn that the young people had met; and they lived together in perfect accord until the winter season began. Nothing, during those months, occurred to disturb their peace. Baishū's love for his gentle wife only strengthened with the passing of time. Yet, strangely enough, he remained ignorant of her history— knew nothing about her family. Of such matters she had never spoken; and, as the Gods had given her to him, he imagined that it would not be proper to question her. But neither the Old-Man-under-the-Moon nor any one else came—as he had feared—to take her away. Nobody even made any inquiries about her. And the neighbors, for some undiscoverable reason, acted as if totally unaware of her presence.

Baishū wondered at all this. But stranger experiences were awaiting him.

One winter morning he happened to be passing through a somewhat remote quarter of the city, when he heard himself loudly called by name, and saw a man-servant making signs to him from the gateway of a private residence. As Baishū did not know the man's face, and did not have a single acquaintance in that part of Kyōto, he was more than startled by so abrupt a summons. But the servant, coming forward, saluted him with the utmost respect, and said, "My master greatly desires the honor of speaking with you: deign to enter for a moment." After an instant of hesitation, Baishū allowed himself to be conducted to the house. A dignified and richly dressed person, who seemed to be the master, welcomed him at the entrance, and led him to the guest-room. When the courtesies due upon a first meeting had been fully exchanged, the host apologized for the informal manner of his invitation, and said:—

"It must have seemed to you very rude of us to call you in such a way. But perhaps you will pardon our impoliteness when I tell you that we acted thus upon what I firmly believe to have been an inspiration from the Goddess Benten. Now permit me to explain.

"I have a daughter, about sixteen years old, who can write rather well,[35] and do other things in the common way: she has the ordinary nature of woman. As we were anxious to make her happy by finding a good husband for her, we prayed the Goddess Benten to help us; and we sent to every temple of Benten in the city a *tanzaku* written by the girl. Some nights later, the Goddess appeared to me in a dream, and said: 'We have heard your prayer, and have already introduced your daughter to the person who is to become her husband. During the coming winter he will visit you.' As I did not understand this assurance that a presentation had been made, I felt some doubt; I thought that the dream might have been only a common dream, signifying nothing. But last night again I saw Benten-Sama in a dream; and she said to me: 'To-morrow the young man, of whom I once spoke to you, will come to this street: then you can call him into your house, and ask him to become the husband of your daughter. He is a good young man; and later in life he will obtain a much higher rank than he now holds.' Then Benten-Sama told me your name, your age, your birthplace, and described your features and

---

35 As it is the old Japanese rule that parents should speak depreciatingly of their children's accomplishments the phrase "rather well" in this connection would mean, for the visitor, "wonderfully well." For the same reason the expressions "common way" and "ordinary nature," as subsequently used, would imply almost the reverse of the literal meaning.

dress so exactly that my servant found no difficulty in recognizing you by the indications which I was able to give him."

This explanation bewildered Baishū instead of reassuring him; and his only reply was a formal return of thanks for the honor which the master of the house had spoken of doing him. But when the host invited him to another room, for the purpose of presenting him to the young lady, his embarrassment became extreme. Yet he could not reasonably decline the introduction. He could not bring himself, under such extraordinary circumstances, to announce that he already had a wife—a wife given to him by the Goddess Benten herself; a wife from whom he could not even think of separating. So, in silence and trepidation, he followed his host to the apartment indicated.

Then what was his amazement to discover, when presented to the daughter of the house, that she was the very same person whom he had already taken to wife!

The same—yet not the same.

She to whom he had been introduced by the Old-Man-under-the-Moon, was only the soul of the beloved.

She to whom he was now to be wedded, in her father's house, was the body.

Benten had wrought this miracle for the sake of her worshippers.

The original story breaks off suddenly at this point, leaving several matters unexplained. The ending is rather unsatisfactory. One would like to know something about the mental experiences of the real maiden during the married life of her phantom. One would also like to know what became of the phantom—whether it continued to lead an independent existence; whether it waited patiently for the return of its husband; whether it paid a visit to the real bride. And the book says nothing about these things. But a Japanese friend explains the miracle thus:—

"The spirit-bride was really formed out of the *tanzaku*. So it is possible that the real girl did not know anything about the meeting at the temple of Benten. When she wrote those beautiful characters upon the *tanzaku*, something of her spirit passed into them. Therefore it was possible to evoke from the writing the double of the writer."

The Gratitude of the Samébito

There was a man named Tawaraya Tōtarō, who lived in the Province of Ōmi. His house was situated on the shore of Lake Biwa, not far from the famous temple called Ishiyamadera. He had some property, and lived in comfort; but at the age of twenty-nine he was still unmarried. His greatest ambition was to marry a very beautiful woman; and he had not been able to find a girl to his liking.

One day, as he was passing over the Long Bridge of Séta,[36] he saw a strange being crouching close to the parapet. The body of this being resembled the body of a man, but was black as ink; its face was like the face of a demon; its eyes were green as emeralds; and its beard was like the beard of a dragon. Tōtarō was at first very much startled. But the green eyes looked at him so gently that after a moment's hesitation he ventured to question the creature. Then it answered him, saying: "I am a *Samébito*,[37]—a Shark-Man of the sea; and until a short

---

36   The Long Bridge of Séta (*Séta-no-Naga-Hashi*), famous in Japanese legend, is nearly eight hundred feet in length, and commands a beautiful view. This bridge crosses the waters of the Sétagawa near the junction of the stream with Lake Biwa. Ishiyamadera, one of the most picturesque Buddhist temples in Japan, is situated within a short distance from the bridge.

37   Literally, "a Shark-Person," but in this story the *Samébito* is a male. The characters for *Samébito* can also be read *Kōjin*—which is the usual reading. In dictionaries the word is loosely rendered by "merman" or "mermaid;" but as the above description shows, the *Samébito* or *Kōjin* of the Far East is a conception having little in common with the Western idea of a merman or mermaid.

time ago I was in the service of the Eight Great Dragon-Kings [*Hachi-Dai-Ryū-Ō*] as a subordinate officer in the Dragon-Palace [*Ryūgū*].[38] But because of a small fault which I committed, I was dismissed from the Dragon-Palace, and also banished from the Sea. Since then I have been wandering about here—unable to get any food, or even a place to lie down. If you can feel any pity for me, do, I beseech you, help me to find a shelter, and let me have something to eat!"

This petition was uttered in so plaintive a tone, and in so humble a manner, that Tōtarō's heart was touched. "Come with me," he said. "There is in my garden a large and deep pond where you may live as long as you wish; and I will give you plenty to eat."

The *Samébito* followed Tōtarō home, and appeared to be much pleased with the pond.

Thereafter, for nearly half a year, this strange guest dwelt in the pond, and was every day supplied by Tōtarō with such food as sea-creatures like.

[*From this point of the original narrative the Shark-Man is referred to, not as a monster, but as a sympathetic Person of the male sex.*]

Now, in the seventh month of the same year, there was a female pilgrimage (*nyonin-mōdé*) to the great Buddhist temple called Miidera, in the neighboring town of Ōtsu; and Tōtarō went to Ōtsu to attend the festival. Among the multitude of women and young girls there assembled, he observed a person of extraordinary beauty. She seemed about sixteen years old; her face was fair and pure as snow; and the loveliness of her lips assured the beholder that their every utterance would sound "as sweet as the voice of a nightingale singing upon a plum-tree." Tōtarō fell in love with her at sight. When she left the temple he followed her at a respectful distance, and discovered that she and her mother were staying for a few days at a certain house

---

38 *Ryūgū* is also the name given to the whole of that fairy-realm beneath the sea which figures in so many Japanese legends.

in the neighboring village of Séta. By questioning some of the village folk, he was able also to learn that her name was Tamana; that she was unmarried; and that her family appeared to be unwilling that she should marry a man of ordinary rank—for they demanded as a betrothal-gift a casket containing ten thousand jewels.[39]

Tōtarō returned home very much dismayed by this information. The more that he thought about the strange betrothal-gift demanded by the girl's parents, the more he felt that he could never expect to obtain her for his wife. Even supposing that there were as many as ten thousand jewels in the whole country, only a great prince could hope to procure them.

But not even for a single hour could Tōtarō banish from his mind the memory of that beautiful being. It haunted him so that he could neither eat nor sleep; and it seemed to become more and more vivid as the days went by. And at last he became ill—so ill that he could not lift his head from the pillow. Then he sent for a doctor.

The doctor, after having made a careful examination, uttered an exclamation of surprise. "Almost any kind of sickness," he said, "can be cured by proper medical treatment, except the sickness of love. Your ailment is evidently love-sickness. There is no cure for it. In ancient times Rōya-Ō Hakuyo died of that sickness; and you must prepare yourself to die as he died." So saying, the doctor went away, without even giving any medicine to Tōtarō.

About this time the Shark-Man that was living in the garden-pond heard of his master's sickness, and came into the house to

---

39 *Tama* in the original. This word *tama* has a multitude of meanings; and as here used it is quite as indefinite as our own terms "jewel," "gem," or "precious stone." Indeed, it is more indefinite, for it signifies also a bead of coral, a ball of crystal, a polished stone attached to a hairpin, etc. Later on, however, I venture to render it by "ruby,"—for reasons which need no explanation.

wait upon Tōtarō. And he tended him with the utmost affection both by day and by night. But he did not know either the cause or the serious nature of the sickness until nearly a week later, when Tōtarō, thinking himself about to die, uttered these words of fare-well:—

"I suppose that I have had the pleasure of caring for you thus long, because of some relation that grew up between us in a former state of existence. But now I am very sick indeed, and every day my sickness becomes worse; and my life is like the morning dew which passes away before the setting of the sun. For your sake, therefore, I am troubled in mind. Your existence has depended upon my care; and I fear that there will be no one to care for you and to feed you when I am dead.... My poor friend!... Alas! our hopes and our wishes are always disappointed in this unhappy world!"

No sooner had Tōtarō spoken these words than the Samébito uttered a strange wild cry of pain, and began to weep bitterly. And as he wept, great tears of blood streamed from his green eyes and rolled down his black cheeks and dripped upon the floor. And, falling, they were blood; but, having fallen, they became hard and bright and beautiful—became jewels of inestimable price, rubies splendid as crimson fire. For when men of the sea weep, their tears become precious stones.

Then Tōtarō, beholding this marvel, was so amazed and over-joyed that his strength returned to him. He sprang from his bed, and began to pick up and to count the tears of the Shark-Man, crying out the while: "My sickness is cured! I shall live! I shall live!"

Therewith, the Shark-Man, greatly astonished, ceased to weep, and asked Tōtarō to explain this wonderful cure; and Tōtarō told him about the young person seen at Miidera, and about the extraor-dinary marriage-gift demanded by her family. "As I felt sure," added Tōtarō, "that I should never be able to get ten thousand jewels, I supposed that my suit would be hopeless. Then I became very unhappy, and at last fell sick. But now, because of your generous weeping, I have many precious stones; and I think that I shall be able to marry that girl. Only—there are not yet quite enough stones; and I beg that you will be good enough to weep a little more, so as to make up the full number required."

But at this request the Samébito shook his head, and answered in a tone of surprise and of reproach:—

"Do you think that I am like a harlot—able to weep whenever I wish? Oh, no! Harlots shed tears in order to deceive men; but creatures of the sea cannot weep without feeling real sorrow. I wept for you because of the true grief that I felt in my heart at the thought that you were going to die. But now I cannot weep for you, because you have told me that your sickness is cured."

"Then what am I to do?" plaintively asked Tōtarō. "Unless I can get ten thousand jewels, I cannot marry the girl!"

The Samébito remained for a little while silent, as if thinking. Then he said:—

"Listen! To-day I cannot possibly weep any more. But to-morrow let us go together to the Long Bridge of Séta, taking with us some wine and some fish. We can rest for a time on the bridge; and while we are drinking the wine and eating the fish, I shall gaze in the direction of the Dragon-Palace, and try, by thinking of the happy days that I spent there, to make myself feel homesick—so that I can weep."

Tōtarō joyfully assented.

Next morning the two, taking plenty of wine and fish with them, went to the Séta bridge, and rested there, and feasted. After having drunk a great deal of wine, the Samébito began to gaze in the direction of the Dragon-Kingdom, and to think about the past. And gradually, under the softening influence of the wine, the memory of happier days filled his heart with sorrow, and the pain of homesickness came upon him, so that he could weep profusely. And the great red tears that he shed fell upon the bridge in a shower of rubies; and Tōtarō gathered them as they fell, and put them into a casket, and counted them until he had counted the full number of ten thousand. Then he uttered a shout of joy.

Almost in the same moment, from far away over the lake, a delightful sound of music was heard; and there appeared in the offing, slowly rising from the waters, like some fabric of cloud, a palace of the color of the setting sun.

At once the Samébito sprang upon the parapet of the bridge, and looked, and laughed for joy. Then, turning to Tōtarō, he said:—

"There must have been a general amnesty proclaimed in the Dragon-Realm; the Kings are calling me. So now I must bid you farewell. I am happy to have had one chance of befriending you in return for your goodness to me."

With these words he leaped from the bridge; and no man ever saw him again. But Tōtarō presented the casket of red jewels to the parents of Tamana, and so obtained her in marriage.

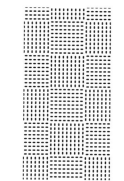

Noctilucæ

··

The moon had not yet risen; but the vast of the night was all seething with stars, and bridged by a Milky Way of extraordinary brightness. There was no wind; but the sea, far as sight could reach, was running in ripples of fire—a vision of infernal beauty. Only the ripplings were radiant (between them was blackness absolute);—and the luminosity was amazing. Most of the undulations were yellow like candle-flame; but there were crimson lampings also—and azure, and orange, and emerald. And the sinuous flickering of all seemed, not a pulsing of many waters, but a laboring of many wills—a fleeting conscious and monstrous—a writhing and a swarming incalculable, as of dragon-life in some depth of Erebus.

And life indeed was making the sinister splendor of that spectacle—but life infinitesimal, and of ghostliest delicacy—life illimitable, yet ephemeral, flaming and fading in ceaseless alternation over the whole round of waters even to the sky-line, above which, in the vaster abyss, other countless lights were throbbing with other spectral colors.

Watching, I wondered and I dreamed. I thought of the Ultimate Ghost revealed in that scintillation tremendous of Night and Sea;— quickening above me, in systems aglow with awful fusion of the past dissolved, with vapor of the life again to be;—quickening also beneath me, in meteor-gushings and constellations and nebulosities of colder fire—till I found myself doubting whether the million ages of the sun-star could really signify, in the flux of perpetual dissolution, anything more than the momentary sparkle of one expiring noctiluca.

Even with the doubt, the vision changed. I saw no longer the sea of the ancient East, with its shudderings of fire, but that Flood whose width and depth and altitude are one with the Night of Eternity—the shoreless and timeless Sea of Death and Birth. And the luminous haze of a hundred millions of suns—the Arch of the Milky Way—was a single smouldering surge in the flow of the Infinite Tides.

Yet again there came a change. I saw no more that vapory surge of suns; but the living darkness streamed and thrilled about me with infinite sparkling; and every sparkle was beating like a heart— beating out colors like the tints of the sea-fires. And the lampings of all continually flowed away, as shivering threads of radiance, into illimitable Mystery....

Then I knew myself also a phosphor-point—one fugitive floating sparkle of the measureless current;—and I saw that the light which was mine shifted tint with each changing of thought. Ruby it some- times shone, and sometimes sapphire: now it was flame of topaz; again, it was fire of emerald. And the meaning of the changes I could not fully know. But thoughts of the earthly life seemed to make the light burn red; while thoughts of supernal being—of ghostly beauty and of ghostly bliss—seemed to kindle ineffable rhythms of azure and of violet.

But of white lights there were none in all the Visible. And I marveled.

Then a Voice said to me:—

"The White are of the Altitudes. By the blending of the billions they are made. Thy part is to help to their kindling. Even as the color of thy burning, so is the worth of thee. For a moment only is thy quickening; yet the light of thy pulsing lives on: by thy thought, in that shining moment, thou becomest a Maker of Gods."

Gothic Horror

I

Long before I had arrived at what catechisms call the age of reason, I was frequently taken, much against my will, to church. The church was very old; and I can see the interior of it at this moment just as plainly as I saw it forty years ago, when it appeared to me like an evil dream. There I first learned to know the peculiar horror that certain forms of Gothic architecture can inspire.... I am using the word "horror" in a classic sense—in its antique meaning of ghostly fear.

On the very first day of this experience, my child-fancy could place the source of the horror. The wizened and pointed shapes of the windows immediately terrified me. In their outline I found the form of apparitions that tormented me in sleep;—and at once I began to imagine some dreadful affinity between goblins and Gothic churches. Presently, in the tall doorways, in the archings of the aisles, in the ribbings and groinings of the roof, I discovered other and wilder suggestions of fear. Even the facade of the organ— peaking high into the shadow above its gallery—seemed to me a frightful thing.... Had I been then suddenly obliged to answer the question, "What are you afraid of?" I should have whispered, "*Those points!*" I could not have otherwise explained the matter: I only knew that I was afraid of the "points."

Of course the real enigma of what I felt in that church could not present itself to my mind while I continued to believe in goblins. But long after the age of superstitious terrors, other Gothic experiences severally revived the childish emotion in so startling a way as to convince me that childish fancy could not account for the feeling. Then my curiosity was aroused; and I tried to discover some rational cause for the horror. I read many books, and asked many questions; but the mystery seemed only to deepen.

Books about architecture were very disappointing. I was much less impressed by what I could find in them than by references in pure fiction to the awfulness of Gothic art—particularly by one writer's confession that the interior of a Gothic church, seen at night, gave him the idea of being inside the skeleton of some monstrous animal; and by a far-famed comparison of the windows of a cathedral to eyes, and of its door to a great mouth, "devouring the people." These imaginations explained little; they could not be developed beyond the phase of vague intimation: yet they stirred such emotional response that I felt sure they had touched some truth. Certainly the architecture of a Gothic cathedral offers strange resemblances to the architecture of bone; and the general impression that it makes upon the mind is an impression of life. But this impression or sense of life I found to be indefinable—not a sense of any life organic, but of a life latent and dæmonic. And the manifestation of that life I felt to be in the *pointing* of the structure.

Attempts to interpret the emotion by effects of altitude and gloom and vastness appeared to me of no worth; for buildings loftier and larger and darker than any Gothic cathedral, but of a different order of architecture—Egyptian, for instance—could not produce a like impression. I felt certain that the horror was made by something altogether peculiar to Gothic construction, and that this something haunted the tops of the arches.

"Yes, Gothic architecture is awful," said a religious friend, "because it is the visible expression of Christian faith. No other religious architecture symbolizes spiritual longing; but the Gothic embodies it. Every part climbs or leaps; every supreme detail soars and points like fire...." "There may be considerable truth in what you say," I replied;—"but it does not relate to the riddle that baffles me. Why should shapes that symbolize spiritual longing create horror? Why should any expression of Christian ecstasy inspire alarm?..."

Other hypotheses in multitude I tested without avail; and I returned to the simple and savage conviction that the secret of the horror somehow belonged to the points of the archings. But for years I could not find it. At last, at last, in the early hours of a certain tropical morning, it revealed itself quite unexpectedly, while I was looking at a glorious group of palms.

Then I wondered at my stupidity in not having guessed the riddle before.

II

The characteristics of many kinds of palm have been made familiar by pictures and photographs. But the giant palms of the American tropics cannot be adequately represented by the modern methods of pictorial illustration: they must be seen. You cannot draw or photograph a palm two hundred feet high.

The first sight of a group of such forms, in their natural environment of tropical forest, is a magnificent surprise—a surprise that strikes you dumb. Nothing seen in temperate zones—not even the huger growths of the Californian slope—could have prepared your imagination for the weird solemnity of that mighty colonnade. Each stone-grey trunk is a perfect pillar—but a pillar of which the stupendous grace has no counterpart in the works of man. You must strain your head well back to follow the soaring of the prodigious column, up, up, up through abysses of green twilight, till at last—far beyond a break in that infinite interweaving of limbs and lianas which is the roof of the forest—you catch one dizzy glimpse of the capital: a parasol of emerald feathers outspread in a sky so blinding as to suggest the notion of azure electricity.

Now what is the emotion that such a vision excites—an emotion too powerful to be called wonder, too weird to be called delight? Only when the first shock of it has passed—when the several elements that were combined in it have begun to set in motion widely different groups of ideas—can you comprehend how very complex it must have been. Many impressions belonging to personal experience were doubtless revived in it, but also with them a multitude of sensations more shadowy—accumulations of organic memory; possibly even vague feelings older than man—for the tropical shapes that aroused the emotion have a history more ancient than our race.

One of the first elements of the emotion to become clearly distinguishable is the æsthetic; and this, in its general mass, might be termed the sense of terrible beauty. Certainly the spectacle of that unfamiliar life—silent, tremendous, springing to the sun in colossal aspiration, striving for light against Titans, and heedless of man in the gloom beneath as of a groping beetle—thrills like the rhythm of some single marvelous verse that is learned in a glance and remembered forever. Yet the delight, even at its vividest, is shadowed by a queer disquiet. The aspect of that monstrous, pale, naked, smooth-stretching column suggests a life as conscious as the

244

serpent's. You stare at the towering lines of the shape—vaguely fearing to discern some sign of stealthy movement, some beginning of undulation. Then sight and reason combine to correct the suspicion. Yes, motion is there, and life enormous—but a life seeking only sun—life, rushing like the jet of a geyser, straight to the giant day.

III

During my own experience I could perceive that certain feelings commingled in the wave of delight—feelings related to ideas of power and splendor and triumph—were accompanied by a faint sense of religious awe. Perhaps our modern æsthetic sentiments are so interwoven with various inherited elements of religious emotionalism that the recognition of beauty cannot arise independently of reverential feeling. Be this as it may, such a feeling defined itself while I gazed;—and at once the great gray trunks were changed to the pillars of a mighty aisle; and from altitudes of dream there suddenly descended upon me the old dark thrill of Gothic horror.

Even before it died away, I recognized that it must have been due to some old cathedral-memory revived by the vision of those giant trunks uprising into gloom. But neither the height nor the gloom could account for anything beyond the memory. Columns tall as those palms, but supporting a classic entablature, could evoke no sense of disquiet resembling the Gothic horror. I felt sure of this—because I was able, without any difficulty, to shape immediately the imagination of such a facade. But presently the mental picture distorted. I saw the architrave elbow upward in each of the spaces between the pillars, and curve and point itself into a range of prodigious arches;—and again the sombre thrill descended upon me. Simultaneously there flashed to me the solution of the mystery.

I understood that the Gothic horror was a *horror of monstrous motion*—and that it had seemed to belong to the points of the arches because the idea of such motion was chiefly suggested by the extraordinary angle at which the curves of the arching touched.

To any experienced eye, the curves of Gothic arching offer a striking resemblance to certain curves of vegetal growth;—the curves of the palm-branch being, perhaps, especially suggested. But observe that the architectural form suggests more than any vegetal comparison could illustrate! The meeting of two palm-crests would indeed form a kind of Gothic arch; yet the effect of so short an arch would be insignificant. For nature to repeat the strange impression of the real Gothic arch, it were necessary that the branches of the touching crests should vastly exceed, both in length of curve and strength of spring, anything of their kind existing in the vegetable world. The effect of the Gothic arch depends altogether upon the intimation of energy. An arch formed by the intersection of two short sprouting lines could suggest only a feeble power of growth; but the lines of the tall mediæval arch seem to express a crescent force immensely surpassing that of nature. And the horror of Gothic architecture is not in the mere suggestion of a growing life, but in the suggestion of an energy supernatural and tremendous.

Of course the child, oppressed by the strangeness of Gothic forms, is yet incapable of analyzing the impression received: he is frightened without comprehending. He cannot divine that the points and the curves are terrible to him because they represent the prodigious exaggeration of a real law of vegetal growth. He dreads the shapes because they seem alive; yet he does not know how to express this dread. Without suspecting why, he feels that this silent manifestation of power, everywhere pointing and piercing upward, is not natural. To his startled imagination, the building stretches itself like a phantasm of sleep—makes itself tall and taller with intent to frighten. Even though built by hands of men, it has ceased to be a mass of dead stone: it is infused with Something that thinks and threatens;—it has become a shadowing malevolence, a multiple goblinry, a monstrous fetish!

Levitation

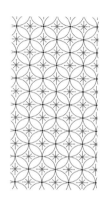

Out of some upper-story window I was looking into a street of yellow-tinted houses—a colonial street, old-fashioned, narrow, with palm-heads showing above its roofs of tile. There were no shadows; there was no sun—only a gray soft light, as of early gloaming.

Suddenly I found myself falling from the window; and my heart gave one sickening leap of terror. But the distance from window to pavement proved to be much greater than I supposed—so great that, in spite of my fear, I began to wonder. Still I kept falling, falling—and still the dreaded shock did not come. Then the fear ceased, and a queer pleasure took its place;—for I discovered that I was not falling quickly, but only *floating* down. Moreover, I was floating feet foremost—must have turned in descending. At last I touched the stones—but very, very lightly, with only one foot; and instantly at that touch I went up again—rose to the level of the eaves. People stopped to stare at me. I felt the exultation of power superhuman;—I felt for the moment as a god.

Then softly I began to sink; and the sight of faces, gathering below me, prompted a sudden resolve to fly down the street, over the heads of the gazers. Again like a bubble I rose, and, with the same impulse, I sailed in one grand curve to a distance that astounded me. I felt no wind;—I felt nothing but the joy of motion triumphant. Once more touching pavement, I soared at a bound for a thousand yards. Then, reaching the end of the street, I wheeled and came back by great swoops—by long slow aerial leaps of surprising altitude. In the street there was dead silence: many people were looking; but nobody spoke. I wondered what they thought of my feat, and what they would say if they knew how easily the thing was done. By the merest chance I had found out how to do it; and the only reason why it seemed a feat was that no one else had ever attempted it. Instinctively I felt that to say anything about the accident, which had led to the discovery, would be imprudent. Then the real meaning of the strange hush in the street began to dawn upon me. I said to myself:—

"This silence is the Silence of Dreams;—I am quite well aware that this is a dream. I remember having dreamed the same dream before. But the discovery of this power is not a dream: *it is a revelation!* ... Now that I have learned how to fly, I can no more forget it than a swimmer can forget how to swim. To-morrow morning I shall astonish the people, by sailing over the roofs of the town."

Morning came; and I woke with the fixed resolve to fly out of the window. But no sooner had I risen from bed than the knowledge of physical relations returned, like a sensation forgotten, and compelled me to recognize the unwelcome truth that I had not made any discovery at all.

This was neither the first nor the last of such dreams; but it was particularly vivid, and I therefore selected it for narration as a good example of its class. I still fly occasionally—sometimes over fields and streams—sometimes through familiar streets; and the dream is invariably accompanied by remembrance of like dreams in the past, as well as by the conviction that I have really found out a secret, really acquired a new faculty. "This time, at all events," I say to myself, "it is impossible that I can be mistaken;—I *know* that I shall be able to fly after I awake. Many times before, in other dreams, I learned the secret only to forget it on awakening; but this time I am absolutely sure that I shall not forget." And the conviction actually stays with me until I rise from bed, when the physical effort at once reminds me of the formidable reality of gravitation.

The oddest part of this experience is the feeling of buoyancy. It is much like the feeling of floating—of rising or sinking through tepid water, for example;—and there is no sense of real effort. It is a delight; yet it usually leaves something to be desired. I am a low flyer; I can proceed only like a pteromys or a flying-fish—and far less quickly: moreover, I must tread earth occasionally in order to obtain a fresh impulsion. I seldom rise to a height of more than twenty-five or thirty feet;—the greater part of the time I am merely skimming surfaces. Touching the ground only at intervals of several hundred yards is pleasant skimming; but I always feel, in a faint and watery way, the dead pull of the world beneath me.

Now the experience of most dream-flyers I find to be essentially like my own. I have met but one who claims superior powers: he says that he flies over mountains—goes sailing from peak to peak like a kite. All others whom I have questioned acknowledge that they fly low—in long parabolic curves—and this only by touching ground from time to time. Most of them also tell me that their flights usually begin with an imagined fall, or desperate leap; and no less than four say that the start is commonly taken from the top of a stairway.

For myriads of years humanity has thus been flying by night. How did the fancied motion, having so little in common with any experience of active life, become a universal experience of the life of sleep?

It may be that memory-impressions of certain kinds of aerial

motion—exultant experiences of leaping or swinging, for example—
are in dream-revival so magnified and prolonged as to create the
illusion of flight. We know that in actual time the duration of most
dreams is very brief. But in the half-life of sleep—(nightmare
offering some startling exceptions)—there is scarcely more than a
faint smouldering of consciousness by comparison with the quick
flash and vivid thrill of active cerebration;—and time, to the
dreaming brain, would seem to be magnified, somewhat as it must
be relatively magnified to the feeble consciousness of an insect.
Supposing that any memory of the sensation of falling, together
with the memory of the concomitant fear, should be accidentally
revived in sleep, the dream-prolongation of the sensation and the
emotion—unchecked by the natural sequence of shock—might
suffice to revive other and even pleasurable memories of airy
motion. And these, again, might quicken other combinations of
interrelated memories able to furnish all the incident and scenery
of the long phantasmagoria.

But this hypothesis will not fully explain certain feelings and
ideas of a character different from any experience of waking-
hours—the exultation of voluntary motion without exertion—the
pleasure of the utterly impossible—the ghostly delight of impon-
derability. Neither can it serve to explain other dream-experiences
of levitation which do not begin with the sensation of leaping or
falling, and are seldom of a pleasurable kind. For example, it
sometimes happens during nightmare that the dreamer, deprived
of all power to move or speak, actually feels his body lifted into
the air and floated away by the force of the horror within him.
Again, there are dreams in which the dreamer has no physical
being. I have thus found myself without any body—a viewless
and voiceless phantom, hovering upon a mountain-road in twilight
time, and trying to frighten lonely folk by making small moaning
noises. The sensation was of moving through the air by mere act

of will: there was no touching of surfaces; and I seemed to glide always about a foot above the road.

Could the feeling of dream-flight be partly interpreted by organic memory of conditions of life more ancient than man—life weighty, and winged, and flying heavily, *a little above the ground?*

Or might we suppose that some all-permeating Over-Soul, dormant in other time, wakens within the brain at rare moments of our sleep-life? The limited human consciousness has been beautifully compared to the visible solar spectrum, above and below which whole zones of colors invisible await the evolution of superior senses; and mystics aver that something of the ultra-violet or infra-red rays of the vaster Mind may be momentarily glimpsed in dreams. Certainly the Cosmic Life in each of us has been all things in all forms of space and time. Perhaps you would like to believe that it may bestir, in slumber, some vague sense-memory of things more ancient than the sun—memory of vanished planets with fainter powers of gravitation, where the normal modes of voluntary motion would have been like the realization of our flying dreams?...

Nightmare-Touch

I

What *is* the fear of ghosts among those who believe in ghosts?

All fear is the result of experience—experience of the individual or of the race—experience either of the present life or of lives forgotten. Even the fear of the unknown can have no other origin. And the fear of ghosts must be a product of past pain.

Probably the fear of ghosts, as well as the belief in them, had its beginning in dreams. It is a peculiar fear. No other fear is so intense; yet none is so vague. Feelings thus voluminous and dim are super-individual mostly—feelings inherited—feelings made within us by the experience of the dead.

What experience?

Nowhere do I remember reading a plain statement of the reason why ghosts are feared. Ask any ten intelligent persons of your acquaintance, who remember having once been afraid of ghosts, to tell you exactly why they were afraid—to define the fancy behind the fear;—and I doubt whether even one will be able to answer the question. The literature of folk-lore—oral and written—throws no clear light upon the subject. We find, indeed, various legends of men torn asunder by phantoms; but such gross imaginings could not explain the peculiar quality of ghostly fear. It is not a fear of bodily violence. It is not even a reasoning fear—not a fear that can readily explain itself—which would not be the case if it were founded upon definite ideas of physical danger. Furthermore, although primitive ghosts may have been imagined as capable of tearing and devouring, the common idea of a ghost is certainly that of a being intangible and imponderable.[40]

Now I venture to state boldly that the common fear of ghosts is *the fear of being touched by ghosts*—or, in other words, that the imagined Supernatural is dreaded mainly because of its imagined power to touch. Only to *touch*, remember!—not to wound or to kill.

But this dread of the touch would itself be the result of experience—chiefly, I think, of prenatal experience stored up in the individual by inheritance, like the child's fear of darkness. And who can ever have had the sensation of being touched by ghosts? The answer is simple:—*Everybody who has been seized by phantoms in a dream.*

Elements of primeval fears—fears older than humanity—doubtless enter into the child-terror of darkness. But the more definite fear of ghosts may very possibly be composed with inherited results of dream-pain—ancestral experience of nightmare. And the intuitive terror of supernatural touch can thus be evolutionally explained.

Let me now try to illustrate my theory by relating some typical experiences.

II

When about five years old I was condemned to sleep by myself in a certain isolated room, thereafter always called the Child's Room. (At that time I was scarcely ever mentioned by name, but only

---

40   I may remark here that in many old Japanese legends and ballads, ghosts are represented as having power to *pull off* people's heads. But so far as the origin of the fear of ghosts is concerned, such stories explain nothing—since the experiences that evolved the fear must have been real, not imaginary, experiences.

referred to as "the Child.") The room was narrow, but very high, and, in spite of one tall window, very gloomy. It contained a fireplace wherein no fire was ever kindled; and the Child suspected that the chimney was haunted.

A law was made that no light should be left in the Child's Room at night—simply because the Child was afraid of the dark. His fear of the dark was judged to be a mental disorder requiring severe treatment. But the treatment aggravated the disorder. Previously I had been accustomed to sleep in a well-lighted room, with a nurse to take care of me. I thought that I should die of fright when sentenced to lie alone in the dark, and—what seemed to me then abominably cruel—actually *locked* into my room, the most dismal room of the house. Night after night when I had been warmly tucked into bed, the lamp was removed; the key clicked in the lock; the protecting light and the footsteps of my guardian receded together. Then an agony of fear would come upon me. Something in the black air would seem to gather and grow—(I thought that I could even *hear* it grow)—till I had to scream. Screaming regularly brought punishment; but it also brought back the light, which more than consoled for the punishment. This fact being at last found out, orders were given to pay no further heed to the screams of the Child.

Why was I thus insanely afraid? Partly because the dark had always been peopled for me with shapes of terror. So far back as memory extended, I had suffered from ugly dreams; and when aroused from them I could always *see* the forms dreamed of, lurking in the shadows of the room. They would soon fade out; but for several moments they would appear like tangible realities. And they were always the same figures.... Sometimes, without any preface of dreams, I used to see them at twilight-time—following me about from room to room, or reaching long dim hands after me, from story to story, up through the interspaces of the deep stairways.

I had complained of these haunters only to be told that I must never speak of them, and that they did not exist. I had complained to everybody in the house; and everybody in the house had told me the very same thing. But there was the evidence of my eyes! The denial of that evidence I could explain only in two ways:—Either the shapes were afraid of big people, and showed themselves to me alone, because I was little and weak; or else the entire household had agreed, for some ghastly reason, to say what was not true. This latter theory seemed to me the more probable one, because I had several times perceived the shapes when I was not unattended;—and the consequent appearance of secrecy frightened me scarcely less than the visions did. Why was I forbidden to talk about what I saw, and even heard—on creaking stairways—behind wavering curtains?

"Nothing will hurt you,"—this was the merciless answer to all my pleadings not to be left alone at night. But the haunters *did* hurt me. Only—they would wait until after I had fallen asleep, and so into their power—for they possessed occult means of preventing me from rising or moving or crying out.

Needless to comment upon the policy of locking me up alone with these fears in a black room. Unutterably was I tormented in that room—for years! Therefore I felt relatively happy when sent away at last to a children's boarding-school, where the haunters very seldom ventured to show themselves.

They were not like any people that I had ever known. They were shadowy dark-robed figures, capable of atrocious self-distortion—capable, for instance, of growing up to the ceiling, and then across it, and then lengthening themselves, head-downwards, along the opposite wall. Only their faces were distinct; and I tried not to look at their faces. I tried also in my dreams—or thought that I tried—to awaken myself from the sight of them by pulling at my eyelids with my fingers; but the eyelids would remain closed, as if sealed.... Many years afterwards, the frightful plates in Orfila's *Traité des Exhumés*, beheld for the first time, recalled to me with a sickening start the dream-terrors of childhood. But to understand the Child's experience, you must imagine Orfila's drawings intensely alive, and continually elongating or distorting, as in some monstrous anamorphosis.

Nevertheless the mere sight of those nightmare-faces was not the worst of the experiences in the Child's Room. The dreams always began with a suspicion, or sensation of something heavy in the air—slowly quenching will—slowly numbing my power to move. At such times I usually found myself alone in a large unlighted apartment; and, almost simultaneously with the first sensation of fear, the atmosphere of the room would become suffused, half-way to the ceiling, with a sombre-yellowish glow, making objects dimly visible—though the ceiling itself remained pitch-black. This was not a true appearance of light: rather it seemed as if the black air were changing color from beneath.... Certain terrible aspects of sunset, on the eve of storm, offer like effects of sinister color.... Forthwith I would try to escape—(feeling at every step a sensation *as of wading*)—and would sometimes succeed in struggling half-way across the room;—but there I would always find myself brought to a standstill—paralyzed by some innominable opposition. Happy voices I could hear in the next room;—I could see light through the transom over the door that I had vainly endeavored to reach;—I knew that one loud cry would save me. But not even by the most frantic effort could I raise my voice above a whisper.... And all this signified only that the Nameless was coming—was nearing—was mounting the stairs. I could hear the step—booming like the sound of a muffled drum—and I wondered why nobody else heard it. A long, long time the haunter would take to come—malevolently pausing after each ghastly footfall. Then, without a creak, the bolted door would open—slowly, slowly—and the thing would enter, gibbering soundlessly—and put out hands—and clutch me—and toss me to the black ceiling—and catch me descending to toss me up again, and again, and again.... In those moments the feeling was not fear: fear itself had been torpified by the first seizure. It was a sensation that has no name in the language of the living. For every touch brought a shock of something infinitely worse than pain— something that thrilled into the innermost secret being of me—a sort of abominable electricity, discovering unimagined capacities of suffering in totally unfamiliar regions of sentiency.... This was commonly the work of a single tormentor; but I can also remember having been caught by a group, and tossed from one to another— seemingly for a time of many minutes.

III

Whence the fancy of those shapes? I do not know. Possibly from some impression of fear in earliest infancy; possibly from some experience of fear in other lives than mine. That mystery is forever insoluble. But the mystery of the shock of the touch admits of a definite hypothesis.

First, allow me to observe that the experience of the sensation itself cannot be dismissed as "mere imagination." Imagination means cerebral activity: its pains and its pleasures are alike inseparable from nervous operation, and their physical importance is sufficiently proved by their physiological effects. Dream-fear may kill as well as other fear; and no emotion thus powerful can be reasonably deemed undeserving of study.

One remarkable fact in the problem to be considered is that the sensation of seizure in dreams differs totally from all sensations familiar to ordinary waking life. Why this differentiation? How interpret the extraordinary massiveness and depth of the thrill?

I have already suggested that the dreamer's fear is most probably not a reflection of relative experience, but represents the incalculable total of ancestral experience of dream-fear. If the sum of the experience of active life be transmitted by inheritance, so must likewise be transmitted the summed experience of the life of sleep. And in normal heredity either class of transmissions would probably remain distinct.

Now, granting this hypothesis, the sensation of dream-seizure would have had its beginnings in the earliest phases of dream-consciousness—long prior to the apparition of man. The first creatures capable of thought and fear must often have dreamed of being caught by their natural enemies. There could not have been much imagining of pain in these primal dreams. But higher nervous development in later forms of being would have been accompanied with larger susceptibility to dream-pain. Still later, with the growth of reasoning-power, ideas of the supernatural would have changed and intensified the character of dream-fear. Furthermore, through all the course of evolution, heredity would have been accumulating the experience of such feeling. Under those forms of imaginative pain evolved through reaction of religious beliefs, there would persist some dim survival of savage primitive fears, and again, under this, a dimmer but incomparably deeper substratum of ancient animal-terrors. In the dreams of the modern child all these latencies might quicken—one below another—unfathomably—with the coming and the growing of nightmare.

It may be doubted whether the phantasms of any particular nightmare have a history older than the brain in which they move. But the shock of the touch would seem to indicate *some point of dream-contact with the total race-experience of shadowy seizure*. It may be that profundities of Self—abysses never reached by any ray from the life of sun—are strangely stirred in slumber, and that out of their blackness immediately responds a shuddering of memory, measureless even by millions of years.

The Story of Mimi-Nashi-Hōïchi

More than seven hundred years ago, at Dan-no-ura, in the Straits of Shimonoséki, was fought the last battle of the long contest between the Heiké, or Taira clan, and the Genji, or Minamoto clan. There the Heiké perished utterly, with their women and children, and their infant emperor likewise—now remembered as Antoku Tennō. And that sea and shore have been haunted for seven hundred years… Elsewhere I told you about the strange crabs found there, called Heiké crabs, which have human faces on their backs, and are said to be the spirits of the Heiké warriors. But there are many strange things to be seen and heard along that coast. On dark nights thousands of ghostly fires hover about the beach, or flit above the waves—pale lights which the fishermen call *Oni-bi*, or demon-fires; and, whenever the winds are up, a sound of great shouting comes from that sea, like a clamor of battle.

In former years the Heiké were much more restless than they now are. They would rise about ships passing in the night, and try to sink them; and at all times they would watch for swimmers, to pull them down. It was in order to appease those dead that the Buddhist temple, Amidaji, was built at Akamagaséki. A cemetery also was made close by, near the beach; and within it were set up monuments inscribed with the names of the drowned emperor and of his great vassals; and Buddhist services were regularly performed there, on behalf of the spirits of them. After the temple had been built, and the tombs erected, the Heiké gave less trouble than before; but they continued to do queer things at intervals—proving that they had not found the perfect peace.

Some centuries ago there lived at Akamagaséki a blind man named Hōïchi, who was famed for his skill in recitation and in playing upon the *biwa*.[41] From childhood he had been trained to recite and to play; and while yet a lad he had surpassed his teachers. As a professional *biwa-hōshi* he became famous chiefly by his recitations of the history of the Heiké and the Genji; and it is said that when he sang the song of the battle of Dan-no-ura "even the goblins [*kijin*] could not refrain from tears."

At the outset of his career, Hōïchi was very poor; but he found a good friend to help him. The priest of the Amidaji was fond of poetry and music; and he often invited Hōïchi to the temple, to play and recite. Afterwards, being much impressed by the wonderful skill of the lad, the priest proposed that Hōïchi should make the temple his home; and this offer was gratefully accepted. Hōïchi was given a room in the temple-building; and, in return for food and lodging, he was required only to gratify the priest with a musical performance on certain evenings, when otherwise disengaged.

One summer night the priest was called away, to perform a Buddhist service at the house of a dead parishioner; and he went there with his acolyte, leaving Hōïchi alone in the temple. It was a hot night; and the blind man sought to cool himself on the verandah before his sleeping-room. The verandah overlooked a small garden

---

41 The *biwa*, a kind of four-stringed lute, is chiefly used in musical recitative. Formerly the professional minstrels who recited the *Heiké-Monogatari*, and other tragical histories, were called *biwa-hōshi*, or "lute-priests." The origin of this appellation is not clear; but it is possible that it may have been suggested by the fact that "lute-priests" as well as blind shampooers, had their heads shaven, like Buddhist priests. The *biwa* is played with a kind of plectrum, called *bachi*, usually made of horn.

in the rear of the Amidaji. There Hōïchi waited for the priest's return, and tried to relieve his solitude by practicing upon his *biwa*. Midnight passed; and the priest did not appear. But the atmosphere was still too warm for comfort within doors; and Hōïchi remained outside. At last he heard steps approaching from the back gate. Somebody crossed the garden, advanced to the verandah, and halted directly in front of him—but it was not the priest. A deep voice called the blind man's name—abruptly and unceremoniously, in the manner of a samurai summoning an inferior:—

"Hōïchi!"

"Hai!"[42] answered the blind man, frightened by the menace in the voice—"I am blind!—I cannot know who calls!"

"There is nothing to fear," the stranger exclaimed, speaking more gently. "I am stopping near this temple, and have been sent to you with a message. My present lord, a person of exceedingly high rank, is now staying in Akamagaséki, with many noble attendants. He wished to view the scene of the battle of Dan-no-ura; and to-day he visited that place. Having heard of your skill in reciting the story of the battle, he now desires to hear your performance: so you will take your *biwa* and come with me at once to the house where the august assembly is waiting."

In those times, the order of a samurai was not to be lightly disobeyed. Hōïchi donned his sandals, took his *biwa*, and went away with the stranger, who guided him deftly, but obliged him to walk very fast. The hand that guided was iron; and the clank of the warrior's stride proved him fully armed—probably some palace-guard on duty. Hōïchi's first alarm was over: he began to imagine himself in good luck;—for, remembering the retainer's assurance about a "person of exceedingly high rank," he thought that the lord who wished to hear the recitation could not be less

---

42 A response to show that one has heard and is listening attentively.

than a daimyō of the first class. Presently the samurai halted; and Hōïchi became aware that they had arrived at a large gateway;—and he wondered, for he could not remember any large gate in that part of the town, except the main gate of the Amidaji. "*Kaimon!*"[43] the samurai called—and there was a sound of unbarring; and the twain passed on. They traversed a space of garden, and halted again before some entrance; and the retainer cried in a loud voice, "Within there! I have brought Hōïchi." Then came sounds of feet hurrying, and screens sliding, and rain-doors opening, and voices of women in converse. By the language of the women Hōïchi knew them to be domestics in some noble household; but he could not imagine to what place he had been conducted. Little time was allowed him for conjecture. After he had been helped to mount several stone steps, upon the last of which he was told to leave his sandals, a woman's hand guided him along interminable reaches of polished planking, and round pillared angles too many to remember, and over widths amazing of matted floor—into the middle of some vast apartment. There he thought that many great people were assembled: the sound of the rustling of silk was like the sound of leaves in a forest. He heard also a great humming of voices—talking in undertones; and the speech was the speech of courts.

Hōïchi was told to put himself at ease, and he found a kneeling-cushion ready for him. After having taken his place upon it, and tuned his instrument, the voice of a woman—whom he divined to be the *Rōjo*, or matron in charge of the female service—addressed him, saying—

"It is now required that the history of the Heiké be recited, to the accompaniment of the *biwa*."

---

43 A respectful term, signifying the opening of a gate. It was used by samurai when calling to the guards on duty at a lord's gate for admission.

Now the entire recital would have required a time of many nights: therefore Hōïchi ventured a question:—

"As the whole of the story is not soon told, what portion is it augustly desired that I now recite?"

The woman's voice made answer:—

"Recite the story of the battle at Dan-no-ura—for the pity of it is the most deep."[44]

Then Hōïchi lifted up his voice, and chanted the chant of the fight on the bitter sea—wonderfully making his *biwa* to sound like the straining of oars and the rushing of ships, the whirr and the hissing of arrows, the shouting and trampling of men, the crashing of steel upon helmets, the plunging of slain in the flood. And to left and right of him, in the pauses of his playing, he could hear voices murmuring praise: "How marvelous an artist!"—"Never in our own province was playing heard like this!"—"Not in all the empire is there another singer like Hōïchi!" Then fresh courage came to him, and he played and sang yet better than before; and a hush of wonder deepened about him. But when at last he came to tell the fate of the fair and helpless—the piteous perishing of the women and children—and the death-leap of Nii-no-Ama, with the imperial infant in her arms—then all the listeners uttered together one long, long shuddering cry of anguish; and thereafter they wept and wailed so loudly and so wildly that the blind man was frightened by the violence and grief that he had made. For much time the sobbing and the wailing continued. But gradually the sounds of lamentation died away; and again, in the great stillness that followed, Hōïchi heard the voice of the woman whom he supposed to be the Rōjo.

She said:—

---

44   Or the phrase might be rendered, "for the pity of that part is the deepest." The Japanese word for pity in the original text is "aware."

"Although we had been assured that you were a very skillful player upon the *biwa*, and without an equal in recitative, we did not know that any one could be so skillful as you have proved yourself to-night. Our lord has been pleased to say that he intends to bestow upon you a fitting reward. But he desires that you shall perform before him once every night for the next six nights—after which time he will probably make his august return-journey. To-morrow night, therefore, you are to come here at the same hour. The retainer who to-night conducted you will be sent for you... There is another matter about which I have been ordered to inform you. It is required that you shall speak to no one of your visits here, during the time of our lord's august sojourn at Akamagaséki. As he is traveling incognito,[45] he commands that no mention of these things be made... You are now free to go back to your temple."

After Hōïchi had duly expressed his thanks, a woman's hand conducted him to the entrance of the house, where the same retainer, who had before guided him, was waiting to take him home. The retainer led him to the verandah at the rear of the temple, and there bade him farewell.

It was almost dawn when Hōïchi returned; but his absence from the temple had not been observed—as the priest, coming back at a very late hour, had supposed him asleep. During the day Hōïchi was able to take some rest; and he said nothing about his strange adventure. In the middle of the following night the samurai again came for him, and led him to the august assembly, where he gave another recitation with the same success that had attended his previous performance. But during this second visit his absence from the temple was accidentally discovered; and after his return in the

---

45 "Traveling incognito" is at least the meaning of the original phrase—"making a disguised august-journey" (*shinobi no go-ryokō*).

morning he was summoned to the presence of the priest, who said to him, in a tone of kindly reproach:—

"We have been very anxious about you, friend Hōïchi. To go out, blind and alone, at so late an hour, is dangerous. Why did you go without telling us? I could have ordered a servant to accompany you. And where have you been?"

Hōïchi answered, evasively—

"Pardon me kind friend! I had to attend to some private business; and I could not arrange the matter at any other hour."

The priest was surprised, rather than pained, by Hōïchi's reticence: he felt it to be unnatural, and suspected something wrong. He feared that the blind lad had been bewitched or deluded by some evil spirits. He did not ask any more questions; but he privately instructed the men-servants of the temple to keep watch upon Hōïchi's movements, and to follow him in case that he should again leave the temple after dark.

On the very next night, Hōïchi was seen to leave the temple; and the servants immediately lighted their lanterns, and followed after him. But it was a rainy night, and very dark; and before the temple-folks could get to the roadway, Hōïchi had disappeared. Evidently he had walked very fast—a strange thing, considering his blindness; for the road was in a bad condition. The men hurried through the streets, making inquiries at every house which Hōïchi was accustomed to visit; but nobody could give them any news of him. At last, as they were returning to the temple by way of the shore, they were startled by the sound of a *biwa*, furiously played, in the cemetery of the Amidaji. Except for some ghostly fires—such as usually flitted there on dark nights—all was blackness in that direction. But the men at once hastened to the cemetery; and there, by the help of their lanterns, they discovered Hōïchi—sitting alone in the rain before the memorial tomb of Antoku Tennō, making his *biwa* resound, and loudly chanting the chant of the battle of Dan-no-ura. And behind him, and about him, and everywhere above the tombs, the fires of the dead were burning, like candles. Never before had so great a host of Oni-bi appeared in the sight of mortal man...

"Hōïchi San!—Hōïchi San!" the servants cried—"you are bewitched!... Hōïchi San!"

But the blind man did not seem to hear. Strenuously he made his *biwa* to rattle and ring and clang;—more and more wildly he chanted the chant of the battle of Dan-no-ura. They caught hold of him;—they shouted into his ear:—

"Hōïchi San!—Hōïchi San!—come home with us at once!"

Reprovingly he spoke to them:—

"To interrupt me in such a manner, before this august assembly, will not be tolerated."

Whereat, in spite of the weirdness of the thing, the servants could not help laughing. Sure that he had been bewitched, they now seized him, and pulled him up on his feet, and by main force hurried him back to the temple—where he was immediately relieved of his wet clothes, by order of the priest. Then the priest insisted upon a full explanation of his friend's astonishing behavior.

Hōïchi long hesitated to speak. But at last, finding that his conduct had really alarmed and angered the good priest, he decided to abandon his reserve; and he related everything that had happened from the time of first visit of the samurai.

The priest said:—

"Hōïchi, my poor friend, you are now in great danger! How unfortunate that you did not tell me all this before! Your wonderful skill in music has indeed brought you into strange trouble. By this time you must be aware that you have not been visiting any house whatever, but have been passing your nights in the cemetery, among the tombs of the Heiké;—and it was before the memorial-tomb of Antoku Tennō that our people to-night found you, sitting in the rain. All that you have been imagining was illusion—except the calling of the dead. By once obeying them, you have put yourself in their power. If you obey them again, after what has already occurred, they will tear you in pieces. But they would have destroyed you, sooner or later, in any event... Now I shall not be able to remain with you to-night: I am called away to perform another service. But, before I go, it will be necessary to protect your body by writing holy texts upon it."

Before sundown the priest and his acolyte stripped Hoïchi: then, with their writing-brushes, they traced upon his breast and back, head and face and neck, limbs and hands and feet—even upon the soles of his feet, and upon all parts of his body—the text of the holy sutra called Hannya-Shin-Kyō.[46] When this had been done, the priest instructed Hoïchi, saying:—

"To-night, as soon as I go away, you must seat yourself on the verandah, and wait. You will be called. But, whatever may happen, do not answer, and do not move. Say nothing and sit still—as if meditating. If you stir, or make any noise, you will be torn asunder. Do not get frightened; and do not think of calling for help—because no help could save you. If you do exactly as I tell you, the danger will pass, and you will have nothing more to fear."

---

46 The smaller Pragña-Pāramitā-Hridaya-Sutra is thus called in Japanese. Both the smaller and larger sutras called Pragña-Pāramitā ("Transcendent Wisdom") have been translated by the late Professor Max Müller, and can be found in volume xlix of the *Sacred Books of the East* ("Buddhist Mahāyāna Sutras"). Apropos of the magical use of the text, as described in this story, it is worth remarking that the subject of the sutra is the Doctrine of the Emptiness of Forms—that is to say, of the unreal character of all phenomena or noumena... "Form is emptiness; and emptiness is form. Emptiness is not different from form; form is not different from emptiness. What is form—that is emptiness. What is emptiness—that is form... Perception, name, concept, and knowledge, are also emptiness... There is no eye, ear, nose, tongue, body, and mind... But when the envelopment of consciousness has been annihilated, then he [the seeker] becomes free from all fear, and beyond the reach of change, enjoying final Nirvana."

After dark the priest and the acolyte went away; and Hōïchi seated himself on the verandah, according to the instructions given him. He laid his biwa on the planking beside him, and, assuming the attitude of meditation, remained quite still—taking care not to cough, or to breathe audibly. For hours he stayed thus.

Then, from the roadway, he heard the steps coming. They passed the gate, crossed the garden, approached the verandah, stopped—directly in front of him.

"Hōïchi!" the deep voice called. But the blind man held his breath, and sat motionless.

"Hōïchi!" grimly called the voice a second time. Then a third time—savagely:—

"Hōïchi!"

Hōïchi remained as still as a stone—and the voice grumbled:—

"No answer!—that won't do!... Must see where the fellow is."...

There was a noise of heavy feet mounting upon the verandah. The feet approached deliberately—halted beside him. Then, for long minutes—during which Hoichi felt his whole body shake to the beating of his heart—there was dead silence.

At last the gruff voice muttered close to him:—

"Here is the *biwa*; but of the *biwa*-player I see—only two ears!... So that explains why he did not answer: he had no mouth to answer with—there is nothing left of him but his ears... Now to my lord those ears I will take—in proof that the august commands have been obeyed, so far as was possible"...

At that instant Hōïchi felt his ears gripped by fingers of iron, and torn off! Great as the pain was, he gave no cry. The heavy footfalls receded along the verandah—descended into the garden—passed out to the roadway—ceased. From either side of his head, the blind man felt a thick warm trickling; but he dared not lift his hands...

Before sunrise the priest came back. He hastened at once to the verandah in the rear, stepped and slipped upon something clammy, and uttered a cry of horror;—for he saw, by the light of his lantern, that the clamminess was blood. But he perceived Hoichi sitting there, in the attitude of meditation—with the blood still oozing from his wounds.

"My poor Hōïchi!" cried the startled priest—"what is this?... You have been hurt?"

At the sound of his friend's voice, the blind man felt safe. He burst out sobbing, and tearfully told his adventure of the night.

"Poor, poor Hōïchi!" the priest exclaimed—"all my fault!—my very grievous fault!... Everywhere upon your body the holy texts had been written—except upon your ears! I trusted my acolyte to do that part of the work; and it was very, very wrong of me not to have made sure that he had done it!... Well, the matter cannot now be helped;—we can only try to heal your hurts as soon as possible... Cheer up, friend!—the danger is now well over. You will never again be troubled by those visitors."

With the aid of a good doctor, Hōïchi soon recovered from his injuries. The story of his strange adventure spread far and wide, and soon made him famous. Many noble persons went to Akamagaséki to hear him recite; and large presents of money were given to him—so that he became a wealthy man... But from the time of his adventure, he was known only by the appellation of Mimi-nashi-Hōïchi: "Hōïchi-the-Earless."

Oshidori

There was a falconer and hunter, named Sonjō, who lived in the district called Tamura-no-Gō, of the province of Mutsu. One day he went out hunting, and could not find any game. But on his way home, at a place called Akanuma, he perceived a pair of *oshidori*[47] (mandarin-ducks), swimming together in a river that he was about to cross. To kill *oshidori* is not good; but Sonjō happened to be very hungry, and he shot at the pair. His arrow pierced the male: the female escaped into the rushes of the further shore, and disappeared. Sonjō took the dead bird home, and cooked it.

That night he dreamed a dreary dream. It seemed to him that a beautiful woman came into his room, and stood by his pillow, and began to weep. So bitterly did she weep that Sonjō felt as if his heart were being torn out while he listened. And the woman cried to him: "Why—oh! Why did you kill him?—of what wrong was he guilty?... At Akanuma we were so happy together—and you killed him!... What harm did he ever do you? Do you even know what you have done?—oh! Do you know what a cruel, what a wicked thing you have done?... Me too you have killed—for I will not live without my husband!... Only to tell you this I came."...

---

47   From ancient times, in the Far East, these birds have been regarded as emblems of conjugal affection.

Then again she wept aloud—so bitterly that the voice of her crying pierced into the marrow of the listener's bones;—and she sobbed out the words of this poem:—

> *Hi kururéba*
> *Sasoëshi mono wo—*
> *Akanuma no*
> *Makomo no kuré no*
> *Hitori-né zo uki!*

["At the coming of twilight I invited him to return with me—! Now to sleep alone in the shadow of the rushes of Akanuma—ah! What misery unspeakable!"][48]

And after having uttered these verses she exclaimed:—"Ah, you do not know—you cannot know what you have done! But to-morrow, when you go to Akanuma, you will see—you will see…" So saying, and weeping very piteously, she went away.

When Sonjō awoke in the morning, this dream remained so vivid in his mind that he was greatly troubled. He remembered the words:—"But to-morrow, when you go to Akanuma, you will see—you will see." And he resolved to go there at once, that he might learn whether his dream was anything more than a dream.

So he went to Akanuma; and there, when he came to the river-bank, he saw the female *oshidori* swimming alone. In the same moment the bird perceived Sonjō; but, instead of trying to escape, she swam straight towards him, looking at him the while in a strange

---

48 There is a pathetic double meaning in the third verse; for the syllables composing the proper name Akanuma ("Red Marsh") may also be read as *akanu-ma*, signifying "the time of our inseparable (or delightful) relation." So the poem can also be thus rendered:—"When the day began to fail, I had invited him to accompany me…! Now, after the time of that happy relation, what misery for the one who must slumber alone in the shadow of the rushes!"—The *makomo* is a short of large rush, used for making baskets.

fixed way. Then, with her beak, she suddenly tore open her own body, and died before the hunter's eyes...

Sonjō shaved his head, and became a priest.

The Story
of O-Tei

A long time ago, in the town of Niigata, in the province of Echizen, there lived a man called Nagao Chosei.

Nagao was the son of a physician, and was educated for his father's profession. At an early age he had been betrothed to a girl called O-Tei, the daughter of one of his father's friends; and both families had agreed that the wedding should take place as soon as Nagao had finished his studies. But the health of O-Tei proved to be weak; and in her fifteenth year she was attacked by a fatal consumption. When she became aware that she must die, she sent for Nagao to bid him farewell.

As he knelt at her bedside, she said to him:—

"Nagao-Sama,[49] my betrothed, we were promised to each other from the time of our childhood; and we were to have been married at the end of this year. But now I am going to die;—the gods know what is best for us. If I were able to live for some years longer, I could only continue to be a cause of trouble and grief for others. With this frail body, I could not be a good wife; and therefore even to wish to live, for your sake, would be a very selfish wish. I am quite resigned to die; and I want you to promise that you will not grieve… Besides, I want to tell you that I think we shall meet again."…

---

49 "Sama" is a polite suffix attached to personal names.

"Indeed we shall meet again," Nagao answered earnestly. "And in that Pure Land[50] there will be no pain of separation."

"Nay, nay!" she responded softly, "I meant not the Pure Land. I believe that we are destined to meet again in this world—although I shall be buried to-morrow."

Nagao looked at her wonderingly, and saw her smile at his wonder. She continued, in her gentle, dreamy voice—

"Yes, I mean in this world—in your own present life, Nagao-Sama... Providing, indeed, that you wish it. Only, for this thing to happen, I must again be born a girl, and grow up to womanhood. So you would have to wait. Fifteen—sixteen years: that is a long time... But, my promised husband, you are now only nineteen years old."...

Eager to soothe her dying moments, he answered tenderly:—

"To wait for you, my betrothed, were no less a joy than a duty. We are pledged to each other for the time of seven existences."

"But you doubt?" she questioned, watching his face.

"My dear one," he answered, "I doubt whether I should be able to know you in another body, under another name—unless you can tell me of a sign or token."

"That I cannot do," she said. "Only the Gods and the Buddhas know how and where we shall meet. But I am sure—very, very sure—that, if you be not unwilling to receive me, I shall be able to come back to you... Remember these words of mine."...

She ceased to speak; and her eyes closed. She was dead.

* * *

Nagao had been sincerely attached to O-Tei; and his grief was

---

50 A Buddhist term commonly used to signify a kind of heaven.

deep. He had a mortuary tablet made, inscribed with her *zokumyō*;[51] and he placed the tablet in his *butsudan*,[52] and every day set offerings before it. He thought a great deal about the strange things that O-Tei had said to him just before her death; and, in the hope of pleasing her spirit, he wrote a solemn promise to wed her if she could ever return to him in another body. This written promise he sealed with his seal, and placed in the *butsudan* beside the mortuary tablet of O-Tei.

Nevertheless, as Nagao was an only son, it was necessary that he should marry. He soon found himself obliged to yield to the wishes of his family, and to accept a wife of his father's choosing. After his marriage he continued to set offerings before the tablet of O-Tei; and he never failed to remember her with affection. But by degrees her image became dim in his memory—like a dream that is hard to recall. And the years went by.

During those years many misfortunes came upon him. He lost his parents by death—then his wife and his only child. So that he found himself alone in the world. He abandoned his desolate home, and set out upon a long journey in the hope of forgetting his sorrows.

One day, in the course of his travels, he arrived at Ikao—a mountain-village still famed for its thermal springs, and for the beautiful scenery of its neighborhood. In the village-inn at which he stopped, a young girl came to wait upon him; and, at the first sight of her face, he felt his heart leap as it had never leaped before. So strangely did she resemble O-Tei that he pinched himself to

---

51   The Buddhist term *zokumyō* ("profane name") signifies the personal name, borne during life, in contradistinction to the *kaimyō* ("sila-name") or *homyō* ("law-name") given after death—religious posthumous appellations inscribed upon the tomb, and upon the mortuary tablet in the parish-temple. For some account of these, see my paper entitled, "The Literature of the Dead," in *Exotics and Retrospectives*.

52   Buddhist household shrine.

make sure that he was not dreaming. As she went and came—
bringing fire and food, or arranging the chamber of the guest—her
every attitude and motion revived in him some gracious memory
of the girl to whom he had been pledged in his youth. He spoke to
her; and she responded in a soft, clear voice of which the sweetness
saddened him with a sadness of other days.

Then, in great wonder, he questioned her, saying:—

"Elder Sister[53], so much do you look like a person whom I knew
long ago, that I was startled when you first entered this room. Pardon
me, therefore, for asking what is your native place, and what is
your name?"

Immediately—and in the unforgotten voice of the dead—she
thus made answer:—

"My name is O-Tei; and you are Nagao Chosei of Echigo, my
promised husband. Seventeen years ago, I died in Niigata: then you
made in writing a promise to marry me if ever I could come back
to this world in the body of a woman;—and you sealed that written
promise with your seal, and put it in the *butsudan*, beside the tablet
inscribed with my name. And therefore I came back."…

As she uttered these last words, she fell unconscious.

Nagao married her; and the marriage was a happy one. But at
no time afterwards could she remember what she had told him in
answer to his question at Ikao: neither could she remember anything
of her previous existence. The recollection of the former birth—
mysteriously kindled in the moment of that meeting—had again
become obscured, and so thereafter remained.

---

53   Direct translation of a Japanese form of address used toward young, unmarried
women.

282

Ubazakura

Three hundred years ago, in the village called Asamimura, in the district called Onsengori, in the province of Iyō, there lived a good man named Tokubei. This Tokubei was the richest person in the district, and the *muraosa*, or headman, of the village. In most matters he was fortunate; but he reached the age of forty without knowing the happiness of becoming a father. Therefore he and his wife, in the affliction of their childlessness, addressed many prayers to the divinity Fudō Myō Ō, who had a famous temple, called Saihōji, in Asamimura.

At last their prayers were heard: the wife of Tokubei gave birth to a daughter. The child was very pretty; and she received the name of Tsuyu. As the mother's milk was deficient, a milk-nurse, called O-Sodé, was hired for the little one.

O-Tsuyu grew up to be a very beautiful girl; but at the age of fiteen she fell sick, and the doctors thought that she was going to die. In that time the nurse O-Sodé, who loved O-Tsuyu with a real mother's love, went to the temple Saihōji, and fervently prayed to Fudō-Sama on behalf of the girl. Every day, for twenty-one days, she went to the temple and prayed; and at the end of that time, O-Tsuyu suddenly and completely recovered.

Then there was great rejoicing in the house of Tokubei; and he gave a feast to all his friends in celebration of the happy event. But on the night of the feast the nurse O-Sodé was suddenly taken ill;

and on the following morning, the doctor, who had been summoned to attend her, announced that she was dying.

Then the family, in great sorrow, gathered about her bed, to bid her farewell. But she said to them:—

"It is time that I should tell you something which you do not know. My prayer has been heard. I besought Fudō-Sama that I might be permitted to die in the place of O-Tsuyu; and this great favor has been granted me. Therefore you must not grieve about my death... But I have one request to make. I promised Fudō-Sama that I would have a cherry-tree planted in the garden of Saihōji, for a thank-offering and a commemoration. Now I shall not be able myself to plant the tree there: so I must beg that you will fulfill that vow for me... Good-bye, dear friends; and remember that I was happy to die for O-Tsuyu's sake."

After the funeral of O-Sodé, a young cherry-tree—the finest that could be found—was planted in the garden of Saihōji by the parents of O-Tsuyu. The tree grew and flourished; and on the sixteenth day of the second month of the following year—the anniversary of O-Sodé's death—it blossomed in a wonderful way. So it continued to blossom for two hundred and fifty-four years—always upon the sixteenth day of the second month;—and its flowers, pink and white, were like the nipples of a woman's breasts, bedewed with milk. And the people called it *Ubazakura*, the Cherry-tree of the Milk-Nurse.

Diplomacy

It had been ordered that the execution should take place in the garden of the *yashiki*[54]. So the man was taken there, and made to kneel down in a wide sanded space crossed by a line of *tobi-ishi*, or stepping-stones, such as you may still see in Japanese landscape-gardens. His arms were bound behind him. Retainers brought water in buckets, and rice-bags filled with pebbles; and they packed the rice-bags round the kneeling man— so wedging him in that he could not move. The master came, and observed the arrangements. He found them satisfactory, and made no remarks.

Suddenly the condemned man cried out to him:—

"Honored Sir, the fault for which I have been doomed I did not wittingly commit. It was only my very great stupidity which caused the fault. Having been born stupid, by reason of my Karma, I could not always help making mistakes. But to kill a man for being stupid is wrong—and that wrong will be repaid. So surely as you kill me, so surely shall I be avenged;—out of the resentment that you provoke will come the vengeance; and evil will be rendered for evil."...

If any person be killed while feeling strong resentment, the ghost of that person will be able to take vengeance upon the

---

54 The spacious house and grounds of a wealthy person is thus called.

killer. This the samurai knew. He replied very gently—almost caressingly:—

"We shall allow you to frighten us as much as you please—after you are dead. But it is difficult to believe that you mean what you say. Will you try to give us some sign of your great resentment—after your head has been cut off?"

"Assuredly I will," answered the man.

"Very well," said the samurai, drawing his long sword;—"I am now going to cut off your head. Directly in front of you there is a stepping-stone. After your head has been cut off, try to bite the stepping-stone. If your angry ghost can help you to do that, some of us may be frightened... Will you try to bite the stone?"

"I will bite it!" cried the man, in great anger—"I will bite it!—I will bite—"

There was a flash, a swish, a crunching thud: the bound body bowed over the rice sacks—two long blood-jets pumping from the shorn neck;—and the head rolled upon the sand. Heavily toward the stepping-stone it rolled: then, suddenly bounding, it caught the upper edge of the stone between its teeth, clung desperately for a moment, and dropped inert.

None spoke; but the retainers stared in horror at their master. He seemed to be quite unconcerned. He merely held out his sword to the nearest attendant, who, with a wooden dipper, poured water over the blade from haft to point, and then carefully wiped the steel several times with sheets of soft paper... And thus ended the cere-monial part of the incident.

For months thereafter, the retainers and the domestics lived in ceaseless fear of ghostly visitation. None of them doubted that the promised vengeance would come; and their constant terror caused them to hear and to see much that did not exist. They became afraid of the sound of the wind in the bamboos—afraid even of the stirring of shadows in the garden. At last, after taking counsel together, they decided to petition their master to have a *Segaki*-service[55] performed on behalf of the vengeful spirit.

"Quite unnecessary," the samurai said, when his chief retainer had uttered the general wish... "I understand that the desire of a dying man for revenge may be a cause for fear. But in this case there is nothing to fear."

The retainer looked at his master beseechingly, but hesitated to ask the reason of the alarming confidence.

"Oh, the reason is simple enough," declared the samurai, divining the unspoken doubt. "Only the very last intention of the fellow could have been dangerous; and when I challenged him to give me the sign, I diverted his mind from the desire of revenge. He died with the set purpose of biting the stepping-stone; and that purpose he was able to accomplish, but nothing else. All the rest he must have forgotten... So you need not feel any further anxiety about the matter."

—And indeed the dead man gave no more trouble. Nothing at all happened.

---

55   A Buddhist service for the dead.

Of a Mirror and a Bell

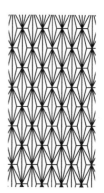

Eight centuries ago, the priests of Mugenyama, in the province of Tōtōmi, wanted a big bell for their temple; and they asked the women of their parish to help them by contributing old bronze mirrors for bell-metal.

[Even to-day, in the courts of certain Japanese temples, you may see heaps of old bronze mirrors contributed for such a purpose. The largest collection of this kind that I ever saw was in the court of a temple of the Jōdo sect, at Hakata, in Kyūshū: the mirrors had been given for the making of a bronze statue of Amida, thirty-three feet high.]

There was at that time a young woman, a farmer's wife, living at Mugenyama, who presented her mirror to the temple, to be used for bell-metal. But afterwards she much regretted her mirror. She remembered things that her mother had told her about it; and she remembered that it had belonged, not only to her mother but to her mother's mother and grandmother; and she remembered some happy smiles which it had reflected. Of course, if she could have offered the priests a certain sum of money in place of the mirror, she could have asked them to give back her heirloom. But she had not the money necessary. Whenever she went to the temple, she saw her mirror lying in the court-yard, behind a railing, among hundreds of other mirrors heaped there together. She knew it by the *Shō-Chiku-Bai* in relief on the back of it—those three fortunate emblems of Pine,

289

Bamboo, and Plumflower, which delighted her baby-eyes when her mother first showed her the mirror. She longed for some chance to steal the mirror, and hide it—that she might thereafter treasure it always. But the chance did not come; and she became very unhappy—felt as if she had foolishly given away a part of her life. She thought about the old saying that a mirror is the Soul of a Woman—(a saying mystically expressed, by the Chinese character for Soul, upon the backs of many bronze mirrors)—and she feared that it was true in weirder ways than she had before imagined. But she could not dare to speak of her pain to anybody.

Now, when all the mirrors contributed for the Mugenyama bell had been sent to the foundry, the bell-founders discovered that there was one mirror among them which would not melt. Again and again they tried to melt it; but it resisted all their efforts. Evidently the woman who had given that mirror to the temple must have regretted the giving. She had not presented her offering with all her heart; and therefore her selfish soul, remaining attached to the mirror, kept it hard and cold in the midst of the furnace.

Of course everybody heard of the matter, and everybody soon knew whose mirror it was that would not melt. And because of this public exposure of her secret fault, the poor woman became very much ashamed and very angry. And as she could not bear the shame, she drowned herself, after having written a farewell letter containing these words:—

"When I am dead, it will not be difficult to melt the mirror and to cast the bell. But, to the person who breaks that bell by ringing it, great wealth will be given by the ghost of me."

—You must know that the last wish or promise of anybody who dies in anger, or performs suicide in anger, is generally supposed to possess a supernatural force. After the dead woman's mirror had been melted, and the bell had been successfully cast, people remembered the words of that letter. They felt sure that the spirit of the writer would give wealth to the breaker of the bell; and, as soon as the bell had been suspended in the court of the temple, they went in multitude to ring it. With all their might and main they swung the ringing-beam; but the bell proved to be a good bell, and it bravely withstood their assaults. Nevertheless, the people were not easily discouraged. Day after day, at all hours, they continued to ring the bell furiously—caring nothing whatever for the protests of the priests. So the ringing became an affliction; and the priests could not endure it; and they got rid of the bell by rolling it down the hill into a swamp. The swamp was deep, and swallowed it up—and that was the end of the bell. Only its legend remains; and in that legend it is called the *Mugen-Kané*, or Bell of Mugen.

Now there are queer old Japanese beliefs in the magical efficacy of a certain mental operation implied, though not described, by the verb *nazoraëru*. The word itself cannot be adequately rendered by any English word; for it is used in relation to many kinds of mimetic magic, as well as in relation to the performance of many religious acts of faith. Common meanings of *nazoraëru*, according to dictionaries, are "to imitate," "to compare," "to liken;" but the esoteric meaning is *to substitute, in imagination, one object or action for another, so as to bring about some magical or miraculous result.*

For example:—you cannot afford to build a Buddhist temple; but you can easily lay a pebble before the image of the Buddha, with the same pious feeling that would prompt you to build a temple if you were rich enough to build one. The merit of so offering the pebble becomes equal, or almost equal, to the merit of erecting a temple… You cannot read the six thousand seven hundred and seventy-one volumes of the Buddhist texts; but you can make a revolving library, containing them, turn round, by pushing it like a windlass. And if you push with an earnest wish that you could read the six thousand seven hundred and seventy-one volumes, you will acquire the same merit as the reading of them would enable you to gain… So much will perhaps suffice to explain the religious meanings of *nazoraëru*.

The magical meanings could not all be explained without a great variety of examples; but, for present purposes, the following will serve. If you should make a little man of straw, for the same reason that Sister Helen made a little man of wax—and nail it, with nails not less than five inches long, to some tree in a temple-grove at the Hour of the Ox[56]—and if the person, imaginatively represented by that little straw man, should die thereafter in atrocious agony—that would illustrate one signification of *nazoraëru*… Or, let us suppose that a robber has entered your house during the night, and carried away your valuables. If you can discover the footprints of that robber in your garden, and then promptly burn a very large *moxa* on each of them, the soles of the feet of the robber will become inflamed, and will allow him no rest until he returns, of his own accord, to put himself at your mercy. That is another kind of mimetic magic expressed by the term *nazoraëru*. And a third kind is illustrated by various legends of the *Mugen-Kané*.

After the bell had been rolled into the swamp, there was, of course, no more chance of ringing it in such wise as to break it. But persons who regretted this loss of opportunity would strike and break objects imaginatively substituted for the bell—thus hoping to please the spirit of the owner of the mirror that had made so much trouble. One of these persons was a woman called Umégaë—famed in Japanese legend because of her relation to Kajiwara Kagésué, a warrior of the Heiké clan. While the pair were traveling together, Kajiwara one day found himself in great straits for want of money; and Umégaé, remembering the tradition of the Bell of Mugen, took

---

56   The two-hour period between 1 AM and 3 AM

a basin of bronze, and, mentally representing it to be the bell, beat upon it until she broke it—crying out, at the same time, for three hundred pieces of gold. A guest of the inn where the pair were stopping made inquiry as to the cause of the banging and the crying, and, on learning the story of the trouble, actually presented Umegae with three hundred *ryō*[57] in gold. Afterwards a song was made about Umégaë's basin of bronze; and that song is sung by dancing girls even to this day:—

> *Umégaë no chōzubachi tataïté*
> *O-kané ga déru naraba*
> *Mina San mi-uké wo*
> *Sōré tanomimasu.*

["*If, by striking upon the wash-basin of Umégaë, I could make honorable money come to me, then would I negotiate for the freedom of all my girl-comrades.*"]

After this happening, the fame of the *Mugen-Kané* became great; and many people followed the example of Umégaë—thereby hoping to emulate her luck. Among these folk was a dissolute farmer who lived near Mugenyama, on the bank of the Ōigawa. Having wasted his substance in riotous living, this farmer made for himself, out of the mud in his garden, a clay-model of the *Mugen-Kané*; and he beat the clay-bell, and broke it—crying out the while for great wealth.

Then, out of the ground before him, rose up the figure of a white-robed woman, with long loose-flowing hair, holding a covered jar. And the woman said: "I have come to answer your fervent prayer as it deserves to be answered. Take, therefore, this jar." So saying, she put the jar into his hands, and disappeared.

---

57 A monetary unit.

Into his house the happy man rushed, to tell his wife the good news. He set down in front of her the covered jar—which was heavy—and they opened it together. And they found that it was filled, up to the very brim, with...

But no!—I really cannot tell you with what it was filled.

Jikininki

Once, when Muso Kokushi, a priest of the Zen sect, was journeying alone through the province of Mino, he lost his way in a mountain-district where there was nobody to direct him. For a long time he wandered about helplessly; and he was beginning to despair of finding shelter for the night, when he perceived, on the top of a hill lighted by the last rays of the sun, one of those little hermitages, called *anjitsu*, which are built for solitary priests. It seemed to be in ruinous condition; but he hastened to it eagerly, and found that it was inhabited by an aged priest, from whom he begged the favor of a night's lodging. This the old man harshly refused; but he directed Muso to a certain hamlet, in the valley adjoining where lodging and food could be obtained.

Muso found his way to the hamlet, which consisted of less than a dozen farm-cottages; and he was kindly received at the dwelling of the headman. Forty or fifty persons were assembled in the principal apartment, at the moment of Muso's arrival; but he was shown into a small separate room, where he was promptly supplied with food and bedding. Being very tired, he lay down to rest at an early hour; but a little before midnight he was roused from sleep by a sound of loud weeping in the next apartment. Presently the sliding-screens were gently pushed apart; and a young man, carrying a lighted lantern, entered the room, respectfully saluted him, and said:—

"Reverend Sir, it is my painful duty to tell you that I am now the responsible head of this house. Yesterday I was only the eldest son. But when you came here, tired as you were, we did not wish that you should feel embarrassed in any way: therefore we did not tell you that father had died only a few hours before. The people whom you saw in the next room are the inhabitants of this village: they all assembled here to pay their last respects to the dead; and now they are going to another village, about three miles off—for by our custom, no one of us may remain in this village during the night after a death has taken place. We make the proper offerings and prayers;—then we go away, leaving the corpse alone. Strange things always happen in the house where a corpse has thus been left: so we think that it will be better for you to come away with us. We can find you good lodging in the other village. But perhaps, as you are a priest, you have no fear of demons or evil spirits; and, if you are not afraid of being left alone with the body, you will be very welcome to the use of this poor house. However, I must tell you that nobody, except a priest, would dare to remain here tonight."

Muso made answer:—

"For your kind intention and your generous hospitality, I am deeply grateful. But I am sorry that you did not tell me of your father's death when I came;—for, though I was a little tired, I certainly was not so tired that I should have found difficulty in doing my duty as a priest. Had you told me, I could have performed the service before your departure. As it is, I shall perform the service after you have gone away; and I shall stay by the body until morning. I do not know what you mean by your words about the danger of staying here alone; but I am not afraid of ghosts or demons: therefore please to feel no anxiety on my account."

The young man appeared to be rejoiced by these assurances, and expressed his gratitude in fitting words. Then the other members of the family, and the folk assembled in the adjoining room, having been told of the priest's kind promises, came to thank him—after which the master of the house said:—

"Now, reverend Sir, much as we regret to leave you alone, we must bid you farewell. By the rule of our village, none of us can stay here after midnight. We beg, kind Sir, that you will take every care of your honorable body, while we are unable to attend upon you. And if you happen to hear or see anything strange during our absence, please tell us of the matter when we return in the morning."

All then left the house, except the priest, who went to the room where the dead body was lying. The usual offerings had been set before the corpse; and a small Buddhist lamp—*tomyo*—was burning. The priest recited the service, and performed the funeral ceremonies—after which he entered into meditation. So meditating he remained through several silent hours; and there was no sound in the deserted village. But, when the hush of the night was at its deepest, there noiselessly entered a Shape, vague and vast; and in the same moment Muso found himself without power to move or speak. He saw that Shape lift the corpse, as with hands, devour it, more quickly than a cat devours a rat—beginning at the head, and eating everything: the hair and the bones and even the shroud. And the monstrous Thing, having thus consumed the body, turned to the offerings, and ate them also. Then it went away, as mysteriously as it had come.

When the villagers returned next morning, they found the priest awaiting them at the door of the headman's dwelling. All in turn saluted him; and when they had entered, and looked about the room, no one expressed any surprise at the disappearance of the dead body and the offerings. But the master of the house said to Muso:—

"Reverend Sir, you have probably seen unpleasant things during the night: all of us were anxious about you. But now we are very happy to find you alive and unharmed. Gladly we would have stayed with you, if it had been possible. But the law of our village, as I told you last evening, obliges us to quit our houses after a death has taken place, and to leave the corpse alone. Whenever this law has been broken, heretofore, some great misfortune has followed. Whenever it is obeyed, we find that the corpse and the offerings disappear during our absence. Perhaps you have seen the cause."

Then Muso told of the dim and awful Shape that had entered the death-chamber to devour the body and the offerings. No person seemed to be surprised by his narration; and the master of the house observed:—

"What you have told us, reverend Sir, agrees with what has been said about this matter from ancient time."

Muso then inquired:—

"Does not the priest on the hill sometimes perform the funeral service for your dead?"

"What priest?" the young man asked.

"The priest who yesterday evening directed me to this village," answered Muso. "I called at his *anjitsu* on the hill yonder. He refused me lodging, but told me the way here."

The listeners looked at each other, as in astonishment; and, after a moment of silence, the master of the house said:—

"Reverend Sir, there is no priest and there is no *anjitsu* on the hill. For the time of many generations there has not been any resident-priest in this neighborhood."

Muso said nothing more on the subject; for it was evident that his kind hosts supposed him to have been deluded by some goblin. But after having bidden them farewell, and obtained all necessary information as to his road, he determined to look again for the hermitage on the hill, and so to ascertain whether he had really been deceived. He found the *anjitsu* without any difficulty; and, this time, its aged occupant invited him to enter. When he had done so, the hermit humbly bowed down before him, exclaiming:—"Ah!

I am ashamed!—I am very much ashamed!—I am exceedingly ashamed!"

"You need not be ashamed for having refused me shelter," said Muso. "You directed me to the village yonder, where I was very kindly treated; and I thank you for that favor."

"I can give no man shelter," the recluse made answer;—and it is not for the refusal that I am ashamed. I am ashamed only that you should have seen me in my real shape—for it was I who devoured the corpse and the offerings last night before your eyes… Know, reverend Sir, that I am a *jikininki*,[58]—an eater of human flesh. Have pity upon me, and suffer me to confess the secret fault by which I became reduced to this condition.

"A long, long time ago, I was a priest in this desolate region. There was no other priest for many leagues around. So, in that time, the bodies of the mountain-folk who died used to be brought here—sometimes from great distances—in order that I might repeat over them the holy service. But I repeated the service and performed the rites only as a matter of business;—I thought only of the food and the clothes that my sacred profession enabled me to gain. And because of this selfish impiety I was reborn, immediately after my death, into the state of a *jikininki*. Since then I have been obliged to feed upon the corpses of the people who die in this district: every one of them I must devour in the way that you saw last night… Now, reverend Sir, let me beseech you to perform a *Segaki*-service[59] for me: help me by your prayers, I

---

58   Literally, a man-eating goblin. The Japanese narrator gives also the Sanscrit term, "Rakshasa;" but this word is quite as vague as *jikininki*, since there are many kinds of Rakshasas. Apparently the word *jikininki* signifies here one of the *Baramon-Rasetsu-Gaki*—forming the twenty-sixth class of pretas enumerated in the old Buddhist books.

59   A *Segaki*-service is a special Buddhist service performed on behalf of beings supposed to have entered into the condition of *gaki* (pretas), or hungry spirits. For a brief account of such a service, see my Japanese Miscellany.

entreat you, so that I may be soon able to escape from this horrible state of existence..."

No sooner had the hermit uttered this petition than he disappeared; and the hermitage also disappeared at the same instant. And Muso Kokushi found himself kneeling alone in the high grass, beside an ancient and moss-grown tomb of the form called *go-rin-ishi*,[60] which seemed to be the tomb of a priest.

---

60 Literally, "five-circle [or five-zone] stone." A funeral monument consisting of five parts superimposed—each of a different form—symbolizing the five mystic elements: Ether, Air, Fire, Water, Earth.

Mujina

On the Akasaka Road, in Tōkyō, there is a slope called Kii-no-kuni-zaka—which means the Slope of the Province of Kii. I do not know why it is called the Slope of the Province of Kii. On one side of this slope you see an ancient moat, deep and very wide, with high green banks rising up to some place of gardens;—and on the other side of the road extend the long and lofty walls of an imperial palace. Before the era of street-lamps and *jinrikishas*, this neighborhood was very lonesome after dark; and belated pedestrians would go miles out of their way rather than mount the Kii-no-kuni-zaka, alone, after sunset.

All because of a Mujina that used to walk there.[61]

The last man who saw the Mujina was an old merchant of the Kyōbashi quarter, who died about thirty years ago. This is the story, as he told it:—

One night, at a late hour, he was hurrying up the Kii-no-kuni-zaka, when he perceived a woman crouching by the moat, all alone, and weeping bitterly. Fearing that she intended to drown herself, he stopped to offer her any assistance or consolation in his power. She appeared to be a slight and graceful person, handsomely dressed; and her hair was arranged like that of a young girl of good family.

---

61 A kind of badger. Certain animals were thought to be able to transform themselves and cause mischief for humans.

"O-jochū,"[62] he exclaimed, approaching her—"O-jochū, do not cry like that!... Tell me what the trouble is; and if there be any way to help you, I shall be glad to help you." (He really meant what he said; for he was a very kind man.) But she continued to weep—hiding her face from him with one of her long sleeves. "O-jochū," he said again, as gently as he could—"please, please listen to me!... This is no place for a young lady at night! Do not cry, I implore you!—only tell me how I may be of some help to you!" Slowly she rose up, but turned her back to him, and continued to moan and sob behind her sleeve. He laid his hand lightly upon her shoulder, and pleaded:—"O-jochū!—O-jochū!—O-jochū!... Listen to me, just for one little moment!... O-jochū!—O-jochū!"... Then that O-jochū turned around, and dropped her sleeve, and stroked her face with her hand;—and the man saw that she had no eyes or nose or mouth—and he screamed and ran away.[63]

Up Kii-no-kuni-zaka he ran and ran; and all was black and empty before him. On and on he ran, never daring to look back; and at last he saw a lantern, so far away that it looked like the gleam of a firefly; and he made for it. It proved to be only the lantern of an itinerant *soba*-seller,[64] who had set down his stand by the road-side; but any light and any human companionship was good after that experience; and he flung himself down at the feet of the soba-seller, crying out, "Ah!—aa!!—*aa!!!*"...

"*Kore! Kore!*"[65] roughly exclaimed the *soba*-man. "Here! What is the matter with you? Anybody hurt you?"

---

62 *O-jochū* ("honorable damsel"), a polite form of address used in speaking to a young lady whom one does not know.

63 An apparition with a smooth, totally featureless face, called a "*nopperabo*," is a stock part of the Japanese pantheon of ghosts and demons.

64 *Soba* is a preparation of buckwheat, somewhat resembling vermicelli.

65 An exclamation of annoyed alarm.

"No—nobody hurt me," panted the other—"only... *Ah!—aa!*"

"—Only scared you?" queried the peddler, unsympathetically. "Robbers?"

"Not robbers—not robbers," gasped the terrified man... "I saw... I saw a woman—by the moat;—and she showed me... *Ah!* I cannot tell you what she showed me!"...

"*He!*[66] Was it anything like THIS that she showed you?" cried the *soba*-man, stroking his own face—which therewith became like unto an Egg... And, simultaneously, the light went out.

66 Well!

Rokuro-Kubi

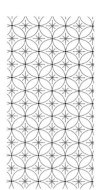

early five hundred years ago there was a samurai, named Isogai Heidazaemon Taketsura, in the service of the Lord Kikuji, of Kyūshū. This Isogai had inherited, from many warlike ancestors, a natural aptitude for military exercises, and extraordinary strength. While yet a boy he had surpassed his teachers in the art of swordsmanship, in archery, and in the use of the spear, and had displayed all the capacities of a daring and skillful soldier. Afterwards, in the time of the Eikyō[67] war, he so distinguished himself that high honors were bestowed upon him. But when the house of Kikuji came to ruin, Isogai found himself without a master. He might then easily have obtained service under another daimyo; but as he had never sought distinction for his own sake alone, and as his heart remained true to his former lord, he preferred to give up the world. So he cut off his hair, and became a traveling priest—taking the Buddhist name of Kwairyo.

But always, under the *koromo*[68] of the priest, Kwairyo kept warm within him the heart of the samurai. As in other years he had laughed at peril, so now also he scorned danger; and in all weathers and all seasons he journeyed to preach the good Law in places where no other priest would have dared to go. For that age was an age of

---

67   The period of Eikyō lasted from 1429 to 1441.

68   The upper robe of a Buddhist priest is thus called.

violence and disorder; and upon the highways there was no security for the solitary traveler, even if he happened to be a priest.

In the course of his first long journey, Kwairyo had occasion to visit the province of Kai. One evening, as he was traveling through the mountains of that province, darkness overcame him in a very lonesome district, leagues away from any village. So he resigned himself to pass the night under the stars; and having found a suitable grassy spot, by the roadside, he lay down there, and prepared to sleep. He had always welcomed discomfort; and even a bare rock was for him a good bed, when nothing better could be found, and the root of a pine-tree an excellent pillow. His body was iron; and he never troubled himself about dews or rain or frost or snow.

Scarcely had he lain down when a man came along the road, carrying an axe and a great bundle of chopped wood. This woodcutter halted on seeing Kwairyo lying down, and, after a moment of silent observation, said to him in a tone of great surprise:—

"What kind of a man can you be, good Sir, that you dare to lie down alone in such a place as this?... There are haunters about here—many of them. Are you not afraid of Hairy Things?"

"My friend," cheerfully answered Kwairyo, "I am only a wandering priest—a 'Cloud-and-Water-Guest,' as folks call it: *Unsui-no-ryokaku*.[69] And I am not in the least afraid of Hairy Things—if you mean goblin-foxes, or goblin-badgers, or any creatures of that kind. As for lonesome places, I like them: they are suitable for meditation. I am accustomed to sleeping in the open air: and I have learned never to be anxious about my life."

"You must be indeed a brave man, Sir Priest," the peasant responded, "to lie down here! This place has a bad name—a very bad name. But, as the proverb has it, *Kunshi ayayuki ni chikayorazu*

---

69   A term for itinerant priests.

['The superior man does not needlessly expose himself to peril'];
and I must assure you, Sir, that it is very dangerous to sleep here.
Therefore, although my house is only a wretched thatched hut, let
me beg of you to come home with me at once. In the way of food,
I have nothing to offer you; but there is a roof at least, and you can
sleep under it without risk."

He spoke earnestly; and Kwairyo, liking the kindly tone of the
man, accepted this modest offer. The woodcutter guided him along
a narrow path, leading up from the main road through mountain-
forest. It was a rough and dangerous path—sometimes skirting
precipices—sometimes offering nothing but a network of slippery
roots for the foot to rest upon—sometimes winding over or between
masses of jagged rock. But at last Kwairyo found himself upon a
cleared space at the top of a hill, with a full moon shining overhead;
and he saw before him a small thatched cottage, cheerfully lighted
from within. The woodcutter led him to a shed at the back of the
house, whither water had been conducted, through bamboo-pipes,
from some neighboring stream; and the two men washed their feet.
Beyond the shed was a vegetable garden, and a grove of cedars and
bamboos; and beyond the trees appeared the glimmer of a cascade,
pouring from some loftier height, and swaying in the moonshine
like a long white robe.

As Kwairyo entered the cottage with his guide, he perceived
four persons—men and women—warming their hands at a little fire
kindled in the ro[70] of the principle apartment. They bowed low to
the priest, and greeted him in the most respectful manner. Kwairyo
wondered that persons so poor, and dwelling in such a solitude,
should be aware of the polite forms of greeting. "These are good

---

70 A sort of little fireplace, contrived in the floor of a room, is thus described.
The ro is usually a square shallow cavity, lined with metal and half-filled with
ashes, in which charcoal is lighted.

people," he thought to himself; "and they must have been taught by someone well acquainted with the rules of propriety." Then turning to his host—the *aruji*, or house-master, as the others called him—Kwairyo said:—

"From the kindness of your speech, and from the very polite welcome given me by your household, I imagine that you have not always been a woodcutter. Perhaps you formerly belonged to one of the upper classes?"

Smiling, the woodcutter answered:—

"Sir, you are not mistaken. Though now living as you find me, I was once a person of some distinction. My story is the story of a ruined life—ruined by my own fault. I used to be in the service of a daimyo; and my rank in that service was not inconsiderable. But I loved women and wine too well; and under the influence of passion I acted wickedly. My selfishness brought about the ruin of our house, and caused the death of many persons. Retribution followed me; and I long remained a fugitive in the land. Now I often pray that I may be able to make some atonement for the evil which I did, and to re-establish the ancestral home. But I fear that I shall never find any way of so doing. Nevertheless, I try to overcome the karma of my errors by sincere repentance, and by helping as far as I can, those who are unfortunate."

Kwairyo was pleased by this announcement of good resolve; and he said to the *aruji*:—

"My friend, I have had occasion to observe that man, prone to folly in their youth, may in after years become very earnest in right living. In the holy sutras it is written that those strongest in wrong-doing can become, by power of good resolve, the strongest in right-doing. I do not doubt that you have a good heart; and I hope that better fortune will come to you. To-night I shall recite the sutras for your sake, and pray that you may obtain the force to overcome the karma of any past errors."

With these assurances, Kwairyo bade the *aruji* good-night; and his host showed him to a very small side-room, where a bed had been made ready. Then all went to sleep except the priest, who began to read the sutras by the light of a paper lantern. Until a late hour he continued to read and pray: then he opened a little window in his little sleeping-room, to take a last look at the landscape before lying down. The night was beautiful: there was no cloud in the sky: there was no wind; and the strong moonlight threw down sharp black shadows of foliage, and glittered on the dews of the garden. Shrillings of crickets and bell-insects[71] made a musical tumult; and the sound of the neighboring cascade deepened with the night. Kwairyo felt thirsty as he listened to the noise of the water; and, remembering the bamboo aqueduct at the rear of the house, he thought that he could go there and get a drink without disturbing the sleeping household. Very gently he pushed apart the sliding-screens that separated his room from the main apartment; and he saw, by the light of the lantern, five recumbent bodies—without heads!

For one instant he stood bewildered—imagining a crime. But in another moment he perceived that there was no blood, and that the headless necks did not look as if they had been cut. Then he thought to himself:—"Either this is an illusion made by goblins, or I have been lured into the dwelling of a Rokuro-Kubi...[72] In the book *Soshinki*[73] it is written that if one find the body of a Rokuro-Kubi without its head, and remove the body to another place, the head will never be able to join itself again to the neck. And the book further

---

71 Direct translation of "*suzumushi*," a kind of cricket with a distinctive chirp like a tiny bell, whence the name.

72 Now a rokuro-kubi is ordinarily conceived as a goblin whose neck stretches out to great lengths, but which nevertheless always remains attached to its body.

73 A Chinese collection of stories on the supernatural.

says that when the head comes back and finds that its body has been moved, it will strike itself upon the floor three times—bounding like a ball—and will pant as in great fear, and presently die. Now, if these be Rokuro-Kubi, they mean me no good;—so I shall be justified in following the instructions of the book.''...

He seized the body of the *aruji* by the feet, pulled it to the window, and pushed it out. Then he went to the back-door, which he found barred; and he surmised that the heads had made their exit through the smoke-hole in the roof, which had been left open. Gently unbarring the door, he made his way to the garden, and proceeded with all possible caution to the grove beyond it. He heard voices talking in the grove; and he went in the direction of the voices—stealing from shadow to shadow, until he reached a good hiding-place. Then, from behind a trunk, he caught sight of the heads—all five of them—flitting about, and chatting as they flitted. They were eating worms and insects which they found on the ground or among the trees. Presently the head of the *aruji* stopped eating and said:—

"Ah, that traveling priest who came to-night!—how fat all his body is! When we shall have eaten him, our bellies will be well filled... I was foolish to talk to him as I did;—it only set him to reciting the sutras on behalf of my soul! To go near him while he is reciting would be difficult; and we cannot touch him so long as he is praying. But as it is now nearly morning, perhaps he has gone to sleep... Some one of you go to the house and see what the fellow is doing."

Another head—the head of a young woman—immediately rose up and flitted to the house, lightly as a bat. After a few minutes it came back, and cried out huskily, in a tone of great alarm:—

"That traveling priest is not in the house;—he is gone! But that is not the worst of the matter. He has taken the body of our *aruji*; and I do not know where he has put it."

At this announcement the head of the *aruji*—distinctly visible in the moonlight—assumed a frightful aspect: its eyes opened monstrously; its hair stood up bristling; and its teeth gnashed. Then a cry burst from its lips; and—weeping tears of rage—it exclaimed:—

"Since my body has been moved, to rejoin it is not possible! Then I must die!... And all through the work of that priest! Before I die I will get at that priest!—I will tear him!—I will devour him!... AND THERE HE IS—behind that tree!—hiding behind that tree! See him!—the fat coward!"...

In the same moment the head of the *aruji*, followed by the other four heads, sprang at Kwairyo. But the strong priest had already armed himself by plucking up a young tree; and with that tree he struck the heads as they came—knocking them from him with tremendous blows. Four of them fled away. But the head of the *aruji*, though battered again and again, desperately continued to bound at the priest, and at last caught him by the left sleeve of his robe. Kwairyo, however, as quickly gripped the head by its topknot, and repeatedly struck it. It did not release its hold; but it uttered a long moan, and thereafter ceased to struggle. It was dead. But its teeth still held the sleeve; and, for all his great strength, Kwairyo could not force open the jaws.

With the head still hanging to his sleeve he went back to the house, and there caught sight of the other four Rokuro-Kubi squatting together, with their bruised and bleeding heads reunited to their bodies. But when they perceived him at the back-door all screamed, "The priest! The priest!"—and fled, through the other doorway, out into the woods.

Eastward the sky was brightening; day was about to dawn; and Kwairyo knew that the power of the goblins was limited to the hours of darkness. He looked at the head clinging to his sleeve—its face all fouled with blood and foam and clay; and he laughed aloud as he thought to himself: "*What a miyage!*[74]—the head of a goblin!" After which he gathered together his few belongings, and leisurely descended the mountain to continue his journey.

Right on he journeyed, until he came to Suwa in Shinano; and into the main street of Suwa he solemnly strode, with the head dangling at his elbow. Then woman fainted, and children screamed and ran away; and there was a great crowding and clamoring until the *torite* (as the police in those days were called) seized the priest, and took him to jail. For they supposed the head to be the head of a murdered man who, in the moment of being killed, had caught the murderer's sleeve in his teeth. As for Kwairyo, he only smiled and said nothing when they questioned him. So, after having passed a night in prison, he was brought before the magistrates of the district. Then he was ordered to explain how he, a priest, had been found with the head of a man fastened to his sleeve, and why he had dared thus shamelessly to parade his crime in the sight of people.

Kwairyo laughed long and loudly at these questions; and then he said:—

"Sirs, I did not fasten the head to my sleeve: it fastened itself there—much against my will. And I have not committed any crime. For this is not the head of a man; it is the head of a goblin;—and, if I caused the death of the goblin, I did not do so by any shedding of blood, but simply by taking the precautions necessary to assure my own safety.".... And he proceeded to relate the whole of the adventure—bursting into another hearty laugh as he told of his encounter with the five heads.

But the magistrates did not laugh. They judged him to be a

---

74 A present made to friends or to the household on returning from a journey is thus called. Ordinarily, of course, the *miyage* consists of something produced in the locality to which the journey has been made: this is the point of Kwairyo's jest.

hardened criminal, and his story an insult to their intelligence. Therefore, without further questioning, they decided to order his immediate execution—all of them except one, a very old man. This aged officer had made no remark during the trial; but, after having heard the opinion of his colleagues, he rose up, and said:—

"Let us first examine the head carefully; for this, I think, has not yet been done. If the priest has spoken truth, the head itself should bear witness for him... Bring the head here!"

So the head, still holding in its teeth the *koromo* that had been stripped from Kwairyo's shoulders, was put before the judges. The old man turned it round and round, carefully examined it, and discovered, on the nape of its neck, several strange red characters. He called the attention of his colleagues to these, and also bade them observe that the edges of the neck nowhere presented the appearance of having been cut by any weapon. On the contrary, the line of leverance was smooth as the line at which a falling leaf detaches itself from the stem... Then said the elder:—

"I am quite sure that the priest told us nothing but the truth. This is the head of a Rokuro-Kubi. In the book *Nan-ho-i-butsu-shi* it is written that certain red characters can always be found upon the nape of the neck of a real Rokuro-Kubi. There are the characters: you can see for yourselves that they have not been painted. Moreover, it is well known that such goblins have been dwelling in the mountains of the province of Kai from very ancient time... But you, Sir," he exclaimed, turning to Kwairyo—"what sort of sturdy priest may you be? Certainly you have given proof of a courage that few priests possess; and you have the air of a soldier rather than a priest. Perhaps you once belonged to the samurai-class?"

"You have guessed rightly, Sir," Kwairyo responded. "Before becoming a priest, I long followed the profession of arms; and in those days I never feared man or devil. My name then was Isogai

Heidazaemon Taketsura of Kyūshū: there may be some among you who remember it."

At the mention of that name, a murmur of admiration filled the court-room; for there were many present who remembered it. And Kwairyo immediately found himself among friends instead of judges—friends anxious to prove their admiration by fraternal kindness. With honor they escorted him to the residence of the daimyo, who welcomed him, and feasted him, and made him a handsome present before allowing him to depart. When Kwairyo left Suwa, he was as happy as any priest is permitted to be in this transitory world. As for the head, he took it with him—jocosely insisting that he intended it for a *miyage*.

And now it only remains to tell what became of the head.

A day or two after leaving Suwa, Kwairyo met with a robber, who stopped him in a lonesome place, and bade him strip. Kwairyo at once removed his *koromo*, and offered it to the robber, who then first perceived what was hanging to the sleeve. Though brave, the highwayman was startled: he dropped the garment, and sprang back. Then he cried out:—"You!—what kind of a priest are you? Why, you are a worse man than I am! It is true that I have killed people; but I never walked about with anybody's head fastened to my sleeve... Well, Sir priest, I suppose we are of the same calling; and I must say that I admire you!... Now that head would be of use to me: I could frighten people with it. Will you sell it? You can have my robe in exchange for your *koromo*; and I will give you five *ryō* for the head."

Kwairyo answered:—

"I shall let you have the head and the robe if you insist; but I must tell you that this is not the head of a man. It is a goblin's head. So, if you buy it, and have any trouble in consequence, please to remember that you were not deceived by me."

"What a nice priest you are!" exclaimed the robber. "You kill men, and jest about it!... But I am really in earnest. Here is my robe; and here is the money;—and let me have the head... What is the use of joking?"

"Take the thing," said Kwairyo. "I was not joking. The only joke—if there be any joke at all—is that you are fool enough to pay good money for a goblin's head." And Kwairyo, loudly laughing, went upon his way.

Thus the robber got the head and the *koromo*; and for some time he played goblin-priest upon the highways. But, reaching the neighborhood of Suwa, he there leaned the true story of the head; and he then became afraid that the spirit of the Rokuro-Kubi might give him trouble. So he made up his mind to take back the head to the place from which it had come, and to bury it with its body. He found his way to the lonely cottage in the mountains of Kai; but nobody was there, and he could not discover the body. Therefore he buried the head by itself, in the grove behind the cottage; and he had a tombstone set up over the grave; and he caused a *Segaki*-service to be performed on behalf of the spirit of the Rokuro-Kubi. And that tombstone—known as the Tombstone of the Rokuro-Kubi—may be seen (at least so the Japanese story-teller declares) even unto this day.

A Dead Secret

A long time ago, in the province of Tamba, there lived a rich merchant named Inamuraya Gensuke. He had a daughter called O-Sono. As she was very clever and pretty, he thought it would be a pity to let her grow up with only such teaching as the country-teachers could give her: so he sent her, in care of some trusty attendants, to Kyoto, that she might be trained in the polite accomplishments taught to the ladies of the capital. After she had thus been educated, she was married to a friend of her father's family—a merchant named Nagaraya;—and she lived happily with him for nearly four years. They had one child—a boy. But O-Sono fell ill and died, in the fourth year after her marriage.

On the night after the funeral of O-Sono, her little son said that his mamma had come back, and was in the room upstairs. She had smiled at him, but would not talk to him: so he became afraid, and ran away. Then some of the family went upstairs to the room which had been O-Sono's; and they were startled to see, by the light of a small lamp which had been kindled before a shrine in that room, the figure of the dead mother. She appeared as if standing in front of a *tansu*, or chest of drawers, that still contained her ornaments and her wearing-apparel. Her head and shoulders could be very distinctly seen; but from the waist downwards the figure thinned into invisibility;—it was like an imperfect reflection of her, and transparent as a shadow on water.

Then the folk were afraid, and left the room. Below they consulted together; and the mother of O-Sono's husband said: "A woman is fond of her small things; and O-Sono was much attached to her belongings. Perhaps she has come back to look at them. Many dead persons will do that—unless the things be given to the parish-temple. If we present O-Sono's robes and girdles to the temple, her spirit will probably find rest."

It was agreed that this should be done as soon as possible. So on the following morning the drawers were emptied; and all of O-Sono's ornaments and dresses were taken to the temple. But she came back the next night, and looked at the *tansu* as before. And she came back also on the night following, and the night after that, and every night;—and the house became a house of fear.

The mother of O-Sono's husband then went to the parish-temple, and told the chief priest all that had happened, and asked for ghostly counsel. The temple was a Zen temple; and the head-priest was a learned old man, known as Daigen Osho. He said: "There must be something about which she is anxious, in or near that *tansu*."—"But we emptied all the drawers," replied the woman;—"there is nothing in the *tansu*."—"Well," said Daigen Osho, "to-night I shall go to your house, and keep watch in that room, and see what can be done. You must give orders that no person shall enter the room while I am watching, unless I call."

After sundown, Daigen Osho went to the house, and found the room made ready for him. He remained there alone, reading the sutras; and nothing appeared until after the Hour of the Rat.[75] Then the figure of O-Sono suddenly outlined itself in front of the *tansu*. Her face had a wistful look; and she kept her eyes fixed upon the *tansu*.

---

75   The Hour of the Rat (*Ne-no-Koku*), according to the old Japanese method of reckoning time, was the first hour. It corresponded to the time between our midnight and two o'clock in the morning; for the ancient Japanese hours were each equal to two modern hours.

The priest uttered the holy formula prescribed in such cases, and then, addressing the figure by the *kaimyō*[76] of O-Sono, said:—"I have come here in order to help you. Perhaps in that *tansu* there is something about which you have reason to feel anxious. Shall I try to find it for you?" The shadow appeared to give assent by a slight motion of the head; and the priest, rising, opened the top drawer. It was empty. Successively he opened the second, the third, and the fourth drawer;—he searched carefully behind them and beneath them;—he carefully examined the interior of the chest. He found nothing. But the figure remained gazing as wistfully as before. "What can she want?" thought the priest. Suddenly it occurred to him that there might be something hidden under the paper with which the drawers were lined. He removed the lining of the first drawer:—nothing! He removed the lining of the second and third drawers:—still nothing. But under the lining of the lowermost drawer he found—a letter. "Is this the thing about which you have been troubled?" he asked. The shadow of the woman turned toward him—her faint gaze fixed upon the letter. "Shall I burn it for you?" he asked. She bowed before him. "It shall be burned in the temple this very morning," he promised;—"and no one shall read it, except myself." The figure smiled and vanished.

Dawn was breaking as the priest descended the stairs, to find the family waiting anxiously below. "Do not be anxious," he said to them: "She will not appear again." And she never did.

The letter was burned. It was a love-letter written to O-Sono in the time of her studies at Kyoto. But the priest alone knew what was in it; and the secret died with him.

---

76 *Kaimyō*, the posthumous Buddhist name, or religious name, given to the dead. Strictly speaking, the meaning of the word is sila-name. (See my paper entitled, "The Literature of the Dead" in *Exotics and Retrospectives*.)

Yuki-Onna

In a village of Musashi Province, there lived two wood-cutters: Mosaku and Minokichi. At the time of which I am speaking, Mosaku was an old man; and Minokichi, his apprentice, was a lad of eighteen years. Every day they went together to a forest situated about five miles from their village. On the way to that forest there is a wide river to cross; and there is a ferry-boat. Several times a bridge was built where the ferry is; but the bridge was each time carried away by a flood. No common bridge can resist the current there when the river rises.

Mosaku and Minokichi were on their way home, one very cold evening, when a great snowstorm overtook them. They reached the ferry; and they found that the boatman had gone away, leaving his boat on the other side of the river. It was no day for swimming; and the woodcutters took shelter in the ferryman's hut—thinking themselves lucky to find any shelter at all. There was no brazier in the hut, nor any place in which to make a fire: it was only a two-mat[77] hut, with a single door, but no window. Mosaku and Minokichi fastened the door, and lay down to rest, with their straw rain-coats over them. At first they did not feel very cold; and they thought that the storm would soon be over.

The old man almost immediately fell asleep; but the boy,

---

77   That is to say, with a floor-surface of about six feet square.

Minokichi, lay awake a long time, listening to the awful wind, and the continual slashing of the snow against the door. The river was roaring; and the hut swayed and creaked like a junk at sea. It was a terrible storm; and the air was every moment becoming colder; and Minokichi shivered under his rain-coat. But at last, in spite of the cold, he too fell asleep.

He was awakened by a showering of snow in his face. The door of the hut had been forced open; and, by the snow-light (*yuki-akari*), he saw a woman in the room—a woman all in white. She was bending above Mosaku, and blowing her breath upon him;—and her breath was like a bright white smoke. Almost in the same moment she turned to Minokichi, and stooped over him. He tried to cry out, but found that he could not utter any sound. The white woman bent down over him, lower and lower, until her face almost touched him; and he saw that she was very beautiful—though her eyes made him afraid. For a little time she continued to look at him;—then she smiled, and she whispered:—"I intended to treat you like the other man. But I cannot help feeling some pity for you—because you are so young... You are a pretty boy, Minokichi; and I will not hurt you now. But, if you ever tell anybody—even your own mother—about what you have seen this night, I shall know it; and then I will kill you... Remember what I say!"

With these words, she turned from him, and passed through the doorway. Then he found himself able to move; and he sprang up, and looked out. But the woman was nowhere to be seen; and the snow was driving furiously into the hut. Minokichi closed the door, and secured it by fixing several billets of wood against it. He wondered if the wind had blown it open;—he thought that he might have been only dreaming, and might have mistaken the gleam of the snow-light in the doorway for the figure of a white woman: but he could not be sure. He called to Mosaku, and was frightened because the old man did not answer. He put out his hand in the dark, and touched Mosaku's face, and found that it was ice! Mosaku was stark and dead...

By dawn the storm was over; and when the ferryman returned to his station, a little after sunrise, he found Minokichi lying senseless beside the frozen body of Mosaku. Minokichi was promptly cared for, and soon came to himself; but he remained a long time ill from the effects of the cold of that terrible night. He had been greatly frightened also by the old man's death; but he said nothing about the vision of the woman in white. As soon as he got well again, he returned to his calling—going alone every morning to the forest, and coming back at nightfall with his bundles of wood, which his mother helped him to sell.

One evening, in the winter of the following year, as he was on his way home, he overtook a girl who happened to be traveling by the same road. She was a tall, slim girl, very good-looking; and she answered Minokichi's greeting in a voice as pleasant to the ear as the voice of a song-bird. Then he walked beside her; and they began to talk. The girl said that her name was O-Yuki[78]; that she had lately lost both of her parents; and that she was going to Yedo[79], where she happened to have some poor relations, who might help her to find a situation as a servant. Minokichi soon felt charmed by this strange girl; and the more that he looked at her, the handsomer she appeared to be. He asked her whether she was yet betrothed; and she answered, laughingly, that she was free. Then, in her turn, she asked Minokichi whether he was married, or pledged to marry; and he told her that, although he had only a widowed mother to support, the question of an "honorable daughter-in-law" had not yet been considered, as he was very young... After these confidences, they

---

78   This name, signifying "Snow," is not uncommon. On the subject of Japanese female names, see my paper in the volume entitled *Shadowings*.

79   Also spelled Edo, the former name of Tōkyō.

walked on for a long while without speaking; but, as the proverb declares, *Ki ga areba, me mo kuchi hodo ni mono wo iu*: "When the wish is there, the eyes can say as much as the mouth." By the time they reached the village, they had become very much pleased with each other; and then Minokichi asked O-Yuki to rest awhile at his house. After some shy hesitation, she went there with him; and his mother made her welcome, and prepared a warm meal for her. O-Yuki behaved so nicely that Minokichi's mother took a sudden fancy to her, and persuaded her to delay her journey to Yedo. And the natural end of the matter was that Yuki never went to Yedo at all. She remained in the house, as an "honorable daughter-in-law."

O-Yuki proved a very good daughter-in-law. When Minokichi's mother came to die—some five years later—her last words were words of affection and praise for the wife of her son. And O-Yuki bore Minokichi ten children, boys and girls—handsome children all of them, and very fair of skin.

The country-folk thought O-Yuki a wonderful person, by nature different from themselves. Most of the peasant-women age early; but O-Yuki, even after having become the mother of ten children, looked as young and fresh as on the day when she had first come to the village.

One night, after the children had gone to sleep, O-Yuki was sewing by the light of a paper lamp; and Minokichi, watching her, said:—

"To see you sewing there, with the light on your face, makes me think of a strange thing that happened when I was a lad of eighteen. I then saw somebody as beautiful and white as you are now—indeed, she was very like you."...

Without lifting her eyes from her work, O-Yuki responded:—

"Tell me about her... Where did you see her?"

Then Minokichi told her about the terrible night in the ferryman's hut—and about the White Woman that had stooped above him, smiling and whispering—and about the silent death of old Mosaku. And he said:—

"Asleep or awake, that was the only time that I saw a being as beautiful as you. Of course, she was not a human being; and I was afraid of her—very much afraid—but she was so white!... Indeed, I have never been sure whether it was a dream that I saw, or the Woman of the Snow."...

O-Yuki flung down her sewing, and arose, and bowed above Minokichi where he sat, and shrieked into his face:—

"It was I—I—I! Yuki it was! And I told you then that I would kill you if you ever said one word about it!... But for those children asleep there, I would kill you this moment! And now you had better take very, very good care of them; for if ever they have reason to complain of you, I will treat you as you deserve!"...

Even as she screamed, her voice became thin, like a crying of wind;—then she melted into a bright white mist that spired to the roof-beams, and shuddered away through the smoke-hold... Never again was she seen.

The Story of Aoyagi

In the era of Bummei [1469–86] there was a young samurai called Tomotada in the service of Hatakeyama Yoshimune, the Lord of Noto. Tomotada was a native of Echizen; but at an early age he had been taken, as page, into the palace of the daimyo of Noto, and had been educated, under the supervision of that prince, for the profession of arms. As he grew up, he proved himself both a good scholar and a good soldier, and continued to enjoy the favor of his prince. Being gifted with an amiable character, a winning address, and a very handsome person, he was admired and much liked by his samurai-comrades.

When Tomotada was about twenty years old, he was sent upon a private mission to Hosokawa Masamoto, the great daimyo of Kyoto, a kinsman of Hatakeyama Yoshimune. Having been ordered to journey through Echizen, the youth requested and obtained permission to pay a visit, on the way, to his widowed mother.

It was the coldest period of the year when he started; and, though mounted upon a powerful horse, he found himself obliged to proceed slowly. The road which he followed passed through a mountain-district where the settlements were few and far between; and on the second day of his journey, after a weary ride of hours, he was dismayed to find that he could not reach his intended halting-place until late in the night. He had reason to be anxious;—for a heavy snowstorm came on, with an intensely cold wind; and the horse showed signs of exhaustion. But in that trying moment, Tomotada unexpectedly perceived the thatched room of a cottage on the summit of a near hill, where willow-trees were growing. With difficulty he urged his tired animal to the dwelling; and he loudly knocked upon the storm-doors, which had been closed against the wind. An old woman opened them, and cried out compassionately at the sight of the handsome stranger: "Ah, how pitiful!—a young gentleman traveling alone in such weather!... Deign, young master, to enter."

Tomotada dismounted, and after leading his horse to a shed in the rear, entered the cottage, where he saw an old man and a girl warming themselves by a fire of bamboo splints. They respectfully invited him to approach the fire; and the old folks then proceeded to warm some rice-wine, and to prepare food for the traveler, whom they ventured to question in regard to his journey. Meanwhile the young girl disappeared behind a screen. Tomotada had observed, with astonishment, that she was extremely beautiful—though her attire was of the most wretched kind, and her long, loose hair in disorder. He wondered that so handsome a girl should be living in such a miserable and lonesome place.

The old man said to him:—

"Honored Sir, the next village is far; and the snow is falling thickly. The wind is piercing; and the road is very bad. Therefore, to proceed further this night would probably be dangerous. Although this hovel is unworthy of your presence, and although we have not any comfort to offer, perhaps it were safer to remain to-night under this miserable roof... We would take good care of your horse."

Tomotada accepted this humble proposal—secretly glad of the chance thus afforded him to see more of the young girl. Presently a coarse but ample meal was set before him; and the girl came from behind the screen, to serve the wine. She was now reclad, in a rough but cleanly robe of homespun; and her long, loose hair had been neatly combed and smoothed. As she bent forward to fill his cup,

Tomotada was amazed to perceive that she was incomparably more beautiful than any woman whom he had ever before seen; and there was a grace about her every motion that astonished him. But the elders began to apologize for her, saying: "Sir, our daughter, Aoyagi,[80] has been brought up here in the mountains, almost alone; and she knows nothing of gentle service. We pray that you will pardon her stupidity and her ignorance." Tomotada protested that he deemed himself lucky to be waited upon by so comely a maiden. He could not turn his eyes away from her—though he saw that his admiring gaze made her blush;—and he left the wine and food untasted before him. The mother said: "Kind Sir, we very much hope that you will try to eat and to drink a little—though our peasant-fare is of the worst—as you must have been chilled by that piercing wind." Then, to please the old folks, Tomotada ate and drank as he could; but the charm of the blushing girl still grew upon him. He talked with her, and found that her speech was sweet as her face. Brought up in the mountains as she might have been;—but, in that case, her parents must at some time been persons of high degree; for she spoke and moved like a damsel of rank. Suddenly he addressed her with a poem—which was also a question—inspired by the delight in his heart:—

> *"Tadzunetsuru,*
> *Hana ka tote koso,*
> *Hi wo kurase,*
> *Akenu ni otoru*
> *Akane sasuran?"*

["Being on my way to pay a visit, I found that which I took to be a flower: therefore here I spend the day... Why, in the time

---

80 The name signifies "Green Willow;"—though rarely met with, it is still in use.

before dawn, the dawn-blush tint should glow—that, indeed, I know not."][81]

Without a moment's hesitation, she answered him in these verses:—

> *"Izuru hi no*
> *Honomeku iro wo*
> *Waga sode ni*
> *Tsutsumaba asu mo*
> *Kimiya tomaran."*

["If with my sleeve I hid the faint fair color of the dawning sun—then, perhaps, in the morning my lord will remain."][82]

Then Tomotada knew that she accepted his admiration; and he was scarcely less surprised by the art with which she had uttered her feelings in verse, than delighted by the assurance which the verses conveyed. He was now certain that in all this world he could not hope to meet, much less to win, a girl more beautiful and witty than this rustic maid before him; and a voice in his heart seemed to cry out urgently, "Take the luck that the gods have put in your way!" In short he was bewitched—bewitched to such a degree that, without further preliminary, he asked the old people to give him their daughter in marriage—telling them, at the same time, his name and lineage, and his rank in the train of the Lord of Noto.

---

81 The poem may be read in two ways; several of the phrases having a double meaning. But the art of its construction would need considerable space to explain, and could scarcely interest the Western reader. The meaning which Tomotada desired to convey might be thus expressed:—"While journeying to visit my mother, I met with a being lovely as a flower; and for the sake of that lovely person, I am passing the day here... Fair one, wherefore that dawn-like blush before the hour of dawn?—can it mean that you love me?"

82 Another reading is possible; but this one gives the signification of the answer intended.

They bowed down before him, with many exclamations of grateful astonishment. But, after some moments of apparent hesitation, the father replied:—

"Honored master, you are a person of high position, and likely to rise to still higher things. Too great is the favor that you deign to offer us;—indeed, the depth of our gratitude therefore is not to be spoken or measured. But this girl of ours, being a stupid country-girl of vulgar birth, with no training or teaching of any sort, it would be improper to let her become the wife of a noble samurai. Even to speak of such a matter is not right... But, since you find the girl to your liking, and have condescended to pardon her peasant-manners and to overlook her great rudeness, we do gladly present her to you, for an humble handmaid. Deign, therefore, to act hereafter in her regard according to your august pleasure."

Ere morning the storm had passed; and day broke through a cloudless east. Even if the sleeve of Aoyagi hid from her lover's eyes the rose-blush of that dawn, he could no longer tarry. But neither could he resign himself to part with the girl; and, when everything had been prepared for his journey, he thus addressed her parents:—

"Though it may seem thankless to ask for more than I have already received, I must again beg you to give me your daughter for wife. It would be difficult for me to separate from her now; and as she is willing to accompany me, if you permit, I can take her with me as she is. If you will give her to me, I shall ever cherish you as parents... And, in the meantime, please to accept this poor acknowledgment of your kindest hospitality."

So saying, he placed before his humble host a purse of gold *ryō*. But the old man, after many prostrations, gently pushed back the gift, and said:—

"Kind master, the gold would be of no use to us; and you will probably have need of it during your long, cold journey. Here we buy nothing; and we could not spend so much money upon ourselves, even if we wished... As for the girl, we have already bestowed her as a free gift;—she belongs to you: therefore it is not necessary to ask our leave to take her away. Already she has told us that she hopes to accompany you, and to remain your servant for as long as you may be willing to endure her presence. We are only too happy to know that you deign to accept her; and we pray that you will not trouble yourself on our account. In this place we could not provide her with proper clothing—much less with a dowry. Moreover, being old, we should in any event have to separate from her before long. Therefore it is very fortunate that you should be willing to take her with you now."

It was in vain that Tomotada tried to persuade the old people to accept a present: he found that they cared nothing for money. But he saw that they were really anxious to trust their daughter's fate to his hands; and he therefore decided to take her with him. So he placed her upon his horse, and bade the old folks farewell for the time being, with many sincere expressions of gratitude.

"Honored Sir," the father made answer, "it is we, and not you, who have reason for gratitude. We are sure that you will be kind to our girl; and we have no fears for her sake."...

[Here, in the Japanese original, there is a queer break in the natural course of the narration, which therefrom remains curiously inconsistent. Nothing further is said about the mother of Tomotada, or about the parents of Aoyagi, or about the daimyo of Noto. Evidently the writer wearied of his work at this point, and hurried the story, very carelessly, to its startling end. I am not able to supply his omissions, or to repair his faults of construction; but I must venture to put in a few explanatory details, without which the rest of the tale would not hold together... It appears that Tomotada rashly took Aoyagi with him to Kyoto, and so got into trouble; but we are not informed as to where the couple lived afterwards.]

…Now a samurai was not allowed to marry without the consent of his lord; and Tomotada could not expect to obtain this sanction before his mission had been accomplished. He had reason, under such circumstances, to fear that the beauty of Aoyagi might attract dangerous attention, and that means might be devised of taking her away from him. In Kyoto he therefore tried to keep her hidden from curious eyes. But a retainer of Lord Hosokawa one day caught sight of Aoyagi, discovered her relation to Tomotada, and reported the matter to the daimyo. Thereupon the daimyo—a young prince, and fond of pretty faces—gave orders that the girl should be brought to the place; and she was taken thither at once, without ceremony.

Tomotada sorrowed unspeakably; but he knew himself powerless. He was only an humble messenger in the service of a far-off daimyo; and for the time being he was at the mercy of a much more powerful daimyo, whose wishes were not to be questioned. Moreover Tomotada knew that he had acted foolishly—that he had brought about his own misfortune, by entering into a clandestine relation which the code of the military class condemned. There was now but one hope for him—a desperate hope: that Aoyagi might be able and willing to escape and to flee with him. After long reflection, he resolved to try to send her a letter. The attempt would be dangerous, of course: any writing sent to her might find its way to the hands of the daimyo; and to send a love-letter to any inmate of the place was an unpardonable offense. But he resolved to dare the risk; and, in the form of a Chinese poem, he composed a letter which he endeavored to have conveyed to her. The poem was written with only twenty-eight characters. But with those twenty-eight characters he was about to express all the depth of his passion, and to suggest all the pain of his loss:—[83]

Koshi o-son gojin wo ou;
Ryokuju namida wo tarete rakin wo hitataru;
Komon hitotabi irite fukaki koto umi no gotoshi;
Kore yori shoro kore rojin.

[Closely, closely the youthful prince now follows after the gem-bright maid;—

The tears of the fair one, falling, have moistened all her robes.

But the august lord, having once become enamored of her—the depth of his longing is like the depth of the sea.

Therefore it is only I that am left forlorn—only I that am left to wander along.]

On the evening of the day after this poem had been sent, Tomotada was summoned to appear before the Lord Hosokawa. The youth at once suspected that his confidence had been betrayed; and he could not hope, if his letter had been seen by the daimyo, to escape the severest penalty. "Now he will order my death," thought Tomotada;—"but I do not care to live unless Aoyagi be restored to me. Besides, if the death-sentence be passed, I can at least try to kill Hosokawa." He slipped his swords into his girdle, and hastened to the palace.

On entering the presence-room he saw the Lord Hosokawa seated upon the dais, surrounded by samurai of high rank, in caps and robes of ceremony. All were silent as statues; and while Tomotada advanced to make obeisance, the hush seemed to his sinister and heavy, like

---

83 So the Japanese story-teller would have us believe—although the verses seem commonplace in translation. I have tried to give only their general meaning: an effective literal translation would require some scholarship.

the stillness before a storm. But Hosokawa suddenly descended from the dais, and, while taking the youth by the arm, began to repeat the words of the poem:—"*Koshi o-son gojin wo ou.*"... And Tomotada, looking up, saw kindly tears in the prince's eyes.

Then said Hosokawa:—

"Because you love each other so much, I have taken it upon myself to authorize your marriage, in lieu of my kinsman, the Lord of Noto; and your wedding shall now be celebrated before me. The guests are assembled;—the gifts are ready."

At a signal from the lord, the sliding-screens concealing a further apartment were pushed open; and Tomotada saw there many dignitaries of the court, assembled for the ceremony, and Aoyagi awaiting him in bride's apparel... Thus was she given back to him;—and the wedding was joyous and splendid;—and precious gifts were made to the young couple by the prince, and by the members of his household.

For five happy years, after that wedding, Tomotada and Aoyagi dwelt together. But one morning Aoyagi, while talking with her husband about some household matter, suddenly uttered a great cry of pain, and then became very white and still. After a few moments she said, in a feeble voice: "Pardon me for thus rudely crying out—but the pain was so sudden!... My dear husband, our union must have been brought about through some Karma-relation in a former state of existence; and that happy relation, I think, will bring us again together in more than one life to come. But for this present existence of ours, the relation is now ended;—we are about to be separated. Repeat for me, I beseech you, the *Nembutsu*-prayer—because I am dying."

"Oh! What strange wild fancies!" cried the startled husband—"you are only a little unwell, my dear one!... lie down for a while, and rest; and the sickness will pass."...

"No, no!" she responded—"I am dying!—I do not imagine it;—I know!... And it were needless now, my dear husband, to hide the truth from you any longer:—I am not a human being. The soul of a tree is my soul;—the heart of a tree is my heart;—the sap of the willow is my life. And someone, at this cruel moment, is cutting down my tree;—that is why I must die!... Even to weep were now beyond my strength!—quickly, quickly repeat the *Nembutsu* for me... quickly!... Ah!..."

With another cry of pain she turned aside her beautiful head, and tried to hide her face behind her sleeve. But almost in the same moment her whole form appeared to collapse in the strangest way, and to sink down, down, down—level with the floor. Tomotada had sprung to support her;—but there was nothing to support! There lay on the matting only the empty robes of the fair creature and the ornaments that she had worn in her hair: the body had ceased to exist...

Tomotada shaved his head, took the Buddhist vows, and became an itinerant priest. He traveled through all the provinces of the empire; and, at holy places which he visited, he offered up prayers for the soul of Aoyagi. Reaching Echizen, in the course of his pilgrimage, he sought the home of the parents of his beloved. But when he arrived at the lonely place among the hills, where their dwelling had been, he found that the cottage had disappeared. There was nothing to mark even the spot where it had stood, except the stumps of three willows—two old trees and one young tree—that had been cut down long before his arrival.

Beside the stumps of those willow-trees he erected a memorial tomb, inscribed with divers holy texts; and he there performed many Buddhist services on behalf of the spirits of Aoyagi and of her parents.

Jiu-Roku-Zakura

··

Jn Wakegori, a district of the province of Iyō, there is a very ancient and famous cherry-tree, called *Jiu-roku-zakura*, or "the Cherry-tree of the Sixteenth Day," because it blooms every year upon the sixteenth day of the first month (by the old lunar calendar)—and only upon that day. Thus the time of its flowering is the Period of Great Cold—though the natural habit of a cherry-tree is to wait for the spring season before venturing to blossom. But the *Jiu-roku-zakura* blossoms with a life that is not—or, at least, that was not originally—its own. There is the ghost of a man in that tree.

He was a samurai of Iyō; and the tree grew in his garden; and it used to flower at the usual time—that is to say, about the end of March or the beginning of April. He had played under that tree when he was a child; and his parents and grandparents and ancestors had hung to its blossoming branches, season after season for more than a hundred years, bright strips of colored paper inscribed with poems of praise. He himself became very old—outliving all his children; and there was nothing in the world left for him to love except that tree. And lo! In the summer of a certain year, the tree withered and died!

Exceedingly the old man sorrowed for his tree. Then kind neighbors found for him a young and beautiful cherry-tree, and planted it in his garden—hoping thus to comfort him. And he thanked them, and pretended to be glad. But really his heart was full of pain; for he had loved the old tree so well that nothing could have consoled him for the loss of it.

At last there came to him a happy thought: he remembered a way by which the perishing tree might be saved. (It was the sixteenth day of the first month.) Along he went into his garden, and bowed down before the withered tree, and spoke to it, saying: "Now deign, I beseech you, once more to bloom—because I am going to die in your stead." (For it is believed that one can really give away one's life to another person, or to a creature or even to a tree, by the favor of the gods;—and thus to transfer one's life is expressed by the term *migawari ni tatsu*, "to act as a substitute.") Then under that tree he spread a white cloth, and divers coverings, and sat down upon the coverings, and performed *hara-kiri* after the fashion of a samurai. And the ghost of him went into the tree, and made it blossom in that same hour.

And every year it still blooms on the sixteenth day of the first month, in the season of snow.

The Dream of Akinosuke

....

In the district called Toichi of Yamato Province, there used to live a *goshi* named Miyata Akinosuke… [Here I must tell you that in Japanese feudal times there was a privileged class of soldier-farmers—free-holders—corresponding to the class of yeomen in England; and these were called *goshi*.]

In Akinosuke's garden there was a great and ancient cedar-tree, under which he was wont to rest on sultry days. One very warm afternoon he was sitting under this tree with two of his friends, fellow-*goshi*, chatting and drinking wine, when he felt all of a sudden very drowsy—so drowsy that he begged his friends to excuse him for taking a nap in their presence. Then he lay down at the foot of the tree, and dreamed this dream:—

He thought that as he was lying there in his garden, he saw a procession, like the train of some great daimyo descending a hill nearby, and that he got up to look at it. A very grand procession it proved to be—more imposing than anything of the kind which he had ever seen before; and it was advancing toward his dwelling. He observed in the van of it a number of young men richly appareled, who were drawing a great lacquered palace-carriage, or *gosho-guruma*, hung with bright blue silk. When the procession arrived within a short distance of the house it halted; and a richly dressed man—evidently a person of rank—advanced from it, approached Akinosuke, bowed to him profoundly, and then said:—

"Honored Sir, you see before you a *kerai* [vassal] of the Kokuo of Tokoyo.[84] My master, the King, commands me to greet you in his august name, and to place myself wholly at your disposal. He also bids me inform you that he augustly desires your presence at the palace. Be therefore pleased immediately to enter this honorable carriage, which he has sent for your conveyance."

Upon hearing these words Akinosuke wanted to make some fitting reply; but he was too much astonished and embarrassed for speech;—and in the same moment his will seemed to melt away from him, so that he could only do as the *kerai* bade him. He entered the carriage; the *kerai* took a place beside him, and made a signal; the drawers, seizing the silken ropes, turned the great vehicle southward;—and the journey began.

In a very short time, to Akinosuke's amazement, the carriage stopped in front of a huge two-storied gateway (*romon*), of a Chinese style, which he had never before seen. Here the *kerai* dismounted, saying, "I go to announce the honorable arrival,"—and he disappeared. After some little waiting, Akinosuke saw two noble-looking men, wearing robes of purple silk and high caps of the form indicating lofty rank, come from the gateway. These, after having respectfully saluted him, helped him to descend from the carriage, and led him through the great gate and across a vast garden, to the entrance of a palace whose front appeared to extend, west and east, to a distance of miles. Akinosuke was then shown into a reception-room of wonderful size and splendor. His guides conducted him to the place of honor, and respectfully seated themselves apart; while

---

84 This name "Tokoyo" is indefinite. According to circumstances it may signify any unknown country—or that undiscovered country from whose bourn no traveler returns—or that Fairyland of far-eastern fable, the Realm of Horai. The term "Kokuo" means the ruler of a country—therefore a king. The original phrase, Tokoyo no Kokuo, might be rendered here as "the Ruler of Horai," or "the King of Fairyland."

serving-maids, in costume of ceremony, brought refreshments. When Akinosuke had partaken of the refreshments, the two purple-robed attendants bowed low before him, and addressed him in the following words—each speaking alternately, according to the etiquette of courts:—

"It is now our honorable duty to inform you... as to the reason of your having been summoned hither... Our master, the King, augustly desires that you become his son-in-law;... and it is his wish and command that you shall wed this very day... the August Princess, his maiden-daughter... We shall soon conduct you to the presence-chamber... where His Augustness even now is waiting to receive you... But it will be necessary that we first invest you... with the appropriate garments of ceremony."[85]

Having thus spoken, the attendants rose together, and proceeded to an alcove containing a great chest of gold lacquer. They opened the chest, and took from it various roes and girdles of rich material, and a *kamuri*, or regal headdress. With these they attired Akinosuke as befitted a princely bridegroom; and he was then conducted to the presence-room, where he saw the Kokuo of Tokoyo seated upon the *daiza*,[86] wearing a high black cap of state, and robed in robes of yellow silk. Before the *daiza*, to left and right, a multitude of dignitaries sat in rank, motionless and splendid as images in a temple; and Akinosuke, advancing into their midst, saluted the king with the triple prostration of usage. The king greeted him with gracious words, and then said:—

"You have already been informed as to the reason of your having been summoned to Our presence. We have decided that you shall

---

85 The last phrase, according to old custom, had to be uttered by both attendants at the same time. All these ceremonial observances can still be studied on the Japanese stage.

86 This was the name given to the estrade, or dais, upon which a feudal prince or ruler sat in state. The term literally signifies "great seat."

become the adopted husband of Our only daughter;—and the wedding ceremony shall now be performed."

As the king finished speaking, a sound of joyful music was heard; and a long train of beautiful court ladies advanced from behind a curtain to conduct Akinosuke to the room in which he bride awaited him.

The room was immense; but it could scarcely contain the multitude of guests assembled to witness the wedding ceremony. All bowed down before Akinosuke as he took his place, facing the King's daughter, on the kneeling-cushion prepared for him. As a maiden of heaven the bride appeared to be; and her robes were beautiful as a summer sky. And the marriage was performed amid great rejoicing.

Afterwards the pair were conducted to a suite of apartments that had been prepared for them in another portion of the palace; and there they received the congratulations of many noble persons, and wedding gifts beyond counting.

Some days later Akinosuke was again summoned to the throne-room. On this occasion he was received even more graciously than before; and the King said to him:—

"In the southwestern part of Our dominion there is an island called Raishu. We have now appointed you Governor of that island. You will find the people loyal and docile; but their laws have not yet been brought into proper accord with the laws of Tokoyo; and their customs have not been properly regulated. We entrust you with the duty of improving their social condition as far as may be possible; and We desire that you shall rule them with kindness and wisdom. All preparations necessary for your journey to Raishu have already been made."

So Akinosuke and his bride departed from the palace of Tokoyo, accompanied to the shore by a great escort of nobles and officials; and they embarked upon a ship of state provided by the king. And with favoring winds they safety sailed to Raishu, and found the good people of that island assembled upon the beach to welcome them.

Akinosuke entered at once upon his new duties; and they did not prove to be hard. During the first three years of his governorship he was occupied chiefly with the framing and the enactment of laws; but he had wise counselors to help him, and he never found the work unpleasant. When it was all finished, he had no active duties to perform, beyond attending the rites and ceremonies ordained by ancient custom. The country was so healthy and so fertile that sickness and want were unknown; and the people were so good that no laws were ever broken. And Akinosuke dwelt and ruled in Raishu for twenty years more—making in all twenty-three years of sojourn, during which no shadow of sorrow traversed his life.

But in the twenty-fourth year of his governorship, a great misfortune came upon him; for his wife, who had borne him seven children—five boys and two girls—fell sick and died. She was buried, with high pomp, on the summit of a beautiful hill in the district of Hanryoko; and a monument, exceedingly splendid, was placed upon her grave. But Akinosuke felt such grief at her death that he no longer cared to live.

Now when the legal period of mourning was over, there came to Raishu, from the Tokoyo palace, a *shisha*, or royal messenger. The *shisha* delivered to Akinosuke a message of condolence, and then said to him:—

"These are the words which our august master, the King of Tokoyo, commands that I repeat to you: 'We will now send you back to your own people and country. As for the seven children, they are the grandsons and granddaughters of the King, and shall be fitly cared for. Do not, therefore, allow your mind to be troubled concerning them.'"

On receiving this mandate, Akinosuke submissively prepared for his departure. When all his affairs had been settled, and the ceremony of bidding farewell to his counselors and trusted officials had been concluded, he was escorted with much honor to the port. There he embarked upon the ship sent for him; and the ship sailed out into the blue sea, under the blue sky; and the shape of the island of Raishu itself turned blue, and then turned gray, and then vanished forever... And Akinosuke suddenly awoke—under the cedar-tree in his own garden!

For a moment he was stupefied and dazed. But he perceived his two friends still seated near him—drinking and chatting merrily. He stared at them in a bewildered way, and cried aloud—

"How strange!"

"Akinosuke must have been dreaming," one of them exclaimed, with a laugh. "What did you see, Akinosuke, that was strange?"

Then Akinosuke told his dream—that dream of three-and-twenty years' sojourn in the realm of Tokoyo, in the island of Raishu;—and they were astonished, because he had really slept for no more than a few minutes.

One *goshi* said:—

"Indeed, you saw strange things. We also saw something strange while you were napping. A little yellow butterfly was fluttering over your face for a moment or two; and we watched it. Then it alighted on the ground beside you, close to the tree; and almost as soon as it alighted there, a big, big ant came out of a hole and seized it and pulled it down into the hole. Just before you woke up, we saw that very butterfly come out of the hole again, and flutter over your face as before. And then it suddenly disappeared: we do not know where it went."

"Perhaps it was Akinosuke's soul," the other *goshi* said;— "certainly I thought I saw it fly into his mouth... But, even if that butterfly was Akinosuke's soul, the fact would not explain his dream."

"The ants might explain it," returned the first speaker. "Ants are queer beings—possibly goblins... Anyhow, there is a big ant's nest under that cedar-tree.".

"Let us look!" cried Akinosuke, greatly moved by this suggestion. And he went for a spade.

The ground about and beneath the cedar-tree proved to have been excavated, in a most surprising way, by a prodigious colony of ants. The ants had furthermore built inside their excavations; and their tiny constructions of straw, clay, and stems bore an odd resemblance to miniature towns. In the middle of a structure considerably larger than the rest there was a marvelous swarming of small ants around the body of one very big ant, which had yellowish wings and a long black head.

"Why, there is the King of my dream!" cried Akinosuke; "and there is the palace of Tokoyo!... How extraordinary!... Raishu ought to lie somewhere southwest of it—to the left of that big root... Yes!—here it is!... How very strange! Now I am sure that I can find the mountain of Hanryoko, and the grave of the princess.".

In the wreck of the nest he searched and searched, and at last discovered a tiny mound, on the top of which was fixed a water-worn pebble, in shape resembling a Buddhist monument. Underneath it he found—embedded in clay—the dead body of a female ant.

Riki-Baka

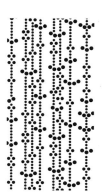

His name was Riki, signifying Strength; but the people called him Riki-the-Simple, or Riki-the-Fool—"Riki-Baka,"—because he had been born into perpetual childhood. For the same reason they were kind to him—even when he set a house on fire by putting a lighted match to a mosquito-curtain, and clapped his hands for joy to see the blaze. At sixteen years he was a tall, strong lad; but in mind he remained always at the happy age of two, and therefore continued to play with very small children. The bigger children of the neighborhood, from four to seven years old, did not care to play with him, because he could not learn their songs and games. His favorite toy was a broomstick, which he used as a hobby-horse; and for hours at a time he would ride on that broomstick, up and down the slope in front of my house, with amazing peals of laughter. But at last he became troublesome by reason of his noise; and I had to tell him that he must find another playground. He bowed submissively, and then went off—sorrowfully trailing his broomstick behind him. Gentle at all times, and perfectly harmless if allowed no chance to play with fire, he seldom gave anybody cause for complaint. His relation to the life of our street was scarcely more than that of a dog or a chicken; and when he finally disappeared, I did not miss him. Months and months passed by before anything happened to remind me of Riki.

"What has become of Riki?" I then asked the old woodcutter

who supplies our neighborhood with fuel. I remembered that Riki had often helped him to carry his bundles.

"Riki-Baka?" answered the old man. "Ah, Riki is dead—poor fellow!... Yes, he died nearly a year ago, very suddenly; the doctors said that he had some disease of the brain. And there is a strange story now about that poor Riki.

"When Riki died, his mother wrote his name, 'Riki-Baka,' in the palm of his left hand—putting 'Riki' in the Chinese character, and 'Baka' in *kana*[87]. And she repeated many prayers for him—prayers that he might be reborn into some more happy condition.

"Now, about three months ago, in the honorable residence of Nanigashi-Sama[88], in Kojimachi[89], a boy was born with characters on the palm of his left hand; and the characters were quite plain to read—'RIKI-BAKA!'

"So the people of that house knew that the birth must have happened in answer to somebody's prayer; and they caused inquiry to be made everywhere. At last a vegetable-seller brought word to them that there used to be a simple lad, called Riki-Baka, living in the Ushigome quarter, and that he had died during the last autumn; and they sent two men-servants to look for the mother of Riki.

"Those servants found the mother of Riki, and told her what had happened; and she was glad exceedingly—for that Nanigashi house is a very rich and famous house. But the servants said that the family of Nanigashi-Sama were very angry about the word 'Baka' on the child's hand. 'And where is your Riki buried?' the servants asked. 'He is buried in the cemetery of Zendoji,' she told them. 'Please to give us some of the clay of his grave,' they requested.

"So she went with them to the temple Zendoji, and showed

---

87   *Kana*: the Japanese phonetic alphabet.

88   "So-and-so": appellation used by Hearn in place of the real name.

89   A section of Tōkyō.

them Riki's grave; and they took some of the grave-clay away with them, wrapped up in a *furoshiki*[90].... They gave Riki's mother some money—ten yen."...[91]

"But what did they want with that clay?" I inquired.

"Well," the old man answered, "you know that it would not do to let the child grow up with that name on his hand. And there is no other means of removing characters that come in that way upon the body of a child: *you must rub the skin with clay taken from the grave of the body of the former birth."*...

---

90   A square piece of cotton-goods, or other woven material, used as a wrapper in which to carry small packages.

91   Ten yen is nothing now, but was a formidable sum then.

Hi-Mawari

....

On the wooded hill behind the house Robert and I are looking for fairy-rings. Robert is eight years old, comely, and very wise;—I am a little more than seven— and I reverence Robert. It is a glowing glorious August day; and the warm air is filled with sharp sweet scents of resin.

We do not find any fairy-rings; but we find a great many pine-cones in the high grass... I tell Robert the old Welsh story of the man who went to sleep, unawares, inside a fairy-ring, and so disappeared for seven years, and would never eat or speak after his friends had delivered him from the enchantment.

"They eat nothing but the points of needles, you know," says Robert.

"Who?" I ask.

"Goblins," Robert answers.

This revelation leaves me dumb with astonishment and awe... But Robert suddenly cries out:—

"There is a Harper!—he is coming to the house!"

And down the hill we run to hear the harper... But what a harper! Not like the hoary minstrels of the picture-books. A swarthy, sturdy, unkempt vagabond, with black bold eyes under scowling black brows. More like a bricklayer than a bard—and his garments are corduroy!

"Wonder if he is going to sing in Welsh?" murmurs Robert.

I feel too much disappointed to make any remarks. The harper poses his harp—a huge instrument—upon our doorstep, sets all the strings ringing with a sweep of his grimy fingers, clears his throat with a sort of angry growl, and begins—

> *Believe me, if all those endearing young charms,*
> *Which I gaze on so fondly to-day...*

The accent, the attitude, the voice, all fill me with repulsion unutterable—shock me with a new sensation of formidable vulgarity. I want to cry out loud, "You have no right to sing that song!" For I have heard it sung by the lips of the dearest and fairest being in my little world;—and that this rude, coarse man should dare to sing it vexes me like a mockery—angers me like an insolence. But only for a moment!... With the utterance of the syllables "to-day," that deep, grim voice suddenly breaks into a quivering tenderness indescribable;—then, marvelously changing, it mellows into tones sonorous and rich as the bass of a great organ—while a sensation unlike anything ever felt before takes me by the throat... What witchcraft has he learned? What secret has he found—this scowling man of the road?... Oh! Is there anybody else in the whole world who can sing like that?... And the form of the singer flickers and dims;—and the house, and the lawn, and all visible shapes of things tremble and swim before me. Yet instinctively I fear that man;—I almost hate him; and I feel myself flushing with anger and shame because of his power to move me thus...

"He made you cry," Robert compassionately observes, to my further confusion—as the harper strides away, richer by a gift of sixpence taken without thanks... "But I think he must be a gipsy. Gipsies are bad people—and they are wizards... Let us go back to the wood."

We climb again to the pines, and there squat down upon the sun-flecked grass, and look over town and sea. But we do not play as before: the spell of the wizard is strong upon us both… "Perhaps he is a goblin," I venture at last, "or a fairy?" "No," says Robert— "only a gipsy. But that is nearly as bad. They steal children, you know.".…

"What shall we do if he comes up here?" I gasp, in sudden terror at the lonesomeness of our situation.

"Oh, he wouldn't dare," answers Robert—"not by daylight, you know.".…

[Only yesterday, near the village of Takata, I noticed a flower which the Japanese call by nearly the same name as we do: Himawari, "The Sunward-turning;"—and over the space of forty years there thrilled back to me the voice of that wandering harper—

As the Sunflower turns on her god, when he sets,
The same look that she turned when he rose.

Again I saw the sun-flecked shadows on that far Welsh hill; and Robert for a moment again stood beside me, with his girl's face and his curls of gold. We were looking for fairy-rings… But all that existed of the real Robert must long ago have suffered a sea-change into something rich and strange… Greater love hath no man than this, that a man lay down his life for his friend…]

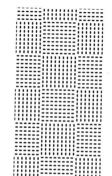

Horai

· ·

Blue vision of depth lost in height—sea and sky interblending through luminous haze. The day is of spring, and the hour morning.

Only sky and sea—one azure enormity… In the fore, ripples are catching a silvery light, and threads of foam are swirling. But a little further off no motion is visible, nor anything save color: dim warm blue of water widening away to melt into blue of air. Horizon there is none: only distance soaring into space—infinite concavity hollowing before you, and hugely arching above you—the color deepening with the height. But far in the midway-blue there hangs a faint, faint vision of palace towers, with high roofs horned and curved like moons—some shadowing of splendor strange and old, illumined by a sunshine soft as memory.

…What I have thus been trying to describe is a *kakemono*—that is to say, a Japanese painting on silk, suspended to the wall of my alcove;—and the name of it is *Shinkiro*, which signifies "Mirage." But the shapes of the mirage are unmistakable. Those are the glimmering portals of Horai the blest; and those are the moony roofs of the Palace of the Dragon-King;—and the fashion of them (though limned by a Japanese brush of to-day) is the fashion of things Chinese, twenty-one hundred years ago…

Thus much is told of the place in the Chinese books of that time:—

In Horai there is neither death nor pain; and there is no winter. The flowers in that place never fade, and the fruits never fail; and if a man taste of those fruits even but once, he can never again feel thirst or hunger. In Horai grow the enchanted plants *So-rin-shi*, and *Riku-go-aoi*, and *Ban-kon-to*, which heal all manner of sickness;— and there grows also the magical grass *Yo-shin-shi*, that quickens the dead; and the magical grass is watered by a fairy water of which a single drink confers perpetual youth. The people of Horai eat their rice out of very, very small bowls; but the rice never diminishes within those bowls—however much of it be eaten—until the eater desires no more. And the people of Horai drink their wine out of very, very small cups; but no man can empty one of those cups— however stoutly he may drink—until there comes upon him the pleasant drowsiness of intoxication.

All this and more is told in the legends of the time of the Shin Dynasty. But that the people who wrote down those legends ever saw Horai, even in a mirage, is not believable. For really there are no enchanted fruits which leave the eater forever satisfied—nor any magical grass which revives the dead—nor any fountain of fairy water—nor any bowls which never lack rice—nor any cups which never lack wine. It is not true that sorrow and death never enter Horai;—neither is it true that there is not any winter. The winter in Horai is cold;—and winds then bite to the bone; and the heaping of snow is monstrous on the roofs of the Dragon-King.

Nevertheless there are wonderful things in Horai; and the most wonderful of all has not been mentioned by any Chinese writer. I mean the atmosphere of Horai. It is an atmosphere peculiar to the place; and, because of it, the sunshine in Horai is *whiter* than any other sunshine—a milky light that never dazzles—astonishingly clear, but very soft. This atmosphere is not of our human period: it is enormously old—so old that I feel afraid when I try to think how old it is;—and it is not a mixture of nitrogen and oxygen. It is not made of air at all, but of ghost—the substance of quintillions of quintillions of generations of souls blended into one immense translucency—souls of people who thought in ways never resembling our ways. Whatever mortal man inhales that atmosphere, he takes into his blood the thrilling of these spirits; and they change the sense within him—reshaping his notions of Space and Time—so that he can see only as they used to see, and feel only as they used to feel, and think only as they used to think. Soft as sleep are these changes of sense; and Horai, discerned across them, might thus be described:—

—*Because in Horai there is no knowledge of great evil, the hearts of the people never grow old. And, by reason of being always young in heart, the people of Horai smile from birth until death—except when the Gods send sorrow among them; and faces then are veiled until the sorrow goes away. All folk in Horai love and trust each other, as if all were members of a single household;—and the speech of the women is like birdsong, because the hearts of them are light as the souls of birds;—and the swaying of the sleeves of the maidens at play seems a flutter of wide, soft wings. In Horai nothing is hidden but grief, because there is no reason for shame;—and nothing is locked away, because there could not be any theft;—and by night as well as by day all doors remain unbarred, because there is no reason for fear. And because the people are fairies—though mortal—all things in Horai, except the Palace of the Dragon-King, are small and quaint and queer;—and these fairy-folk do really eat their rice out of very, very small bowls, and drink their wine out of very, very small cups...*

—Much of this seeming would be due to the inhalation of that ghostly atmosphere—but not all. For the spell wrought by the dead is only the charm of an Ideal, the glamor of an ancient hope;—and something of that hope has found fulfilment in many hearts—in the simple beauty of unselfish lives—in the sweetness of Woman...

—Evil winds from the West are blowing over Horai; and the magical atmosphere, alas! Is shrinking away before them. It lingers now in patches only, and bands—like those long bright bands of cloud that train across the landscapes of Japanese painters. Under these shreds of the elfish vapor you still can find Horai—but not everywhere... Remember that Horai is also called *Shinkiro*, which signifies Mirage—the Vision of the Intangible. And the Vision is fading—never again to appear save in pictures and poems and dreams...

The Mirror Maiden

n the period of the Ashikaga Shōgunate the shrine of Ogawachi-Myōjin, at Minami-Isé, fell into decay; and the daimyō of the district, the Lord Kitahataké, found himself unable, by reason of war and other circumstances, to provide for the reparation of the building. Then the Shintō priest in charge, Matsumura Hyōgo, sought help at Kyōto from the great daimyō Hosokawa, who was known to have influence with the Shōgun. The Lord Hosokawa received the priest kindly, and promised to speak to the Shōgun about the condition of Ogawachi-Myōjin. But he said that, in any event, a grant for the restoration of the temple could not be made without due investigation and considerable delay; and he advised Matsumura to remain in the capital while the matter was being arranged. Matsumura therefore brought his family to Kyōto, and rented a house in the old Kyōgoku quarter.

This house, although handsome and spacious, had been long unoccupied. It was said to be an unlucky house. On the northeast side of it there was a well; and several former tenants had drowned themselves in that well, without any known cause. But Matsumura, being a Shintō priest, had no fear of evil spirits; and he soon made himself very comfortable in his new home.

In the summer of that year there was a great drought. For months no rain had fallen in the Five Home-Provinces; the river-beds dried up, the wells failed; and even in the capital there was a dearth of water. But the well in Matsumura's garden remained nearly full; and the water—which was very cold and clear, with a faint bluish tinge—seemed to be supplied by a spring. During the hot season many people came from all parts of the city to beg for water; and Matsumura allowed them to draw as much as they pleased. Nevertheless the supply did not appear to be diminished.

But one morning the dead body of a young servant, who had been sent from a neighboring residence to fetch water, was found floating in the well. No cause for a suicide could be imagined; and Matsumura, remembering many unpleasant stories about the well, began to suspect some invisible malevolence. He went to examine the well, with the intention of having a fence built around it; and while standing there alone he was startled by a sudden motion in the water, as of something alive. The motion soon ceased; and then he perceived, clearly reflected in the still surface, the figure of a young woman, apparently about nineteen or twenty years of age. She seemed to be occupied with her toilet: he distinctly saw her touching her lips with *béni*[92]. At first her face was visible in profile only; but presently she turned towards him and smiled. Immediately he felt a strange shock at his heart, and a dizziness came upon him like the dizziness of wine, and everything became dark, except that smiling face—white and beautiful as moonlight, and always seeming to grow more beautiful, and to be drawing him down—down—down into the darkness. But with a desperate effort he recovered his will and closed his eyes. When he opened them again, the face was gone, and the light had returned; and he found himself leaning down over the curb of the well. A moment more of that dizziness—a moment more of that dazzling lure—and he would never again have looked upon the sun...

92　A kind of rouge, now used only to color the lips.

Returning to the house, he gave orders to his people not to approach the well under any circumstances, or allow any person to draw water from it. And the next day he had a strong fence built round the well.

About a week after the fence had been built, the long drought was broken by a great rain-storm, accompanied by wind and lightning and thunder—thunder so tremendous that the whole city shook to the rolling of it, as if shaken by an earthquake. For three days and three nights the downpour and the lightnings and the thunder continued; and the Kamogawa rose as it had never risen before, carrying away many bridges. During the third night of the storm, at the Hour of the Ox, there was heard a knocking at the door of the priest's dwelling, and the voice of a woman pleading for admittance. But Matsumura, warned by his experience at the well, forbade his servants to answer the appeal. He went himself to the entrance, and asked—

"Who calls?"

A feminine voice responded:—

"Pardon! it is I—Yayoi![93]... I have something to say to Matsumura Sama—something of great moment. Please open!"...

Matsumura half opened the door, very cautiously; and he saw the same beautiful face that had smiled upon him from the well. But it was not smiling now: it had a very sad look.

"Into my house you shall not come," the priest exclaimed. "You are not a human being, but a Well-Person.... Why do you thus wickedly try to delude and destroy people?"

The Well-Person made answer in a voice musical as a tinkling of jewels (*tama-wo-korogasu-koë*):—

"It is of that very matter that I want to speak.... I have never

---

93 This name, though uncommon, is still in use.

wished to injure human beings. But from ancient time a Poison-Dragon dwelt in that well. He was the Master of the Well; and because of him the well was always full. Long ago I fell into the water there, and so became subject to him; and he had power to make me lure people to death, in order that he might drink their blood. But now the Heavenly Ruler has commanded the Dragon to dwell hereafter in the lake called Torii-no-Iké, in the Province of Shinshō; and the gods have decided that he shall never be allowed to return to this city. So to-night, after he had gone away, I was able to come out, to beg for your kindly help. There is now very little water in the well, because of the Dragon's departure; and if you will order search to be made, my body will be found there. I pray you to save my body from the well without delay; and I shall certainly return your benevolence."...

So saying, she vanished into the night.

Before dawn the tempest had passed; and when the sun arose there was no trace of cloud in the pure blue sky. Matsumura sent at an early hour for well-cleaners to search the well. Then, to everybody's surprise, the well proved to be almost dry. It was easily cleaned; and at the bottom of it were found some hair-ornaments of a very ancient fashion, and a metal mirror of curious form—but no trace of any body, animal or human.

Matusmura imagined, however, that the mirror might yield some explanation of the mystery; for every such mirror is a weird thing, having a soul of its own—and the soul of a mirror is feminine. This mirror, which seemed to be very old, was deeply crusted with scurf. But when it had been carefully cleaned, by the priest's order, it proved to be of rare and costly workmanship; and there were wonderful designs upon the back of it—also several characters. Some of the characters had become indistinguishable; but there could still be discerned part of a date, and ideographs signifying, *"third month, the third day."* Now the third month used to be termed *Yayoi* (meaning, the Month of Increase); and the third day of the third month, which is a festival day, is still called *Yayoi-no-sekku*. Remembering that the Well-Person called herself "Yayoi," Matsumura felt almost sure that his ghostly visitant had been none other than the Soul of the Mirror.

He therefore resolved to treat the mirror with all the consideration due to a Spirit. After having caused it to be carefully repolished and resilvered, he had a case of precious wood made for it, and a particular room in the house prepared to receive it. On the evening of the same day that it had been respectfully deposited in that room, Yayoi herself unexpectedly appeared before the priest as he sat alone in his study. She looked even more lovely than before; but the light of her beauty was now soft as the light of a summer moon shining through pure white clouds. After having humbly saluted Matsumura, she said in her sweetly tinkling voice:—

"Now that you have saved me from solitude and sorrow, I have come to thank you.... I am indeed, as you supposed, the Spirit of the Mirror. It was in the time of the Emperor Saimei that I was first brought here from Kudara; and I dwelt in the august residence until the time of the Emperor Saga, when I was augustly bestowed upon the Lady Kamo, Naishinnō of the Imperial Court.[94] Thereafter I became an heirloom in the House of Fuji-wara, and so remained until the period of Hōgen, when I was dropped into the well. There I was left and forgotten during the years of the great war.[95] The

---

94 The Emperor Saimei reigned from 655 to 662; the Emperor Saga from 810 to 842. Kudara was an ancient kingdom in southwestern Korea, frequently mentioned in early Japanese history. A *Naishinnō* was of Imperial blood. In the ancient court-hierarchy there were twenty-five ranks or grades of noble ladies; that of *Naishinno* was seventh in order of precedence.

95 For centuries the wives of the emperors and the ladies of the Imperial Court were chosen from the Fujiwara clan. The period called Hōgen lasted from 1156 to 1159: the war referred to is the famous war between the Taira and Minamoto clans.

Master of the Well[96] was a venomous Dragon, who used to live in a lake that once covered a great part of this district. After the lake had been filled in, by government order, in order that houses might be built upon the place of it, the Dragon took possession of the well; and when I fell into the well I became subject to him; and he compelled me to lure many people to their deaths. But the gods have banished him forever.... Now I have one more favor to beseech: I entreat that you will cause me to be offered up to the Shōgun, the Lord Yoshimasa, who by descent is related to my former possessors. Do me but this last great kindness, and it will bring you good-fortune.... But I have also to warn you of a danger. In this house, after to-morrow, you must not stay, because it will be destroyed."... And with these words of warning Yayoi disappeared.

Matsumura was able to profit by this premonition. He removed his people and his belongings to another district the next day; and almost immediately afterwards another storm arose, even more violent than the first, causing a flood which swept away the house in which he had been residing.

Some time later, by favor of the Lord Hosokawa, Matsumura was enabled to obtain an audience of the Shōgun Yoshimasa, to whom he presented the mirror, together with a written account of its wonderful history. Then the prediction of the Spirit of the Mirror was fulfilled; for the Shōgun, greatly pleased with this strange gift, not only bestowed costly presents upon Matsumura, but also made an ample grant of money for the rebuilding of the Temple of Ogawachi-Myōjin.

---

96 In old-time belief every lake or spring had its invisible guardian, supposed to sometimes take the form of a serpent or dragon. The spirit of a lake or pond was commonly spoken of as *Iké-no-Mushi*, the Master of the Lake. Here we find the title "Master" given to a dragon living in a well; but the guardian of wells is really the god Suijin.

The Story of Itō Norisuké

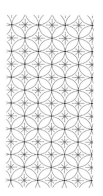

In the town of Uji, in the province of Yamashiro, there lived, about six hundred years ago, a young samurai named Itō Tatéwaki Norisuké, whose ancestors were of the Heiké clan. Itō was of handsome person and amiable character, a good scholar and apt at arms. But his family were poor; and he had no patron among the military nobility—so that his prospects were small. He lived in a very quiet way, devoting himself to the study of literature, and having (says the Japanese story-teller) "only the Moon and the Wind for friends."

One autumn evening, as he was taking a solitary walk in the neighborhood of the hill called Kotobikiyama, he happened to overtake a young girl who was following the same path. She was richly dressed, and seemed to be about eleven or twelve years old. Itō greeted her, and said, "The sun will soon be setting, damsel, and this is rather a lonesome place. May I ask if you have lost your way?" She looked up at him with a bright smile, and answered deprecatingly: "Nay! I am a *miya-dzukai*,[97] serving in this neighborhood; and I have only a little way to go."

By her use of the term *miya-dzukai*, Itō knew that the girl must be in the service of persons of rank; and her statement surprised him, because he had never heard of any family of distinction residing

---

97 August-residence servant.

in that vicinity. But he only said: "I am returning to Uji, where my home is. Perhaps you will allow me to accompany you on the way, as this is a very lonesome place." She thanked him gracefully, seeming pleased by his offer; and they walked on together, chatting as they went. She talked about the weather, the flowers, the butter-flies, and the birds; about a visit that she had once made to Uji, about the famous sights of the capital, where she had been born;— and the moments passed pleasantly for Itō, as he listened to her fresh prattle. Presently, at a turn in the road, they entered a hamlet, densely shadowed by a grove of young trees.

[Here I must interrupt the story to tell you that, without having actually seen them, you cannot imagine how dark some Japanese country villages remain even in the brightest and hottest weather. In the neighborhood of Tōkyō itself there are many villages of this kind. At a short distance from such a settlement you see no houses: nothing is visible but a dense grove of evergreen trees. The grove, which is usually composed of young cedars and bamboos, serves to shelter the village from storms, and also to supply timber for various purposes. So closely are the trees planted that there is no room to pass between the trunks of them: they stand straight as masts, and mingle their crests so as to form a roof that excludes the sun. Each thatched cottage occupies a clear space in the plan-tation, the trees forming a fence about it, double the height of the building. Under the trees it is always twilight, even at high noon; and the houses, morning or evening, are half in shadow. What makes the first impression of such a village almost disquieting is, not the transparent gloom, which has a certain weird charm of its own, but the stillness. There may be fifty or a hundred dwellings; but you see nobody; and you hear no sound but the twitter of invisible birds, the occasional crowing of cocks, and the shrilling of cicadæ. Even the cicadæ, however, find these groves too dim, and sing faintly;

being sun-lovers, they prefer the trees outside the village. I forgot to say that you may sometimes hear a viewless shuttle—*chaka-ton, chaka-ton*;—but that familiar sound, in the great green silence, seems an elfish happening. The reason of the hush is simply that the people are not at home. All the adults, excepting some feeble elders, have gone to the neighboring fields, the women carrying their babies on their backs; and most the children have gone to the nearest school, perhaps not less than a mile away. Verily, in these dim hushed villages, one seems to behold the mysterious perpetuation of conditions recorded in the texts of Kwang-Tze:—

"The ancients who had the nourishment of the world wished for nothing, and the world had enough:—they did nothing, and all things were transformed:—their stillness was abysmal, and the people were all composed."]

... The village was very dark when Itō reached it; for the sun had set, and the after-glow made no twilight in the shadowing of the trees. "Now, kind sir," the child said, pointing to a narrow lane opening upon the main road, "I have to go this way." "Permit me, then, to see you home," Itō responded; and he turned into the lane with her, feeling rather than seeing his way. But the girl soon stopped before a small gate, dimly visible in the gloom—a gate of trellis-work, beyond which the lights of a dwelling could be seen. "Here," she said, "is the honorable residence in which I serve. As you have come thus far out of your way, kind sir, will you not deign to enter and to rest a while?" Itō assented. He was pleased by the informal invitation; and he wished to learn what persons of superior condition had chosen to reside in so lonesome a village. He knew that sometimes a family of rank would retire in this manner from public life, by reason of government displeasure or political trouble; and he imagined that such might be the history of the occupants of the dwelling before him. Passing the gate, which his young guide opened for him, he found himself in a large quaint garden. A miniature landscape, traversed by a winding stream, was faintly distinguishable. "Deign for one little moment to wait," the child said; "I go to announce the honorable coming;" and hurried toward the house. It was a spacious house, but seemed very old, and built in the fashion of another time. The sliding doors were not closed; but the lighted interior was concealed by a beautiful bamboo curtain extending along the gallery front. Behind it shadows were moving—shadows of women;—and suddenly the music of a *koto* rippled into the night. So light and sweet was the playing that Itō could scarcely believe the evidence of his senses. A slumbrous feeling of delight stole over him as he listened—a delight strangely mingled with sadness. He wondered how any woman could have learned to play thus—wondered whether the player could be a woman—wondered even whether he was hearing earthly music; for enchantment seemed to have entered into his blood with the sound of it.

The soft music ceased; and almost at the same moment Itō found the little *miya-dzukai* beside him. "Sir," she said, "it is requested that you will honorably enter." She conducted him to the entrance, where he removed his sandals; and an aged woman, whom he thought to be the *Rōjo*, or matron of the household, came to welcome him at the threshold. The old woman then led him through many apartments to a large and well-lighted room in the rear of the house, and with many respectful salutations requested him to take the place of honor accorded to guests of distinction. He was surprised by the stateliness of the chamber, and the curious beauty of its decorations. Presently some maid-servants brought refreshments; and he noticed that the cups and other vessels set before him were of rare and costly workmanship, and ornamented with a design indicating the high rank of the possessor. More and more he wondered what noble person had chosen this lonely retreat, and what happening could have inspired the wish for such solitude. But the aged attendant suddenly interrupted his reflections with the question:

"Am I wrong in supposing that you are Itō Sama, of Uji—Itō Tatéwaki Norisuké?"

Itō bowed in assent. He had not told his name to the little *miyadzukai*, and the manner of the inquiry startled him.

"Please do not think my question rude," continued the attendant. "An old woman like myself may ask questions without improper curiosity. When you came to the house, I thought that I knew your face; and I asked your name only to clear away all doubt, before speaking of other matters. I have some thing of moment to tell you. You often pass through this village, and our young Himégimi-Sama[98] happened one morning to see you going by; and ever since that moment she has been thinking about you, day and night. Indeed, she thought so much that she became ill; and we have been very uneasy about her. For that reason I took means to find out your name and residence; and I was on the point of sending you a letter when—so unexpectedly!—you came to our gate with the little attendant. Now, to say how happy I am to see you is not possible; it seems almost too fortunate a happening to be true! Really I think that this meeting must have been brought about by the favor of Enmusubi-no-Kami—that great God of Izumo who ties the knots of fortunate union. And now that so lucky a destiny has led you hither, perhaps you will not refuse—if there be no obstacle in the way of such a union—to make happy the heart of our Himégimi-Sama?"

For the moment Itō did not know how to reply. If the old woman had spoken the truth, an extraordinary chance was being offered to him. Only a great passion could impel the daughter of a noble house

---

98 A scarcely translatable honorific title compounded of the word *himé* (princess) and *kimi* (sovereign, master or mistress, lord or lady, etc.)

to seek, of her own will, the affection of an obscure and masterless samurai, possessing neither wealth nor any sort of prospects. On the other hand, it was not in the honorable nature of the man to further his own interests by taking advantage of a feminine weakness. Moreover, the circumstances were disquietingly mysterious. Yet how to decline the proposal, so unexpectedly made, troubled him not a little. After a short silence, he replied:—

"There would be no obstacle, as I have no wife, and no betrothed, and no relation with any woman. Until now I have lived with my parents; and the matter of my marriage was never discussed by them. You must know that I am a poor samurai, without any patron among persons of rank; and I did not wish to marry until I could find some chance to improve my condition. As to the proposal which you have done me the very great honor to make, I can only say that I know myself yet unworthy of the notice of any noble maiden."

The old woman smiled as if pleased by these words, and responded:—

"Until you have seen our Himégimi-Sama, it were better that you make no decision. Perhaps you will feel no hesitation after you have seen her. Deign now to come with me, that I may present you to her."

She conducted him to another larger guest-room, where preparations for a feast had been made, and having shown him the place of honor, left him for a moment alone. She returned accompanied by the Himégimi-Sama; and, at the first sight of the young mistress, Itō felt again the strange thrill of wonder and delight that had come to him in the garden, as he listened to the music of the *koto*. Never had he dreamed of so beautiful a being. Light seemed to radiate from her presence, and to shine through her garments, as the light of the moon through flossy clouds; her loosely flowing hair swayed about her as she moved, like the boughs of the drooping willow bestirred by the breezes of spring; her lips were like flowers of the peach besprinkled with morning dew. Itō was bewildered by the vision. He asked himself whether he was not looking upon the person of Amano-kawara-no-Ori-Himé herself—the Weaving-Maiden who dwells by the shining River of Heaven.

Smiling, the aged woman turned to the fair one, who remained speechless, with downcast eyes and flushing cheeks, and said to her:—

"See, my child!—at the moment when we could least have hoped for such a thing, the very person whom you wished to meet has come of his own accord. So fortunate a happening could have been brought about only by the will of the high gods. To think of it makes me weep for joy." And she sobbed aloud. "But now," she continued, wiping away her tears with her sleeve, "it only remains for you both—unless either prove unwilling, which I doubt—to pledge yourselves to each other, and to partake of your wedding feast."

Itō answered by no word: the incomparable vision before him had numbed his will and tied his tongue. Maid-servants entered, bearing dishes and wine: the wedding feast was spread before the pair; and the pledges were given. Itō nevertheless remained as in a trance: the marvel of the adventure, and the wonder of the beauty of the bride, still bewildered him. A gladness, beyond aught that he had ever known before, filled his heart—like a great silence. But gradually he recovered his wonted calm; and thereafter he found himself able to converse without embarrassment. Of the wine he partook freely; and he ventured to speak, in a self-deprecating but merry way, about the doubts and fears that had oppressed him. Meanwhile the bride remained still as moonlight, never lifting her eyes, and replying only by a blush or a smile when he addressed her.

Itō said to the aged attendant:—

"Many times, in my solitary walks, I have passed through this village without knowing of the existence of this honorable dwelling. And ever since entering here, I have been wondering why this noble household should have chosen so lonesome a place of sojourn.... Now that your Himégimi-Sama and I have become pledged to each other, it seems to me a strange thing that I do not yet know the name of her august family."

At this utterance, a shadow passed over the kindly face of the old woman; and the bride, who had yet hardly spoken, turned pale, and appeared to become painfully anxious. After some moments of silence, the aged woman responded:—

"To keep our secret from you much longer would be difficult; and I think that, under any circumstances, you should be made aware of the facts, now that you are one of us. Know then, Sir Itō, that your bride is the daughter of Shigéhira-Kyō, the great and unfortunate San-mi Chūjō."

At those words—"Shigéhira-Kyō, San-mi Chūjō"—the young samurai felt a chill, as of ice, strike through all his veins. Shigéhira-Kyō, the great Heiké general and statesman, had been dust for centuries. And Itō suddenly understood that everything around him—the chamber and the lights and the banquet—was a dream of the past; that the forms before him were not people, but shadows of people dead.

But in another instant the icy chill had passed; and the charm returned, and seemed to deepen about him; and he felt no fear. Though his bride had come to him out of Yomi—out of the place of the Yellow Springs of death—his heart had been wholly won. Who weds a ghost must become a ghost;—yet he knew himself ready to die, not once, but many times, rather than betray by word or look one thought that might bring a shadow of pain to the brow of the beautiful illusion before him. Of the affection proffered he had no misgiving: the truth had been told him when any unloving purpose might better have been served by deception. But these thoughts and emotions passed in a flash, leaving him resolved to accept the strange situation as it had presented itself, and to act just as he would have done if chosen, in the years of Jü-ei, by Shigéhira's daughter.

"Ah, the pity of it!" he exclaimed; "I have heard of the cruel fate of the august Lord Shigéhira."

"Ay," responded the aged woman, sobbing as she spoke;—"it was indeed a cruel fate. His horse, you know, was killed by an arrow, and fell upon him; and when he called for help, those who had lived upon his bounty deserted him in his need. Then he was taken prisoner, and sent to Kamakura, where they treated him shamefully, and at last put him to death.[99] His wife and child—this dear maid here—were then in hiding; for everywhere the Heiké were being sought out and killed. When the news of the Lord Shigéhira's death reached us, the pain proved too great for the mother to bear, so the child was left with no one to care for her but me—since her kindred had all perished or disappeared. She was only five years old. I had been her milk-nurse, and I did what I could for her. Year after year we wandered from place to place, traveling in pilgrim-garb.... But these tales of grief are ill-timed," exclaimed the nurse, wiping away her tears;—"pardon the foolish heart of an old woman who cannot forget the past. See! the little

---

99 Shigéhira, after a brave fight in defense of the capital—then held by the Taïra (or Heiké) party—was surprised and routed by Yoshitsuné, leader of the Minamoto forces. A soldier named Iyénaga, who was a skilled archer, shot down Shigéhira's horse; and Shigéhira fell under the struggling animal. He cried to an attendant to bring another horse; but the man fled. Shigéhira was then captured by Iyénaga, and eventually given up to Yoritomo, head of the Minamoto clan, who caused him to be sent in a cage to Kamakura. There, after sundry humiliations, he was treated for a time with consideration—having been able, by a Chinese poem, to touch even the cruel heart of Yoritomo. But in the following year he was executed by request of the Buddhist priests of Nanto, against whom he had formerly waged war by order of Kiyomori.

maid whom I fostered has now become a Himégimi-Sama indeed!—
were we living in the good days of the Emperor Takakura, what a
destiny might be reserved for her! However, she has obtained the
husband whom she desired; that is the greatest happiness.... But the
hour is late. The bridal-chamber has been prepared; and I must now
leave you to care for each other until morning."

She rose, and sliding back the screens parting the guest-room
from the adjoining chamber, ushered them to their sleeping apartment. Then, with many words of joy and congratulation, she
withdrew; and Itō was left alone with his bride.

As they reposed together, Itō said:—

"Tell me, my loved one, when was it that you first wished to
have me for your husband."

(For everything appeared so real that he had almost ceased to
think of the illusion woven around him.)

She answered, in a voice like a dove's voice:—

"My august lord and husband, it was at the temple of Ishiyama,
where I went with my foster-mother, that I saw you for the first
time. And because of seeing you, the world became changed to me
from that hour and moment. But you do not remember, because our
meeting was not in this, your present life: it was very, very long
ago. Since that time you have passed through many deaths and
births, and have had many comely bodies. But I have remained
always that which you see me now: I could not obtain another body,
nor enter into another state of existence, because of my great wish
for you. My dear lord and husband, I have waited for you through
many ages of men."

And the bridegroom felt nowise afraid at hearing these strange
words, but desired nothing more in life, or in all his lives to come,
than to feel her arms about him, and to hear the caress of her voice.

* * *

But the pealing of a temple-bell proclaimed the coming of dawn. Birds began to twitter; a morning breeze set all the trees a-whispering. Suddenly the old nurse pushed apart the sliding screens of the bridal-chamber, and exclaimed:—

"My children, it is time to separate! By daylight you must not be together, even for an instant: that were fatal! You must bid each other good-bye."

Without a word, Itō made ready to depart. He vaguely understood the warning uttered, and resigned himself wholly to destiny. His will belonged to him no more; he desired only to please his shadowy bride.

She placed in his hands a little *suzuri*, or ink-stone, curiously carved, and said:—

"My young lord and husband is a scholar; therefore this small gift will probably not be despised by him. It is of strange fashion because it is old, having been augustly bestowed upon my father by the favor of the Emperor Takakura. For that reason only, I thought it to be a precious thing."

Itō, in return, besought her to accept for a remembrance the *kōgai*[100] of his sword, which were decorated with inlaid work of silver and gold, representing plum-flowers and nightingales.

Then the little *miya-dzukai* came to guide him through the garden, and his bride with her foster-mother accompanied him to the threshold.

As he turned at the foot of the steps to make his parting salute, the old woman said:—

"We shall meet again the next Year of the Boar, at the same hour of the same day of the same month that you came here. This being the Year of the Tiger, you will have to wait ten years. But,

---

100   This was the name given to a pair of metal rods attached to a sword-sheath, and used like chop-sticks. They were sometimes exquisitely ornamented.

for reasons which I must not say, we shall not be able to meet again in this place; we are going to the neighborhood of Kyōto, where the good Emperor Takakura and our fathers and many of our people are dwelling. All the Heiké will be rejoiced by your coming. We shall send a *kago*[101] for you on the appointed day."

Above the village the stars were burning as Itō passed the gate; but on reaching the open road he saw the dawn brightening beyond leagues of silent fields. In his bosom he carried the gift of his bride. The charm of her voice lingered in his ears—and nevertheless, had it not been for the memento which he touched with questioning fingers, he could have persuaded himself that the memories of the night were memories of sleep, and that his life still belonged to him.

But the certainty that he had doomed himself evoked no least regret: he was troubled only by the pain of separation, and the thought of the seasons that would have to pass before the illusion could be renewed for him. Ten years!—and every day of those years would seem how long! The mystery of the delay he could not hope to solve; the secret ways of the dead are known to the gods alone.

Often and often, in his solitary walks, Itō revisited the village at Kotobikiyama, vaguely hoping to obtain another glimpse of the past. But never again, by night or by day, was he able to find the rustic gate in the shadowed lane; never again could he perceive the figure of the little *miya-dzukai*, walking alone in the sunset-glow.

The village people, whom he questioned carefully, thought him bewitched. No person of rank, they said, had ever dwelt in the settlement; and there had never been, in the neighborhood, any such garden as he described. But there had once been a great Buddhist

---

101   A kind of palanquin.

temple near the place of which he spoke; and some gravestones of the temple-cemetery were still to be seen. Itō discovered the monuments in the middle of a dense thicket. They were of an ancient Chinese form, and were covered with moss and lichens. The characters that had been cut upon them could no longer be deciphered.

Of his adventure Itō spoke to no one. But friends and kindred soon perceived a great change in his appearance and manner. Day by day he seemed to become more pale and thin, though physicians declared that he had no bodily ailment; he looked like a ghost, and moved like a shadow. Thoughtful and solitary he had always been, but now he appeared indifferent to everything which had formerly given him pleasure—even to those literary studies by means of which he might have hoped to win distinction. To his mother—who thought that marriage might quicken his former ambition, and revive his interest in life—he said that he had made a vow to marry no living woman. And the months dragged by.

At last came the Year of the Boar, and the season of autumn; but Itō could no longer take the solitary walks that he loved. He could not even rise from his bed. His life was ebbing, though none could divine the cause; and he slept so deeply and so long that his sleep was often mistaken for death.

Out of such a sleep he was startled, one bright evening, by the voice of a child; and he saw at his bedside the little *miya-dzukai* who had guided him, ten years before, to the gate of the vanished garden. She saluted him, and smiled, and said: "I am bidden to tell you that you will be received to-night at Ōhara, near Kyōto, where the new home is, and that a *kago* has been sent for you." Then she disappeared.

Itō knew that he was being summoned away from the light of the sun; but the message so rejoiced him that he found strength to sit up and call his mother. To her he then for the first time related the story of his bridal, and he showed her the ink-stone which had been given him. He asked that it should be placed in his coffin—and then he died.

The ink-stone was buried with him. But before the funeral ceremonies it was examined by experts, who said that it had been made in the period of *Jō-an* (AD1169), and that it bore the seal-mark of an artist who had lived in the time of the Emperor Takakura.

Stranger
than Fiction

Jt was a perfect West Indian day. My friend the notary and I were crossing the island by a wonderful road which wound up through tropic forest to the clouds, and thence looped down again, through gold-green slopes of cane, and scenery amazing of violet and blue and ghost-gray peaks, to the roaring coast of the trade winds. All the morning we had been ascending—walking after our carriage, most of the time, for the sake of the brave little mule;—and the sea had been climbing behind us till it looked like a monstrous wall of blue, pansy-blue, under the ever heightening horizon. The heat was like the heat of a vapor-bath, but the air was good to breathe with its tropical odor—an odor made up of smells of strange saps, queer spicy scents of mould, exhalations of aromatic decay. Moreover, the views were glimpses of Paradise; and it was a joy to watch the torrents roaring down their gorges under shadows of tree-fern and bamboo.

My friend stopped the carriage before a gateway set into a hedge full of flowers that looked like pink-and-white butterflies. "I have to make a call here," he said;—"come in with me." We dismounted, and he knocked on the gate with the butt of his whip. Within, at the end of a shady garden, I could see the porch of a planter's house; beyond were rows of cocoa palms, and glimpses of yellowing cane. Presently a negro, wearing only a pair of canvas trousers and a great straw hat, came hobbling to open the gate—followed by a multitude, an astonishing multitude, of chippering chickens. Under the shadow of that huge straw hat I could not see the negro's face; but I noticed that his limbs and body were strangely shrunken—looked as if withered to the bone. A weirder creature I had never beheld; and I wondered at his following of chickens.

"Eh!" exclaimed the notary, "your chickens are as lively as ever!... I want to see Madame Floran."

"*Moin ké di*," the goblin responded huskily, in his patois; and he limped on before us, all the chickens hopping and cheeping at his withered heels.

"That fellow," my friend observed, "was bitten by a *fer-de-lance* about eight or nine years ago. He got cured, or at least half-cured, in some extraordinary way; but ever since then he has been a skeleton. See how he limps!"

The skeleton passed out of sight behind the house, and we waited a while at the front porch. Then a *métisse*—turbaned in wasp colors, and robed in iris colors, and wonderful to behold—came to tell us that Madame hoped we would rest ourselves in the garden, as the house was very warm. Chairs and a little table were then set for us in a shady place, and the *métisse* brought out lemons, sugar-syrup, a bottle of the clear plantation rum that smells like apple juice, and ice-cold water in a *dobanne* of thick red clay. My friend prepared the refreshments; and then our hostess came to greet us, and to sit with us—a nice old lady with hair like newly minted silver. I had never seen a smile sweeter than that with which she bade us welcome; and I wondered whether she could ever have been more charming in her Creole girlhood than she now appeared—with her kindly wrinkles, and argent hair, and frank, black, sparkling eyes....

In the conversation that followed I was not able to take part, as it related only to some question of title. The notary soon arranged whatever there was to arrange; and, after some charmingly spoken words of farewell from the gentle lady, we took our departure. Again the mummified negro hobbled before us, to open the gate—followed by all his callow rabble of chickens. As we resumed our places in the carriage we could still hear the chippering of the creatures, pursuing after that ancient scarecrow.

"Is it African sorcery?" I queried.... "How does he bewitch those chickens?"

"Queer—is it not?" the notary responded as we drove away. "That negro must now be at least eighty years old; and he may live for twenty years more—the wretch!"

The tone in which my friend uttered this epithet—*le misérable!*—somewhat surprised me, as I knew him to be one of the kindliest men in the world, and singularly free from prejudice. I suspected that a story was coming, and I waited for it in silence.

"Listen," said the notary, after a pause, during which we left the plantation well behind us; "that old sorcerer, as you call him, was born upon the estate, a slave. The estate belonged to M. Floran—the husband of the lady whom we visited; and she was a cousin, and the marriage was a love-match. They had been married about two years when the revolt occurred (fortunately there were no children)—the black revolt of eighteen hundred and forty-eight. Several planters were murdered; and M. Floran was one of the first to be killed. And the old negro whom we saw to-day—the old sorcerer, as you call him—left the plantation, and joined the rising: do you understand?"

"Yes," I said; "but he might have done that through fear of the mob."

"Certainly: the other hands did the same. But it was he that killed M. Floran—for no reason whatever—cut him up with a cutlass. M. Floran was riding home when the attack was made—about a mile below the plantation.... Sober, that negro would not have dared to face M. Floran: the scoundrel was drunk, of course—

raving drunk. Most of the blacks had been drinking tafia, with dead wasps in it, to give themselves courage."

"But," I interrupted, "how does it happen that the fellow is still on the Floran plantation?"

"Wait a moment!... When the military got control of the mob, search was made everywhere for the murderer of M. Floran; but he could not be found. He was lying out in the cane—in M. Floran's cane!—like a field-rat, like a snake. One morning, while the gendarmes were still looking for him, he rushed into the house, and threw himself down in front of Madame, weeping and screaming, '*Aïe-yaïe-yaïe-yaïe!—moin té tchoué y! moin té tchoué y!—aïe-yaïe-yaïe!*' Those were his very words:—'I killed him! I killed him!' And he begged for mercy. When he was asked why he killed M. Floran, he cried out that it was the devil—*diabe-à*—that had made him do it!... Well, Madame forgave him!"

"But how could she?" I queried.

"Oh, she had always been very religious," my friend responded—"sincerely religious. She only said, 'May God pardon me as I now pardon you!' She made her servants hide the creature and feed him; and they kept him hidden until the excitement was over. Then she sent him back to work; and he has been working for her ever since. Of course he is now too old to be of any use in the field;—he only takes care of the chickens."

"But how," I persisted, "could the relatives allow Madame to forgive him?"

"Well, Madame insisted that he was not mentally responsible—that he was only a poor fool who had killed without knowing what he was doing; and she argued that if *she* could forgive him, others could more easily do the same. There was a consultation; and the relatives decided so to arrange matters that Madame could have her own way."

"But why?"

"Because they knew that she found a sort of religious consolation—a kind of religious comfort—in forgiving the wretch. She imagined that it was her duty as a Christian, not only to forgive him, but to take care of him. We thought that she was mistaken— but we could understand.... Well, there is an example of what religion can do.".

The surprise of a new fact, or the sudden perception of something never before imagined, may cause an involuntary smile. Unconsciously I smiled, while my friend was yet speaking; and the good notary's brow darkened.

"Ah, you laugh!" he exclaimed—"you laugh! That is wrong!— that is a mistake!... But you do not believe: you do not know what it is—the true religion—the real Christianity!"

Earnestly I made answer:—

"Pardon me! I do believe every word of what you have told me. If I laughed unthinkingly, it was only because I could not help wondering".

"At what?" he questioned gravely.

"At the marvelous instinct of that negro."

"Ah, yes!" he returned approvingly. "Yes, the cunning of the animal it was—the instinct of the brute!... She was the only person in the world who could have saved him."

"And he knew it," I ventured to add.

"No—no—no!" my friend emphatically dissented—"he never could have known it! He only *felt* it!... Find me an instinct like that, and I will show you a brain incapable of any knowledge, any thinking, any understanding: not the mind of a man, but the brain of a beast!"